The Runaway Family

DINEY COSTELOE is the bestselling author of *The Throwaway Children*. She has three children and seven grandchildren, so when she isn't writing, she's busy with family. She and her husband divide their time between Somerset and West Cork.

Also by Diney Costeloe

The Girl With No Name
The Lost Soldier
The Sisters of St Croix
The Throwaway Children

The Runaway Family

DINEY COSTELOE

HEAD
ᵎ ZEUS

First published in the UK in 2009 by Castlehaven Books
as *Evil on the Wind*

This edition first published in the UK in 2016 by Head of Zeus Ltd

9 7 5 3 1 2 4 6 8

A catalogue record for this book is available
from the British Library.

ISBN (PB) 9781784972646
ISBN (E) 9781784972622

Typeset by Adrian McLaughlin
Printed in the UK by Clays Ltd, St Ives Plc

Head of Zeus Ltd
Clerkenwell House
45–47 Clerkenwell Green
London EC1R 0HT

WWW.HEADOFZEUS.COM

*To all those who suffered under Nazi tyranny…
those who survived and those who did not.*

*"If men could learn from history,
what lessons it might teach us."*
Samuel Taylor Coleridge

*"Those who cannot remember the past
are condemned to repeat it."*
George Santayana

The Nuremberg Laws on Citizenship and Race:
September 15, 1935

Article 4 (1) A Jew cannot be a citizen of the Reich. He cannot exercise the right to vote; he cannot hold public office. (2) Jewish officials will be retired as of December 31, 1935. In the event that such officials served at the front in the World War either for Germany or her allies, they shall receive as pension, until they reach the age limit, the full salary last received, on the basis of which their pension would have been computed. They shall not, however, be promoted according to their seniority in rank. When they reach the age limit, their pension will be computed again, according to the salary last received on which their pension was to be calculated. (3) These provisions do not concern the affairs of religious organisations. (4) The conditions regarding service of teachers in public Jewish schools remains unchanged until the promulgation of new laws on the Jewish school system.

Article 5 (1) A Jew is an individual who is descended from at least three grandparents who were, racially, full Jews... (2) A Jew is also an individual who is descended from two full-Jewish grandparents if: (a) he was a member of the

Jewish religious community when this law was issued, or joined the community later; (b) when the law was issued, he was married to a person who was a Jew, or was subsequently married to a Jew; (c) he is the issue from a marriage with a Jew, in the sense of Section I, which was contracted after the coming into effect of the Law for the Protection of German Blood and Honour of September 15, 1935; (d) he is the issue of an extramarital relationship with a Jew, in the sense of Section I, and was born out of wedlock after July 31, 1936.

Article 6 (1) Insofar as there are, in the laws of the Reich or in the decrees of the National Socialist German Workers' Party and its affiliates, certain requirements for the purity of German blood which extend beyond Article 5, the same remain untouched...

Article 7 The *Fuehrer* and Chancellor of the Reich is empowered to release anyone from the provisions of these administrative decrees.

*Law for the Protection of German Blood
and German Honour
September 15, 1935*

Thoroughly convinced by the knowledge that the purity of German blood is essential for the further existence of the German people and animated by the inflexible will to safeguard the German nation for the entire future, the Reichstag has resolved upon the following law unanimously, which is promulgated herewith:

Section 1 1 Marriages between Jews and nationals of German or kindred blood are forbidden. Marriages concluded in defiance of this law are void, even if, for the purpose of evading this law, they are concluded abroad. 2 Proceedings for annulment may be initiated only by the Public Prosecutor.

Section 2 Relations outside marriage between Jews and nationals for German or kindred blood are forbidden.

Section 3 Jews will not be permitted to employ female nationals of German or kindred blood in their households.

Section 4 1 Jews are forbidden to hoist the Reich and national flag and to present the colours of the Reich. 2 On the other hand they are permitted to present the Jewish colours. The exercise of this authority is protected by the State.

Section 5 1 A person who acts contrary to the prohibition of section 1 will be punished with hard labour. 2 A person who acts contrary to the prohibition of section 2 will be punished with imprisonment or with hard labour. 3 A person who acts contrary to the provisions of section 3 or 4 will be punished with imprisonment up to a year and with a fine or with one of these penalties.

Section 6 The Reich Minister of the Interior in agreement with the Deputy of the *Fuehrer* will issue the legal and administrative regulations which are required for the implementation and supplementation of this law.

Section 7 The law will become effective on the day after the promulgation, section 3 however only on January 1, 1936.

Nuremberg, the 15th day of September 1935 at the Reich Party Rally of Freedom.

The Fuehrer and Reich Chancellor Adolf Hitler
The Reich Minister of the Interior Frick
The Reich Minister of Justice Dr Goertner

One

The crash of shattering glass and the sound of shouting in the street below startled Laura awake. More shouting and banging, a piercing scream and then more breaking glass. Laura sat bolt upright in bed, her eyes wide with fear as she listened in the darkness to the uproar outside, the shouts, bangs and crashes getting nearer. People were chanting something, Laura couldn't make out what, but their voices, combining into the throaty roar of a mob, were angry and frightening.

It was dark outside, though the faint light of a streetlamp gleamed through the gap in the curtains, but there was another light too, a flickering light, dancing and leaping, casting weird shadows on the ceiling. What was happening down there? What was going on?

Laura stole out of bed and crept to the window. Cautiously she lifted the corner of the curtain and peeped out. She stared down into the street in fascinated horror. A crowd was surging along the road, their snarling faces lit by the streetlamps and the flaming torches some of them carried. Many brandished stout walking sticks in the air, others carried stones, bricks and iron bars. They were led by men in uniform, guns held high, urging the crowd on. The windows of the baker's shop across the way were already smashed, and its door hanging on a broken hinge. Even as she watched, Laura saw a man throw another brick, this time at the windows of the apartment above the shop. There was a cheer as the glass shattered, its shards flying inwards.

"Jews out! Jews out! Jews out!" She could hear what they were chanting now as the voices grew louder, stronger, as more and more people joined the crowd.

"Laura, what's happening?" Inge, her seven-year-old sister, asked sleepily from the other bed.

"I don't know," Laura said, shrinking back behind the curtain, but somehow unable to turn away. "There're people outside throwing stones and shouting."

There was another sound too, the crackle of flames, and Laura realised with growing horror that the dancing light she had seen through the curtains was fire. There was smoke now, and the red and gold tongues of flame appeared at the windows of the synagogue further up the road. Even as Laura watched, horrified, the door burst open and Rabbi Rosner came rushing out, shouting for the fire brigade. He ran straight into the crowd that bayed with delight at his terror, and brandishing their sticks and hurling stones, they chased him back into the burning building.

"I don't like it!" Inge was wailing. "Where's Mutti?"

At that moment the bedroom door opened and Ruth Friedman, the girls' mother, came quickly into the room, her face white with fear.

"Laura! Come away from the window!" she cried and, rushing over, dragged her daughter away. "Out of here, quickly." She scooped Inge off the bed and clutching her in her arms, pushed Laura in front of her as she hurried them into her own bedroom at the back of the house. Her husband, Kurt, was already in the room with the twins, Peter and Hans, aged just three; both were crying at having been awoken so suddenly and their father was trying to hush them. Ruth turned the key in the lock, and, placing Inge on the bed, went to the twins.

"Papa, the synagogue's on fire." Laura tugged at her father's sleeve. "It's burning down, and Rabbi Rosner is inside."

"Don't worry, darling," her father put an arm round her. "He'll have got out safely."

"No, Papa," Laura insisted, her eyes wide, "when he ran out some people chased him back inside. They were hitting him!"

Before her father could answer, there came a thundering on their own front door, the splintering of wood and the sound of breaking glass as the window in the shop below became the target for the bricks. Ruth drew the twins closely into her arms, and Kurt gathered the now screaming Inge against him, his other arm still firmly round Laura.

"Ssh! Ssh!" he hushed them. "It'll be all right. Mutti and Papa are here! It'll be all right."

But it wasn't. Within moments they heard heavy footsteps on the stairs, and then a voice, which bellowed, "Come out, Jews! Come out, dirty Jews! Come out of your holes!"

Before they could do anything, there was a crash and the door flew open, the lock hanging sideways where a jackboot had kicked it free. A tall man in storm-trooper's uniform, his cap – with its death's head badge – dark over his fair hair, stood on the threshold, a gun in his hand, towering over the family who crouched together around the bed. Behind him two others moved along the landing, kicking open the

7

bedroom doors, and shouting down to the mob below, "Jews up here!"

"You, Jew, you're under arrest!" The first man advanced on Kurt, who pushed his daughters behind him in an effort to shield them.

"Why? What for?" It was Ruth who asked, her voice cracking with fear. "He's done nothing wrong."

"He's a Jew. He's under arrest!"

"But..." Ruth began to protest.

"Shut up," bellowed the man, "or I'll arrest the lot of you!"

"Don't worry, Ruth," Kurt said, trying to keep his voice steady. "I'll go with him. I'm sure there's some mistake and I'll be back in no time." For a moment their eyes met, hers wide and fearful. Kurt's strong face was calm and determined, but fear flickered behind his eyes too, and, seeing it, Ruth began to shake.

"You look after the children, I'll be back soon. And if not," there was the slightest tremor in his voice, "go to Herbert."

"Out!" The storm trooper grasped him by the shoulder, and spinning him round, shoved him roughly through the door. "Out! Out!" Immediately the two men on the landing grabbed his arms, one punching him violently in the stomach so that he doubled over, groaning with pain, before they dragged him, still bent double, down the stairs.

The storm trooper, still in the bedroom, glanced across at the trembling woman surrounded by her four children. "You'll stay up here if you know what's good for you," he said coldly, and turning on his heel, stamped his way back down the stairs.

For a moment there was silence in the bedroom and then Inge began to wail again. "Where's Papa gone? I want Papa."

Ruth suppressed the cry that rose in her throat that she wanted him too, and tried to soothe the terrified children.

"Don't cry," she said, rocking Peter on her knee and holding Inge to her with the other arm. "Don't cry, Peter, there's a good boy. Look, Hansi isn't crying. Laura, give Hansi a cuddle, he's being very brave. Come on now, you must be brave, all of you. That's what Papa would want. We must all be brave!"

She gathered the four children close, rocking them comfortingly, and as they huddled together on her bed, she listened to shattering glass and splintering wood as the mob downstairs ransacked the shop, their voices raised in shouts of glee. Then with the bang of a door and shouts of laughter, the baying mob moved onward down the street. The stillness they left behind was, if anything, more terrifying than their animal howls. What was happening down there? Had the mob moved on somewhere else? Was it safe to come out of the bedroom? Ruth went quietly across the room, and, opening the door, peeped out onto the landing. The apartment was empty; there was no sound from downstairs.

"You'll stay up here if you know what's good for you," the trooper had said, but Ruth could not. She had to go down, to find out what had happened.

"Stay here," she said to the children and quietly crossed into the girls' bedroom to look out into the street below. She lifted the corner of the curtain as Laura had done and looked down. Their street was almost empty now, the mob had moved on to the next. She could still hear its animal roar, but more distant, the chanting indistinct. She looked over towards the synagogue. There were still flames behind the windows, but she could see the shadows of people running around inside, trying to douse the fire before it really took hold and burned the place to the ground. The smell of smoke was bitter and acrid as it billowed out from the broken windows, wafting along the street.

Ruth returned to her bedroom door. "Stay here, Laura," she said. "Look after the little ones. I'll be back in a minute." Steeling herself to what she might find below, Ruth crept downstairs. She was still afraid the storm troopers might be there lying in wait for her, but as she peered round the corner into the shop there was no one. Complete chaos greeted her eyes, and for a long moment she stood, aghast at what she saw. In the few minutes the mob had given its attention to Friedmans' Grocery, they had destroyed everything they could find.

The till had been broken open and lay upended on the counter, with what little money there had been in it, gone. Broken jars and bottles littered the floor, their contents mixed with the shards of glass from the window. Sacks of flour, too heavy to carry, had been ripped open and tipped out, tea and rice, coffee, jam and oil all added to the glutinous mess that covered the floor. Ruth crossed to the cold store and opened the door. Where there should have been cheese and butter, eggs and milk, the shelves were empty. Trays of eggs had been tossed to the floor, a milk churn upended. Two large cheeses, wrapped in their linen cloths, had disappeared. For a moment she stared at the mess in sick dismay. Then she smelled the smoke.

At first she thought it must be coming from the burning synagogue along the street, but then she realised that it was in the shop with her. Looking round wildly she saw that smoke was seeping out from under the door of the storeroom where they kept all the dry goods. Running into the kitchen, Ruth grabbed a bucket from under the sink and quickly filled it with water. Cautiously she edged the storeroom door open, her bucket poised to douse the fire, but with the draught from the outer door drawing them, the flames leapt towards her. Her tossed bucket of water made no impression on the fire and in that moment Ruth knew it was already too late to save the shop and their home. Feeding on oil which had been liberally emptied onto floor and shelves, it was a glorified chip-pan fire and had too firm a hold to be controlled; water would only make matters worse.

With a shriek of terror, Ruth tried to slam the storeroom door shut, but the heat from within was too great and flames had already laid claim to the door. Ruth's one thought now was to save her children from the fire. As she fled back up the stairs she could hear the crackle of the fire almost at her heels. There was a door at the top of the stairs separating the apartment from the shop below and she slammed this behind her, hoping to keep the fire at bay, but even with this door safely closed the smoke was wreathing its way underneath, wafting along the landing.

"Hurry," she cried as she flew into the bedroom where the children waited. "Hurry! Hurry! There's a fire, we must get out now. Laura, you carry Hans, I'll take Peter. Inge, stop crying, darling, and hold tight to my skirt."

Laura reached out for Hans, gathering him into her arms and holding him against her body. "Come on, Hansi, put your arms round my neck," she said, trying to ease the dead weight of his body as he snuggled against her. Obediently he reached up and she felt his arms snake round her neck, the hair on the top of his head soft under the curve of her chin. She turned for the door, following her mother who had Peter on her hip and was holding Inge's hand firmly in her own. Ruth strode along the landing to the door at the top of the stairs. The smoke was thicker now, forcing its way under the door in thick black coils, making them cough. Even before she eased the door open, Ruth knew that they were too late. The fire had taken hold of the stairs, crackling merrily as it ate up the tinder-dry wood of the ancient staircase.

"Back! Go back!" Ruth cried as she flung the door closed again and pushed them back along the landing. For a moment she stood in the bedroom, the bedroom she had shared with Kurt for almost fifteen years, the room where all the children had been conceived and born, and which now seemed likely to be their grave. Putting Peter back onto the bed she ran into the front room and looked down into the street again. A few people had ventured outside to stare in horror at the trail of destruction the mob had left behind, the mob that even now howled its rage on other Jewish homes, other Jewish businesses. Leah Meyer was standing outside her husband's baker's shop, trying to take in the damage that had been inflicted on it so suddenly and so swiftly. Other shadows appeared by the synagogue, from which smoke was still pouring in a thick dark cloud, though the combined efforts of the neighbours seemed to have doused the flames, their flickering light no longer dancing in the windows.

Nobody had noticed that Friedmans' Grocery was also on fire. Ruth threw up the window and began calling for help. At first no one seemed to hear her frantic cries, but at last Leah Meyer looked up and seeing Ruth at the window raised her hand in salute.

"Help!" Ruth screamed. "Help us! We're trapped. The stairs are on fire! Help! Oh, help us, please!"

Frau Meyer seemed to be turning away again, but Ruth screamed at her, calling her by name. "Leah! Leah! Get help! My children will be burned alive!"

At last the words seemed to register in the old lady's brain and she ran towards the synagogue and went inside. Within moments people came rushing out. One woman ran to the shop door, but was driven back by the flames that now completely engulfed the ground floor.

"Jump!" she shouted. "You must jump! We can't get in to rescue you."

"I can't!" shrieked Ruth in panic. "The children can't jump from this high."

"Get a sheet and lower them down," the woman shouted. "Quickly, tie them to a sheet and let them down. We'll catch them."

Ruth nodded and, dashing back to her bedroom, hustled the children into the girls' room. "Look after the twins," she instructed the girls as she grabbed the sheet from Laura's bed. Tearing at it, she tried to rip it in half, but the quality was too good, the hems too strong to be torn. With a bellow of frustration, she ran into her bedroom and grabbed the manicure set off her dressing table. The nail scissors were small, but they cut enough to start the tear.

Smoke was pouring along the landing now, and, choking, Ruth slammed the bedroom door closed. She concentrated on ripping the sheet into two strips to tie together for a makeshift rope. Dragging the bedstead to the window, she made one end fast to the metal frame and dropped the other out of the window. It was too short. There were still at least six feet to drop to the ground. Grasping the quilt from the bed, she tossed it out of the window. Willing hands below grabbed it

13

and held it taut, to make a makeshift landing place.

"You first, Laura," Ruth said. "Remember, grip the rope with your feet as well as your hands so you don't go too fast." She gave her daughter a hug. "Come on, darling, be brave, I need you down there to catch the twins."

The smoke was pouring under the door now and the other children began to cough, their eyes streaming as it coiled round them, hiding them from their mother. Laura sat on the windowsill, and with a terrified glance at her mother, slid down the rope, the taut linen ripping at her hands, so that she screamed with pain and fear as she reached the end and landed in a crumpled heap in the middle of the quilt. The moment the rope was free, Ruth hauled it up and knotted it tightly round Peter's waist, then even as he screamed and clung to her in terror she edged him off the sill and lowered him down to the waiting arms reaching up from below.

The flames were crackling outside the bedroom door now, and it was buckling under the increasing heat. Frantically Ruth knotted the rope round Hans's waist and slipped him over the sill, lowering him to the safety of the ground below. All this was done to the accompanying screams of Inge, who lay on the floor, drumming her heels in fear and rage. As Ruth hauled the rope up again, the door finally gave way and the fire exploded into the room, the flames spreading and feeding on the furnishings. With one backward glance, Ruth gathered up the bellowing Inge in her arms and dragged her to the window. There was no time to tie her safely into the rope of sheets, so with a warning cry to those gathered below, she tipped the little girl out of the window onto the quilt that was spread ready to catch her. Even as the child landed and was gathered into waiting arms, Ruth felt the heat on her back as her clothes began to smoke and smoulder. With another warning cry, she jumped.

Laura watched in horror as her mother fell from the bedroom window, arms flailing as she tried to grasp the linen rope to slow her fall. Her fall was broken by Rabbi Rosner as he reached up his arms to try and catch her. They collapsed together in a heap on the ground, their arms and legs entwined as if in some passionate embrace, the wind knocked out of the old man as Ruth landed heavily on his chest.

Forgetting the pain in her hands, Laura rushed over to her mother, crying out as she saw her lying on the ground. "Mutti! Are you all right? Mutti!"

Her mother lay still, and Laura thought she was dead until she heard a faint moan and saw her legs twitch. Ruth, winded by her fall, couldn't answer for a moment, and in truth she didn't know the answer. Every inch of her felt bruised, she could still feel the heat on her back, and her ankle felt as if it had been pierced by a red-hot needle. Underneath her Rabbi Rosner groaned, and Ruth tried to disentangle herself so that he could get up. Frau Rosner hurried up, and, pulling Laura out of the way, knelt beside her husband. The twins, being looked after by Frau Meyer, began to whimper and Inge, who had never ceased wailing, increased the volume of her crying to maximum. The savage roar of the mob surged back through the darkness as it circled round to continue its way along a parallel street.

There was an anguished cry. "They're coming back. They're coming back!"

The few people gathered in the street melted away into the darkness, scurrying for the illusory safety of their homes as they heard the monstrous crowd baying for its prey.

"We must get away from here," Frau Rosner urged. "Come on, Samuel! You must get up." She pulled at Ruth's arm to try and move her out of the way so that the rabbi could get to his feet. "They're coming back!" she cried, terrified by the sound of the shouting. "We must get off the street! Samuel!"

Ruth dragged herself clear and Laura and Inge rushed to her side. "Mutti!" Laura clutched at her hand: "Are you all right?"

This time Ruth did manage to answer. "Yes, darlings, I'm all right. Just a bit bruised. I think I may have sprained my ankle."

"They're coming back!" Leah Meyer shouted, her voice cracking with fear. "We must get off the street." She took the twins firmly by the hand and dragged them back towards her own home, above her husband's shop.

"We must call the fire brigade," cried Ruth as she looked up and saw the flames devouring the curtains at the window of the bedroom, reaching out to lick at the overhanging wooden eaves.

"They won't come!" snapped Frau Rosner as she pushed her still-wheezing husband ahead of her. But she was wrong. Within a few minutes a fire engine was racing down the street and the powerful hoses were trained on what was left of the Friedmans' home. Ruth had not had to call them, they had come at the summons of another neighbour whose home backed onto the Friedmans'; a neighbour who was not Jewish and so didn't deserve to have his house burned down.

The Friedman family were taken in and given refuge by the Meyers. Although their shop had been damaged and daubed with paint, the brick through the first-floor window was the only damage to their living quarters above. With infinite care, Frau Meyer, who had no children of her own, bathed Laura's rope burns in cold water a[...] hands with clean strips of linen. She warmed so[...] the younger children, and then took the twins into t[...] spare bedroom and placed them top to toe under the qui[...] on its single bed, crooning to them softly as they fell into exhausted sleep.

Ruth sat in an armchair, her injured foot up on a footstool. It was so swollen that when they had taken off her shoe she could hardly see her toes. Leah had put on a cold compress.

"Tomorrow we will try and get Dr Kohn to have a look," she said.

"It'll be much better in the morning," Ruth assured her, her face pale and pinched with the pain that shot through her ankle if she so much as moved it an inch. "I don't need a doctor."

"We'll see in the morning," Leah insisted. "It may be broken."

Laura, her hands a little less painful now, looked anxiously across at her mother. Inge had finally stopped crying and was curled beside her, her fair hair hiding her face as she buried her head in Mutti's shoulder.

Laura saw Mutti wince with pain as Inge shifted to get more comfortable, and she said sharply, "Inge! Sit still, you're hurting Mutti!"

Inge ignored her, snuggling closer, and Mutti said, "It's all right, darling. I'm all right." She smiled weakly across at Laura and added, "How are your hands?"

Laura looked down at the bandages and said, "Frau Meyer says she'll get Dr Kohn to look if he comes to see you."

At last Inge had drifted into an uneasy sleep against her mother's shoulder. Leo Meyer lifted her gently and placed her in the big double bed in his own room.

ttle thing," he said. He added, as
ner mother, "Be careful now, Laura.
ruised. It is a miracle she wasn't killed!"
hat we weren't all killed," Frau Meyer was
thought, it's always Inge. She's allowed to sit

then, Laura, time you got some sleep as well," said
the old lady. "You can go in the bed next to Inge, all right?"

"I can't sleep," Laura insisted, her voice trembling, on the
verge of tears. "How *can* I sleep? Where's Papa?"

But sleep she did. When Frau Meyer had tucked her into
the bed beside the sleeping Inge, Laura had buried her face in
the pillow, and with muffled sobs cried herself to sleep; she
didn't wake until several hours later, needing the bathroom.
Inge was no longer in the bed beside her, just a damp patch
across the sheet. Inge had also needed the bathroom, but she
hadn't been able to wait. Laura screwed up her nose at the
sour smell of the damp sheet, and felt scarlet with embarrass-
ment that her sister should have done such a thing in someone
else's bed.

A wet bed, however, was the least of the household's
worries that morning. Leo Meyer went out to find out what
was happening and to try and discover what had happened
to Kurt Friedman, but no one knew. So many of their friends'
homes had been damaged; other men had been dragged off as
Kurt had been. As he learned more of what had happened to
so many Jewish families that night, Leo could hardly believe
he had not been arrested too.

Ruth managed to convince Leah that she didn't need Dr
Kohn to come to see her. She had no money, and she hated
to become even more indebted to the Meyers. The old lady

replaced the compress, and as they could both see that the swelling had lessened a little, she said no more about the doctor.

"I think you should be keeping it up though," she said.

"I'm sure you're right," Ruth agreed, "but I can't sit here and do nothing. I have to go over to the shop and see what can be salvaged before anyone else does." Very gingerly she lowered her foot to the floor. Leah understood. She found an old walking stick and helped Ruth get to her feet.

"I'll mind the little ones," she said. "You take Laura with you and go and have a look."

Using Laura's shoulder and Leah's stick for support, Ruth emerged from the bakery. Outside she paused, looking along Gerbergasse, the street where she had lived all her married life. A narrow twisting street that wound its way through a largely Jewish neighbourhood, and dominated by the synagogue at one end, it had been the centre of her community life; doors left open, children running in an out of each other's homes, neighbours gossiping on the pavement, a street vibrant with life. Now, not a soul was abroad; Gerbergasse was deserted. Several of the buildings showed superficial damage, caused in the riot, but it was when Ruth turned her eyes to her shop, her home, that despair flooded through her. Leaning heavily on Laura and the stick, she hobbled across the road to contemplate what was left of it. The shop window was a smoke-blackened gaping hole and the remains of the charred front door hung from one hinge. As Laura pushed against the hanging door, the single hinge creaked ominously before the weight of the door was too much and it crashed inwards, allowing Ruth and Laura to see what was left of the family business. There was nothing. The shop had been completely destroyed. An acrid pall still hung in the air. They gazed in despair at the blackened shell. Only a few tins lay on the floor. Gone were the counter and the shelves, gone the staircase leading to the apartment above.

Ruth fought back the tears that sprang to her eyes. Everything they had in the world was gone, and she had to face it all alone. They had taken Kurt, and now it was she who would have to find somewhere for herself and the children to live. How were they going to survive? What were they going to live on? They couldn't stay with the Meyers more than another couple of days, they had problems of their own. Ruth felt a wave of panic rising within her, black fear filling her head and threatening to engulf her. Everything they had possessed had gone and she couldn't even stand on her own feet.

"Mutti!" Laura's small voice brought her back and she realised that she had been gripping her daughter's arm so tightly that it hurt.

Forcing herself to relax her grip she said, "Sorry, darling. Come on, let's go. There's nothing for us here."

"Shouldn't we get the box from the garden?" asked Laura. For a moment her mother looked at her blankly and Laura said again, "You know, Papa's box. The one he buried?"

The deed box. For a moment Ruth looked stunned. She had forgotten all about the deed box. Kurt, no longer trusting the bank to deal fairly with its Jewish customers, had put all their important documents into a strong metal box and had buried it in the garden beneath one of the paving slabs outside the back door. How could she have forgotten?

"Good girl! Come on!" With new purpose, Ruth hobbled through the burnt-out shop and down the steps into the tiny yard below at the back. She remembered which stone Kurt had raised, but it seemed as firmly embedded as those around it.

"We need something to lever up the stone slab," she said, looking round to see what they might use.

"I'll look in the shed," Laura said, and crossed to the lean-to shed that stood against the back wall. Inside she found the coal shovel and returned to the yard. "This should do." She put the blade of the shovel under the edge of the paving stone and leaned hard on the handle. She felt a little movement, but wasn't strong enough to lift the slab. For a moment or two she heaved in vain.

"I can't shift it, Mutti!" she said despairingly. "It's too heavy! Shall I run and get Herr Meyer?"

"No." Her mother's reply was sharp. "No, this is private family business. Here, hold this stick and let me have a go." Ruth handed the walking stick to Laura, and balancing awkwardly on one leg tried to lever the stone. "Here, Laura, put your weight on it too."

Time and again they leaned on the shovel, and gradually they felt the stone loosening.

"We're getting there," Ruth said breathlessly. "At least Papa didn't cement it back down. One more go!"

This time the stone shifted enough to allow the edge of the shovel to slide right in underneath it.

"Now we need something to wedge it open," puffed Ruth, and then gave a little cry as she stepped back onto her sprained ankle, and sat down hard on the ground.

"Mutti! Are you all right?" cried Laura.

The stab of pain had taken her breath away, but she managed to say, "Yes, Laura, I'm fine. See what you can find to hold the stone up, so we can get at the box."

Laura went back into the shed and came out moments later

carrying a brick. "There are more of these in there," she said. "We can put them under the edge of the stone."

At last it was done. The heavy paving stone was resting on bricks and Laura was able to reach in underneath and pull out the strongbox her father had hidden there.

"Well done," said her mother. "Let's put the stone back, and then we'll go." It was a struggle to put the slab back in place, but Ruth was determined that there should be as little evidence of the hiding place as possible. Who knew when they might need it again? Once the stone was flat, she instructed Laura to push the loose dust back round it, pressing it down into the cracks, so that at a casual glance anyway there was nothing to see. Laura put the shovel and the bricks back into the shed. They, too, might serve again another day. She helped Ruth to her feet, handed her the stick and then picked up the box.

"We don't want anyone to see this," Ruth said. "I'll go to the front door, and if there's no one about, you carry it quickly to the Meyers'."

"What about you?" asked Laura anxiously.

"I can't move fast enough," Ruth replied. "You take the box to safety, I can manage on my own. Try not to let anyone see what you've got. Hide it under the bed for now."

"Not even Frau Meyer?"

"Better not," answered her mother. "If she does, never mind, but better if she doesn't. Come on." Ruth was anxious to get their valuable box to safety. She couldn't remember all it contained, but, apart from the clothes they stood up in, it was all they had left in the world, and she wanted to take no risks. "Wait, while I have a look outside." She edged past the broken front door and looked along the narrow street. There were a few people still moving in and out of the synagogue, but no one seemed to be coming in their direction.

"Go! Fast!" Ruth stood back to let her daughter slip out of the door and dart across the road to the comparative safety of the Meyers' home. Once she saw that Laura was safely inside, Ruth set out to hobble the thirty yards or so to join her. As she negotiated the uneven cobbles of the street, two boys wearing the uniform of the Hitler Youth came round the corner, carrying a bucket of red paint.

"Here's one," cried the first. "Give me the brush!" He snatched a large paintbrush from his companion and dipping it in the bucket daubed two words in red paint on the remains of the Friedmans' shop window. *Jüden Raus! Jews Out!*

Unable to stop herself, Ruth turned round, as he laughed and began chanting "Jews out! Jews out!"

His friend took up the chant, and then seeing Ruth standing unsteadily in the middle of the street, he pointed a finger. "Poor old Jew!" he jeered. "Poor old Jew! She's got a bad leg."

Before she realised what he was going to do, the boy came up behind Ruth and kicked her savagely in the back of the leg, so that her knees buckled and she fell to the ground with a cry.

"Jew! Jew! Dirty Jew!" chorused the boys, as they pranced round her. The one with the paintbrush still in his hand slashed it across her face, the red paint running into her eyes, and as she reached up to dash it away, the other gave her a brutal kick, his boot ramming into her side. Ruth curled up in the road, sobbing as he aimed one last kick at her head before they marched on down the street chanting, "Jews out! Heil Hitler! Jews out!" and daubing other shop windows as they went.

Ruth pulled herself up onto her hands and knees, and began to crawl the last few yards to the Meyers' shop door. It, too, had received the red-paint treatment, but the youths were too keen to daub as many doors as possible to bother breaking in again. As she reached it, the door opened and Laura erupted into the street.

"Mutti! Mutti! Are you all right? Oh Mutti!" Laura was sobbing as she tried to help her mother to her feet. Leah Meyer came out behind her and together they eased Ruth into the shop and onto a chair. "Frau Meyer wouldn't let me come to you!"

"She was quite right," wheezed Ruth, still winded from the kicks. "Worse if you'd come out."

This time Leah insisted on calling Dr Kohn. "We'll pay him," she said, guessing at Ruth's dilemma. "You can pay us back in happier times."

Feeling so completely battered, Ruth could only accept their generosity. She hoped there was some money in the deed box.

Dr Kohn came as dusk was falling, gratefully accepting the coffee Leah Meyer offered him. After examining Ruth, he said he thought that there was no permanent damage done, just very heavy bruising. He treated the bruises with ointment, gently rubbing it in while Ruth winced at every touch.

"You were lucky," he said. "They could have ruptured a kidney with kicks like that! Try and get some rest." With a smile, he shook his head at the proffered money. "Not after last night," he said.

"What will you do, Ruth?" asked Leah, when only she, her husband and Ruth were left in the living room. "Where will you go?"

"Of course you can stay here for as long as you want," Leo had said, but Ruth had caught the glance that flashed between husband and wife and knew, though the offer had had to be made, it was not possible for her to accept. For one thing there was no room for them all. Already the Meyers had

24

given up their bed, and she was propped up on the only other piece of furniture on which one might lie down.

Ruth was pale with exhaustion and fear, her eyes huge and dark in her stark white face. Her ankle throbbed, she ached all over and her brain felt like cotton wool.

What am I going to do, she thought wearily? We can't stay here and we can't go home... we've no home to go to.

"It's very kind of you both," she said, "but I shall take the children to Kurt's brother. I know he'll take us in and... and," her voice broke, "that's where Kurt will come to find us."

"We'll think about it in the morning," Leah said kindly. "What you need now is a good night's rest. I've got some aspirin. You take two of those and try and get some sleep."

Ruth took the proffered aspirin gratefully, but insisted on sleeping with the girls so that the Meyers could at least have the sofa to sleep on that night. "We can easily fit into that big bed," she said, "and you need your sleep too."

When at last she was settled beside the girls, Ruth thought about the deed box she and Laura had rescued that afternoon. It was hidden under the bed, but she couldn't examine its contents because the box was securely padlocked, and she had no key. Kurt had the key hidden somewhere, but that somewhere was in the ruins of the shop and Ruth had no idea where. It had never occurred to Kurt that he would not be there when the box was needed.

There's no alternative, Ruth decided. Tomorrow I'll have to borrow some sort of tool from Leo and break the lock. Then we'll go to Herbert.

With the decision taken, Ruth tried to get some sleep, but her brain would not rest. Endlessly it re-played the riot, the storm troopers, the raid on the shop, the fire, and as a soundtrack to it all the baying of the mob, terrifying in its savagery, thundered in her head. Did that sound really only emanate from human throats? Her physical aches were as nothing compared with her mental torment. Her only concern was to keep her children safe, and with Kurt arrested, it was now up to her.

Leo had reported back that the riots had been localised. "Just in our part of Kirnheim," he'd said, "but they were carefully orchestrated…storm troopers whipping up the mob, encouraging the Hitler Youth to take part. Small riots, but breaking out everywhere!"

"Didn't seem like a small riot to me!" remarked his wife.

It didn't seem like a small riot to Ruth, either. It seemed to her that all Germany had gone mad; that persecution of Jews had become a national pastime. Going to Herbert seemed to be the only chance of safety. Herbert and Kurt were not close as brothers. Kurt had been happy to take over and run the family business, whereas Herbert had set out to better himself and worked as a clerk for a large legal practice in Munich. Ruth didn't know him well, but surely Herbert would stand by his brother's family in their time of need, it was just a question of getting to him.

Eventually, lulled by the regular breathing of her daughters, Ruth dozed off and slept fitfully until the fingers of dawn pierced the curtains and woke her once again to the stark reality of what had happened to them all.

Two

As Frau Meyer sat the children down for some breakfast, Ruth presented Leo with the box.

"All our important papers are in here," she told him. "Kurt has the key. Please can you break it open for me?"

Leo inspected the padlock and then went to his toolbox and produced a chisel and a hammer.

"I'll have to break the hasp," he said. "I've nothing strong enough to deal with the actual padlock. Hold the box steady."

With Ruth holding the box firmly in her hands, Leo placed the end of the chisel and levered it against the hasp. With a resounding snap the hasp broke away from the box, allowing the lid to come free.

"There you are," he said cheerfully, and turned away to replace the tools, leaving Ruth to open the box and inspect its contents unobserved.

Settling the box on her knees, Ruth lifted the lid. Inside were several documents; the family's birth certificates, her and Kurt's marriage certificate, the deeds to the shop, which the family had owned for more than thirty years. There was Kurt's passport and her own, which she had used when she had taken the girls to Vienna for her nephew Paul's bar mitzvah, and a small bundle of money, held together with an elastic band. In a small box was a gold brooch, a present from her mother, and in another was a pair of pearl earrings that Kurt's mother had given her on their wedding day. Ruth stared down, dry-eyed, at the contents of the box, all that was left of their family fortune. She didn't weep, she was already beyond tears.

"You've got to be strong," she told herself, "so that we're all safe when Kurt comes back."

Kurt not coming back could not be contemplated, and in the meantime there was Herbert.

She told the Meyers of her decision as soon as the children had been fed.

"You mustn't feel you have to go," Leo said. "What are neighbours for if not to help in time of trouble?"

"You have helped, more than I could have dreamed of asking, but now it is time for us to move on," replied Ruth. "I must take the children to their uncle. He will look after us until Kurt is released, and Kurt will know where to find us."

"Well, if you are quite sure…" In spite of herself, Leah could not hide the note of relief that crept into her voice. Taking in a woman and four children had stretched her home to breaking point, not to mention the danger to which it exposed her and Leo. The Nazis were out looking for Jews, and if you were a Jew it was best to keep your head down and pray that they passed by without noticing you. She knew it, her husband knew it and Ruth knew it.

Ruth reached out and grasped her hands. "Quite sure," she said, "we've burdened you enough."

"No burden," smiled Leo, but Ruth could see the relief in his eyes as well, and knew that her decision was the right one.

"How will you get there?" Leah, ever the practical one, asked.

"We'll take the train into the city and then the bus. It shouldn't be difficult."

"Have you money?" asked Leah.

Ruth had counted the notes in the elastic band, and had been relieved at how much Kurt had hidden. She smiled at her neighbour and said, "Yes, enough to get us there, anyway, and to pay back what I owe you, dear Leah."

The morning after the fire, Leah had looked at the children in their nightclothes and disappeared to the market. When she returned, each child had one set of clothes to wear, a pair of shoes and an extra set of underwear. Ruth had only the clothes she stood up in, but at least she had not been in bed when the riot started. The old lady had asked Ruth for nothing, but Ruth was relieved that she could now reimburse her for her outlay.

"You've been so kind to us," Ruth said, "but we can't stay with you any longer."

"How will you contact your brother-in-law?" asked Leo.

"I won't," Ruth replied. "He has a telephone of course, but I think it is better that we arrive at his house, unannounced. Then he must take us in, for Kurt's sake."

"Do you think that he won't?" asked Leah, surprised.

"To be honest, Leah, I really don't know. We were never close; perhaps if I telephoned he would think of some reason why we should not come, but," she shrugged philosophically, "if we are all standing on his doorstep with nowhere else to go, I doubt if he would actually turn his brother's family away."

"Surely that is not the only money you have?" asked Leo. "Did your husband not have a bank account?"

"We did, but when things began to get difficult for us, he

was afraid the bank might not pay us our money if we asked for it. He withdrew it all."

"And that's what was in your strongbox?" Leo Meyer was incredulous.

"Some of it," admitted Ruth, not keen to let even the Meyers know just how much she had found in the box. "The rest he put in different places..." Her voice trailed away as she remembered the extra cash that had been hidden in the apartment and was now almost certainly ashes. She smiled bravely at her neighbour. "Please don't worry, Leo," she said. "You've both been kindness itself. I can manage on what I've got until I get to Herbert."

They insisted that she stay to rest her ankle and recover from her bruises for one more day, and Ruth allowed herself to be persuaded. She wasn't looking forward to taking the four children into the city. As they left the following morning Ruth felt a rush of affection for the Meyers, and it was with tears in her eyes that she bid them goodbye.

"There are some tins on the floor in the shop," she said. "Please take them. I can't carry them, they're too heavy. I don't know what's in them, the labels have all burned off, but if they're still all right, please have them. A sort of thank you...for everything."

The journey from Kirnheim wasn't easy, but with Laura holding the hand of each twin and Inge clinging on to her mother, they took the train into Munich and then negotiated the two buses needed to reach Herbert's suburb.

"You must be very good on the train," she warned the children. "We may have to sit in special seats. If anyone speaks to you, just smile, but don't answer. Even if they are unkind," she reiterated to the two girls, "don't answer."

There had been some comments as they clambered aboard, but they were able to sit altogether in the corner of a carriage. The children, overawed by the strange journey, had behaved well, and the little family had been left alone. When they finally alighted in the district where Herbert lived, they were all tired. Laura carried Peter, Ruth carried Hans, and Inge walked between them, gripping her mother's skirt firmly in her hand. Ten minutes later they were outside the building where Herbert had his apartment. Inside the porch, at the bottom of a stone staircase they were faced with a column of doorbells, each with a name beside it. Drawing a long breath, Ruth pressed the one marked Friedman. At first there was no response, then from above them a woman's voice came echoing down the stairwell.

"Yes, who is it?"

Ruth looked up the stairs to see a face peering down at them. "It's Ruth Friedman," she called. "I've come to see Herr Herbert Friedman."

"What do you want?"

"I want to see Herr Friedman," replied Ruth, wondering who the woman was.

"He isn't here." The face disappeared and Ruth heard a door close.

Ruth rang the bell again, but there was no further response.

"Come on," she said to the waiting children. "We'll go up." Trailed by the children, she set off up the stone stairs, pausing at each landing to read the names beside the front doors. On the third of the four floors there were three apartments. Hartmann, Gruber and Friedman. She pressed the Friedman bell. Nothing happened. Inge began to pull urgently at her skirt.

"I need the bathroom, Mutti," she whispered.

"Hold on, darling," Ruth replied. "Won't be long." She placed her finger on the bell again and held it there. She could hear its insistent ring inside the apartment, but she did not remove her finger. Inge was dancing up and down beside her now, clutching at herself, and Ruth knew that the child wouldn't be able to hold on much longer. She put her mouth to the door and called, "If you don't want a pool of urine on your doorstep, I suggest you open the door and let us in." She continued her pressure on the bell, and at last the door opened a fraction and an elderly woman looked out at them, her face twisted with rage.

"Go away!" she bellowed. "Herr Friedman isn't here."

"Then we will wait until he is," snapped Ruth. "In the meantime, my daughter needs the bathroom."

"You can't come in."

Ruth was placatory. "Madam, I am Herr Friedman's sister-in-law. These are his nephews and nieces. We have come with messages from his brother. Please let us in."

The woman looked at the little family standing on the landing, the mother leaning heavily on a stick, one of the children hopping up and down, clutching at her knickers, and with a sigh, she stood aside, saying as she did so, "First door on the left."

With a muttered thank you, Ruth hurried Inge into the bathroom, leaving Laura to bring the twins inside. The woman closed the door behind them with a snap and then led the way down a short passage to the room at the end. Moments later Ruth joined them with a much-relieved Inge and returned to the bathroom with the twins.

Laura looked round her as she waited for her turn.

The room was not large, but comfortably furnished, with a wide window that looked out over the street to a public garden beyond.

Uncle Herbert's got a nice view, she thought, as she looked at the joyful colours of the late summer flowers in the garden below. Tall trees gave welcome shade to a corner where several nursemaids sat gossiping, their charges blissfully asleep in their perambulators, and older children played on the grass, their laughter drifting up to the open windows above.

Laura watched them enviously. How long was it since she had been to the park to play with her school friends? School friends. She had few of those now. Since Herr Hitler had become Chancellor, everything had changed. Her friends, or those Laura had thought were her friends, were no longer allowed to play with her. At school she and the other Jewish children had been made to sit at the back of the classroom. It was as if they had become invisible. Their teacher Fräulein Lederman, whom Laura had loved, had left and been replaced by another, Fräulein Karhausen. Fräulein Karhausen ignored them, leaving them in the back row to learn what they could without any further explanations. They were no longer allowed to play with the other children in the yard in break times, they had to eat their lunch in the classroom, listening to their erstwhile playmates running and shouting in the fresh air outside. Gradually the other children had changed from being the friends she had known much of her life into unkind strangers, at first simply avoiding or ignoring her and then actively hostile, calling after her in the street, "Dirty Jew!" Even Wanda, who had been her best friend ever since they had started school together.

Her mother had tried to explain that "things" had changed.

Laws had changed. People were afraid to speak to Jews, afraid for their own families if they were seen to do so.

"They must put their families first," Ruth had said when she had found Laura in tears one afternoon. "Wanda's parents are afraid that someone will report them to the authorities if they are seen to be friendly with us."

"But she didn't have to shout 'Dirty Jew' at me," cried Laura, and her mother could only agree.

Now it was the summer holidays, and there was no school. Laura played with the other Jewish children, but she missed her other friends. Until "things" had changed Laura had been almost unaware of her Jewishness. Her family went to synagogue on a Saturday morning. Wanda's family went to church on a Sunday. It hadn't mattered before. Laura watched the children playing in the gardens below and wondered if any of them were Jews.

"I'm sorry to intrude on you like this," she heard her mother say as she came back into the room, "but I do have to see Herr Friedman."

The old woman who had let them in was standing in the room as if to see that they didn't steal anything.

"I told you, he isn't here," she said flatly.

"But he'll be back," Ruth said with a cheerfulness she didn't feel. "We'll wait." She looked across at the dour face of the older woman and said again, "I'm Ruth Friedman, Herr Friedman's sister-in-law." She held out a hand, but the woman ignored it, so she let it fall to her side and said, "And you are Frau—?"

The question hung in the air before, at last, the woman replied. "I'm Frau Schultz...I'm Herr Friedman's housekeeper."

"His housekeeper?" Ruth couldn't keep the surprise out of her voice. "We didn't know...I mean...I see."

"I come in most days," Frau Schultz said. "I'll be going home when I've finished preparing his supper." She moved to the door. "He won't be home till this evening. You going to wait that long?"

"Yes," replied Ruth firmly, relieved that the woman was not a live-in servant. While the children had been using the bathroom, she had gained some idea of the size of the apartment, and although there were several doors opening off the main passage, it was a very small apartment to house an extra five people. "I've brought some food with me, I'll prepare it for the children when you've finished in the kitchen."

"I don't know as I can leave you in the place on your own," Frau Schultz said sourly. "How do I know that you're who you say you are?"

Ruth had had enough of the woman's obstruction. "You don't," she agreed crisply, "so perhaps you'd better stay until Herr Friedman comes home." As she spoke she noticed the telephone standing on a small table in the passage. "You could always phone Herr Friedman at his office. Do you have the number? I'll ring myself if you like."

Still stony-faced, Frau Schultz opened the little drawer in the telephone table and pulling out a piece of paper, she thrust it at Ruth. "Help yourself," she sniffed, and, turning away, opened one of the doors and disappeared into the kitchen.

Ruth turned back to the children who, except for Laura, who was still standing by the window, were seated in a neat row on a sofa.

"I'm just going to ring Uncle Herbert," she said. "You sit

still like good children, and then we'll have something to eat. Laura, just keep an eye on the twins while I'm on the phone."

Ruth picked up the phone and gave the operator the number on the piece of paper.

"Durst, Hartmann and Weber. Good afternoon, how may I help you?"

"I'd like to speak to Herr Herbert Friedman, please."

"Herr Friedman. Whom shall I say is calling?"

"Ruth Friedman."

"Hold the line, please."

There was a long pause and then a man's voice. "Herbert Friedman. May I help you?"

"Herbert? It's Ruth."

"Frau Friedman." His voice was neutral; clearly Herbert was not going to acknowledge her on the telephone. Ruth decided she must be direct.

"I am at your apartment, with the children. Frau Schultz doesn't want me to wait for you."

There was a moment's silence at the other end and then Herbert said, "That is quite in order, Frau Friedman. Thank you for calling. Good afternoon." The line went dead.

Herbert arrived an hour later, his face red with the exertion of running up the stairs. He came into the apartment, and, shedding his hat and coat in the little hallway, walked into the sitting room to greet his sister-in-law.

"Ruth!" He extended a hand and placed a token peck on her cheek. He looked at the children ranged along his sofa, but immediately turned his attention back to their mother. "Where's Kurt?"

Ruth, who had risen at his entrance, sank back into the armchair where she had been sitting. "Taken by the storm

36

troopers." Briefly she told him what had happened.

"Kurt told me to come to you," she said at length, "so here we are. This is where he will look for us."

"But my dear Ruth, you can't stay here!"

"Where else can we go? Everything we had has gone, Herbert, I've almost no money and four children to look after. They have the clothes they stand up in, as do I. They're your brother's children, would you put them on the street?"

"Who knows you are here? Who else have you told about me?"

Ruth was puzzled. "What do you mean, who else knows about you? I haven't told anyone about you. Kurt will know where to find us when he is released."

"Thank God for that," breathed Herbert. He looked again at the little family camped in his living room. "Well, you'll have to stay for tonight, obviously, but tomorrow we must find you somewhere else to live."

"We only need one room, Herbert, and you have one to spare."

Herbert's face turned a darker shade of red. "You have searched my apartment? How dare you, madam!"

"Of course I haven't *searched* your apartment," snapped Ruth. "I have, however, opened the doors and glanced into the rooms. You have two bedrooms. I assume you only sleep in one." With an effort she softened her tone, it wouldn't help to antagonise her brother-in-law. "I agree it's not ideal, Herbert. If we were able to find somewhere else we would, but I have no money to pay any rent. If we stay here, I will ensure that the children don't disturb you when you are at home. I will also keep house for you, if you wish."

"I have Frau Schultz," Herbert said, grasping at a straw.

"Indeed you have," agreed Ruth. "I saw what she'd left for your supper. I have made you stew with dumplings. It is hot and waiting in the oven now."

Three

Ruth made the children as comfortable as she could in Herbert's second bedroom. It was not large, but it had a double bed in it, and by moving this against the wall, she was able to make space for some pillows on the floor beside it. The twins and Inge she tucked into the big bed, and Laura she settled on the pillows.

"Where will you sleep, Mutti?" asked Laura anxiously.

"I'll be on the sofa in the sitting room," replied her mother, "just across the passage. If you need me in the night, you only have to call."

Once the children were settled, Ruth returned to the living room. Herbert was sitting at the table, the remains of his meal in front of him.

"They seem well-behaved children," he remarked. "Have they gone to sleep?"

"They will very shortly," answered Ruth. "They've had a long day, and a very frightening few days before it. They can feel safe here." She sat down at the table opposite him. "I'm sorry we had to come, Herbert. I know it's inconvenient to you, but we had nowhere else to go. The dear people who took us in had no room for us either, and they had their own problems."

"Don't we all!" said Herbert testily. "You shouldn't have rung me at the office, Ruth."

Ruth was startled at his sudden vehemence. "I'm sorry, Herbert, I didn't know what else to do. Frau Schultz refused to let us stay, and I preferred not to stand in the street with the children until you came home."

Herbert shuddered. "No, that would have been worse. One can't afford to have attention drawn to one these days."

"Has there been trouble here, too?" asked Ruth.

"My dear Ruth, there has been trouble everywhere. Even those of us who are fully assimilated are being watched. I am lucky to keep my place at the office. It's only because the senior partner is Jewish that I have not been replaced. That is why I cannot afford to draw attention to myself by receiving private phone calls in office hours."

"I see. Well, I'm sorry, Herbert. I won't phone again. I am sure Kurt will be home soon, and then we can move away and try and start again."

Ruth was sure of no such thing, but she knew Herbert had to get used to the idea of housing his brother's family indefinitely. He was a bachelor, set in his ways and she could quite understand how he shuddered at such an invasion. He had her sympathy, but it was not going to stop her doing what was best for her children.

"In the meantime," she continued, "I can look after you as well. When does Frau Schultz come? I don't want to get in her way."

"She won't come again until Friday," Herbert replied. He got up from the table and picking up his newspaper, carried it to his chair. It was a firm indication that the conversation was over, and that he expected Ruth to clear away the meal.

The rest of the evening was passed in silence. Once the dishes were done, Ruth went into the bathroom and washed the children's clothes. Tomorrow she would have to set about finding them some more. At last Herbert bid her goodnight and she was able to settle herself down on the sofa, trying to get comfortable with the pillow and the blanket he had found for her. Despite feeling exhausted by the events of the day, and with her shoulder and her ankle both aching abominably, it was a long time before she slept.

When Herbert had left for work the next day, Ruth set about the housekeeping. Frau Schultz had clearly been doing the minimum she could get away with, and the state of the kitchen left a lot to be desired. First, however, she had to occupy the children. Herbert had found them each a notepad, the sort he used in his office, and provided a pencil for each from his desk, so Ruth sat them round the table in the living room with some schoolwork. Laura and Inge each had a page of sums to do. The twins joined the dots she had drawn on the page to form letters.

When the front door opened and Frau Schultz made her appearance, every one of them was fully occupied.

"Good morning, Frau Schultz," said Ruth, surprise in her voice. "I didn't think you came to Herr Friedman today."

The old woman ignored the remark and pushed her way into the kitchen, demanding, "What do you think you are doing in my kitchen?"

"Cleaning it," replied Ruth succinctly. "It's dirty."

"Herr Friedman doesn't complain."

"I'm sure he doesn't," agreed Ruth, "but it doesn't alter the fact that it needs a good clean."

"In which case, I'll leave you to clean it," replied Frau

Schultz. "You can tell Herr Friedman I'm not working for him while the place is a Jewish orphanage. If he wants me back, he can come and find me. And you can tell him he owes me a week's wages, which I'll come and collect on Saturday." With that, she turned abruptly and left the apartment, slamming the front door behind her.

Ruth sighed. Now Herbert had lost his housekeeper, not that she deserved that name if the grime round the gas stove and the state of the floor were anything to go by; but Ruth could only hope that she could be persuaded back when she and the children had moved out.

There was little food in the larder, and just one plate of cold meat in the tiny refrigerator that stood in a corner of the kitchen. Certainly not enough to feed them all, so when the kitchen was clean, Ruth gathered up the children, and with a little of her carefully hoarded money in her purse set out to buy a few basic groceries. The children's clothes would have to wait a little longer.

It was a glorious summer's day, and as they emerged from the apartment building Ruth felt the sun on her face, and for the first time in days her spirits lifted. They were in an area where no one knew them; for a while they would have the luxury of not being branded Jews. Gathering the children round her, she made her way down the street to the shops she had seen when they arrived. There was no kosher butcher of course, but she soon found a grocer's where she could buy bread and cheese, some eggs, potatoes, flour and butter. She had left the children outside the shop in charge of Laura.

She found herself in a shop very like her own, though it was clearly not Jewish, with a flitch of bacon hanging up behind the counter. Ruth averted her eyes, and gave her attention to the shopkeeper, a large, comfortable-looking woman with grey hair scraped back into a bun. Her eyes, a faded blue, peered at her customer from a wealth of wrinkles, and she smiled.

"Good morning," she said, "isn't it a beautiful one?"

"Good morning," Ruth replied, returning the smile. "It is indeed."

"What I can I get you?"

Ruth went through her list, and the woman placed the packages on the counter. As Ruth counted the money from her purse, the woman said casually, "I haven't seen you round here before. Have you just moved in to the area?"

"No." Ruth was immediately on her guard. "No, we are just visiting family. Only here for a few days, I'm afraid. Thank you." She picked up her purchases and put them into the shopping bag she'd found in Herbert's kitchen. "I think I'll take the children to the gardens on our way home."

The woman glanced out of the window to where the children were waiting patiently on the pavement. "They'll enjoy that," she said. "Lovely looking children, especially the little girl...such pretty blond hair."

"Indeed. Thank you." Ruth forced a smile and left the shop. As she did so she made way for another customer to enter, and saw with some dismay that it was Frau Schultz. The woman glared at her, pushed roughly past her into the shop, and said to the shopkeeper, "Well, Frau Schneider, I see you met the Jewish orphanage."

The door swung closed on her malice, and Ruth hurried the children away, urging them along the road, back towards the apartment.

"Mutti, you said we could play in the gardens on our way

home," Inge said, looking longingly across the road at the open iron gates that gave onto the park.

"Not just now," Ruth replied. "We have to go home and eat some lunch first, and the twins need their nap afterwards. Then perhaps we'll go."

"That's not fair," Inge wailed. "You *said* we could go." She dragged her feet as her mother hurried her along the pavement. "You *promised*, Mutti, I want to play on the swings."

"I didn't promise," snapped Ruth. "I said we might go, and we still might, but not if you make a fuss now. Come along, it's time for lunch."

The little group trailed back up the stairs to Herbert's flat. Once inside, Ruth locked the door and put the bolt across. She didn't want Frau Schultz to think she could walk in whenever she chose. Laura returned to her station by the window. She too was disappointed that they weren't going to spend some time in the gardens. She had been looking forward to the freedom of playing in the sunshine. She didn't know why her mother had changed her mind, but she knew that moaning like Inge wouldn't make her change it back again, so she sat down with the boys and played pat-a-cake with them while her mother put some food on the table.

Ruth had been dismayed as she heard Frau Schultz's comment. Their anonymity had been lost; they were now marked as Jews in this area as well. Her instinct had been to get the children back to the safety of Herbert's flat as soon as possible, but now as she gave them their lunch she looked at their pale faces and anger stirred again. Why shouldn't her children play in the gardens, run among the trees, slide down the slide? Why should she hide them in this dreary apartment on a glorious summer's day, when other children were outside with sun on their faces?

"When the boys have had a nap, we'll go to the park," she said as she cleared the plates away. "You should rest, too, Inge. Lie on the bed for half an hour, and then we'll go out."

*

Frau Schultz and Frau Schneider watched through the shop window as Ruth gathered up her children and led them back along the street.

"What did you mean...Jewish orphanage?" asked Frau Schneider as the little family disappeared from view.

"Turned up on Herr Friedman's doorstep yesterday afternoon, didn't they!" replied Frau Schultz. "Demanding to come in. Said she was his sister-in-law. Said she had nowhere else to go."

Frau Schneider's eyes were wide. "Did you let them in?"

"Had to, didn't I? She rang him at his office, and he said they could stay. Had to, didn't want a rabble like that standing on his doorstep, did he?"

"You wouldn't know they were Jews," Frau Schneider remarked. "The little girl, anyway, lovely fair hair and blue eyes."

"Yes, that's what's so awful," agreed Frau Schultz. "You could be fooled into thinking they were true Germans!"

"But you work for Herr Friedman," pointed out her friend, "and he's a Jew."

"Not anymore I don't," snapped Frau Schultz. "Went in this morning to see if I could be of help, and found that woman cleaning my kitchen. Told me it was dirty! Dirty!

That's the word I'd use for them. Dirty Jews. I told her, I said if that's what she thought she could tell Herr Friedman that I wasn't working there anymore and I'd collect my money on Saturday."

"But I suppose Herr Friedman isn't a proper Jew," Frau Schneider said thoughtfully. "I mean, he doesn't go to the synagogue on Saturdays or anything. If you hadn't said, I wouldn't have known he was a Jew either."

"A Jew is a Jew is a Jew," said Frau Schultz judiciously. "I'll be more choosy who I work for in the future, I can tell you."

"You might not be able to find another job that easy," pointed out her friend.

Frau Schultz knew that there was a lot of truth in that, and it was not comforting. "That's what I mean," she snarled. "Them Jews are keeping good honest Germans out of work. Taking all the jobs."

"Will they be staying with him long?" wondered Frau Schneider, ignoring this tirade. "There can't be much room for them all in that apartment."

"More room than we've got," Frau Schultz snapped. "I live in one room and share a bathroom. You have only two rooms above your shop for you and Herr Schneider. What does a single man need with all the space he has?"

"Well, he hasn't much space now," Frau Schneider laughed. "Poor man can't know what's hit him with those four kids descending on him! Now," she smiled, "what can I get you today?"

Frau Schultz made her purchases and then walked back to the tiny room she rented above the tobacconist shop in the next street. As she passed the gardens she glanced in, but there was no sign of the Jewish children playing there. She smiled grimly. That woman must have read the notice that had been placed there only last week. *Jüden Verboten! No Jews Allowed!* More and more, Jews were being made to understand their place. Herr Hitler was right, they were at the root of all Germany's problems. Get rid of the Jews and there would be plenty of jobs, plenty of houses, plenty of money for ordinary Germans like herself. The German people could reclaim their own country and make it strong again. Widows, like herself, wouldn't have to struggle to make a living.

When she had first gone to work for Herr Friedman, Eva Schultz had not known that he was a Jew. He was a man who kept himself to himself; a quiet man who went nowhere but his office and hardly knew his neighbours. She was well pleased with the work, it was in no way arduous. She went in three days a week, to clean, to do the laundry and to prepare Herr Friedman's evening meals. One meal she would leave in the oven for that night, and another, cold, on a plate in his refrigerator for the next day. Frau Schultz envied him that refrigerator. Fancy a man on his own having such a luxury. However, he paid well, and left money for her to do the shopping. That was a bonus. It was easy enough to buy some extra slices of meat, a few more eggs, another small piece of cheese, charging it up to him. He had little idea of the price of food and simply left her some money for the house-keeping each week. She was careful to leave him the change each week, amounts that varied slightly, so that he didn't ask any awkward questions. Then she had discovered that he was Jewish. Snooping among his papers one day, she read a letter he'd received from his brother about the family going to Vienna for a bar mitzvah. Bar mitzvah! Herr Friedman was a Jew! She was working for a Jew. After that she stole from him more regularly and without compunction. She didn't like the idea of working for a Jew, but it was worth putting in the minimal amount of time she gave to cleaning his apartment, to enable her to help herself to the extras to which she felt she was entitled. The arrival of his sister-in-law with her hordes had now put paid to that. It was clear that woman had already realised what she was up to, and no doubt she would tell Herr Friedman when he got home this evening...and her job really would be gone. Another example of Jews taking the bread from the mouths of a good, honest German.

Back in her room, Eva dumped her shopping onto the table. She filled the kettle from the single, cold-water tap over the basin in the corner and set it to boil on the gas ring that stood beside it. Kicking off her shoes, she flopped into the one easy chair that stood in front of the gas fire. Behind her was an alcove, curtained to conceal her bed. She looked round her, taking in again the dreariness of her accommodation. She had lived here for five years now, ever since her husband, Ernst, had been killed in an accident on the building site where he had worked as a labourer. The chain of a hoist, lifting a pallet of bricks to the first-floor scaffolding, had snapped and the bricks had fallen on Ernst, killing him instantly. An accident, a dreadful accident, the building firm had said. Very sad...their condolences to the grieving widow. Ernst had had no pension, they had had no savings, and despite the whip-round organised by his mates, Eva Shultz had found herself almost destitute. She had to move out of the small apartment they rented, and had found this dismal room only through the good offices of one of Ernst's workmates, whose sister was married to the tobacconist in the shop below. The whip-round had provided her with the first month's rent and then she had had to find some work to support herself, and find it quickly. It was a card in the tobacconist's window that caught her eye. *Housekeeper wanted for quiet, single gentleman.* Eva applied, got the job and began working for Herbert Friedman.

As she drank the weak coffee she had made, Eva thought now about the family who had arrived so unexpectedly. Clearly they were in some sort of trouble, or they wouldn't have descended on Herbert so suddenly. Where was the husband, she wondered, the one who was Herbert's brother? Little had been said during the phone conversation she had overheard, but it was clear that they had nowhere else to go. The idea that they, too, had been turned out of their home gave Eva a certain satisfaction, and it was that and the conversation she'd had with Frau Schneider in the shop that had given her the glimmerings of an idea. As she sipped her coffee, she wondered if it might work, and then shivered at her own temerity. She would ponder it, she decided, look into how it could be done. The seed was sown, and as she got to her feet to put away her meagre provisions, the last she would buy with Herbert Friedman's money, she thought about his refrigerator, and smiled.

*

Ruth was as good as her word, and when the twins awoke from their nap, she took the children down the stairs and across the road to the gardens opposite. The wrought-iron gates stood wide and welcoming, but the newly painted sign mounted on a pole just inside made her pause.

No Jews allowed!

Of the children, only Laura could read the words, and she glanced anxiously at her mother. Ruth gave her a reassuring smile, marched determinedly through the gate and took the path that led to the children's playground. This was surrounded by a low fence, with another, more succinct sign on its gate. *No Jews.* Ignoring it, Ruth pushed open the gate and let the children run in. Inge headed straight for the slide, and the twins ran happily across to the sandpit where two small girls were digging a sand castle. Laura followed the boys, while Ruth called to Inge to hold tight as she climbed the steps to the top of the slide.

A nursemaid, with a pram beside her, was sitting on a bench, uninterestedly watching the little girls in the sandpit. She hardly noticed the twin boys and their elder sister who joined them. The boys had nothing to dig with except their hands, but they set to work piling sand into a heap for their castle, laughing and chatting to each other as they did so. Her charges watched for a moment, pausing in their own efforts.

"Would you like to help?" Laura asked the little girls. "Hansi and Peter would love you to help them."

The elder of the two girls, aged about six, nodded shyly, and they both edged nearer to the twins.

"What's your name?" Laura asked the older sister.

"Angela," replied the girl. "Come on, Erna, come and help."

The five children played together. The boys digging energetically with their hands, the girls filling their bucket, and Laura upending it carefully to make turrets for the castle.

Inge had moved from the slide to the swings, and Ruth, seeing that Laura was looking after the twins, went across and pushed Inge, so that she squealed with delight as she sailed up into the air. All the children were laughing and shouting with pleasure as they played together in the sunshine. The nursemaid was now dozing on her bench in the heat of the afternoon sun, and the baby lay waving its arms, batting the rattles that were strung across the pram. Having had her fill of swinging, Inge jumped off and ran across to the sandpit to see what the others were doing. Ruth followed her and together they admired the splendid castle that now stood in the middle, a turret on each corner and a feather as a flag.

"No Jews allowed!"

The harsh voice behind them made her jump and Ruth spun round to see a uniformed park keeper, accompanied by Frau Schultz.

"I beg your pardon?" Ruth replied.

"No Jews allowed. Can't you read?"

"The notice is on both gates," Frau Schultz put in sweetly. "I'd have thought you'd have seen it," adding with venom, "or are you blind...as well?"

The nursemaid started up from the bench, one hand grasping the pram as if it might escape her, the other beckoning frantically to the two little girls in the sandpit.

"Angela, Erna, come away at once!" As the surprised girls moved towards her, she grabbed Erna by the hand, and called Angela again. "Come away, Angela. Come away from those dirty children. Whatever would your mother say?"

She pulled the children away, and, pushing the pram, hurried off down the path. As she went, Ruth heard the younger girl pipe, "Nanny, what's a Jew?" If she gave one, the nursemaid's answer was lost as she sped her charges away.

"Out!" The park keeper was pointing at the gate. "Out of here, out of the gardens, and don't come back or I'll call the law."

"Come along, children," Ruth said quietly. "We must go

home now." She took the twins by the hand, and, edging the girls in front of her, made her way to the gate.

"Trouble is," she heard the park keeper saying, "you wouldn't know they was Jews, would you? Not from the look of them."

"That's why you have to be so vigilant," replied Frau Schultz. "But don't worry, Herr Maus, I won't report you... this time."

"Vile woman," murmured Ruth under her breath. "Vile and evil woman!"

"What did you say, Mutti?" asked Inge.

"Vile and evil woman! Vile and evil woman!" chanted the twins, delighted with the words.

Ruth jerked them to a halt, so roughly that they cried out. "Be quiet!" she admonished. "Be quiet and don't speak again until we get home, or I'll take a wooden spoon to you!"

As they crossed the road to the apartment block, Ruth risked a glance back over her shoulder. The park keeper had moved away, but Frau Schultz still stood by the sandpit, watching them leave. She was too far away to see the expression on her face, but the set of her head and shoulders shouted "triumph" as loudly as if she had actually called after them.

She must have heard me say that I'd take the children there, thought Ruth, as she hurried them up the stairs to Herbert's apartment. She must have been watching, so that she could report us.

Herbert listened in horror to the events of the day when Ruth related them to him that evening.

"How could you have been so stupid?" he raged at her. "How could you have drawn such attention to yourselves? Can't you read, you stupid woman? Didn't you see the sign that says 'No Jews'?"

52

"I saw it," Ruth replied, trying to keep her own anger in check. "I saw it, but who was to know round here that we are Jews?"

"Frau Schultz!" Herbert almost shrieked. "As you discovered."

"Well, we won't go again," sighed Ruth.

"You'd better not!" Herbert snapped. "You'll be watched now," he went on bitterly. "You'll be watched, I'll be watched, we'll all be watched from now on. You should have gone to your mother, that's where you should have gone. You should have gone to your mother, not come here with your brood."

"I came here, because Kurt...your brother, Kurt...told me to," hissed Ruth. "It is here he will come looking for us. Here he will come looking for his brood. They're your brother's children, Herbert. Your nieces and nephews. They're family. I am his wife. We're family."

"Yes, yes," Herbert replied testily, "but family is no protection these days."

"You mean we've put you in danger, Herbert, by coming here. Is that what you mean?"

"No, no." Herbert waved a placatory hand. "But all Jews are in some sort of danger these days, especially..." he paused, trying to choose the right words, "...especially practising Jews. They are noted. I haven't been to the synagogue for years. I no longer follow the dietary requirements. I am not a Jew in any real sense. I'm German through and through, the fact that I had Jewish parents is beyond my control."

"Beyond your control," agreed Ruth, "but true none the less. As far as the authorities are concerned you're a Jew. The new laws apply to you as they do to the rest of us."

Ruth could see Herbert was about to argue, and she was

too tired. "Never mind," she sighed, "let's not argue now. Come to the table, I've made dinner for you."

Herbert was happy enough to do as he was bid. The food, though plain, was a great improvement on what Frau Schultz had been in the habit of leaving him, and he found himself looking forward to the meal that would be waiting for him when he got home.

Laura's Diary
24th July 1937

We have come to stay with Uncle Herbert in Munich. He wasn't very pleased to see us and I don't like it here. We are all sleeping in one room, except for Mutti and she's got to sleep on the sofa in the living room. I wish we could go home again, but I know we can't. I wish Papa was here. Uncle Herbert is his brother, but he's not like him. Papa is always kind, but Uncle Herbert is always cross. He has a cross voice and a cross face and it's nice when he goes to his office.

Laura paused, chewing her pencil thoughtfully, and then wrote,

25th July 1937

We can't go out like we did at home, there is nowhere to play. Mutti took us to the park. Hansi and Peter played in the sandpit. I helped them. We made a castle with two girls. A man came and told us to leave. He said Jews weren't allowed to play in the park. The nasty lady who was here when we got here was with him. She was smiling, but she was horrible.

Laura stopped writing and looked at what she had written in the notebook Mutti had found for her. Mutti had suggested she write a story. Laura had always loved writing stories and had done so as long as she could remember. At school the teachers used to encourage her, especially Fräulein Lederman, but that was until everything changed, when Fräulein Lederman had to leave and Fräulein Karhausen took her place. From then on Laura was left out. Oh, not from the actual classroom, just from the activities that went on inside it. She and two other Jewish children, Olga and Elfriede, were made to sit at the back...where they were ignored. Fräulein Karhausen never asked them to provide answers in class, even when nobody else could; she never looked at the work they produced, never corrected it, no stars were given, indeed their names weren't even on the star chart. But Laura had continued writing. She began to keep a diary, which she wrote every evening when she had finished her homework, homework that was required but never looked at. Papa had given her a beautiful notebook in which to write her diary, but that, like everything else she owned, had been destroyed in the fire. All her thoughts and ideas had vanished in the smoke that billowed from the window into the night sky.

Ruth had not suggested that Laura start her diary again, she thought it would be unhealthy to keep a record of the dreadful things that had happened. They were best forgotten as soon as possible, so that the slithering skein of life could be grasped once more, and some sort of normality could be re-established.

"Why don't you write a story?" she suggested. "One you could read to the twins. They always love your stories." It was true, Hansi and Peter did always love her stories, begging

55

her for new ones, but today there were no stories in her head, only the events of the last few days, churning and bubbling like an over-boiling saucepan. The men coming to the apartment. Papa being arrested. The fire. Staying with the Meyers. Finding the box. Suddenly their lives had been turned upside down, and Laura felt that if she didn't write it all down, set it in some sort of order in her mind, it would overwhelm her and she would sink under its weight. Mutti needed her help. She, Laura, was almost eleven, after all. She must be strong and help Mutti, especially with the twins. They had always been her beloved brothers. She loved Inge, of course she did, but Peter and Hansi...she would be strong for them. They were too young to understand what was happening.

"When's Papa coming?" Hansi had suddenly asked as he was being got ready for bed.

"Will he be here soon?" Peter had chimed in, finishing as he so often did his twin's thought.

"Soon," his mother had soothed, but Laura knew that she had lied. She didn't know when and was only trying to comfort the little boys.

I should start this diary from the night of the fire, Laura thought now, and crossing out what she had written, began again.

19th July 1937

They took Papa away and we haven't seen him since...

On the first Friday evening after their arrival at Herbert's, Ruth had set the table for the Sabbath evening meal, carefully ironing the only white linen tablecloth she could find, before washing and laying out the silver and china she had discovered packed away in the sideboard. She polished two rather tarnished candlesticks, which still had the remnants of candles stuck into them, and set them in the middle of the table. Murmuring the familiar prayers, she lit them, and waited for Herbert to come home. As the children waited for him, seated round the table, they too seemed to be soothed by the familiar ritual of Friday evening. The meal would start when the man of the house, normally Kurt, but in this case Herbert, came home, but this evening Herbert did not come home. Kurt would have been to the synagogue, but Ruth knew that was the last place Herbert would be. She knew there was a synagogue not that far away, for she had discussed it with her brother-in-law. But when she had suggested she might take the children there on Saturday morning he had been adamant.

"It would be madness to go," Herbert had stated. "I forbid you to go! Do you want to draw even more attention to your children? I forbid you to go."

No, wherever Herbert was, he would not be at the synagogue this evening. Eventually she said the prayers herself and served the meal.

When the children were safely in bed Ruth sat in the living room, the table uncleared, and waited. At last she heard Herbert's key in the lock, and as she turned to greet him saw the shock at what he saw before him register on his face.

"What's all this mess?" he demanded, looking at the remains of the meal on the table.

"It's your supper, Herbert," she replied quietly. "It's the Sabbath."

"Well, I don't want it!" he snapped. "You can clear it

away." When she hesitated he rounded on her. "You may not work on the Sabbath in your own home, Ruth," he growled, "but you do in mine. I have no intention of sitting looking at this stuff. Put it in the kitchen. I don't want it. I've eaten."

"If you'd said you were going out, I wouldn't have cooked dinner for you." Ruth forced herself to speak mildly, though she could feel the anger welling up inside her.

"Oh? So now I have to account to you for my movements, do I?"

"Of course not," Ruth replied, "but it seems a pity to waste food when we have so little of it."

Herbert suddenly seemed to sag, and dropping into his chair said, "Just put it in the kitchen, Ruth, you can leave the washing-up until tomorrow evening if you must."

Accepting this compromise, Ruth got up. After all, with the changed state of things, there was no way she could do no work on the Sabbath. She cleared the table, stacking the dishes neatly beside the kitchen sink, which was where Frau Schultz saw them the next morning when she called to demand her money.

"And she had the audacity to call *my* kitchen dirty," she said to Frau Schneider, as she recounted her visit. "Dirty crockery and cutlery, in heaps by the sink. Nasty Jewish food. Beginning to smell in this heat, I can tell you." She sniffed as if the smell was still in her nostrils. "No German would live in a pigsty like that."

"No, indeed." Frau Schneider nodded judiciously, even as she thought of the squalid state of her own kitchen upstairs where no one had washed a plate for days. "Just the Jews."

Over the next few days Ruth slipped into a routine of cooking and cleaning for Herbert, for Frau Schultz, true to her word, and much to Ruth's relief, did not reappear. Ruth spent time with her children, making them do some lessons every day, before taking them out for some fresh air in the afternoon. Not to the gardens, though. She dared not venture there again. She knew she had been stupid to ignore the notice and take the children there in the first place. She had put them at risk, and she was determined not to do so again.

Nor did she return to Frau Schneider's shop, but walked the children further afield, to shops where they were not known, buying her groceries in different places, so that they were not recognised as "locals". Herbert had given her some money, and so she managed to buy them all another set of clothes, pinafores and blouses for the girls, shorts and shirts for the twins. There was no money for shoes. Once she thought she saw Frau Schultz walking along the street behind them, but when she looked back a second time there was no sign of the woman, and she decided she must have been mistaken. Surely not even Frau Schultz would bother to trail them round the area to warn the shopkeepers that they were dealing with Jews. Surely not.

Four

The days turned to weeks, and still there was no news of Kurt. In many ways Ruth wished they had found some way to remain in Gerbergasse, where at least they would be surrounded by people they knew. There might be news of the men who had been taken the night of the riot; such news would spread swiftly through the neighbourhood. There might be news of Kurt.

Ruth had written to Frau Meyer to thank her for her kindness and to tell her that they had reached Herbert's in safety She'd asked if anything had been heard of those arrested. The letter she received in reply did nothing to raise her spirits.

Dear Frau Friedman,

Thank you for your letter. I am glad you and the children are safe with your brother-in-law. You are certainly safer than you would be here. Terror stalks our streets now, and we walk in fear of our lives.

Herr Rosen came back the other day. He's been held in some sort of camp. A place called Dachau. He says that all the men from here are being held there. The conditions there are very bad. He has been let out because he has agreed to

60

leave Germany with his family and never return. He came to collect them, but they have had to leave everything behind.

Everything except what they could put into one suitcase, and that was searched by the Gestapo to make sure they weren't taking anything of value. They went three days ago, and already another family have moved into their apartment.

So far nothing has been done with your shop. Leo boarded up the door, but it remains a burnt-out shell.

If your husband comes here I will tell him where you are, but I shall not write to you again, and ask you not to write to me. Who can tell if the post is safe?

God bless you all,

L

There was no return address on the letter, nothing other than the single initial to identify the writer, but its content struck fear into Ruth's heart. She had done the right thing moving the children out of the area; she could only pray that Kurt would soon be let out of this Dachau place, wherever it was, and be able to come for them. If it meant leaving Germany, Ruth wouldn't mind. What was left for people like them here, after all? Encouraged by the government and orchestrated by the Gestapo, the persecution was getting worse, more frequent, the ways of degrading and humiliating Jews becoming more inventive, more brutal.

This isn't how I want my children to live, Ruth thought as she read and re-read the letter. Better we leave now. But where, with no money, no possessions? America? England? Palestine? How can we go? What should we live on?

She would show the letter to Herbert when he got home that

evening and see what he thought about it. Probably he would say that Leah Meyer was being alarmist. He still thought that Jews who kept their heads down were in no real danger. He had become less concerned about her and the children being in his home recently, now that she was so careful to do nothing more to draw attention to them. He even played with the children sometimes, in the evening when he came in. He genuinely had difficulty in telling the twins apart, and often called them by the wrong name, which sent them off into paroxysms of laughter, and once he discovered that he could make them laugh, he found that he enjoyed doing so. One day he had come home with a present for each of them; soft toy rabbits dressed in striped trousers for the twins, some crayons for Inge and a book for Laura. The delight on the children's faces as they opened the parcels was mirrored in his own, and Ruth could see he was becoming genuinely fond of them.

This evening, however, he came home late, well after the children were in bed, and at once Ruth could see that something was wrong. He seemed to have aged ten years since the morning. He looked pale, his skin, the colour of parchment, seemed more tightly drawn over his cheekbones. His shoulders sagged and his whole body seemed to have shrunk. Only his eyes gleamed, and they gleamed not with life, but with fear, continually darting in all directions as if he expected an attack.

"Herbert? Are you all right? What's happened?"

For answer he simply shook his head and sank down into his armchair, burying his head in his hands.

"Herbert?" Ruth waited, but it was some time before her brother-in-law looked up at her, his eyes wide with fear and disbelief.

"Herr Durst," he said. "Herr Durst has left."

Ruth knew that Herbert thought the light of day shone out of Herr Jacob Durst, the senior partner. She had often had to listen to Herbert extolling the abilities, the intellect, the steadfast character of Herr Durst, the mainstay of the firm.

"Left? Left the office?"

"They've thrown him out!"

"Thrown him out? Who's thrown him out?"

"The other partners."

"The other partners? Why? Why would they do that?"

"The firm was losing clients," replied Herbert wearily. "Nobody wants a Jewish lawyer anymore. Just having his name on the letterheads has made the clients look elsewhere."

"So, what's going to happen?" asked Ruth.

"It's already happened," Herbert said. "They had a meeting today...without him, and after it they called him in and told him to leave...there and then. To leave everything in his desk and his files...everything. When he went back to the office for his coat, his desktop was clear...there was nothing on it, except the photograph of his wife and daughters stuffed into a brown paper bag."

"And he just accepted this? It was his firm; you told me he founded the firm." Ruth was incredulous. "And he let them simply throw him out?"

Herbert let out a shuddering sigh. "What else could he do? Wait to be manhandled out of the building? They were already changing the locks on the doors as I followed him out."

"You followed him out?" repeated Ruth.

Herbert gave a mirthless laugh. "You don't think they'd keep me on once he'd gone, do you? I was at my desk as he passed my door, and within two minutes Herr Hartmann was in the room, saying, 'Out, Friedman! We don't want your sort here either!' I sat there staring at him, because I didn't know then what had happened to Herr Durst.

"I must have looked very stupid, because he crossed over to the desk and put his face right down next to mine and spoke very slowly and distinctly as if I was an idiot. 'Get out of this office, Friedman, and don't come back.'"

"What did *you* say?"

"I didn't know what to say. He simply turned away saying, as he walked out of the door, 'Collect your wage packet from Fräulein Weiss. You're lucky to get it.' I was still too shocked to move, I just stared at him and then he said, 'And if you're still here in five minutes' time, you won't be paid!'"

"Did you get it?" Ruth asked anxiously. "Did they pay you what they owed?" Her own money had dwindled to almost nothing, and would have run out long ago if Herbert hadn't given her housekeeping money…the money he no longer paid Frau Schultz.

"Yes, they've paid me to the end of the week. It's not much."

"But if you left so early, where have you been since?" wondered Ruth.

"When I'd collected my money from Fräulein Weiss, I went after Herr Durst. He was outside in the street, looking up at the office building as if he couldn't believe what he was seeing. We were hardly out of the door before we saw someone not only changing the locks on the front door, but replacing the brass plate beside it."

"The brass plate?"

"With the name of the firm. As from today the firm has a new name. Hartmann and Weber." Herbert shook his head sadly. "This must all have been planned for some time," he went on. "How else would they have had the new nameplate ready? When I came out, Herr Durst looked across at me and said, 'You too, Friedman? I'm sorry about that. No Jews allowed.' 'What will you do now, sir?' I asked him."

"What did he say?"

"He said, 'Perhaps set up on my own again, and deal only with Jewish clients. Let's face it,' he said, 'there are plenty of Jews who need my help just now.' 'Will you have work for me?' I asked him. 'I need a job too.' He said, 'Come and have a drink and we'll talk about it.'"

"So that's where you've been." Ruth sounded relieved.

"We went to a bar where Herr Durst is known, and they did serve us, but it was clear they overcharged us. When I said as much to Herr Durst, he said that it had been so for some time now, but that it meant he could still buy a drink there if he wanted to."

"So, did he give you a job?"

"No. He gave me advice." Herbert fell silent.

"What?" demanded Ruth at last. "What did he say?"

"He said I should get out while I could."

"Get out?" echoed Ruth. "Get out of where?"

"Germany. He said I was single and that it would be easy for me to leave now, but he thought things were going to get much worse. That the time would come when it would be too late. Jews wouldn't be allowed to leave."

"And is he going to get out?" enquired Ruth.

"No," answered Herbert, "but he has a family, it's not so easy for him simply to up sticks and go."

"Exactly! He has family! You'd think he would be trying to get them out as soon as he can."

"He said he'd thought of it," Herbert said, "but he's not sure it's necessary for a family like his."

"A family like his?" Ruth spoke with the utmost scorn. "Does he really think he's too well connected to be in any danger? Does he think the Nazis pay any attention to that? He's a Jew. All Jews are at risk." Ruth pulled Leah Meyer's letter out of her pocket and handed it to Herbert. "Read that," she said. "Jews are being rounded up and sent to this dreadful camp, well the men are anyway, and they are only being allowed out if they agree to leave Germany for good. Kurt is in this camp…at least I assume he is, as he was arrested the same night as Martin Rosen. God knows if he will be offered the same chance to leave, but in the meantime things are getting worse, you know they are. Look what she says here, 'terror stalks the streets', she means the Gestapo."

"I know it, you know it. But there's nothing we can do about it except keep out of the way."

"That's not going to work forever," Ruth said. "Only today when I was out with the children we heard them marching towards us. There was nowhere to hide, and as they came towards us those dreadful boots they wear crashing on the road, they sounded like an enemy army. They took no notice of us this time, but I was terrified for the children."

"You shouldn't be taking them out," Herbert said.

"I have to. They can't stay prisoners in here all day and every day. Oh Herbert, I wish I knew what to do!"

Herbert nodded wearily. "So do I," he said.

Ruth hardly slept that night, churning everything over in her mind, considering and discarding ideas as to what they might do. Herbert losing his job meant that his income had dried up, which meant that hers had too. What were they

66

going to live on? How was she going to feed four hungry children, not to mention herself and Herbert? It wasn't just money for food that she had to find. The winter was coming, they would need warm clothes. She could try and get work herself, but there were so few jobs, and almost none that might be given to a Jew. Ruth didn't mind hard work, would welcome it if it meant that her children were warm and fed, but she knew there would be little on offer.

And even if I can get work, she wondered, who'll look after the children? It'll have to be Laura; though she's only ten, she'll have to look after them if I do manage to find something.

Herbert might be more lucky, she thought. He, unlike her with her dark hair and eyes, her slightly hooked nose and wide mouth, was not so obviously Jewish. He might find himself a job of some sort, even if not the kind of work he was used to. He won't be able to be choosy about what he does, she thought. He'll have to take anything that's offered.

At last she drifted off into fitful sleep, from which she woke in the morning, un-refreshed, her eyes as heavy as her heart.

Herbert left at his usual time next morning, as if he were going to the office. Ruth was pleased he did, it prevented any awkward questions from Laura, who was quite old enough and bright enough to notice a change in routine. At the end of the week he gave Ruth her usual housekeeping money, but though he had been looking for work every day, he told her, "There's no work for anyone. I did call on Herr Durst again, but he was not at home."

"Not at home, or not at home to you?" asked Ruth.

Herbert shrugged. "It's all one when it comes down to it,"

he said. "He's not going to be able to give me any work, even if he gets something set up for himself. He has two sons. They will keep anything like that in the family. It's everyone for himself these days."

Ruth could only agree with him. There had been unrest all over the country, though not, thank goodness, in their immediate locality. All Jews were constantly looking over their shoulders now. Frau Meyer's words lived in her mind: "terror stalks our streets". Ruth, like almost all Jews, had become more and more aware of the tramp of jackboots, and the casual cruelty of the Hitler Youth who haunted the Jewish districts, hunting in gangs. She seldom took the children far these days, just a short walk each day to give them some exercise and fresh air. They were virtually prisoners in the apartment, and although she tried to keep up a pretence of normality, they were changing from the cheerful, rosy-cheeked children she had brought from Gerbergasse, to restive, fractious children, pale-faced and hollow-eyed.

It was over a week later that Herbert finally dropped his bombshell.

"I'm going to Argentina," he told Ruth when the children were safely in bed and they were alone in the living room. They were sitting across the dining table from each other, the remains of a frugal meal between them.

Ruth stared at him, aghast. "You're what?"

"I'm going to Argentina," he repeated, "I've booked my passage on a ship. I leave from Hamburg next week. There's nothing to keep me here."

Ruth continued to stare at him. "Nothing to keep you here," she echoed flatly.

Herbert continued as if she hadn't spoken, "I've no family,

and it's no good me waiting to see if Herr Durst is going to set up another firm. I'm getting out while I still can."

"Nothing to keep you here," Ruth said again. "No family. What about Kurt's children? Kurt's family? Don't you think we might need you?"

Herbert looked a little uncomfortable, but he spoke firmly. "I have thought about you and the children...of course I have. I would take you, but Kurt will be coming to look for you here. Otherwise I'd take you with me, of course I would...But you said yourself that this is where Kurt will come to find you." His eyes showed a gleam of...what? Ruth wasn't sure as she listened to him cap his lies with the argument she had used to get him to allow them to stay with him.

"Here," she repeated. "But if you've gone..."

"My dear Ruth," Herbert said soothingly, "you don't think I am just going to walk away and leave you with nowhere to live, do you?"

It was *exactly* what Ruth was thinking, so she didn't reply as she waited for him to continue. "Of course not." He shook his head firmly. "It would be wrong to take you with me, but you can stay here. The rent on this flat is paid up until the end of the year. You can stay here, just as you are now until Kurt comes for you. If they're letting them out of that camp, it won't be long before he's here with you again."

"And you've actually booked your passage? Bought your ticket? You have your ticket in your hands?"

"Not yet, but I've paid for it. I collect it from the office of the shipping company tomorrow."

"Let's hope there is one for you," snapped Ruth bitterly.

Once he had told her, Herbert's demeanour began to change. He had made his decision some days ago, but now he had admitted it to Ruth there came a sense of relief, a sense of purpose. He still looked older than his years, but a little colour began to creep back into his cheeks. He got up from his chair and went to the sideboard where he poured himself a glass of schnapps. Turning back towards Ruth he saw her watching him, her eyes dull with worry.

"Would you like a drink, Ruth?" he asked awkwardly. "I'm sorry, I should have asked you."

Ruth was about to refuse when she thought, "Why not?" She seldom drank alcohol, but suddenly she felt in need of...whatever it might supply. She nodded and Herbert poured another, smaller measure into a glass and handed it to her.

"Prosit!" he said.

Ruth took the glass and took a sip. The drink was fiery in her throat, and she coughed, before downing the rest in one draught, and coughing again.

"Steady," Herbert said. "You're not used to it." He tilted his own glass and he, too, downed the contents in one, before pouring each of them another.

Later, as Ruth lay on the sofa, feeling a little woozy from the unaccustomed schnapps, she went over and over what Herbert had said.

"You can stay here in the flat. You'll be fine."

"And what do you suggest we live on?" she had demanded angrily. "Fresh air?"

"Of course not," Herbert soothed. "I will give you some money. It's the least I can do. I have some money saved. Most of it I must take with me, to start again in Argentina...but of course I will leave you enough to keep you going until Kurt gets here."

"And supposing he doesn't?" demanded Ruth, staring at him icily. "Supposing he doesn't get here?"

Herbert had returned her stare. "Then you'll be on your own, Ruth. I'll have done everything I can for you, and it'll be up to you."

"Will they let you take your money with you?" she'd asked a little later. "I thought you weren't allowed to take anything valuable with you."

"Don't worry, I've thought of that," Herbert replied. "I'm not taking it in actual cash. I've converted it into something more portable; something easier to hide. I'll get it out all right."

Ruth didn't ask what, or where he would conceal it. She didn't want to know. She didn't want to know how much he was taking, or how. She simply asked, "When do you go?" She knew that whatever she said or did, Herbert would leave and she and the four children would be on their own.

"I collect my ticket tomorrow," he replied, "and then take the train to Hamburg. The boat leaves next week."

So this time tomorrow, Ruth thought, it'll just be me and the children.

She fought to keep the rising panic at bay. She fought the tears of frustration and desperation that threatened to overwhelm her. This was no time to give way to tears. It was only her strength that was going to keep them alive.

Herbert had spent much of the night packing. Ruth could hear him moving round his bedroom, opening and closing drawers and the wardrobe. There was the occasional creak of bedsprings, and then as the grey of a false dawn lightened the sky, one final groan of the bed as Herbert lay down.

Ruth wondered if he had actually managed to go to sleep,

or whether he, too, was lying in the dark, afraid of what the future might hold.

Next morning he ate his breakfast in silence, paying no attention to the chatter of the children, and they, picking up the strange atmosphere, gradually slipped into silence. As soon as they had finished eating, Ruth sent them to their bedroom, telling them to play in there until she called them to do their lessons.

Herbert looked at his sister-in-law across the table. "I'll be off soon," he said. He reached into his pocket and pulled out a bundle of notes and handed them across to her. "This should keep you going for a while," he said. "As I told you, the rent is paid until the end of the year. You'll have a roof over your heads until then at least."

Ruth nodded, and reaching for the money put it into her pocket. "Thank you for that," she said, getting to her feet. "I wish you the best of luck in your new life, Herbert."

"As soon as I get settled there, I'll be in touch. Kurt can bring you all over to join me... and," Herbert paused as if not knowing quite how to phrase what he wanted to say next, before continuing awkwardly, "and, if he hasn't come back by then, perhaps you should consider joining me anyway... to keep the children safe."

"Yes, well..."

"Yes, well..." Herbert turned away and went into his bedroom. Ruth was still standing beside the breakfast table when he reappeared a few moments later, wearing his overcoat and a felt hat and carrying a large suitcase.

"Obviously I haven't been able to take all my clothes with me," he said. "Kurt can have them when he gets here." For a moment he gave his sister-in-law a long look, then he put

72

the case on the floor and reached out to take her hand. For a moment Ruth thought he was going to put his arms round her, but he simply shook her hand and said, "Goodbye, Ruth. I'll be in touch."

Ruth nodded. She knew that she should be thanking him properly for the money, for housing them all for so long, for making sure they weren't hungry and homeless. She knew that he had done all he could for them, but the words wouldn't come. She felt so bereft at his leaving, she could only let him shake her hand before he laid his keys on the table and, without another word, walked out of the apartment. As the door closed behind him, and she heard his feet on the stairs, Ruth looked at the keys, and finally accepted that Herbert wasn't coming home again. No man who thinks he might come back leaves the keys to his home on the table. She moved to the window and looking down into the street watched him walk away, suitcase in hand, his head bent against the late October drizzle.

"Goodbye, Herbert," she whispered. Then with a deep breath she turned back to the room and slowly and methodically began to clear the breakfast table. When it was done she called the children to come and do their lessons.

"Uncle Herbert's gone away for a holiday," she told them. "He says you girls can use his bedroom while he's away. That's kind of him, isn't it?"

"Will he want it back when he comes home again?" asked Inge.

"Of course he will," said Laura. "It's his room." She glanced across at her mother and added, "But it will be nice to sleep in there for now."

When they had finished their lessons, while Ruth made

up Herbert's bed with clean sheets, the girls moved their few possessions into his bedroom. They moved the clothes he had left behind into one corner of the wardrobe and began to settle in.

Ruth made the other bedroom more comfortable for the twins, deciding that she would continue to sleep on the sofa in the living room. That way everyone had a little more space. She had counted the money Herbert had given her, and she had to admit he had done his best. If she were careful she could make it last for two or even three months. They would not eat well, but they would not starve either, as they waited for Kurt to come. She divided the notes up into several smaller bundles, which she hid in different places in the apartment. One crammed between the lavatory cistern and the wall, another buried in a tin of flour in the kitchen, a third under the mattress in the twins' room, and a fourth, the largest, tucked into her own underwear. The rest she put into the cashbox with the passports and other personal documents that was locked in their suitcase. Ruth did not know why she felt compelled to do this. It was unlikely burglars would break into a third-floor apartment, but she remembered how important the cashbox buried in the garden had been, and although there was no garden in which to hide it here, she was determined not to have all her money in the same place. She told Laura where the money was hidden. It was Laura, after all, who had remembered the box buried in the garden.

"If anything should happen to me," she said gently, "you'll know where to find the money."

Laura stared at her in horror. "*You* won't leave us, will you, Mutti?" she whispered.

Ruth gathered her into her arms and said, "No, darling. I won't leave you, but we have to look after the children now, you and I, and if there was an accident or something…" Ruth's voice trailed off as Laura's arms tightened round her and she buried her face in her mother's neck. For a long moment they hugged each other close. "You are my strength, now, Laura," Ruth said. "You must help me with the younger ones."

After lunch, they all trailed down the stairs and out into the autumn wind. The earlier drizzle had stopped, but there was a distinct chill in the air, and Ruth realised that it wouldn't be long before she had to find the children warmer clothes if they were going out of the apartment at all. Ruth led them briskly along the street, away from the gardens, towards the canal that carried sluggish brown water behind the apartment buildings. There was a path on either side, joined by two bridges that spanned the water giving pedestrian access to the neighbourhood beyond. The children loved to walk by the canal, running ahead of their mother to drop sticks from one bridge into the slow-moving water, and rushing to the other bridge to see them arrive there.

Ruth had been afraid to let the twins play this game at first, for fear that they might fall into the canal as they raced along the path, but, holding the hand of each, she too ran between the bridges, encouraging the sticks they had dropped. It was harmless fun, it gave the children some exercise, brought a little colour to their cheeks, and laughter to their lives. Nowhere was there a sign banning Jews from the towpath.

Today when they returned from this excursion, climbing the stairs to the apartment, it felt to Ruth, for the first time, as if they were coming home. She unlocked the door and the children tumbled inside, the girls rushing into their new bedroom, the twins stumping across to the window to watch the streetlamps come on in the quiet street below.

For the first time since they had arrived in Munich, that night Ruth lay down upon the sofa, and drifted off into an easy sleep. Things were still going to be difficult, she knew that, but as she said her prayers, praying as always for Kurt to come and find them soon, she thought that maybe God was listening to her after all, and she knew the glimmerings of hope. Herbert had left them, but they had a roof, some money and each other. As she had stood beside the children's beds, the twins, curled up together in the bed like kittens in a basket, Inge flat on her face, one arm thrown over her head and Laura, almost invisible under the quilt, she felt a sudden and overwhelming flood of love for them. Whatever happened, it was her job to protect them.

The first crash on the door made it shudder. The second splintered the wood around the lock and the third made it swing open drunkenly on its hinges. The noise set the children screaming, and Ruth shot to her feet, her heart hammering. Two men burst into the room, shouting. "Out! Out! Out!"

At first they were huge, dark figures, bursting into the apartment, making the children scream with terror, but then they were revealed as long-coated, jackbooted storm troopers, carrying guns.

Behind them was Frau Schultz.

Ruth and the children had just finished their midday meal and were still round the table.

One of the men strode through the apartment, peering into each room while the other marched over to Ruth and grabbed her violently by the hair.

"You've got ten minutes to pack," he growled, yanking at Ruth's hair so that she gasped in pain. "This place is too good for Jews. Out! The lot of you! Out! Out now!"

"Where? Where shall we go?" faltered Ruth, leaning towards her captor to try and ease the tearing at her scalp. Her words were almost drowned by the screams of the children, and the other man suddenly backhanded a slap across Inge's face.

"Shut up!"

Inge's hysterical screams stopped abruptly, and were replaced by a soft whimper. A white-faced Laura gathered the boys into her arms, doing her best to soothe their terrified cries, while struggling to stop her own.

"You're terrifying the children," Ruth stammered. "Please leave them alone. We'll go if we must, but let me collect their things together."

"Ten minutes." The man released her hair. "And you can only take what you can carry."

Frau Schultz walked across to the sofa and sat down, her back erect, her handbag on her knees, watching. Her eyes gleamed with triumph as she said, "And don't take anything that belongs to me!"

"To you?" Ruth couldn't help herself. "Belongs to you?"

"All this belongs to me now. I've earned it!"

Earned it? Somehow Frau Schultz was taking over Herbert's apartment. How had she earned it? Ruth's mind was in a spin, but there was no time for further exchange, let alone explanation, the ten minutes were ticking away, and the two Gestapo were standing waiting, waiting for an excuse to strike again.

Released from the man's grasp, Ruth hurried into the boys'

bedroom, and pulled the suitcase from the wardrobe. The old deed box was still inside it. Hurriedly she threw the boys' clothes into the case, covering the box, but with the man watching from the door, she didn't dare retrieve the money she'd hidden under the mattress.

"Laura," she called, putting her own clothes in on top of the boys', "get your things. Bring them here." The man glanced over his shoulder into the living room, but there was still no time to reach under the mattress for the money.

Laura came into the room, her arms draped with the few clothes she and Inge had between them, her precious diary tucked in among them. The man watched as Ruth piled them into the case and closed the lid.

"Good girl." With force of will, Ruth managed to keep her voice calm though fear was coursing through her and she was shaking. Suppose the men decided to search the case? She looked across at the younger children. Inge was sitting on the floor, whimpering like a whipped puppy. Hans and Peter stood together, wide-eyed, no longer crying, but staring, almost rigid with fear, at the men in uniform who towered over them. "Now, take the boys to the bathroom while I finish packing our things."

Laura stared at her for a moment and then nodded. Grasping a twin with each hand she dragged them into the bathroom and began to help them with their trousers. Hoping to distract the watching Gestapo from what Laura was doing, Ruth went into the kitchen, picked up her shopping basket and began to pack food into it.

"What are you taking?" demanded Frau Schultz, leaping to her feet and peering round the kitchen door. "What are you stealing? All the food in that fridge is mine."

"Just a little flour, and some rice," replied Ruth shakily. "Some bread and a few apples. I must have something to feed the children. I beg you."

One of the Gestapo gave a cruel laugh. "Yes, dirty Jew! Beg! On your knees! Go on! On your knees. Beg!"

Gripping the precious basket tightly, Ruth forced herself onto her knees. "Please, Frau Schultz, let me take this basket of food for my children."

Frau Schultz shrugged, and turned away, and Ruth made as if to get up, but the trooper kicked out, sending her sprawling.

"You haven't begged me, yet," he jeered. "Beg me, on your knees!"

Ruth begged.

The second man came to the door and yet again she had to beg, but at last, tiring of the game, they let her get up and carry her basket to the door. As she passed the Gestapo man, he took hold of the basket, and reaching into it selected an apple, biting into it with sharp white teeth before he let go of the handle again, and allowed Ruth to hand the basket to a white-faced Laura.

"You carry this, Laura," she said. "I'll get the suitcase." She went back into the bedroom and picked up the case that now held everything that they had left in the world. She didn't know if Laura had remembered the money hidden in the bathroom, and could only pray that she had, and had managed to retrieve it. The cash under the mattress would have to remain there. No doubt Frau Schultz would find it soon enough.

She gathered the children together and was helping them put on their coats, when Hans suddenly looked at Peter and saw he was clutching Flop-Ear, the rabbit Herbert had given him. Hans let out a wail, "Where's Bunnkin? I want

79

Bunnkin." Pulling free of Laura's restraining hand, he darted back to his bedroom to find his own rabbit. Diving among the tumbled bedcovers, he retrieved the rabbit, still dressed in his striped trousers and hugged it to him.

"Wait a minute!" One of the Gestapo grabbed Hans by the scruff of the neck and lifted him clean off his feet, snatching the rabbit from him as he did so. "Better make sure you've nothing hidden in this." He dropped Hans unceremoniously to the floor and ripped the head off the rabbit. Pulling out the stuffing, he peered into its insides before tossing it aside. Hans, grabbing the remains of his rabbit, began to scream, and immediately Peter joined in.

"Get them out of here! Out! Out!" The Gestapo man pointed at Laura. "You, take them out."

Terrified, Laura grabbed at the boys, and still clutching the basket of food dragged them out of the apartment. Inge, moaning softly, clung to her mother, her face buried in Ruth's skirt.

"You're lucky," remarked one of the Gestapo. "You're free to go. Your brother-in-law has been arrested."

Ruth stared at him. "Arrested?" she echoed faintly. "Herbert? Why?"

"He was caught," replied the man. "Smuggling diamonds out of the country."

"Diamonds? Herbert?"

"Yes!" smirked Frau Schultz, "and now he's been caught...and it's all thanks to me! I've been watching you," she went on gleefully. "I've been watching all of you. I saw him sneaking round, going to different jewellers, buying precious stones. I saw him getting ready to run. I saw him buying his ticket...and I reported him. They took him yesterday when he went to collect his ticket...and he had diamonds in the heels of his shoes!"

One of the Gestapo gave a scornful laugh. "In his shoes! It's the first place we look!"

"And now I have my reward for being a good German," crowed Frau Schultz. "I have a new home and you are back where you belong...in the gutter!"

"And if I see you anywhere round here again," the Gestapo man said grimly, "you'll find yourself in prison and your children in an orphanage. Now get out."

Ruth picked up the suitcase in one hand, and pulling Inge along with the other, walked out of the flat, down the stairs, to where Laura and the twins were waiting for her in the street.

Five

The night he had been arrested, Kurt had been frog-marched along the street to a waiting tarpaulin-covered lorry. There, along with several other men, he had been forced into the lorry, already so full of crushed humanity that it seemed impossible to cram in any more. Kurt stood, his arms pinned to his sides, with his face pressed against shoemaker Martin Rosen's back. Manfred Schmied, the tailor from along the street, leaned heavily against him, and Rudy Stein, who had once been a teacher at the local school, was actually standing on Kurt's feet. More and more were pushed into the lorry at gunpoint, until finally even the Gestapo could see there was no room for more. The engine roared into life and with a sudden jolt the lorry pulled away. In the back men cried out as the movement tipped and twisted them, crushing them violently against their fellows. Someone's bladder failed and there was a strong smell of urine close to where Kurt stood. Someone began to sob quietly to himself, and the noise of general lamentation filled the lorry.

Kurt lost track of time as the lorry rumbled and bounced its way out of the town. He could no longer feel his feet. He could hardly breathe, for the smell of sweat, urine and faeces that had filled the covered lorry was almost tangible.

Others had been overcome by it and the stench of vomit was added to the mix. When they finally stopped, Kurt had no idea of how long they had been travelling in the nightmare vehicle. The stop was only for a moment or two. Outside they could hear shouted orders and then the lorry jerked forward again, bumping across an unpaved surface, before it came to a halt once more, and at last the canvas flaps were thrown up, letting the warm night air flood in. They were still unable to move, but gradually those at the back either fell or were hauled out, and the crush began to lessen.

"Out! Out! All out!" The guards prodded them with rifles, jabbing ribs with the barrels, or smashing the butts across heads if anyone moved too slowly.

"My God! What a stink!" cried one of the guards as he climbed up on the tailgate. "You can tell this lot are Jews! The truck stinks to high heaven!"

Kurt heaved himself awkwardly off the lorry, and at the prod of a rifle followed Martin and Rudy into the line of men that had formed up outside. Manfred was soon beside them, and they stood and waited as the last of the men were unloaded. Some were unable to stand, their cramped legs giving way under them, but kicks from the SS guards and the lash of a whip soon had them crawling over to the column of men and hauling themselves upright.

An SS man barked an order, and the column shuffled through a set of heavy gates, above which were inscribed the words "Work Makes You Free".

"We've been brought to a work camp," Kurt thought, and an icy-cold fear crept through him. There had been rumours of such camps, but they were for Communists, criminals, enemies of the state. Why had he and the others been arrested?

He knew, of course, knew that it was because they were Jews. Jews with businesses. Jews who had no business to make money out of honest Germans. Jews who recently had come together to form a local committee to try and protect themselves from the ever-increasing persecution. Jews who were making a nuisance of themselves. Jews.

Someone further up the line fell over, and was almost trampled as the column continued past him, stepping over him, before coming to a halt in front of a squat, square building. With Rudy Stein on one side of him and Manfred Schmied on the other, Kurt waited. The sun came up behind the building, and out of the corner of his eye he could see other buildings away in the distance, surrounded by barbed wire.

And so they waited, and waited, as the sun rose higher, its heat pounding their unprotected heads. Some, unable to withstand the heat, keeled over, collapsing in a heap on the ground. No one made a move to help them, no one dared move as the SS guards stalked the lines, whips in hand, pistols in their belts, looking for signs of rebellion. The sun rose to its zenith, and still they stood there until at last an SS officer appeared from inside the building. He strode out in front of the drooping column of men, and raising his voice began to harangue them.

"I am Oberführer Hans Loritz, commandant of this camp," he announced, adding ominously, "and you will get to know me." He pointed his finger, drawing it along the line of men. "You are the dregs of humanity. You are enemies of the Reich, and now you have been brought here you will work for the good of the German people. You will stay here until you have, through hard work and re-education, understood the error of your ways and can be returned to society in safety. You will stay here for as long as is takes." His voice had risen as he spoke and now it was almost a screech. "In the meantime you will work. You will be obedient to the guards. No disobedience or weakness will be tolerated. My guards have been well trained and they will be watching you. If you fail to obey an order, you will be punished. If you are slow to obey an order, you will be punished. If you break camp regulations, you will be punished. If you incite other prisoners to rebel, you will be punished. If you don't work hard, you will be punished. If you show lack of respect to your guards, you will be punished. You are here because you are not fit to live among decent Germans. You will stay here until you are fit to return...however long that takes." He walked over to one of the men who had collapsed in the heat, and kicked him in the ribs. "While you are on parade you will remain at attention at all times...or you will be punished." His eyes roved the phalanx of men standing before him, as if searching out resistance, recalcitrance. The prisoners remained rigid, unmoving, as the guards continued to stalk between the lines.

"Registration will now begin!" With this order Hans Loritz turned on his heel and strode back to the building.

When he had disappeared the guards marched the first rank of prisoners to the door, where again they waited in line. The rest continued to stand in the sun. No one spoke. No one moved. The commandant's words echoed in their heads and the roving SS guards ensured that there was no break in the ranks.

At last their turn came and their line moved forward. Kurt stood in front of a desk and gave his name, address and date of birth. The SS sergeant wrote it down meticulously in his ledger. He then looked up at Kurt.

"Why have you been arrested?" he asked.

"I don't know," Kurt replied. As the words left his mouth he was struck a powerful blow in the back. He staggered forward, only just maintaining his feet.

"Stand to attention, scum!" screamed a voice behind him, and Kurt caught himself from turning and managed to draw himself upright again.

"You are here because you are an agitator, a dirty Jew stirring up other Jews," said the sergeant, continuing in a bored drawl, without looking up. "Based on article one of the Decree of the Reich President for the Protection of People and State of 28th February 1933, you are taken into protective custody in the interest of public security and order. Reason: suspicion of activities inimical to the state . . . or as I said," and now he did look up again, his eyes narrowing, "you're a dirty Jew stirring up other Jews, and until you've learnt better, you'll stay here . . . and work!"

Work Kurt did. Work they all did, from first light, throughout the day, until they dragged themselves back to their huts to sleep. The prisoners' compound was surrounded by coils of barbed wire, overlooked by five watchtowers, where ever-vigilant sentries manned machine guns. The sleeping quarters were housed in bare concrete buildings that had once been an explosives factory. Within a wall and surrounded by a high electric fence, they stood in ranks on either side of a track that led to the parade ground. Kurt, Rudy, Martin and Manfred were assigned to the same hut.

Once their details had been taken, they were photographed, had their heads shaved, were stripped of their clothes and given prison garb, little more than ill-fitting white overalls. Any personal possessions they had, including money, had been logged in another ledger and taken from them.

86

"There is a canteen where you can buy what you need," said the corporal who listed their effects. "The cost will be deducted from your money."

"What happens when it runs out?" Manfred had dared to ask.

"Then you can buy nothing more," snapped the man. "What do you think this is? A charity home?" He gave a harsh laugh. "Your family can send you more money. That is how it works."

"But they don't know where I am!" Manfred had not yet learned to keep his mouth shut. A sudden lash from behind made him stagger, crying out and clasping his neck where a dark red weal sprang to life.

Kurt, Rudy and Martin, waiting in line, kept their eyes rigidly ahead. The guard with the whip had turned his attention to them. He walked along the waiting line, flicking his whip at the unmoving prisoners, enjoying the fear in their staring eyes. The SS, indeed well trained for such work, had begun their work of dehumanising their prisoners.

Once their "registration" was completed, their group was lined up again, and clutching the few possessions they had been given, a few items of clothing, a bowl, mug, knife, fork and spoon, they were marched into the prisoners' compound to the huts they'd been assigned.

As new prisoners they had to find bunk space among the already occupied bunks. Shuffling into the hut, they were confronted by a tall prisoner with an aggressive face, and few teeth.

"I'm Horst Kleiber," he told them. "I'm the sergeant of this hut. I'm in charge of everything in here. You do what I tell you, at the double, and we'll rub along. You don't, you'll be in dead trouble because then we're all in the shit. Got it?" They got it, but it was almost impossible to comply with all the regulations. The first morning, Kurt was struggling to make his bed. His was a top bunk, and as he wrestled with the bed sheet his feet disturbed the bed of the man below him.

"Watch your sodding feet!" roared the man. "They'll be here in two minutes!"

In less than that time, two SS guards came into the hut and checked the beds and the cupboards. Manfred's cupboard was deemed to be untidy, though he had only the socks and the mess tins handed out to him the previous day. One of the guards upended the cupboard onto the floor and then beat him with steady blows of his whip until the contents were replaced. Everyone else in the hut stood to attention in silence as this punishment was inflicted, each praying that his bed, his cupboard, would pass muster.

Life in the camp was sheer hell. Every morning they got up at first light, and once the hut had been passed as tidy by the guards, which seldom happened at first inspection, Kleiber led the section out to parade as a platoon for roll call. Then it was labour. Hard labour. The camp was to be rebuilt, extended, to accommodate more prisoners, with improved quarters for the SS guards and their families. All the old buildings had to be torn down and replaced. Everything was done at the double, and any man seen flagging was kicked or beaten.

Kurt and Manfred were on the same work detail and spent much of their day as human draft horses, pulling huge wagons laden with stone from place to place. Always at the double, always at the mercy of the whips and rifle butts. Rudy, who was older and smaller, was on a similar work detail, but he struggled to keep up. He needed glasses, but even though it meant he had difficulty in seeing where he was going, he seldom wore them.

"Take 'em off, mate," advised Horst Kleiber. "They always pick on blokes with specs, think you're intellectuals!"

He was right. After two such encounters with the SS guards, Rudy took his glasses off.

Horst had been arrested several years before because he was a Communist. As an old hand, he knew how best to work the system to make life fractionally easier. He was a fierce hut sergeant, roaring at anyone who risked getting the whole hut punished, but he was also scrupulously fair when it came to division of food, his Communist principles allowing every man equal shares. Kurt, Manfred, Martin and Rudy were the only Jews in the hut, but though Horst would probably have had no truck with them outside, here he ensured that they received their fair share. He was responsible for discipline in the hut, and that affected everyone alike. As the four friends settled in, other inmates taught them tricks that helped them escape the attentions of the guards. No one in the hut wanted to draw the attention of the SS.

As the weeks progressed there was an awful inevitability about their lives. They had each been allowed to send one postcard to their family at home, to say where they were, and to ask for money.

"They make a nice little profit on their canteen," Horst pointed out when Kurt expressed surprise that they were allowed to communicate with the outside world. "They need you to have money to spend so that they can insist on your spending it!"

The canteen provided some of the necessities of camp life.

It was possible to buy, at a price, a little extra food, and although this was often almost inedible, they ate it anyway; anything to stave off the ever-present gnawing hunger. Clothes had to be repaired, and precious funds had to be used to buy needles and thread. Clothes in disrepair were the excuse for further beatings at the hands of the guards.

Rudy grew steadily weaker. The others helped him whenever they could, but on work detail it was every man for himself. Helping a struggling comrade almost certainly earned you the lash of a whip or the kick of a jackboot and did the comrade no good at all.

"I'm going to die in this place," Rudy said dismally one evening when they had collapsed on their bunks after an extended evening roll call. "I can't go on like this."

"You can and you must!" insisted Kurt. "Don't give them the satisfaction." He looked across at his old friend, and took in his emaciated state. They had all lost weight, the meagre diet and hard physical work had ensured that, but he saw now that Rudy was in a worse state than the rest of them. The flesh had fallen away from his face, so that his skull seemed to strain through the parchment of his skin. His arms and legs, poking from under his camp overalls, looked skeletal in the harsh light of the lamp. But it was his eyes that told Kurt that Rudy was right. There was nothing in his eyes, sunk into the hollows of his face, but a blank stare; the life had gone out of his eyes.

"It's all right for you," Rudy said. "Most of the time I can't even see where I'm going. They shout 'Tempo! Tempo! Los! Los!' and I don't know which way to run."

The next day he was detailed to break up the concrete blocks from one of the demolished buildings. Swinging the heavy hammer was beyond him, and one of the guards, a sadistic bully called Schuller, grabbed the sledgehammer from Rudy's grasp and swung it himself, smashing it down onto Rudy's legs. With an agonised scream, Rudy collapsed, his legs useless beneath him. Blood streamed, soaking through his grubby white overalls, as he writhed on the ground with pain.

Schuller looked down at him dispassionately and said, "That is how you swing a sledgehammer." He looked round the rest of the crew. "Why aren't you working?" he bawled. "Does anyone else want a demonstration?" The rest of the detail turned away from Rudy, trying to close their ears to his agonised cries. Schuller looked down at him with contempt and then pointed to the man nearest to him. "You! You take him back to his hut. On the double! You've five minutes to be back here!"

It was Kleiber whom he'd chosen. Kleiber dropped his hammer and bent to Rudy. There was no way he could carry him without subjecting him to further agony, so he simply picked him up and hoisted him over his shoulder, his smashed legs dangling behind, his blood pouring onto the gravel. Kleiber took him back towards the ranks of huts with Schuller's bellow of "Tempo! Tempo!" echoing in his ears. When he reached the hut he laid Rudy on his bunk. He was no longer screaming, he had passed out with the pain. Kleiber tried to straighten the damaged legs, but he could see that Rudy would never walk again.

"Poor bugger! Better off unconscious," Kleiber muttered as he looked down at the motionless body. "Better off dead, now."

When they returned to the hut at the end of the day, they

found Rudy was indeed dead. His bed was soaked in blood, his pale face a mask of agony.

Kleiber told them what had happened. "Nothing we could have done for him, poor bugger," he said. "He was a goner as soon as that bastard Schuller raised the sledge."

Kurt looked down at the man whom he'd known all his life. Rudy, the teacher that all the children had loved, lying in a pool of blood with his legs smashed.

"What happens to him now?" he asked Kleiber.

"We take him out to roll call," replied Kleiber. "Now!"

"We what?" Kurt was incredulous.

"He's not reported dead yet, is he?" Kleiber sounded weary. "If he's not on parade the numbers won't tally and we'll all be out there all night. Remember last week?"

How could they forget it? For some reason the numbers at evening roll call had been out and the entire camp had stood there for six hours under the glare of the searchlights before being allowed to crawl back to their huts for a couple of hours' sleep before reveille.

"He's your mate, you can carry him," ordered Kleiber, and Kurt and Martin lifted the now stiffening body of Rudy Stein and solemnly carried him out onto the parade ground to be counted. By the next evening Rudy's body had been disposed of, and his bunk, scrubbed for an hour by Manfred to remove the blood, had been taken by a new prisoner.

That night Kurt lay on his bunk and thought of home, aching for his beloved Ruth and his children. It was at night that he was at his most wretched. Despite the need for sleep, he found that he lay awake, in dread of what the following day would bring. Would he even survive it, or would he, like Rudy, be murdered by one of the guards? How long would he be in this hellish place? He had been called to the administration office, and a list of his "crimes" had been read out to him. Joining his local Jewish committee made him a troublemaker. Until it was clear that he had atoned for this, had renounced such action again, he would not be set free. He was sent back to his work detail with the SS officer's words ringing in his ears.

"We're watching you, Friedman. You're an agitator. We're watching you!"

It was a week later that Martin Rosen disappeared. In the morning he was at roll call, at the end of the day he was not. As the men paraded ready for roll, Kleiber was shouting at them. "Where the fuck is he? Someone must know!" But no one did, and as they lined up for roll, they knew that it would be their hut's fault that the numbers didn't tally. The wrath of the SS would come down on them. Pale-faced and rigid with fear, Kleiber's platoon took their place on the parade ground.

Then a miracle happened. Roll was called but Martin Rosen's name wasn't. Incredulous, they were dismissed, and within minutes of returning to the hut, a new prisoner came through the door. Kleiber allotted him Martin Rosen's bed.

"Where can he be?" Kurt muttered to Manfred as they ate their meagre evening meal. "What's happened to him?"

"Daren't even think about it, after what happened to poor Rudy," Manfred said, scraping his bowl with his fingers to scoop up the last drop of the slop that had been in it.

Klaus Herman, another in their hut, looked across from where he sat. "He was in our work party this morning," he said. "He was called to Nero's office. Haven't seen him since."

Kurt gave an involuntary shudder. Nero was the prisoners' name for the commandant. A call to his office usually meant some great punishment was about to be administered, usually in front of the full complement of prisoners. It was Oberführer Loritz's way of reminding them all that they were at his mercy...and that he never showed any. What could Martin have done, he wondered? Was he even now being tortured in the punishment block?

"Whatever's happened to him, he's not coming back here," Kleiber told them. "They've filled his bunk!"

What had happened to Martin Rosen remained a mystery, and that mystery was only revealed to Kurt when he too was called to the commandant's office a few weeks later. He was working in a detail that was digging foundations for the new huts. It was backbreaking work, and was carried on with little respite, though the winter weather had made the ground rock-hard. They had stopped for the half-hour allowed for their midday meal when Kurt had received the summons. He stood up shakily. His legs felt like jelly, but he managed to walk across to the gate which led from the compound to the administrative block. He was taken to a cell, and told to stand to attention while he waited to be called. He stood, stiff and still for over an hour, wondering why he had been called. Trying to remember anything that he had done...or not done...that might have earned him a stint in the punishment block, but he could think of nothing. Not that that mattered to the SS. There didn't have to be a reason for them to punish you, they simply did it because they felt like it, because they enjoyed it. These thoughts were no comfort to Kurt as he stood, still to attention, waiting.

At last the door swung open and at a barked order from an SS corporal he marched out and followed the man along a corridor, through a door into another part of the building, and was finally brought into an office. Here seated behind a large desk sat Oberführer Loritz. He paid no attention to Kurt at all. Simply went on writing something in a large book before him. Kurt waited rigidly to attention, as did his escort, until finally the commandant looked up.

"Who is this?" he demanded and the corporal snapped out a "Heil Hitler" before replying. "Kurt Friedman, sir. Jew."

"Thank you, Corporal, you may leave us."

The corporal snapped his heels and saluted again, before leaving the room.

For a long moment the commandant stared at Kurt, and Kurt, terrified of making eye contact, stared at a spot above the Oberführer's head.

"Friedman," the commandant said at last. "A Jew. Do you know what we want to do with all Jews, Friedman?"

Kurt hesitated for a moment. Which was the right answer? Yes or no? Which did the commandant want to hear?

"We want to get rid of the lot of you," Oberführer Loritz answered his own question. "One way or another we want to get rid of the lot of you. Do you understand, Friedman?"

"Yes, sir." Kurt's voice was hardly more than a croak.

"Yes, sir," mimicked the commandant. "I doubt it, Friedman. I doubt it. But you," he pointed at Kurt with a pudgy finger, "you are lucky. You are going to be given the chance to leave here."

Kurt's head began to spin.

"To leave here provided you promise to take you family and leave Germany." Loritz paused a moment and then went on. "Are you prepared to give that undertaking?"

Kurt gulped for air, enough air to allow him to speak. "Yes, sir."

"And where would you go? Do you have relations abroad?"

Kurt's mind continued to spin. He had no relations abroad, his family had lived in Kirnheim all his life, had run the grocery in Gerbergasse for most of it. No, he had no relations outside Germany.

"A cousin in America, sir," he said, without actually deciding to say it.

Oberführer Loritz sniffed. "America is full of Jews," he remarked. "It will be their downfall." His eyes drilled into Kurt. "And this cousin, will he vouch for you?"

"I'm sure he will, sir."

"And then there is the question of your property here. You own property, I understand."

"A shop, sir," replied Kurt, adding when this elicited no comment, "with an apartment above it."

"Your property would be forfeit of course. You will have no need of it and it can be sold to a good honest German family." His eyes bored into Kurt. "And the money will, of course, revert to the state."

Kurt swallowed. "Of course, sir." The money might revert to the state, but much more likely to Nero's bank account.

How would they live if the money paid for his property didn't come to him? How would he live if he didn't get out of this hellhole camp? There was only one way to get out of here, one way to get back to his family and try and get them to safety somewhere, and that was to agree to whatever this man said. If Kurt said anything but "Yes, sir" he would be back in the prisoners' compound and he might never see his family again.

Oberführer Loritz pulled a paper from under the book in which he had been writing, and pushed it across to Kurt. "You will sign this to say you and your family will be out of the country in three weeks, that your property will revert to

the state, and that you will never return to Germany again."
He looked up at Kurt. "Do you have title deeds to this shop?"

"Yes, sir."

"They must be lodged with the Emigration Office in Munich. Within the three weeks." The commandant held out a pen. "Sign!"

Kurt grasped the proffered pen and signed. He had no chance to read the document he had signed. He had no idea whether he had agreed to any other conditions not stipulated by the commandant, but he knew it was his only chance of freedom, so he took it...and signed.

"One more thing, Friedman," snapped the Oberführer. "I want to hear no slander about how this camp is run. Prisoners here work hard, but they are well fed, and rewarded for their work." He paused and his eyes held Kurt's. "Is that understood, Friedman?"

"Yes, sir, quite understood."

"I'm glad to hear it." Oberführer Loritz's voice was ice-cold. "If you are found to be spreading malicious lies about the camp and its staff, you will be arrested and returned here immediately. Immediately! Do you understand?"

"Yes, sir," replied Kurt, ready to agree to anything. "Yes, sir, I understand."

Things moved very quickly after that. He was taken back to the Jourhaus, the building where they had all been registered on the first day, and was given his own clothes back. He changed into them, but they no longer fitted him, hanging off him like a big brother's cast-offs.

"You look like a scarecrow," scoffed the SS soldier who oversaw his departure. He picked up Kurt's wallet and peered into it before handing it back to him. It was exceedingly light.

Kurt doubted if he even had the bus fare home, but he didn't care. All he wanted to do was to slip out through those fearsome gates and run for his life.

The gates clanged shut, but Kurt didn't dare run; he walked away from the camp without a backward glance. He knew if he looked back one of the guards would shout at him, drag him back inside, and close those awful gates behind him. He had been allowed to leave, but even as he hurried away, he dreaded hearing his name called. It would be a game to them.

"Halt, Friedman! Where do you think you're going?" And if he didn't stop he would be shot in the back. Shot while trying to escape. He'd seen it happen.

Fear crawled over him as he continued to walk away. Surely this hope of release would be withdrawn; surely this was yet another cruel punishment. Let him think he was free and then, as he actually, actually began to believe it, bring him back, back into the nightmare that was Dachau.

Despite his determination to keep walking, Kurt's panic overtook him and he began to run. Running was easy. Running was what he'd been doing for the past four months, running in the camp had kept him alive, but even as his feet pounded on the road that led to the town of Dachau, he expected the guard dogs to be unleashed, to hear them give tongue, to feel their teeth tear into him. When, daring at last to glance over his shoulder, he realised he was no longer within sight of the camp, and there was no pursuit, he allowed his pace to ease a little, caught his breath and then settled down to a steady jog.

When he got off the bus in Kirnheim, Kurt walked from the bus station, along the familiar streets of his childhood, and turned into Gerbergasse. It was late Monday afternoon, a time when people would normally still be out and about their business, but the street, though not quite deserted, seemed to Kurt abnormally quiet. Then he realised what the difference was. There were no children to be seen. No children playing in the street; no sound of little girls chanting as the skipping rope slapped the pavement, no excited shouts from boys playing football or scuffling in the dust. There was not a child in sight.

He walked on, past the synagogue, which, he noticed, had new doors, not the ornately carved ones he had always loved and admired, but plain, untreated timber on utilitarian black hinges. His step hastened as he passed familiar shops, some with boarded-up windows, to the corner where his own shop was...had been. He stared in horror at what he saw. It, too, was boarded up, but not just the window, the door as well, a haphazard criss-cross of planks nailed into a blackened doorframe. Dark swathes of soot streaked the walls, and the blackened frames of the upstairs windows gaped to the open air. For a long, disbelieving moment, Kurt stood quite still, staring at the ruin of his home. Terror clutched his heart, a physical pain. Ruth! Where's Ruth? The children? Were they there when the fire broke out? Are they safe? Did this happen the night of his arrest, or later on? Where are they now?

Turning his back on the burnt-out blackened shell of his home, he rushed into the Meyers' bakery on the other side of the street. Leah Meyer was behind the counter as he crashed through the door. She looked up, fear leaping in her eyes, to see who had burst in so violently. The fear turned to astonishment and then pleasure as despite his scarecrow appearance, hollow cheeks and shaved head, she recognised him.

"Herr Friedman!" she cried. "You're back! God be praised! You're home." She hurried round from behind the counter to clasp his hand and pump it up and down.

"Where's my family?" demanded Kurt. "Are they safe? What happened?"

"Yes, yes," she assured him. "Don't worry! They're safe. They escaped the fire. Your wife took them to your brother. They are living with him."

Kurt sank onto the chair beside the counter, suddenly exhausted. "Thank God!" he murmured. "Thank God for that." He gave Frau Meyer a weak smile. "I'm sorry," he said. "I didn't mean to frighten you. What happened? What happened to the shop? How did it catch fire?"

At that moment Leo Meyer came into the shop from the bakery behind. When he saw Kurt sitting by the counter he rushed over to him, clapping him on the shoulder. "You've come back, Kurt. Thank God you're safe." He turned to his wife.

"Put up the shutters, Leah. Let's close up." He turned back to Kurt. "We don't stay open after dark anymore, it isn't safe. It's bad enough in the daytime. You'll stay with us for the night, eh? Before you go to Munich to find them?"

He helped his wife put sturdy wooden shutters in place across the window. "Protects the glass from stray bricks," he explained as he slid the metal bar into its socket and snapped the padlock closed. "Wouldn't stop anyone determined to break in, but it slows them down."

Once the shop was secured, the Meyers led the way up the stairs, to the apartment above.

"I expect you're hungry," Frau Meyer said, and without waiting for Kurt to admit it, went into the kitchen to prepare some food. She had taken in his emaciated face and the way his clothes hung off his body.

"Tell me what happened," Kurt said to her husband as he sat down. Leo took out a cigarette case and passed it over to Kurt, before taking a cigarette himself and lighting both.

"It was the night of the riot, the night you were arrested," he said. "You saw the mob, the frenzy they were in." Leo shuddered at the recollection of that night. "We were lucky that night, we only had our windows broken. We locked ourselves into the bakery, or they would probably have arrested me too." Leo inhaled deeply on his cigarette, letting the smoke fill his lungs. "Well, when the SS took you away, the mob set fire to your shop. They'd already tried to burn the synagogue, and they got the taste for fire. They weren't people anymore, not people, just one huge howling beast. Your shop was there, it belonged to a Jew and so they set it on fire."

"But Ruth? The children? You said they were all right. They weren't hurt? They got out in time?"

"Thanks to the courage of your wife," Leo replied, "they all got out. But it was close. She managed to lower them down from the upstairs window. She had to jump herself. She sprained her ankle, but amazingly that was all." Leo drew hard on his cigarette. "She is a brave woman, your Ruth."

Over the meal that Leah had prepared, the Meyers told Kurt how Ruth had found the deed box; how she'd been attacked by the Hitler Youth; how she'd refused to burden the Meyers any longer.

"She was determined to take them to your brother," said Leah. "She wouldn't stay with us any longer. She did write though, just once to say they'd arrived."

"It's where I told her to go if necessary," Kurt said, "but I didn't really think she'd have to." He looked across the table at his neighbours, a couple he had known for years, but with whom he had never been close. "Thank you," he said simply. "Thank you for all you did."

Leah raised her hands. "Who would not?"

"She was right to go," Leo told him. "No one's safe round here. Oh, we try and get on with our daily lives, but it is more and more difficult. Our shops are continual targets for the Hitler Youth and as soon as we make repairs they come by again. Several of the local children have been beaten up by these gangs, and there's no redress, no justice. Parents are keeping them indoors now. Since the new laws, we have no status."

"For the first time in my life, I'm glad we weren't blessed with children," Leah said. "All my married life I prayed for children, begged God to give me just one child, but now I see the wisdom of His refusal. We won't have to watch as our children are bullied, humiliated, injured, maybe even killed."

The silence that followed the bitterness of these words lengthened as all three of them contemplated the dark void of the future.

"You'll stay with us tonight," Leo said at last. It wasn't a question and Kurt felt another wave of gratitude for this couple's generosity.

"Thank you," he said. "I will. Then in the morning I'll go to Munich."

"Did you see the others, the others who were arrested the same night?" asked Leah tentatively. "Martin Rosen came home, just for a few days, and then he took his whole family and left. He didn't say much."

Kurt wasn't surprised, Martin would certainly have been

warned as he had. "Yes, Martin was there," he said. "He got out before me. So, he's gone?"

Leo nodded. "Yes, he's gone."

"But he had to leave everything behind," said Leah. "All the tools in his workshop, all the furniture in his house. The Gestapo watched him pack up. They wouldn't let him take anything that the family couldn't carry between them as they walked out of the door."

"One day they were there, the next they were gone." Leo shook his head in disbelief. "There's another family living in there now. Not Jews of course, but some official who works on the railway." He looked across at Kurt. "Reckon someone would have moved into your place if it hadn't been so badly damaged. No one can afford to repair it." Leo passed Kurt another cigarette, and Kurt drew on it gratefully. He had no intention of telling the Meyers, or anyone else, that he had agreed that the state should take over his property.

"I shall go and have a look at it tomorrow before I go," he said. "Just in case there is anything else I can salvage." His mind flicked to the money he had hidden in the unused bread oven beside the stove in the living room. Was there any possibility it would still be there?

"Were Rudy Stein, or Manfred Schmied with you?" Leah was asking. "Do you know anything about them?"

Kurt forced his mind back to her question. "We were all together in one hut," he said, "Rudy...died. He found the camp regime difficult and...and he wasn't strong enough. I think Mannie is still there." He drew deeply on his cigarette. "He may be released. I was let out because I agreed to collect my family and leave the country. I've got three weeks to prove to the authorities that we are emigrating...somewhere, otherwise I shall be sent back to Dachau, and the children will be put in an orphanage." His face was bleak as he explained, "And God knows what will happen to Ruth." He shook his head in despair. "I told them I had a cousin in America."

"And have you?"

Kurt shook his head. "No, but unless I could convince them I had somewhere to go, they wouldn't have let me out. This way at least we have a chance."

Kurt spent the night in the bedroom his children had shared weeks earlier, and as he lay on the hard little bed he thought about them all. Ruth, his Ruth, so brave, so resourceful, saving the children from the fire. Finding the box, taking them all to Munich. Thank God they had got there safely. At least Herbert was there to look after them all until he, Kurt, could get there. Kurt thought of his children. Laura, only ten, but far older than her years, made to grow up too fast by what her life had become in the last few years. Inge, beautiful, spoilt, only six, but used to getting her own way. She seemed almost unaware of the animosity that surrounded them all. And then the twins, just three, prattling happily together as they played, so wrapped up in each other that they only seemed to be complete when both were there. His beloved family. Somehow he had to get them away, out of this benighted country, his family's home for generations, which no longer accepted them as citizens, regarded them as subhuman.

He thought of his father, Amos, wounded fighting in the trenches for the Kaiser and the Fatherland. It hadn't mattered then that he was a Jew, when the army was haemorrhaging men and every soldier was needed at the front. He'd been good enough to be a German then. And when he came home, limping from the shrapnel still lodged in his leg, Amos had slipped back into life as a shopkeeper, and brought his sons up to be both good Jews and good Germans.

Kurt had lied to them in Dachau and he knew it was a risk. He had no cousin in America, something the SS could discover easily enough if they bothered. He knew they had little chance of going to America, but they had to get out somewhere, and he had such a short time to make the arrangements. Thank God Ruth had found the deed box. She would have all the family documents safely with her, but, most important now, the deeds for the shop, which he must deliver to the Emigration Office in Munich. She had their passports, too, except for the twins'. Although Kurt didn't expect the authorities to make it easy, they would probably allow him to put them on his, simply to get rid of them all.

But where they were going to go, and where the money was going to come from, he didn't know. He had his watch and Ruth had her wedding ring, and he thought he remembered there were a brooch and some earrings in the box, which might fetch something. Otherwise they had no money. Any cash there might have been would, he realised, have been spent long ago.

Eventually, sleep overtook him, but it was a sleep beset with dreams; dreams of Dachau, dreams of the lorry that had taken him there, of the children calling his name, and the nightmare that finally startled him awake, Ruth on fire. She was running towards him, flames devouring her clothes, crackling through her hair, Ruth screaming, screaming to him for help, and he rooted to the spot unable to move as the fire engulfed her.

Kurt sat bolt upright in bed, his heart pounding, cold

sweat running down his back, staring into the darkness. He could still hear her screams echoing in his head, and see the agony on her face.

There was no going back to sleep. Indeed Kurt didn't dare, the nightmare had been so vivid, so real, he knew if he closed his eyes it would return. He switched on the light, and sitting with his eyes wide open waited for his racing heart to slow. He spent the rest of the night planning what he would do.

As soon as it was light, before much of the street was awake, he crossed the road again, and, with a claw hammer borrowed from Leo, levered the planks from the door and went into his shop. It was cold, dark and dank. Rain had blown in through the gaps in the planking, and the smell of damp soot was strong and acrid.

The shop had been gutted by the fire. There was nothing left but a smoke-blackened shell. The staircase was gone, and parts of the ceiling had collapsed, leaving the charred rafters exposed above.

Kurt looked up at the rafters, and then went back across the road to the bakery.

"Have you got a ladder I can borrow?" he asked Leo. "I need to try and get into the apartment, and the stairs have gone."

"I have," Leo said, leading him out to the back, "but be very careful, the whole building must be very unsafe."

"I will," promised Kurt, hefting the ladder over his shoulder.

"And don't be long," warned Leo. "If you're seen, someone will report you for looting."

"Hardly looting, it's my own property!"

"Since when did that make any difference to the Gestapo?" replied Leo.

Kurt took the ladder over to the shop and set it up where the stairs should have been. Cautiously he climbed, not even sure if the beam supporting the ladder would take his weight. It appeared to do so and he scrambled up onto one of the more solid-looking rafters. The floor had burned away, but the old timbers of the house were thick and strong, and although they were scorched and blackened, most of them seemed to have survived the fire. Carefully Kurt edged his way along the landing till he reached the doorway of his bedroom. There was little left to see, all the furnishings and furniture were ash. He crossed the landing and looked into the girls' room. Here it was the same, with only the remains of the old iron bedstead, a twisted misshapen mess, melted against the window. Water had been poured in to quench the fire, and with windows open to the rain the room was cold and dank. Reluctantly Kurt looked into all the rooms. The boys' room had fared little better, and the comfortable kitchen living room, which had been the centre of their family life, was a blackened mess. Here, however, the damage had been caused more by smoke and water than by fire. Kurt edged his way into the room, fighting back tears as he saw what was left of their home. Then something caught his eye, stuffed into the corner of a chair. He reached out and pulled it clear.

"Bella!" he cried aloud, and hugged the doll, Inge's favourite toy, convulsively to his chest. "Bella!"

Then, at last, he turned his attention to the old bread oven. Crossing the floor gingerly, he opened the heavy oven door and looked inside. There, kept safe from the smoke and the flames by the cast iron of the oven walls, lay the envelope into which he had put some of the money he'd taken from the bank. A wave of relief washed over him. He had what he'd come for. Now perhaps they had a chance. Hurriedly Kurt stuffed the envelope into one pocket of his jacket, and catching up Bella stuffed her into the other. Then he made his way back through the apartment, to the top of the ladder. As he passed the broken window that overlooked the street, he suddenly heard the tramp of marching feet. He didn't have to look out of the window to know who was approaching. He was trapped in his own apartment, with his own money hidden in his coat, and the SS were coming down the street.

Kurt thought of Leo's warning about looting. He reached the ladder, but realised that if he went down now, he would be caught coming out of the shop. He had no proof that it was his, and even if he had, it would probably make no difference. As the tramping feet drew closer, he made a grab for the top of the ladder, and heaved, pulling it upwards, out of sight. The weight of it made him stagger backwards, and he sat down hard on a beam, but his foot pushed through the remains of the burnt-out ceiling, protruding into the shop. Frantically he struggled, trying to pull free so that he could finish pulling the ladder out of sight from below. Outside the sound of marching feet grew louder, and then, at a barked order, they stopped. As Kurt finally extricated his foot from the ceiling, and heaved the ladder upwards, he heard a raised voice from the street.

"Someone has broken in here. Weissen! Müller! See what's going on here!"

There was the sound of feet, and a crack of timber as more of the planks were ripped away from the front door.

"No one here, sir," called a voice.

"What about upstairs?"

"There aren't any stairs, sir. Place is burnt out."

"Any sign of looters?"

"Nothing worth looting here, sir."

"Clearly someone's broken in, Weissen. You're to stay here. Guard the door until we can come back and investigate properly."

"Yes, sir." Weissen sounded resigned to his duty. Outside another order was given and the tramping feet resumed, as the rest of the troop marched away.

Kurt found he had been holding his breath. Now he let it out, and as silently as he could eased himself out from under the ladder. For a long moment he listened. Weissen was still in the shop, but when Kurt heard the scratch of a match and the smell of cigarette smoke, he knew that the soldier below wasn't taking his guard duty very seriously. He didn't think there was anyone there, and he wasn't expecting anyone to challenge him from the street.

But Kurt was still trapped, and they were coming back. He felt the panic rise within him, as he listened to the movements of the man below. He had to get out, but there was no escape that way.

Get a grip on yourself, Kurt thought fiercely. Get a grip on yourself and think!

He edged back along the landing until he reached his bedroom. Here the window overlooked the small yard below. Treading softly on the remaining rafters, Kurt crossed to the window and looked down. It was quite a drop, for the yard was lower than the level of the shop floor.

It's the only way out, he thought, and I have to try. He considered bringing the ladder along the landing, but realised straightaway that this was almost impossible. The ladder was heavy and unwieldy and would almost certainly make a noise that would alert the guard below. Reluctantly he dismissed the ladder and looked down again into the yard. The buildings next door overlooked it as well, but there was nothing he could do about that. He would have to risk being seen, it was a lesser risk than staying where he was, waiting to be discovered...with the money in his pocket.

It was impossible to open the window as the metal frame had been distorted by the heat, but that same heat had shattered the glass. A few shards were still embedded in the frame, but the gap was wide enough for Kurt to slide through if he were careful. With one final glance behind him, he reached through and grasped the top of the frame outside. Sitting on the sill, his legs still inside the room, he edged himself through the gap until he was crouching on the broad outer windowsill. Once he glanced below and shuddered. It seemed a long way down. Shutting his eyes for a moment he calmed himself, and then began to ease himself over the edge of the sill. Grasping the bottom of the window frame, he lowered himself until he was hanging, arms extended, down the side of the building. There was no going back, and no hanging on for much longer either. He gave a quick glance downward and then, steeling himself to let go, dropped the final twelve feet onto the paved yard. The drop jarred his ankles, but he flexed his knees to absorb some of the jolt as he landed and rolled over on the stones. His hands were bleeding from where they had caught on the embedded glass, but otherwise he had no real injury, and he was quickly on his feet again. He scrambled over the wall at the end of the yard into the alley beyond, and made his way along its narrow length towards the street.

Before he emerged he blotted the blood from the cuts on his hands on the tail of his shirt, and, praying he wouldn't meet the Gestapo, walked as slowly as he dared back towards the bakery, entering it as just another customer.

Leo looked at him in horror and murmured, "You must go, now." His eyes flicked to the door, and Kurt, following his look, saw the SS soldier standing outside his own burnt-out shop.

"I'm sorry," Kurt said, "if I have put you in danger."

Leo thrust a newly baked loaf into his hands and said, "Go and find your family, Kurt. Go now. We can't do anything more for you here." He turned away from the window, and Kurt, with the loaf in his hands, left the shop, walking away along Gerbergasse for the last time, without a backward glance.

He didn't reach Herbert's apartment block until late in the afternoon. He had never been to his brother's home before, and he was relieved to find it was in a respectable suburban area. It was clearly not a Jewish enclave, as Gerbergasse was. The shop windows, displaying their various goods, were unbroken; there was no red paint daubed on their doors. Indeed some had notices proclaiming "No Jews served here". If Herbert lived and worked in such a place, then he must be completely accepted by his neighbours, and Ruth and the children would be safe.

Suddenly Kurt ached to see them, to hold them in his arms once more. He went into the apartment building and peered at the names beside the column of bell pushes in the hallway.

None of them was Friedman. He ran his eye over them again to be sure he hadn't missed it. No Friedman. He went back into the street to check the number displayed on the building itself, wondering if he had walked into the wrong block. No, on the outside wall, clear for all to see was the number 15. Elbestrasse 15 Apartment 3c. That was definitely Herbert's address. Kurt went back inside and looked at the number on the door of one of the ground-floor flats. 1a. The others were 1b and 1c. 3c must be on the third floor. He climbed the stairs and stopped outside the door of 3c. The name beside it was Schultz. Kurt rang the bell.

"I'm sorry to trouble you," he said to the old woman who opened the door a crack and peered out at him, "but I am looking for Herr Friedman."

The woman scowled. "He doesn't live here anymore."

"But he did? You said 'anymore'. I'm his brother."

"Another Jew," remarked the woman with distaste. "Well he's gone. I live here now!" She began to shut the door, but frantic for news of Ruth and the children, Kurt stuck his foot in the doorway.

"I'm looking for my wife…my children," he began.

"Oh!" the woman gave an unpleasant smile. "The Jewish orphanage! They've gone too."

"But…gone where?"

The woman shrugged. "How should I know?"

"But where did Herbert take them?" As he spoke Kurt took a step back and the woman immediately slammed the door.

"Nowhere," she cackled from inside the flat. "He didn't take them anywhere. The Gestapo took him! He's been arrested."

Six

"Where are we going, Mutti?" Laura asked as she trudged along the street behind her mother, still carrying the food basket in one hand and gripping Hansi tightly with the other. Ruth didn't answer. She didn't have an answer. All she knew was that they had to get away from the apartment building and out of sight before the Gestapo decided to come down after them.

"Just follow me," she said. "Inge, hold Peter's hand." Carrying the suitcase, she led the little procession along the street, turning off along the first side road that presented itself.

Once they were off the main road they continued along the smaller streets towards the canal. On the far side of the bridge there was a bench overlooking the water. Here Ruth paused and setting the suitcase down took the basket from Laura. It was quite heavy, and Laura had been struggling with it, but in it was the precious flour bag with a small roll of banknotes concealed inside.

"I'm tired, Mutti!" Inge this time, her voice a wail of despair. "Where are we going?"

"You'll see," replied Ruth, but Inge's despair echoed in her own heart. Where were they going? She had no idea.

The chilly dampness that had been in the air over the

last few days had again turned into a steady drizzle. The children were getting cold and wet, and she had nowhere to take them.

There must be somewhere we can go, Ruth thought. We have to find some shelter, and soon.

Then she thought of the synagogue she had found when she first arrived. At Herbert's insistence she had kept well away from it, but now it seemed to her that it was their only hope. Surely the rabbi would help them. It wasn't that far. That's where they'd go.

"Come on," she said. "It's not far. I'll take the basket and the case. Laura, you and Inge look after the twins."

It wasn't very far, but although Ruth knew the general direction, they took a couple of wrong turns and by the time they finally reached it, the children were all soaking wet and exhausted. Ruth opened the unlocked door and led them inside.

"Wait here," she said, "while I find the rabbi. Laura, do you understand? You are not to move from here."

Rabbi Rahmer was a small man with a greying beard and a balding head. When his wife, who was considerably larger, led Ruth into his study, he got to his feet to greet her, peering at her with sharp black eyes, over a pair of half-moon spectacles.

"How can I help you, Gnädige Frau?" he asked courteously. He indicated that she should take a seat beside his desk, before returning to his own place behind it.

Ruth introduced herself and explained how she had brought the children to Herbert's home after they had been burnt out of their own.

"Now he's been arrested," she went on, "and we've been turned out onto the street. I'll have to try and find us somewhere to live, but we've nowhere to go while I look. Do you know anyone who would take us in, just for a few days?" She looked at the rabbi hopefully. "I can pay...a little... but I know a hotel won't take us, and anyway it would be too expensive."

Rabbi Rahmer stroked his beard and looked thoughtful. "It's not easy," he said. "Life is difficult for us all. Haven't you any other family you can go to?"

"There is my mother," Ruth said, "but it would take time to arrange. She is an old lady, and she lives miles away."

Rabbi Rahmer looked relieved. "But she would want to see her grandchildren safe, I'm sure," he said. "I think you should try and go there. Surely that is where your husband will look for you when he is set free."

"He'll look for me here," Ruth said. "He'll come to Herbert's apartment."

"But he won't find you," pointed out the rabbi. "Surely, then, he'll go to your mother's. He'll guess that's where you'd turn for help."

"Even if that is the best thing and I do take the children to her," Ruth said wretchedly, "I can't go today. I have to find out how to get there from here, which trains and when they run. We must have somewhere to stay for at least one night, possibly two. Is there nowhere you can suggest?" Her eyes held his, beseeching him to help her. "I'm desperate," she said quietly. "They are standing, soaking wet, in your synagogue. I must get them somewhere warm and dry. Please, I'm begging you to help us."

"We'd better go and fetch them." The rabbi sighed, and, getting to his feet, once again led Ruth out of his study, calling to his wife. "I'm just going across to the synagogue to see these children. We'll have to get them dried off over here. Can you find some towels?"

That night the family slept in the meeting room at the back of the synagogue. Frau Rahmer gave them bread and some thick broth in her kitchen and when they were warm, dry and fed, she found blankets and pillows and took them over to the meeting room. Using these, Ruth contrived a bed for them on the floor. When at last exhaustion had taken over and they were all asleep on the makeshift bed, Ruth sat on one of the chairs and went through their meagre belongings, considering their options.

When she had taken the twins to the bathroom, Laura had managed to retrieve the money Ruth had hidden there; and there was the flour-bag money. With what Ruth had on her person and the last few Reichmarks in the deed box, they had enough for a while, but she knew she would have to eke it out very carefully. Ruth grimaced as she thought of the money Frau Schultz would find when she stripped the bed in the boys' room. But then, she thought, perhaps Frau Schultz won't find it. Perhaps as Jews had slept in it she'll consign the whole bed and bedding to be burned. Somehow Ruth doubted it. No, Frau Schultz would find it and then begin scouring the apartment for any other hidden money. Tipping out drawers, upending Herbert's bed, tearing the cushions from the sofa, and realising that there must have been money hidden in the basket of food she'd so casually allowed Ruth to carry with her. Frau Shultz's imagined rage at being duped by a Jew gave Ruth a brief moment of triumph, but it was only momentary. She thought of how the woman had spied on them all, watching as they went about their lives, noting where they went and what they did, and then going to the Gestapo and informing on them. Did she really hate Jews that much, or had she simply seen it as a way to steal Herbert's apartment from them? For a moment, Ruth felt an overpowering fury at the injustice of it all, but even as it flooded through her, she knew that she had to forget the malicious and vengeful Frau Schultz and find a way to protect her children from others, equally malicious and vengeful.

She knew she couldn't stay here in Munich; here she knew no one, and had no friends. It was pointless to return to Kirnheim; there was nothing left for them there. There were only two other possibilities. To go to her mother, an elderly widow, or to go to her sister, who'd married an Austrian doctor and now lived in Vienna. Her mother lived in Vohldorf, a village not far from Stuttgart, in the house where Ruth and her sister Edith had been born. Edith lived in a large apartment in Vienna, with her husband, who was an orthopaedic surgeon, and their three children. Edith had, as her mother said, "married above her", and Ruth knew she would not welcome a homeless sister, with four dependent children.

Ruth had heard from neither her mother nor her sister since she had come to Munich, though she had written to both to tell them what had happened and where she was. She wasn't particularly surprised that Edith hadn't bothered to reply, but she was surprised that she had heard nothing from her mother.

It would be easier to get to Mother's, she thought now. It's an easier journey and we shan't need passports. From here we simply take the train to Stuttgart and then go by bus to Vohldorf. In the morning I'll go to the railway station and find out the times of the Stuttgart trains.

With this decision made, she lay down beside the children

and fell into an uneasy sleep. Next morning she gave the children an apple each and the last of the bread in the basket. The bags of flour and rice she took over to the rabbi's wife.

"I am going to the station to find out about trains to Stuttgart," she told her. "If we can travel there today, we will, but we can't carry these with us when we go." She passed over the two bags. "I'm sure you can make use of them."

Frau Rahmer thanked her gravely. "Where are the children now?" she asked.

"Laura's looking after them in the meeting room," replied Ruth. "I hope I shan't be very long."

The journey to the station was easy enough. Travelling alone, Ruth attracted little attention, and she had soon discovered they had missed the morning train, but there was another later that afternoon. It would mean that they arrived in Stuttgart after it was dark, but she felt certain that they could reach her mother's house that evening. Last night's decision confirmed, she bought five tickets.

When she reached the meeting room again, it was to find it empty. No children, no luggage. Her heart almost stopped at the sight of the empty room. Had the Gestapo come for them there? Then more rational thought returned and she hurried across to the rabbi's house. Frau Rahmer was in her kitchen, the children round her, the suitcase and the basket tidily in the corner.

"I thought it would be better if they were here with me," Frau Rahmer said.

"I said we should stay, Mutti," burst out Laura. "But she took the twins."

"She gave us gingerbread," reported Peter.

"And honey," added Hans.

"But I brought everything with us," went on Laura, pointing to the luggage.

"It's all right, Laura," her mother reassured her. "You did the right thing." She turned back to Frau Rahmer. "Thank you for looking after them for me," she said. "I've got our tickets. We leave almost at once."

"I've put some bread and cheese in your basket," Frau Rahmer said, "to eat on the journey. You'll all be hungry before you get there."

Ruth smiled at her with true gratitude. "You've been very kind," she said.

Frau Rahmer shrugged. "We've done what we can," she said, and Ruth saw what she had seen in the Meyers' eyes when they had left there, relief that they were moving on. And she understood it. Life was difficult enough and dangerous enough without taking on other people's problems.

"If by any chance my husband comes looking for us," Ruth said as they said goodbye, "please tell him where to find us."

"Of course," promised Rabbi Rahmer. "May God protect you."

They reached Stuttgart without a problem, and Ruth led them to the bus station. She knew where she was now, Stuttgart was where her parents had brought her and Edith for treats when they were children. They were in time to catch the last bus to Vohldorf, and it was with great relief that Ruth settled them all in seats at the back. They were on the final leg of their journey.

She had been so concerned at getting them out of Munich, away from the danger that lurked there, that she had given little thought as to how they might be received in the village of her childhood. Here there would be people who had known her as a child; friends and neighbours who would recognise her, or, if not actually recognise her after the years she'd been away, would know who she was when they moved in with her mother.

How will they react when they find out I've come back, she wondered? Will old childhood friendships stand, or will I find, as Laura has with her school friends, that they'll all turn against me, all our shared happiness forgotten?

As the bus trundled through the dank, winter countryside, Ruth found herself longing for the comfort of her mother's arms. She needed to be a child again herself. She'd been brave for her own children, but the nearer she came to her childhood home, the more she ached to see her mother, and just for one moment slough off the responsibility of being a parent.

At last the bus dropped them in the market square and rumbled off into the night. Several other people had got off as well, hurrying away to the warmth of their own homes, leaving Ruth and her children standing alone in the familiar square. It was bathed in peaceful moonlight, the silence broken only by the soft splash of a fountain at its centre, the fountain where Ruth and Edith had sat and chatted with their friends as they dawdled their way home from school. At the far end the church tower reached up into the night, moonlight gleaming on its clock face and the hands which showed ten minutes past nine.

We'll be home by half past nine, thought Ruth. "Nearly there now," she said cheerfully. "It's not far to Oma's house. We can walk it easily from here. There's enough moon to see where we're going." She picked up the case and the depleted basket. "Come on, Laura, don't lose the boys in the dark.

Inge, you can help me carry the basket."

It was cold and she set off at a brisk pace, leading the children along the lane that led away from the centre of the village, passing the small cottages crouching on either side of the road, the larger homes set back behind gates, and past the tall gateposts of the Great House. All were bathed in peaceful moonlight, and the quiet serenity of the night as she took the familiar road lifted Ruth's spirits. Yes, she thought, we're nearly there, now.

Her mother lived on the edge of the village, in a row of houses that wound up the hill to fields and woodland beyond. As children, Ruth, Edith and their friends had played in those woods, picnicking under the trees, gathering wild flowers, playing hide and seek. Such a carefree childhood. Perhaps here, in this quiet village, her own children would be able to reclaim something of their childhood; be able to play in the woods and fields as she had done, with no shadow of fear haunting their play.

When they reached the house Ruth was surprised to find the gate closed. There'd always been a gate, but she'd never seen it shut before. Pushing it open, she led the children up the path to the front door. Lights shone welcomingly from the windows, and a trail of smoke from the chimney filled the night air with the scent of apple wood. Mother would have finished her evening meal, but Ruth had no doubt she would be able to find something warm and filling for them all. Food might be getting scarce in the towns, but here in the country there would be plenty, and Mother had always been a wonderful cook.

Ruth rang the bell, and as she heard the bolts being pulled back from the door, prepared herself for the astonishment in her mother's eyes as she found her daughter and grandchildren standing on her doorstep... astonishment and delight.

The door creaked open, and there standing in the familiar hallway was a woman whom Ruth had never seen before.

"Yes?" she said.

"I was looking..." Ruth began, "I mean... is Frau Heber at home?"

"Frau Heber? Frau Heber doesn't live here anymore."

"Doesn't live here?" echoed Ruth. "Why? I mean when, when did she move? Where's she gone?"

"Oh, she's still in the village," replied the woman airily. "Who are you?"

"I'm her daughter. Where is she?"

"Her daughter? Well, you'll find her in Kreuzstrasse."

"Kreuzstrasse!" Ruth was aghast.

"Yes. Kreuzstrasse. That's where she lives now." And with that the woman closed the door.

"Was that Oma?" asked Hans, who had only met his grandmother once and had no recollection of her. "I don't like her!"

"No," agreed Peter stoutly. "I don't like her."

"I want to go home," wailed Inge. "Mutti, I don't like it here."

"If Oma isn't here," Laura said in a tremulous voice, "where shall we go?"

"She is here," Ruth said firmly. "It's just that she's moved house. I know where Kreuzstrasse is, so we'll go and find her."

Tiredly, with the children dragging their feet, they trailed back to the village, from where Ruth led them through an alley that ran behind the shops fronting the square. As they walked, Ruth's mind was whirling. Kreuzstrasse! She knew

Kreuzstrasse all right, it was the poorest part of the village, where old houses crouched together, their roofs patched, their grimy windows small, their rooms dark and poky, with a shared tap at the front and a shared outhouse at the back. How could her mother be living in one of these dilapidated houses? Why had she moved out of her own home? Even as these questions raced through her mind, Ruth knew the answers. Her mother had been turned out of her home too, and the place she had moved to was one of the hovels in Kreuzstrasse. There would be little room for five extra people.

There were three houses in Kreuzstrasse. Ruth chose the middle one and knocked on the door.

From inside came a soft voice that Ruth recognised at once. "Who's there? What do you want?"

"Mother! It's me, Ruth. Open the door, Mother. Open the door."

There was the sound of a bolt and a key turning before the door eased open, and Ruth saw her mother, Helga Heber, peering out through the crack. Then it was just as Ruth had imagined. She stared at her daughter in astonishment, before her face broke into the delighted smile. She flung the door wide and gathered her Ruth into her arms.

"Oh, Ruth, my darling girl!" and for a moment Ruth was a child again, sheltered in her mother's embrace.

"Now let me have a look at you all," Helga cried, reaching out to the exhausted children. "Come inside and let Oma have a look at you."

Later, when the children were once again settled down on a makeshift bed in one of the two tiny bedrooms, Ruth sat in the kitchen with her mother and told her everything that had happened.

"I wrote and told you when we moved in with Herbert," she said, "but I suppose you didn't get the letter."

"No, I didn't. And I wrote to you to tell you I'd had to move, but of course I sent that to Gerbergasse."

"And I didn't get it. Mother, what happened here? Who made you leave your home?"

"I knew I had to leave. There's an SS unit stationed outside the village. All the Jewish families were being moved. There was no way that I was going to be allowed to stay there. The Müllers, who live there now, used to live just off the square, but they'd always liked our house, so they offered to buy it from me."

"To buy it?"

"Yes. I was lucky. They didn't offer much for it of course, but if I'd refused to sell, I'd have been put out anyway and had nothing to show for it. They said as much."

"Then why did they bother paying you anything?" asked Ruth bitterly.

Helga shrugged. "Guilt?" she suggested. "Your father and I used to play cards with them every week."

"They were your friends and they stole your house," Ruth said flatly.

"Darling, be realistic! If they hadn't had it, someone else would have. At least I still have somewhere to live and a little money to live on. Jews were being turned out all over the village. The bakery's closed, the butcher's closed. You remember Moises' grocers?"

"Of course."

"Well, they've gone. Their shop's taken over by a family from Stuttgart, called Wessel. Not Jews of course."

"I shall always remember the wonderful smell in Moises',"

Ruth mused, "a mixture of all my favourite food smells combining into one glorious aroma. And Frau Moise behind the counter watching us children like a hawk with those beady eyes."

"Well, they've gone and the Wessels are here. Anyway," Helga went on, "the Müllers paid me for the house and I moved in here."

"You're very philosophical about it, Mother," Ruth said.

"It's the only way to be if you're going to keep your sanity," replied her mother. "Otherwise fear and anger take over your life."

"They've certainly taken over mine," said Ruth sharply. "And that's how I keep my sanity. My anger at the injustice of it all keeps me sane...that and protecting the children are what keep me going. But," her shoulders sagged with weariness, "what am I going to do now? I thought we could come and live with you for a while, I thought you'd have plenty of room for us."

"Well, you can stay here with me for as long as you like," said Helga. "You know that, but it will certainly be close quarters!"

"Oh, I wish Kurt was here!" Ruth's cry exploded from her. "I don't know where he is, or even if he's still alive!"

Helga reached out and took her hands. "My darling, you've been so brave. Never doubt that Kurt will find you. He'll follow you to Herbert's, and when you're not there he'll come here. That is what we have to hold on to. He will come. And," she went on, "you're not on your own now. You've got me. Between us we'll keep the children safe. We'll keep them safe until Kurt finds you."

Ruth looked across at her mother, a diminutive, grey-haired

old lady, but one who had never lacked determination or courage. Through her own tears she could see the tears on her mother's face, and in that moment she knew, indeed, that she was no longer alone. She might not have Kurt beside her, but she had the next best person. She returned her mother's grasp and whispered, "Yes, we will."

Neither woman voiced the possibility that Kurt wasn't coming back, his release was a hope that they would cling to, but each felt in her heart that as they had heard nothing for nearly four months, it was becoming less and less likely.

Next day they set to work to re-organise the house to accommodate them all. The only room of any size was the kitchen, and it was here that they spent the better part of their time. Ruth tried to keep some structure to the children's day with lessons in the morning, and play in the afternoon... but seldom out of doors. No chance of the carefree play in the woods Ruth had hoped for.

"Certainly not the woods," Helga had said. "There's an SS training camp there now. It's not really safe to let them play outside at all. It won't be long before it's round the village that you've come home. Everyone knows we're Jews and though some people aren't actively hostile, there is no sign of friendship either."

"But I can't keep them indoors all day," protested Ruth.

"But you can't let them play outside either," answered her mother. "Adults probably won't pay any attention to them, it'll be the other children. It's what they're taught at school now, that Jews are inferior, not really human. They can torment them in any way they like, and no one will tell them to stop."

20th October 1936

We were turned out of Uncle Herbert's apartment, so we have come to stay with Oma. She doesn't live in her old house anymore, where Mutti used to live, but in a much smaller one. We have to go to an outhouse in the yard when we want to be excused. I don't like it. It's very smelly and very cold.

I am cold all the time now. It's winter and we haven't got any warm clothes. Mutti says she will try and get us some, but I know she hasn't got any money. Oma gave us girls each one of her cardigans the other day when we said we were cold. We haven't taken them off since. They are far too big for us, and we do look funny, but we are a bit warmer. We sit in the kitchen with Oma most of the time. It is the only warm room in the house. There is a stove, which burns wood, but there isn't much wood left, so soon it will go out. The twins talk to each other all the time, but not to the rest of us. They don't speak German much at all, just some funny language of their own. I don't like it here, but we haven't got anywhere else to go. I like Oma. She tells us stories about when Mutti was a little girl.

Laura wrote her diary every day. "It's to show Papa when he comes back," she explained to Oma. "He'll want to know what happened to us while he was away."

As the days passed they gradually fell into a routine, and apart from when Helga went out to buy food, they didn't leave the safety of the house. The grocery store in the village displayed the required notice in the window, *No Jews*, but the Wessels saw the serving of the few Jewish customers who were left in the village as a business opportunity. For extortionate prices, they sold Helga goods that they couldn't sell to anyone else. She had to pay a far higher price than Aryan customers for even the most basic food; pay it or starve. The family remained fed, but the money was fast dwindling.

As November came and went, they faced another, potentially more difficult, problem. There was almost no wood left for the stove, their only source of heat. Helga tried to buy logs from the woodcutter, Franz Beider, whom she met in the market square. He had always supplied her with logs at her old house, but now he refused to sell her any.

"I haven't enough to be wasting them on Jews," he snapped, when she asked. "Need them for the rest of the village."

"It's not for myself, Herr Beider, as much as for my grandchildren," she explained. "We've no wood for the stove. It's very cold this winter, we shall freeze." But Franz Beider simply walked away, saying loudly to Frau Wessel from the grocery store, "She's got a nerve!"

That night, however, there was a tap on the door, and when Ruth opened it a crack, Franz Beider stood outside. He pushed at the door, and she was so surprised that she allowed him to step past her and come into the house. He walked into the tiny kitchen, where the whole family was huddled round the stove.

"Got some logs for you outside," he said in a half-whisper, as if he could be overheard. "Get 'em indoors quick, before someone sees."

They put the light out before they opened the door again, and he hastily manoeuvred a wheelbarrow into the room. Tipping it up, the logs cascaded onto the floor.

"We ain't all Nazis," he said to Helga. "You was good to me in the old days. I'll try and bring you a barrowful now and then. Can't promise…if someone informed…" He nodded to Ruth, whom he had known as a child, "I'll do me best."

"How much?" began Ruth, but the man shook his head.

"Better days will come," he said. "You can pay me then. In the meantime, keep the little uns indoors, eh?" Then he opened the door once more and slipped out into the night.

Ruth and Helga stared at each other. They both found they had tears in their eyes, it had been so long since one of their neighbours had treated them with anything but abuse, let alone generosity. They stacked the logs neatly beside the stove; if they were careful, thanks to Franz Beider, there was another week's warmth there.

"Only potatoes and cabbage," Helga said, one afternoon a week later as she put the shopping basket on the table. "And it's definitely round the village that you're here."

"Mother! You're bleeding." Ruth rushed over to Helga and, pulling the hair away from her forehead, inspected the cut above her eyebrow that was oozing blood. "What happened?"

"Hitler Youth," replied her mother, allowing Ruth to dab at the cut with cold water. "Hitler Youth in the square. They saw me coming out of the shop and began their usual chanting, then one of them marched over to me and said, 'There's Jewish spawn in your house. All you dirty Jews crammed in together. We don't want any more Jews here. Get rid of them!' Then another joined in. 'Yeah,' he said 'Get rid of them… or we will!'"

Ruth stared at her mother in horror. "What did you say?" she whispered.

"Say? I didn't say anything. You don't answer those boys back, Ruth. You know that. No, I just turned away, and that's when they started throwing stones. One hit me on my head."

"And anywhere else? Did they hit you anywhere else?" asked Ruth anxiously.

"Only bruises...no more blood."

That night, as they finished the vegetable broth that had been their supper, there was a loud crash against the front door. Memory of the Gestapo raid on Herbert's flat sent Inge off into hysterical screams. The twins began to whimper and Laura stared white-faced at her mother and grandmother. There was another bang on the door, as if someone had hit it with a hammer, and then the chanting began. "Jews out! Jews out! Jews out!" followed by shouts of laughter and a brick that smashed the kitchen window, showering the floor with glass. The children huddled together, all of them crying now.

"Let's move the children upstairs," Helga hissed, as she cradled against her.

Ruth shook her head. "No," she said vehemently. "Never upstairs again." However, she went upstairs herself and peered down into the alley. There was a small group of boys outside, happily chanting and firing stones and bricks at the house, but none of them seemed to come nearer than the lane, and after a while they gave one final shout and raced off, back towards the square.

"I don't think we can stay here," Helga said to Ruth when they had finally settled the frightened children. "The children aren't safe here."

"They aren't safe anywhere," pointed out Ruth. "And anyway, where else can we go? It's the same everywhere. At least here we know the people. They may taunt and torment us, but surely they wouldn't do us any physical harm."

"It isn't just people from the village, though, is it?" replied Helga. "New people have moved in, people who only know us as the Jews that are left. They'd like to get rid of us."

"No one would want to live in this house," said Ruth bitterly.

"Probably not," Helga agreed, "but they don't want us to live in it either. No, I seriously think we should consider moving away."

"But where?" Ruth tried to keep the irritation out of her voice. It was all very well for Mother to say they should move on, but they had very little money and no obvious place to go. At least here they still had a roof over their heads. "Where do you suggest we go, Mother?"

"To Edith, of course."

"But Edith's in Vienna."

Helga shrugged. "So, we go to Vienna."

"Mother, I don't think we can. They may not let us out of Germany. They caught Herbert trying to leave."

"He was trying to take money with him," said Helga. "Didn't you say he hid diamonds in his shoes?"

"And the twins aren't on my passport."

"So, we'll get them put on." Helga was not to be deterred. "They want us to leave, Ruth. So, we'll leave. We may end up with just the clothes we stand up in, but we shall be out of Germany and safe. When we get to Vienna, Edith will take us in, just until we find somewhere. Things are different in Austria. We'll find somewhere to live, you can get a job of some sort, the girls can go back to school and I'll look after the twins and keep house."

"That all sounds very fine, Mother," said Ruth, "but it's not going to be easy. I'm sure we'll have to get permits to leave."

"Then we'll get them," snapped her mother. "Come on, Ruth! This isn't like you. We can't stay here waiting for someone to give us up to the Gestapo. Do you want the children to be put into an orphanage?"

"No! Of course not."

"Well, that will happen if we stay here. I thought we might be allowed just to live here quietly, but now the Youth have found us it won't be long before the Gestapo do. Better to move away, and keep moving."

"And what do you suggest we live on?" demanded Ruth. "I have very little of Herbert's money left. We can't live on fresh air, you know!"

"I know," answered her mother soothingly. "But I still have some money, remember, from my house. Enough to get us to Vienna."

Ruth sank her head into her hands. "Oh Mother, I don't know what to do!"

"Tomorrow you go into Stuttgart and you go to the government offices and find out what permits you need. You have your passport, with the girls already on it?"

"Yes."

"Well, you take that and get the boys put on as well. Take mine too. We'll all need permits if they are going to let us go...and if they aren't..."

"Suppose they seize the passports?"

"That's a risk we have to take, Ruth. Otherwise we sit here and wait for the Gestapo to come and find us."

Ruth looked across at her mother, so small and upright. "You're very strong, Mother," she said.

"So are you, darling," replied Helga. "Look how far you've already brought the children on your own! Now we have each other, and so we're doubly strong."

They agreed that Ruth should take with her all the documents in the deed box.

"You don't know what information and proof of identity they're going to ask for," Helga said when Ruth wondered if it was wise to have everything with her. "If you have your birth and marriage certificates, they can register the numbers if they need to. Let's face it, you don't want to be sent home for more documentation, do you? We need to get all this organised as soon as possible."

"Oh God, I hope we've made the right decision," murmured Ruth.

"It's the only decision," replied her mother firmly. "Apart from everything else, if Franz doesn't manage to bring us some more fuel, we're going to freeze to death in this house!"

Seven

Next morning Ruth left the children with Helga and set out to catch the morning bus to Stuttgart. When it pulled up in the market square, she took her place at the back of the group waiting to board. She stepped up inside and paused to pay the driver.

"You! Jew! Out!" shouted a voice from inside the bus.

She ignored the shout and handed the driver her cash, who took it from her, putting it into the money satchel beside him, but instead of handing her a ticket, said, "No Jews on this bus!"

"But I've just bought a ticket," cried Ruth in dismay.

"No you haven't," grinned the driver. "If you'd just bought a ticket, you would have it in your hand, wouldn't you? Now get off! You're holding up my bus." He gave her a shove and she almost fell back out of the door. There was a cheer from inside, and then the driver revved the engine and pulled away, leaving Ruth standing, in a cloud of exhaust, at the side of the road.

She stared after it, and then gritting her teeth set off along the road towards Stuttgart. It was fifteen kilometres to the edge of the city, but Ruth hoped that she wouldn't have to walk the whole way. There were other villages along the way where she was not known, and she hoped to be able to get on a bus in one of these. With her shopping basket, in which she had the deed box, covered with a cloth, she looked like any countrywoman on her way into the city.

It took her four hours, two buses and a five-kilometre walk to reach the city, and when she did she was exhausted. Her clothes were dusty from the road, and her arm ached from the weight of the shopping basket, but she had made it. Now she had to discover how she could get the boys put on her passport so they could all leave for Vienna.

She went first to the city hall where she made enquiries about the twins. She was sent to one office after another, and each place she had to wait until there was someone to deal with her enquiry.

"Can you prove these children are yours?"

Ruth produced their birth certificates.

"Are you married to the father?"

Ruth produced her marriage certificate.

"Where is their father? They should be registered on his passport, not yours."

Ruth explained that she didn't know where Kurt was, finally admitting that he had been arrested.

"You are Jews. Your husband is a Jewish agitator." It was a statement, not a question.

"No. I mean yes, we are Jews, but my husband isn't an agitator."

Wrong answer. "If he wasn't an agitator, he wouldn't have been arrested! Wait over there."

She waited and was sent to another office.

"Why do you wish to leave Germany?"

"We want to visit my sister who lives in Vienna."

"You have no passports for your sons."

"That is why I have come. To ask you to register my sons on my passport."

"Are they legitimate?"

"Of course they are."

"Let me see your marriage certificate."

Ruth produced her marriage certificate.

"Let me see their birth certificates."

Ruth produced their birth certificates.

"We cannot deal with this! You are Jews. You must go to the Office of Jewish Affairs."

Another office building, another wait in another draughty corridor, but eventually Ruth was sent into a small office where an elderly man with grey hair and steel-rimmed glasses sat behind a desk. He wore civilian clothes, though there was a silver swastika pinned to his lapel, but he had the upright bearing of a military man.

"What can I do for you, Gnädige Frau?" he asked with a smile.

Ruth was so surprised at the politeness of his tone that she didn't reply at once. The man waved her to a chair in front of his desk.

"Please sit down."

Still more astonished, Ruth sat. At all the interviews so far she had been left standing while the official remained seated.

"I need..." she began and then hesitated.

"Yes?" The man was encouraging.

"I need to have my sons' names added to my passport," she said, the words all coming out in a rush. "We are hoping to visit my sister in Vienna and..."

"You have the passport there?"

136

Ruth opened the deed box, and withdrawing her passport put it into the man's outstretched hand. He opened it, glancing at the photograph, and then looked across at her. "I'm sure I can arrange this for you, Frau Friedman," he said smoothly, "for a consideration."

"A consideration?" Ruth was uncertain. Was he asking for money? Presumably he was, but how much? Had she got enough? The questions flew through her mind before he replied, "These things normally take a great deal of time." He looked at her slyly and added, "And I don't think you have much of that particular commodity…do you?" His smile, which had appeared friendly at the outset, now took on a sinister quality, and Ruth dropped her eyes. "No," he went on, "I don't think so. But I can speed the process up…if we can come to some agreement."

"What sort of agreement?" whispered Ruth. "How much do you want?"

"How much have you got?" The eyes glittered behind the glasses.

"Not much," Ruth said. "Almost nothing."

"What else is hidden in that deed box, I wonder?" He raised an interrogatory eyebrow. "What other treasures do you have tucked away in there?" He placed the passport on the desk and held out his hand.

Ruth's grip tightened on the precious box. "Our birth and marriage certificates," she said.

His hand was still extended. "And?"

"Some earrings my mother-in-law gave me as a wedding present."

"I'd like to see those," he remarked conversationally, as if she had wanted to show her present off.

Ruth opened the deed box, and taking the earrings out reached over and dropped them into his hand.

The man looked at them consideringly, holding them up to the light to view them better.

"Pretty baubles," he said, "but not worth much. What else?"

"Just a brooch of my mother's." Ruth knew that there would be nothing she could do if this man, at first more sympathetic than any she had seen, and now so greedy, decided to take any of her jewellery. Again he held out his hand, and she passed the brooch over. He looked at it for a moment and then turned his attention back to Ruth.

"This is like drawing teeth," he said. "I think the best thing you can do is to hand the box over to me and I'll have a look myself." He got to his feet, and walking round the desk towered over her. Without another word he simply reached down, and scooping the box from her hands tipped its contents out onto the desk.

"This looks more like it," he said, and picked up the title deed to the Friedmans' shop. "I think this would work." He studied the document for several minutes before glancing back at Ruth, who sat white-faced on the chair.

"Now," he said, "here's the deal. I add your sons' names to your passport. For that you pay me one pair of pearl earrings and one gold brooch. I also get you five exit permits, which allow you and your family to travel to Vienna. For that you pay me one set of title deeds." He smiled broadly. "Sounds fair to me."

It's robbery! Ruth wanted to shriek. Bare-faced robbery! She bit the words back, almost gulping them down into her throat before she said, "The title deeds aren't mine to give. They belong to my husband."

"Indeed they do," agreed the man affably. "But he's not here, is he? *You* have the deeds, and it is you who are asking me for a favour." His voice took on an edge of steel. "Don't you think he would want you to use them to save your children? Or don't dirty Jews feel the same way about their children as normal human beings do?"

Of course we do, Ruth wanted to scream at him, that's why scum like you can use them as a lever to get what you want. It's because we love our children so much that we do anything, anything we can to protect them from monsters like you.

But of course she said none of this. She just sat shaking on the chair in front of him.

"Well?" he snapped. "I'm losing patience with you, Gnädige Frau." This time the salutation was imbued with vitriol. "You have this one chance." He picked up the passport and the jewellery and slipped them into a drawer of his desk, then he folded the title deeds. "What is it to be?"

Ruth raised her head with as much dignity as she could muster and said, "It's a deal."

"Good." The man tucked the folded deeds into an inside pocket and stood up. "Back here, eight o'clock tomorrow morning. Don't be late."

Ruth stood as well. "Will you give me the permits then, sir?"

The man beamed at her. "You'll find out tomorrow at eight, won't you?" He rang a bell on his desk and a young SS man came in.

"This woman is leaving, Schwarz," he said. "Make sure she does."

"Who do I ask for?" Ruth realised in panic that she had never learned the man's name. "In the morning? Who do I ask for?"

"Standartenführer Unger. Standartenführer Paul Unger of the SS."

That night Ruth hid in a wooden shelter in a park. She had nowhere to go, and as she had been told to present herself at eight o'clock the next morning at the Gestapo headquarters, there was no way she could get back to Vohldorf for the night and be back in time. She knew that her mother would be worried sick when she did not come home, but there was nothing she could do about that. She found the shelter, little more than a summer arbour in a quiet part of a public garden and curled up in the corner trying to keep out of the wintry wind. As always there was a *No Jews* notice on the iron gates, but then she wasn't allowed to be out on the streets either, and there was no question of finding a room, so she was at risk whatever she did.

She had hardly slept at all. Standartenführer Unger had taken everything of value that she had, and there was no guarantee that he would keep his side of the bargain. What a fool she'd been, to have left the deeds in the box when she had come into the city. She should have taken those out and left them safely with her mother. The fear that consumed her now made her feel physically sick. Tears of despair coursed down her face, streaking her cheeks with dark rivulets. He had taken everything and given her nothing. For all his smiles, he was more sinister than the men who had come and arrested Kurt. And what was Kurt going to say when he found out she'd given away the shop? Of course he would understand. Of course he wouldn't mind if it saved his beloved family, but suppose she'd been tricked by this evil man? They would have lost everything and gained nothing. Oh God, she prayed, let the colonel keep his side of the bargain.

As dawn broke she slipped out of the park gates. She was stiff with cold, and exhausted, and she needed the lavatory. She had found a public convenience the night before, and she returned there now, hoping it would be open this early. She was in luck, the attendant was just unlocking the metal gates.

The woman eyed Ruth suspiciously, taking in her crumpled clothes and dishevelled hair. "You're about early," she said.

Ruth managed a smile and replied, "Yes, I have to get to the market." Once locked into a cubicle she used the lavatory and dragged a comb through her hair. When she came out again, the attendant was nowhere to be seen, so Ruth hastily washed her hands and face and hurried out into the cold morning air. As she turned a corner in search of a café, she caught sight of the attendant returning to the lavatory block, followed by a man in uniform. Ruth didn't wait to see which uniform it was, she fled down the street, turning into smaller side streets until she was lost, and, she hoped, they were too.

She emerged into a small square where she found a café serving breakfast to early risers. She needed food, she'd had nothing since the morning before, and she felt hollow inside and a little light-headed. She went into the café, and sitting at a small table at the back ordered herself a plate of bread and cheese and a cup of hot, black liquid which was advertised as coffee. The waitress brought her food, after which no one paid her any attention at all. The bread was fresh, and the cheese tasty. Ruth could have eaten several such plates, but had no money for such extravagance, and forced herself to eat slowly. She sipped the bitter coffee, grateful for its warmth if not for its flavour, and considered what to do.

She would go to the Jewish Affairs Office at eight o'clock,

and ask to see Standartenführer Unger. Then she could only pray that he would indeed have the updated passport and the exit permits. If he didn't...well, then she'd have to decide what she was going to do.

At exactly eight o'clock she presented herself at the desk in the reception area, and was told to wait. She waited for five hours. Officials walked past her as she stood in the passage. No one spoke to her, or even acknowledged her existence, and still she waited. The young officer, Schwartz, who had seen her off the premises, came by several times, and at last she plucked up courage to speak to him.

"Please, sir," she said. "I was here at eight o'clock as the Herr Standartenführer told me to be. Is he here?"

"He's busy," snapped Schwartz. "You'll have to wait."

Ruth continued to wait, but was becoming increasingly aware that she needed the lavatory again. She tried not to think about it, but as time passed she knew that unless she was to disgrace herself here in the corridor she had to find a toilet. She returned to the front desk and asked. The woman seated at the desk looked outraged.

"You certainly can't use one in this building," she said. "The lavatories here are not for Jews. You'll have to go and find one somewhere else." She returned to her typewriter and Ruth knew there was no point in asking again. She hurried out into the street, and within three or four hundred metres found a public lavatory.

Ten minutes later she was back at the front desk of the Jewish Affairs Office. The woman at the desk looked up as she came back in.

"You Friedman?" she asked.

"Yes," replied Ruth, "Yes, I'm Ruth Friedman."

"The Herr Standartenführer sent for you, but I told him you'd left."

Ruth stared at her in absolute horror. "You told him what?" she whispered.

"I told him you were here, but you'd left."

"Did you tell him why I left?" demanded Ruth angrily. "Did you explain why?"

The woman sniffed. "As if the Herr Standartenführer would be interested in your incontinence!"

It took all Ruth's self-control not to reach over the desk and shake the smug young woman until her teeth rattled. Hardly incontinence, she wanted to shout. I've been here more than five hours, in which time you've been to the ladies' room twice. She bit back the words, knowing they would only make matters worse.

"Please," she forced herself to speak politely, "please would you be so good as to tell the Herr Standartenführer that I am back now."

"Oh, he's gone now," said the girl airily. "He said that if you did bother to show up again that you should come back again tomorrow at the same time."

Ruth left the building, her emotions running the gamut from rage through humiliation to despair. There was nothing she could do except turn up again the next morning and hope that he would see her and give her the precious passes he had promised. She spent another very cold and uncomfortable night in the open, in a different park this time, trying to get some sort of rest. She thought of her mother and the children. They must be going out of their minds with worry now that she'd spent two nights away. Her mother would think she'd been arrested, and the children would be terrified that she had suddenly disappeared like their father.

Next morning she drank no coffee and having spruced herself up at the public conveniences that she'd found near the Jewish Affairs Office she presented herself once more at exactly eight o'clock. This time the wait was nearly six hours, standing in the same draughty corridor, ignored by all that used it as they went about their duties. This time she spoke to no one and at last she was summoned to Standartenführer Unger's office.

"I hear you left the building yesterday," he said by way of opening. "That was extremely foolish of you."

"I'm sorry, I needed the lavatory and..."

"I imagine you'd have thought of that before you came." Standartenführer Unger raised a supercilious eyebrow.

"Yes, sir," murmured Ruth "I'm very sorry."

"So you should be. It inconvenienced me greatly. Now—" he reached down and slid open the drawer of his desk "— here are your passports and the permits to travel to Vienna. They are valid for one week. Make sure you use them by then...and make sure you don't come back." He pushed the passport and the permits across the table and Ruth, unable to believe that they were actually there, snatched them up and stuffed them into the basket. "It's feckless families like yours that bring our great country down," he went on. "Now get out."

Ruth muttered, "Thank you, Herr Standartenführer," and left the room, before he could change his mind. Once safely outside the fearsome building, Ruth found a quiet street and looked at the papers she had been given, terrified that even now he had tricked her and that they were worthless. She held them up in the fading light and saw that they were made out in the right names and were dated and stamped with an SS stamp.

This time she had no problems with the bus driver, and seated quietly at the back of the bus drew no attention to herself. The other passengers ignored her, and she was able to stay on the bus until it dropped her in the Vohldorf market square. Keeping her head down and clutching her basket, she hurried along the narrow alley to Kreuzstrasse.

Helga opened the door, and burst into tears as she gathered her daughter into her arms.

"It's all right, Mutti, it's all right," she soothed, not even noticing she had reverted to the childhood name, as she tried to console her. "I've got everything we need. We leave for Vienna tomorrow."

Eight

Kurt stood for a moment, dumbfounded, outside the slammed door and then walked slowly back down the stairs to the street below. His mind began racing. Where were Ruth and the children? Where could they have gone now? And what had happened to Herbert? Why had he been arrested? Was it simply because he, too, was a Jew? Or was there something more? Was he even now learning how to survive in Dachau, or some other such camp? Where were Ruth and the children? Where were Ruth and the children?

Kurt stepped out onto the pavement and for a moment looked up at the building. Which was Herbert's flat? Third floor. And then he knew exactly which one it was, as the old woman stood there by the window, staring down into the street. When she saw him looking up she gave him a triumphant Heil Hitler and then drew the curtains across, as if to shut him out.

What a vile woman, Kurt thought furiously! How had she come to be living in Herbert's apartment? She had referred to Kurt's family as "the Jewish orphanage". Clearly they had been made homeless yet again, so where had they gone?

It was dusk now, and Kurt knew he needed somewhere to stay. He doubted if he would be able to pick up the trail tonight, even if there was one. People were more than reluctant to open their doors to a strange man after dark. He set off down the street at a brisk pace, looking for a small hotel or guesthouse where he might stay for the night. He was loath to spend the money, but although there was no official curfew that he knew about, it would be foolhardy to be out alone after dark. For a while he wandered the streets, looking for somewhere suitable, and finally saw a card in a window. Room to let.

He knocked on the door and waited. At length it was opened by a young woman in an apron. She peered at him as he stood in the dim light in her hallway. She clearly was not impressed with what she saw.

"Yes?"

"Good evening," Kurt said. "I'm looking for a room, and I saw the card in your window."

The woman eyed him suspiciously. "How long for?"

"One night, maybe two."

"Only let by the week," she replied and began to shut the door.

"I may stay a week?" asked Kurt hurriedly. "How much would it be?"

The woman paused and then told him the price. "Week in advance! No meals! Take it or leave it."

Kurt took it. He realised that she knew he was a Jew and the price she had asked reflected that, but he had to have somewhere to stay, and he didn't know how long it was going to take him to track down his family.

The room she showed him was small and poky, furnished with a single bed, a chest of drawers with a mirror and a washstand on which stood a bowl and a ewer of water. The bathroom was down the landing. However, Kurt was grateful to be off the street. He knew that with the way he looked and no luggage, nowhere more salubrious was going to take him. When he looked in the mirror and saw the hollow-cheeked, stubble-faced, pallid ghost that returned his stare, he was amazed that the woman had agreed to let him have the room at any price. Clearly she, too, was facing hard times and couldn't be too choosy about her guests.

Longing to see his family, Kurt had travelled straight to Munich with little thought given to his appearance. He had only the clothes he'd been arrested in, and they were grubby, hanging off his emaciated frame. His hair had begun to grow again, but sprouted in tufts over his head, where the rough strokes of the camp barber's razor had shaved him unevenly. His reflection told him that he must change his appearance, and fast. Looking like a convict was as dangerous as looking like a Jew, and he looked like both. First thing in the morning he must do something about it.

As he lay in the narrow bed that night, he considered how to set about finding his family. Where would Ruth have taken them? If it had been him, where would he have gone? His parents were both dead, and Herbert was his only sibling. He had no other family, so there was no lead there. Ruth's father was dead, but her mother lived in the old family house in Vohldorf. Perhaps Ruth might have taken the children there. Or there was her sister, Edith, who lived in Vienna. Could she have gone there? They'd be safer there, but it was a long way to travel with four small children, and there was the problem of crossing into Austria without passports for the twins. No, he decided, it was more likely that she had gone to her mother's...if she'd been able to go anywhere. What money had she? If she were destitute where would she go for help? She knew no one else in Munich. To the synagogue, that was the obvious place. But which synagogue? Where were the synagogues here? There was no question of asking. In the morning he would have to wander round and find them for himself.

At last he closed his eyes, and managed to sleep several hours before the nightmares began to crowd his dreams and he woke, as he did so often now, drenched in a cold sweat and shaking.

As soon as it was daylight Kurt left the house and went in search of food. He'd eaten nothing since the previous morning and he was very hungry. He found a workman's café where he ate some breakfast, after which he felt better and went in search of a street market. He had to conserve the money he had found in the bread oven, but new clothes and some toiletries were a must, and he reckoned that street traders would pay less attention to him, and be cheaper than trying to buy from shops, many of which wouldn't even let him cross the threshold. He found what he was looking for in a small square, flanked by tall medieval houses, where market traders' stalls of all sorts were set up round a central fountain. He bought himself a change of clothes from a second-hand clothes stall, a razor and some soap and a small case to carry them in, and hurried back to his room. Once he had washed and shaved and changed into his new clothes, he felt infinitely better. Now he could set out to search for his family without looking like a scarecrow. He pulled his new hat down over his ears so that his peculiar haircut was less visible, buttoned his overcoat against the chill of the wind and headed back out onto the street.

He spent the day looking for synagogues. Once he had found the first one, though the rabbi knew nothing about Ruth, it was easier. Each rabbi he spoke to pointed him in the direction of someone else. Rabbi Rahmer was the fourth that he visited.

"Yes," said the rabbi. "Your wife was here. She and the children stayed a night in our meeting room and then went to stay with her mother. Somewhere near Stuttgart, I think she said."

"Vohldorf," said Kurt.

"Yes, that's right. Well, she asked us to tell you where she'd gone if you ever came looking for her." The rabbi gave a sad smile. "I didn't really think you would."

"How long ago was she here?"

"Four...five weeks?" The rabbi was vague.

Next morning Kurt took the early train to Stuttgart, and reached Vohldorf by mid-afternoon. It was a cold wet day, but he didn't mind. The thought of seeing his family, of holding them all in his arms again, buoyed him up, and when he got off the bus in the market square his heart was racing. He had been to his parents-in-law's house only twice, but he thought he remembered where it was, and set out at a brisk pace. With only one wrong turn, he reached it and saw welcoming light flooding from a window into the damp dusk. The gates were shut, to stop the twins from straying, Kurt supposed, as he opened them and then closed them carefully behind him. For a brief moment he stood outside the front door, then he drew a deep breath and rang the bell.

"What do you want? We'll have no vagrants here!" The man who had come to the door stared at Kurt belligerently. He was tall and broad, a much larger man than Kurt, and he thrust his head aggressively forward as he spoke.

Kurt took an involuntary step back. "I'm...I'm looking for my wife..." he began.

"Well, she's not here! Be off, before I set the dogs on you."

"Frau Heber..." Kurt tried again, though he didn't like the sound of the dogs he could hear barking inside the house.

"No one called Heber in this house," snapped the man. "Get lost." He turned inside and called, "Lotte...let the dogs out!"

Kurt beat a hasty retreat.

"And don't come back, Jew. We don't want your sort in this village."

Kurt hurried away from the house, the sound of the dogs loud on the evening air. He had always liked dogs, until he went to Dachau. There the guard dogs were terrifying, and Kurt knew he would never look at a dog in the same way again.

Once he was out of sight he slowed his pace. There were tears in his eyes as he realised he had lost them all again, and this time he had no trail to follow. Helga Heber had lost her home, and he had no idea where she had gone, nor if Ruth and the children were with her.

"Think!" he admonished himself. "There must be some way I can pick up the trail again. Just take time and think."

With leaden feet he walked back into the market square. The dusk had deepened to darkness now, but there were still lights in the shops that edged the square, and Kurt decided to ask in those. He chose the grocer's, and pushed open the door. A large woman in an enveloping white apron was standing behind the counter, chatting to a customer. They both turned as Kurt came in and looked at him with interest. A stranger. Not someone from the village.

"Good evening," said the shopkeeper pleasantly. "Can I help you?"

"Good evening," Kurt replied with a smile. "Yes, I am looking for Frau Heber, Frau Helga Heber."

The shopkeeper's face hardened. "Are you, indeed?"

"Yes," Kurt kept his smile fixed to his face. "She's my mother-in-law."

"Is she now?" The woman waved her hand about the shop. "Well," she said, "she's not in here, is she?"

"No. It's just that she's moved and I wondered if you could tell me where she is living now. Is she still in the village?"

"No."

"No. Do you know where she went?"

"No. Now if you aren't going to buy anything, you can get out. I've got work to do."

Kurt left the shop and stood outside in the square. He saw, now, the sign in the window, which he hadn't noticed before: *No Jews*. As soon as he'd mentioned Helga Heber's name, the woman had realised he must also be a Jew. He looked in through the window of the shop next door, a small general store. Inside a man was unpacking some boxes. There was no sign on this window and Kurt was about to go in when someone bumped into him from behind. He spun round to see the customer from the grocer's.

"Kreuzstrasse," she murmured. "She's in Kreuzstrasse." But before Kurt could answer, the woman had hurried away across the square without a backward glance and disappeared into the darkness.

Kreuzstrasse. Had he heard her right, and if so where was Kreuzstrasse? It was clear that she didn't want to be seen talking to him, so he did not try to follow her. She had done what she could. He would have to try and find the place himself. Feeling the eyes of the grocer's wife upon him, he moved out of the light and walked across the square towards the church. As he reached it, the door opened and the priest came hurrying out. When he saw Kurt, he hesitated and then turned away.

The hesitation was enough. Kurt called across to him, "Excuse me."

The priest stopped and turned back, "Yes?"

"I'm looking for Kreuzstrasse," Kurt said. "Please can you tell me where it is?"

For a moment the priest said nothing, and Kurt was about to ask again when he pointed down a lane that ran off the square. "Down there," he said. "There's an alley at the end of the lane, that's Kreuzstrasse."

"Thank you," Kurt said fervently, "thank you very much."

The priest seemed about to say something else, but thought better of it, and with a brief nod, he, too, turned and hurried away.

Kurt followed the directions he'd been given, and found himself in the alley. There were three tiny houses there, each clothed in darkness. Surely this couldn't be where his mother-in-law was living. He stood outside in the silent street, wondering which house she lived in. There was no sign of life in any of them, no smoke from the chimneys, no chink of light from the dark windows. Was everybody out? Surely someone would be at home on such a cold and miserable evening. Kurt walked up to the front of the middle house. In the faint light of a streetlamp at the end of the alley, he could see that the front window had been broken and had been patched with cardboard. Despite the dampness in the air, the cardboard was still relatively dry; it couldn't have been there for very long. Someone must be living here. He knocked on the door. The sound of the knock seemed swallowed by the darkness, so he knocked again, more loudly, but there was no reply. He pressed his ear to the door in the hope of hearing movement inside, but there was nothing. He was about to turn away and try one of the other houses, when, on impulse, he tried the handle. To his astonishment the door opened. He pushed it wide and then stepping just inside, called out.

"Is there anyone there?" His words hung in the silence, but there was no reply. Cautiously he went inside and found himself in a kitchen, the only room downstairs. He felt for a light switch, but when he pressed it nothing happened. Feeling his way across the room he found the stove. It was cold. The last fire had been some time ago. As he felt round the top of the stove his fingers found a stub of candle on a saucer and a box of matches. Kurt struck a match and lit the candle. Shadows jumped around him as he held it high to look at the room.

There was a wooden table, two old chairs, some plates on a shelf, and a tin basin on a stand. He looked at the window. It had been carefully patched, but when he looked on the floor he found several tiny shards of glass. Kurt went up the narrow staircase to the two tiny rooms above. Here there was no furniture at all, but in each room an old mattress lay on the floor. The rooms were freezing cold, but the mattresses were not damp. They had been used fairly recently, Kurt thought. He went downstairs again. Had Ruth and the children really all been living here with her mother, or had they been in one of the other houses? Shielding the flickering candle with his hand he went back out into the alley and looked at the other two houses. He tried the one on the left, and when there was no reply to his knock he tried the door. It opened reluctantly, squeaking on its hinges. This house was the same as the other, except that it was clear no one had lived here for months. Cobwebs festooned the ceiling, there was no furniture at all, and the stale smell of damp pervaded the room. Holding the candle high, Kurt saw that there were a few sticks heaped beside the stove, but otherwise the room was empty. He did not bother to go upstairs. No one lived here, it must have been deserted for years. Carefully he closed the front door and turned to the third house. The door to this one did not open, and there was no reply when he knocked. He pressed his face against the filthy window that gave onto the kitchen, holding the candle against the glass, but the flame reflected back at him, and he could see nothing.

Then it dawned on him; the middle house, despite being sparsely furnished and cold, was clean. There were no cobwebs hanging in the corners, or trailing down to tickle his face. The floor had been swept, the stacked plates were clean, the surface of the table, though old, had been scrubbed. If Helga had lived in Kreuzstrasse, then it was in this house, and if Helga had lived here so had Ruth and the children. Kurt stood in the kitchen once more and drew in deep breaths, trying to sense the presence of his family. It was cold here, but it had been a roof over their heads, so why had they left?

He could go no further tonight, and so decided to sleep in the house and try and find out where they had gone in the morning. It was bitterly cold, so he crept back to the house next door and scooping up the pile of sticks carried it back and lit the stove. The leaping flames made the grim little kitchen more cheerful. He had nothing to eat, but at least he had a roof over his head. He heated some water on the stove and drank it, grateful for the warmth it brought. He dragged one of the mattresses down the stairs. Wrapped in his overcoat, Kurt lay down in front of the stove; and with Bella, Inge's doll, held tightly against his cheek, he tried to sleep. But despair crept up on him once more as he realised that he had missed them again, and as he lay in the flickering light cast by the flames, he began to weep. The trail had gone cold, and he was no nearer to finding Ruth and the children.

Finally Kurt slept, and when he awoke the fire had gone out and he was stiff and cold. The grey of dawn was lightening the sky and he was able to see his surroundings properly for the first time. From the window at the back he could see an outhouse in an overgrown yard. Had his family really been reduced to this? A tap outside the front door and a privy in the garden? Again he searched the rest of the house, and it was upstairs in one of the bedrooms that he made his discovery. Beneath the old mattress he found a piece of paper, and on it was written, *An Elephant Story for the Twins. Once upon a time there was an elephant and he lived in the jungle with his mummy and daddy. They hid among the trees where no one could find them*...Kurt stared at the paper and the writing, Laura's writing. Laura writing a story for her little brothers as she so often did. They *had* been here. Now he knew for sure. They had been here living in this house; but why on earth had they moved? Had they been forced to move? Turned out, even from this hovel of a home? He would have to try and find out.

If I knew why they'd gone, he thought, I might be able to work out where they've gone.

It was hunger that drove Kurt back to the market square. He had to get something to eat, as he'd had nothing since he'd got on the bus for Vohldorf yesterday. He looked round the shops that fronted the old cobbled square. He was determined not to go back into the grocer's unless he absolutely had to. On the opposite side, beyond the fountain, he saw a bakery, and he decided to try his luck there. As well as selling bread and pastries, the little shop offered a couple of white-clothed tables, and Kurt was served hot coffee, a pancake and a large slice of apple tart. He also bought fresh bread and another apple tart to take back to the house. Feeling much refreshed, he left the bakery and walked back towards Kreuzstrasse. The grocer's wife was standing outside her shop talking to a man with a pony cart. When she saw Kurt leaving the bakery, she pointed at him and the man turned round to look. She was gesticulating, and Kurt could imagine her tirade about Jews. He paid no attention, just kept on walking as if he hadn't seen her, but as he turned into the lane beside the church he heard her shout, "Dirty Jew! We don't want your sort in our village! Dirty Jew!"

Kurt gave no indication that he'd heard her, simply walked round the corner and into the lane. He let himself back into the house, put his purchases onto the table and sat down to consider what to do next. The girl in the bakery hadn't realised that he was a Jew, she had served him quite happily, and thinking back to the night before, it was only after he had mentioned Helga Heber by name that the woman in the grocer's had become hostile. With his dark hair, dark eyes and a high-bridged nose, Kurt knew he had a Semitic cast to his features, but his face did not shriek "Jew" and he could pass unnoticed if he was careful. He had never worn a beard, as many of his friends and neighbours had, but now he was going to be extra careful about shaving, keeping his face smooth and unremarkable. He filled the tin basin from the tap outside the house and got out his razor. As he lathered a little of his precious soap onto his face, there was a knock at the door. Kurt turned, but before he could go to the door it opened and a man slipped inside, pulling the door closed behind him. It was the man who had been talking with the grocer's wife.

Kurt stood, razor in hand, face half-covered in soap. "What the—?" he began.

"No time to talk," hissed the man. "You're Frau Heber's son-in-law?"

"Yes, but..."

"My name's Franz Beider. I've known Frau Heber for many years. You have to get away from here, now, at once."

"But..."

"Don't hesitate, man, there's no time. The woman at the grocer's, Frau Wessel, is going to the Gestapo to report you for moving in here. You have to leave now. They will be here within half an hour to arrest you."

Kurt turned pale. He wiped the soap from his cheeks and said shakily, "But where shall I go? They'll soon pick me up in this tiny place."

"Get your stuff and go out the back. I'll bring my cart along that lane and pick you up. Hurry, man, they'll be here any time." Franz Beider went to the front window and looked out into the alley. "I'll be there in five minutes. If you aren't, I shan't wait."

"But why?" began Kurt, his mind racing. Could he trust this man who only moments ago had been talking to a strongly anti-Semitic woman? Why would he offer help? Was it a trap? Then a mental picture of the parade ground at Dachau flashed into his mind and the decision was made.

"Thank you," was all he could say.

"We're not all Nazi scum round here," Franz Beider said. "Now, get a move on. If you aren't there," he repeated, "I shan't wait." With another anxious look into the street, he opened the door and disappeared.

For a moment Kurt stood frozen to the spot, then he grabbed his few possessions and the food he had just bought at the bakery, and crammed them into his case. It was clear someone had passed the night in the house, but he could do nothing about that. Frau Wessel would have told them that already, so it hardly mattered. He locked the front door, though he knew that wouldn't keep anyone out for long, then he opened the small door that led out into the backyard. It was overlooked by the other two houses, but no other buildings. He hurried past the rickety outhouse, and tossing the case over ahead of him, clambered over the back wall into the lane beyond. There was nowhere to hide, and as he waited for Franz Beider to appear, Kurt was terrified that someone else might come into the lane and see him waiting. After what seemed an age, he heard the unhurried clip-clop of a horse's hoofs, and then the pony cart came round the corner, with Franz sitting up on the driver's seat. As soon as he drew level with Kurt, he jumped down from the cart.

"Into the back," he said. "Hurry! Under the logs."

Kurt scrambled up onto the cart and Franz pushed the little suitcase in with him before covering him with a tarpaulin. Then he began piling logs on top of him. They were heavy and sharp, and pressed painfully into his body, but Kurt lay still as the weight increased, and the log load covered the shape of his body under the tarpaulin.

"For God's sake don't move," Franz instructed him.

"Whatever happens don't move until I let you out. Both our lives are at stake here."

With the breath all but crushed out of him, Kurt could do little more than grunt in reply. He felt the cart tilt as Franz climbed back up onto the box, and then the rocking movement as the cart turned and began to trundle back along the lane. Kurt had no idea where they were going, he simply lay as still as he could in the bumping cart and prayed that they wouldn't be stopped.

The journey became even more uncomfortable as the cart entered the market square, jolting its way across the cobbles. Some of the logs shifted and dug into new and different parts of his body, but Kurt didn't dare ease himself underneath them for fear of them moving even more and revealing him underneath. As they rumbled slowly across the square he heard a shout, and the sound of marching feet. The cart slowed to a halt as the feet tramped past. Frau Wessel had clearly made good her threat and had been to the Gestapo; SS troops had been summoned from the training camp. Then he heard her voice.

"You see, Herr Beider?" she called. "I was right. The Gestapo did want to hear that another dirty Jew had moved in."

"Indeed, Frau Wessel," Kurt heard his driver reply. "You were quite right. No doubt they'll find him hiding in his hole."

The woman laughed. "We'll get rid of them all in the end, Herr Beider. We'll get rid of them all in the end."

"And good riddance," agreed Herr Beider. Then he clicked his tongue and the horse moved on again.

Once they had left the cobbled square the road was smoother and the horse and cart picked up a little more speed, but it was another half hour before it creaked to a halt. Kurt could hear the sound of someone chopping wood. He stayed absolutely still under the logs, hardly daring to breathe.

"Dieter!" Kurt heard Franz call. "Dieter!"

The chopping stopped and a voice called back, "Yes, Herr Beider?"

Footsteps approached the cart and a young man's voice said, "You want me to unload the cart?"

"No, not now. You can take that barrow-load of logs I promised your mother, and eat with her. Back here in an hour though, all right?"

"Yes, sir! Thank you, sir! Ma'll be very grateful for the logs."

"Take the big barrow and load it up, then," ordered his boss.

Kurt heard Dieter tossing logs into a metal barrow, and then the rattle of it being wheeled away.

"Back in an hour, sir," called Dieter, "and thanks again for the logs."

Kurt tried to ease the pain in his legs, but as he moved he heard Franz Beider hiss, "Stay still!" He froze.

It seemed an age before Franz Beider began unloading the logs from the cart. When he finally emerged from under the tarpaulin, Kurt was grubby, bruised and ached all over. Franz helped him down, steadying him as he tried to stand on stiff and painful legs. They were in a yard beside an old stone house. All round the yard were piles of logs, stacked neatly under sheltering roofs to keep them dry. An axe lay on the ground beside a pile of split logs. On the far side of the yard there was a stable and a barn, with a hayloft above; clearly where Franz kept his horse and cart.

"Go into the barn and climb up into the hayloft," instructed Franz. "I doubt anyone will come looking for you here, but I don't want you found in the house."

"Of course," Kurt agreed. "If I am found here, you'll know nothing about it." He held out his hand to the woodman, who took it. "Thank you, Herr Beider, for getting me away, for risking your own life."

Franz Beider nodded, and then said, "Up to the hayloft then. I'll bring you some food and water in a little while." He gave Kurt a brief smile. "Don't worry," he said, "I live alone and Dieter only comes in during the day. You should be safe here for a while, till we can get you right away."

Kurt settled himself in the hay, and with the winter sun shining in through the skylight in the roof, warm and comfortable for the first time in days, fell into a deep sleep. He didn't hear the horse and cart leave the yard again, nor did he hear it return. When he woke it was to find dusk was falling. Franz stood over him with a basket in his hand.

"You've slept well," Franz said, putting the basket down in the hay. "Here, eat something." He handed him some bread and cheese, and as Kurt ate it he told him what was going on in the village.

"I went back with the cart and made my usual deliveries," he said. "The SS had been to the house and found you'd gone, so they've been searching for you. They asked me if I'd seen anyone on the road, and I told them I hadn't. Frau Wessel is having her day, telling everyone how she flushed you out. They're searching the surrounding area, but I doubt if they'll worry too much about finding you. All they want to be sure of is that you've gone."

Kurt drank thirstily from the bottle of water that was in

the basket and then asked the question that had been consuming him ever since he had climbed into the cart.

"Did the same thing happen to my family? Did the Gestapo come for them too?"

"No, they left in time. Frau Heber had to move from her old house some time ago, but no one took much notice of her once she was living in Kreuzstrasse...not until Ruth turned up with the children."

"You know Ruth?" breathed Kurt.

Franz smiled. "Known her since she was a child. Bit of a surprise to find she had four kiddies, though."

"So, tell me what's happened to them," begged Kurt. "I've been trying to find them."

"They left a few days ago," replied Franz. "Things were getting very difficult for them. The house was far too small for so many, the Wessels were charging them exorbitant prices for food, and when winter came on they could have died of cold in that house. I did get some logs to them, but I couldn't do it regular, like. And then the Hitler Youth began to take an interest in them."

"So, where have they gone?"

Franz shook his head. "I don't know. They took the bus to Stuttgart, but where they were going from there I wouldn't know. Didn't know they were actually leaving until I saw them in the square that morning, getting on the bus." He thought for a moment and then added, "The driver wasn't keen to take them, but they showed him some paper or other, and he let them get on."

Kurt stayed in Franz Beider's hayloft for two more days. Dieter arrived every morning and spent the day working in the yard, sawing up waiting tree trunks, chopping and stacking

163

logs. While he was there, Kurt stayed silently in the hay, listening to the work going on below. He offered to chop logs himself when Dieter had gone, but Franz refused his offer.

"Can't risk you being surprised in the yard," he said. "They're still out looking for you."

Two days later, when Dieter had finished his day's work, Franz climbed up into the loft. "It's time to move you out," he said as Kurt ate the food he had brought. "Tomorrow I'll hide you in the cart again and take you over to Dost. It's a small town, on the main line to Stuttgart, you'll be able to catch a train from there." He cut short Kurt's thanks. "It won't be a comfortable journey," he warned. "I'm afraid you'll have to travel under the logs again. We pass within a mile or two of the SS camp." He gave Kurt one of his rare smiles and said, "I'd better bring you some water to shave! You really do look like an undesirable vagrant, now."

Early next morning, while it was still dark, Kurt was once again hidden under the tarpaulin, weighed down with logs. As daylight crept into the sky, Franz put the horse in the shafts and they set out. They trundled along the country lanes, and occasionally there would be a shouted greeting, which Franz answered cheerfully, but the cart never stopped.

Kurt lost track of time. The weight of the logs seemed to increase as they travelled, until he felt that he was being crushed into one huge bruise. He had no idea how long they had been on the road, but at last he heard Franz say, "We're coming to the outskirts of Dost now. I'm going to let you out here."

The cart finally halted, and moments later Franz was hauling Kurt out from under the woodpile. As before, Kurt was so stiff and sore he could hardly stand, but he slipped over the back of the cart and staggered to his feet. As soon as he was clear, Franz started reloading the logs. They were in a small clearing at the edge of a wood, partially concealed from the road by the trees and underbrush.

"We can't stay here long," he said. "Get yourself dusted down, or you really will cause comment when you get to the town."

Obediently Kurt brushed at his trousers and coat, which were both covered in sawdust. He combed the dust from his hair, and spitting on his hands wiped the dirt from his face as best he could. The only good thing about the tarpaulin and the logs was that they had kept him comparatively warm. Now even standing in the shelter of the little wood, Kurt realised how cold it had become. He shivered, and blew on his fingers.

"Could snow later," Franz said as he tossed the last of the logs back onto the cart. "You should try and catch a train today. Go anywhere. Just don't stay in Dost, or you may attract unwanted attention to yourself." He looked across at Kurt. "This is as far as I can take you," he said. "There is nowhere nearer the town to let you get off unseen." He reached into the cart and handed Kurt a packet of bread and cheese. "Something to keep you going," he said.

Kurt took the parcel and slipped it into his pocket. "I don't know how to thank you..." he began, but Franz Beider waved the words away.

"One day this madness will end," he said, "then come back and thank me. I'll be pleased to see you. Good luck and God speed." He swung himself up onto the cart once more, and gathering the reins, clicked his tongue to his horse and was off, back the way they had come.

Kurt watched him from the cover of the trees until he was out of sight, then he picked up his suitcase and began to walk into the town in search of the railway station.

Nine

"What did you expect me to do with them?" Edith demanded, facing her husband, David, across the bedroom. "Put them out into the street?" She seldom raised her voice to David, but his annoyance at returning home to find his mother-in-law, his sister-in-law and her four children all camped out in his house, had made her angrily defensive.

"No, of course not," snapped David, as he began to get undressed. "But you know perfectly well we haven't got room for them. They'll have to find somewhere else to stay as soon as they can."

Ruth was saying exactly the same thing to her mother in the spare room they were sharing with the twins at the other end of the landing. They lay in the darkness, listening to the snuffling sleep of the two little boys, safe at last after the nightmare of the past few weeks.

"Mother, we can't stay here for long. We must find a place of our own. It's very clear that David doesn't want us here, and Edith never stands up to him, you know."

Helga sighed. "I know," she said, "but they'll have to put up with us for a few days, we're flesh and blood after all."

"The fewer the better," said Ruth darkly. "We haven't survived everything so far simply to be regarded as poor relations by my own sister." She lapsed into silence as she thought of their escape...from the fire, from Munich, from Vohldorf, from Germany.

The journey from Stuttgart had been slow and cold, the train chugging steadily through the winter countryside, towards the Austrian border. After four hours in the chill of an unheated compartment, Ruth, Helga and the children had had to change trains at Munich. They waited two hours for their connection, but at least that gave them a chance to buy some more food for the journey. The waiting room had a large notice, *No Jews*, and, not wanting to draw any attention to themselves, they hadn't tried to go in. Ruth sat them all down on a bench on the platform, their two precious suitcases close beside them, and gave them the bread, cheese and apples Helga had bought from a station stall.

When the train to Vienna finally steamed out of the station, it was full; all the compartments crowded with people going home after their day's work in the city. Ruth and her family stood in the corridor, the twins sitting on the cases, their heads hanging uncomfortably in exhausted sleep.

Laura looked out of the window, watching the cold countryside race by. As it became dusk, lamps were switched on in the houses, warm beacons of light to welcome fathers home at the end of the day.

Who lives in those houses, Laura wondered? Who are the children waiting eagerly for their papa to come home? She felt a sudden ache of longing for her own papa. Where was he? Would she ever see him again? Tears filled her eyes and coursed silently down her cheeks. Determined that her mother shouldn't see them, Laura turned her face resolutely to the window again, seeing the passing landscape through the blur of her tears.

A pale moon had risen, occasionally breaking free from the scudding cloud, to bathe the country in cold, silver light. Scattered villages emerged from the night, bright clusters of warm light, only to vanish as the train passed on. They steamed through small towns where the streetlamps marked the pattern of the roads, and the buildings crowded together in an untidy sprawl. Sometimes the train stopped, and there was the noise and bustle of a station, people climbing on and off the train; guards and porters shouting, the shriek of the engine letting off steam. Then with the shrill of the guard's whistle, the train would chuff away again, gathering speed as it left the station behind to race onwards through the night.

Gradually the train emptied a little, and when at last they were able to find space in a compartment, they tried to get comfortable for the rest of the journey.

We've still got a long way to go, thought Ruth, as she settled the children as comfortably as she could. The train will stop several times before we reach the border, but at least we don't have to change trains again.

She was still worried about the border crossing. Suppose they weren't allowed across into Austria? Suppose the SS colonel had tricked them and their papers weren't in order? A wave of panic flooded through her, but she forced it down. No point in worrying about it until it happened, she tried to make herself believe. It would be all right. It *had* to be all right.

The morning after Ruth had returned with the travel permits, the little family had left Vohldorf on the morning bus to Stuttgart. She and Helga had spent all night packing up ready to travel. They had the travel permits in their hands and neither of them dared waste a day in setting out in case those permits were rescinded.

They had just two suitcases, and into these they packed as many of their belongings as they could. Ruth and the children had few enough clothes, and Helga selected hers from the small number she had been able to bring from her old house. Helga picked up the worn leather photo frame she always carried with her. For a long moment she stared down at her beloved husband, Hans-Peter, after whom the twins were named, so young and so handsome on his wedding day. His eyes were alight with joy, his arm protectively round her as she stood beside him, smiling shyly into the camera.

"Oh my darling," Helga murmured. "I'm so glad you didn't live to see this dreadful day, with your grandchildren hounded out of the country."

In the other half of the folding frame, Ruth and Edith, one dark, the other fair, hair plaited and tied with ribbons, sat side by side on a sofa, beaming into the camera; her lovely daughters; how had their family come to this?

With a sigh Helga tucked the photograph in among her clothes and turned to help the girls with their packing. Laura's diary and the single pencil she had to write it with, went into the other case, along with the twins' rabbits. Bunnkin had survived his encounter with the Gestapo officer, and carefully repaired by Helga he was Hansi's constant comfort. It was with extreme reluctance that he allowed Ruth to pack the rabbit in the case.

"But darling," she reasoned, "he'll be much safer in there. Suppose you dropped him on the bus!"

"I'd pick him up again," replied Hans. "He won't like being in the case, Mutti. He won't be able to breathe."

"But Flop-Ear will be lonely without him," Ruth pointed out as she put the two toys into the top of the case, "and when we get to Aunt Edith's house you can get them both out to play with."

Inge had no toys, but she had developed an attachment to an old silk scarf of her grandmother's, winding it round her neck or, thumb in mouth, rubbing its luxurious softness against her cheek. This, too, was carefully packed into one of the cases.

A diary with a stub of pencil, an old silk scarf and two battered rabbits were the sum total of the children's private possessions, and Ruth was determined that they should not lose them.

It's no good worrying about the border, Ruth thought as the train rattled onwards. We must all try and get some sleep.

It was some time later that a ticket inspector came along the train. He looked at the family crammed into the compartment. Ruth and Helga each had a twin fast asleep on her knee, Inge was cuddled up against her grandmother, and Laura was crushed between the two other occupants of the carriage, two large elderly ladies.

"Tickets please!"

Ruth fumbled in her bag and produced the tickets. The inspector wore a swastika armband on the sleeve of his uniform, and he spoke in the peremptory tones of a small man with a modicum of power. He studied the tickets and then looked up.

"You're going all the way to Vienna?" he said, suspiciously. "Have you got passports?"

Ruth tried to sound unconcerned. "Yes, of course. Do you want to see them?"

She knew it was a mistake as soon as the words were out

of her mouth. The man nodded and held out his hand. With an inward sigh she passed them over and watched his face as he read the names.

"Friedman," he said. "Jews." He looked up at Ruth with a sneer of disgust. "You shouldn't be sitting in this compartment with these good German ladies," he said, "squashing them into a corner with your dirty children. Indeed you probably shouldn't be on the train."

"We have permits to travel." Ruth faced him down bravely. "Issued by Herr Standartenführer Unger of the SS, in Stuttgart."

"Have you indeed? Let me see them!"

"They're here." Ruth held them out for him to see, but she didn't let go of them herself. She didn't trust the man not to tear them up, or throw them out of the window. The inspector glanced at the signature and the stamp and hurriedly passed them back. Even he was not prepared to question the authority of an SS colonel.

He took refuge in more bluster. "Well you can't sit in here with these ladies, you can just move your lot out into the corridor."

Helga spoke for the first time. "Excuse me, Herr Inspector, but have you looked at these children? They are exhausted. They are doing no harm sitting in here. I am happy to move into the corridor if that's what you wish, but let the children stay asleep in here."

The inspector was about to reply when one of the other women in the compartment stood up and said with a look of distaste, "I will certainly move to another carriage. The Jews can stay in here. They'd be a great inconvenience to everyone else on the train, Herr Inspector, if they were standing about in the corridor." She walked to the door, before turning to the other woman. "Won't you come with me," she asked, "to a more salubrious carriage?"

"I think I will." The second woman got up and crossed to the door, kicking Laura sharply on the ankle as she passed. Laura smothered her cry of pain with a sharp intake of breath, but the woman affected not to notice what she had done and stalked out of the compartment, followed by the ticket inspector, who slid the door closed with a resounding crash. For a moment the first woman looked back through the glass, a flicker of sympathy in her eyes, then she disappeared down the corridor to find another seat.

Helga began to settle the children again, while Ruth stuffed the passports, tickets and permits back into the depths of her bag. She found she was shaking. How close had they come to being put off the train? Or at least stuck in the corridor? She thought with gratitude of the woman who had come to their aid, while appearing to disparage them. Few people could risk being labelled as a Jew-lover, but there were still good people who were ashamed of how so many of their countrymen treated the Jews.

When at last they reached the border the train came to a halt. German officials swarmed onto the train, demanding papers. When they reached the Friedmans' carriage Ruth prepared herself for more trouble, but the passports seemed to be in order. All the official asked was which child was which. As he was leaving the compartment he looked across at Ruth.

"I shouldn't come back if I were you," he said, and moved on down the corridor.

There were shouts from outside, and, peering out of the window again, Laura could see the officials climbing down off the train onto the platform. Then after further whistles, shouts and arm-waving, the train chugged forwards, only to stop again with a loud shriek of steam at the Austrian check-point a hundred metres down the track. Here their papers were given no more than a cursory glance, and they were safely out of Germany and into Austria. Ruth could have wept with relief, and Helga, who was nearly as exhausted as the children, was suddenly on the verge of tears.

"We made it, Mother," Ruth whispered, adding as she fought back her own tears of relief and sorrow, "if only Kurt was with us."

There was still a distance to go, with stops at Salzburg and Linz and other smaller stations along the way, but passengers who boarded at these places could see that the compartment where Ruth and her family were sitting was already full, and no one made any attempt to climb in. When at last the train steamed into the Westbahnhof, it was daylight, and a weak sun was forcing its way through the layer of cloud that covered the city. Tired and stiff, they all clambered down onto the platform, Helga gathering the children round her, while Ruth managed the luggage. The station was huge and busy with people. The hiss of steam, the shrill of whistles and the clatter of trains arriving and departing added to the cacophony that surrounded them; but it was Austrian noise. They were safely out of Germany.

"Come on, Mother, let's get out of here." Ruth led the way resolutely along the platform while the children trailed after her, Helga shepherding them from behind. Once they were away from the platform and they could hear themselves speak, they paused and decided what to do.

"We take a taxi," Helga said. "We don't know the way

to Edith's from here. David met us when we came for Paul's bar mitzvah."

"We haven't money for a taxi, Mother!" protested Ruth.

"Edith will have. Come on."

They found a waiting taxi and all piled in while the driver stowed their cases. Helga gave him the address and they were off through the streets of Vienna. When they reached Edith's house the door was opened by a uniformed parlour maid.

"Good morning, Anna," Ruth said briskly, pleased that a quick search of her memory had produced the maid's name. "Please would you tell Frau Bernstein that her mother and sister are here."

Anna eyed the invasion of children with disfavour, said she would see if Madam was at home, and, leaving them standing in the hall, with an anxious taxi driver hovering on the front step, she disappeared up the stairs.

"Ruth! Mother! Why on earth didn't you warn me you were coming?" cried Edith as she hurried down the stairs to greet them. She stared at them all, ranged in her front hall, where Anna had left them. "Come in! Come in here and sit down." She moved towards the door on her right, but Ruth laid her hand on her sister's arm.

"Sorry, Edith, but we need some money for the taxi. I'm afraid we haven't any schillings."

Edith stared at her uncomprehendingly for a moment, so that Helga had to say, "Edith, dear, please pay the taxi driver so that we can all come into the warm."

"Oh, yes, of course, Mother. I'll get my bag." She ran back up the stairs and returned moments later with money in her hand. She paid the relieved-looking taxi driver and closed the front door behind him. Anna, watching all this wide-eyed, was hovering beside the door leading to the kitchen. Edith turned to her.

"We'll be in the morning room," she said. "Please bring some coffee, Anna, and some milk for the children."

The maid disappeared to the kitchen and Edith opened the door off the hallway. "Now then, all of you, come in here and sit down." She turned to the children who had trailed into the room behind their mother. "You'd like a drink of milk, wouldn't you?"

"I'm hungry," whined Inge. No one told her to be quiet and not to be rude. Inge spoke for all of them; they were all hungry.

"I'm sure you are, pet," cooed her Aunt Edith. "Anna shall bring you a biscuit."

"I'm afraid she needs more than a biscuit, Edith," Ruth said quietly. "She hasn't eaten since yesterday. None of us has!"

"What!" cried Edith. "You poor things, you must be starving!" She went back out into the hall and called the maid back again. "Anna, please ask Cook to prepare a meal for my sister and her family, and have it laid out in the dining room...straightaway."

Anna murmured, "Very good, madam," but it was clear that she didn't welcome the intrusion of so many people.

"Now," Edith said brightly, "sit down, all of you, and tell me why you're here."

Before Ruth could reply, Helga spoke. "We're here, Edith dear, because Kurt has been arrested, Ruth's home has been burnt down round her ears, and I have been turned out of mine." Her tone was terse. She was angry at her elder daughter's lack of thought.

Edith gasped. "Kurt arrested? How awful! What did he do?"

176

"He didn't *do* anything," snapped her mother. "He's a Jew! No further reason is needed."

"Well, thank goodness it isn't like that here!" exclaimed Edith. She turned to Ruth. "What happened to the shop? How awful for you! How did it catch fire?"

"It didn't just 'catch fire', Edith," said Ruth. "It was set on fire. There was a riot one night in Kirnheim. A mob rampaged through the town, Kurt was taken away by the storm troopers, and the shop was set on fire. The children and I only just escaped with our lives." She gave her sister a hard stare. "I did write and tell you what had happened and that we'd had to go to Munich and stay with Herbert, Kurt's brother."

"Did you?" Edith's eyes flickered. "I never got your letter...or I'd have answered, of course. Offered you a home with us."

"Well, that's all right, then," Helga said. "Because that's why we've come to you now. We've nowhere else to go, and we need somewhere to stay."

Ruth saw the dismay flash in Edith's eyes before she said, "Of course, Mother. You're all very welcome."

"Don't worry," Ruth said. "We just need a place for a few days, until we can find somewhere of our own."

"That's fine!" Edith said cheerfully. "We can always squeeze you in for a few days."

At that moment the door burst open and Paul, Edith's son, came bounding into the room. He was a good-looking boy, tall for his fifteen years, with deep-set dark eyes, and a mop of dark curls, cropped short in a vain attempt to keep them in order.

"Oma!" he cried, hugging his grandmother. "Anna told me you were here! How lovely to see you! And Aunt Ruth...have you come to stay? Are these my cousins? Laura, Inge, all grown up." He gave each girl a hug before crouching down to look at the twins. "Well," he said, "I haven't met you two before. Peter and Hans, isn't it? Which one of you is which? How will I ever tell?"

The twins gurgled with laughter. "I'm Peter," said Hans.

"And I'm Hansi," said Peter.

"Other way round," said Ruth, smiling for the first time since they had come into her sister's house. "It's their new game, to pretend to be each other. Peter has a small mole on his cheek. That's how you tell until you know!"

"Well, I shall call you both Hans-Peter," Paul told them cheerfully, "then I can't ever be wrong, can I?" He turned to Ruth. "Is Uncle Kurt with you, Aunt Ruth? Where's he?"

"I'm afraid not," began Ruth, but Edith cut in smoothly.

"Your uncle can't come this time," she said. "Now, go and find Naomi and wash your hands. We're having an early lunch. Your cousins have come a long way and they are hungry."

"OK, Mother," said Paul cheerfully, heading for the door in search of his sister.

"And don't say OK, Paul," reprimanded his mother. "It's common."

Paul gave her a grin, "OK," he said, and left the room.

"He's growing into such a good-looking boy," Helga said, "and so welcoming!"

Edith glanced sharply in her mother's direction to see if the comment was directed at her, but Helga was smiling fondly after Paul. "It's lovely to see him again. I can't wait to see Naomi."

"Well," Edith said, "while we're waiting for Cook to prepare lunch, I'd better show you your rooms. It will be a bit of a crush, I'm afraid, we don't have a big house, you know, but I'm sure you won't mind that." She turned to the four children who were still standing silently round their mother. "Come along, children, and then we can all have some lunch." She led the way upstairs, and along a landing to a room at the end. Pushing open the door, she stood aside to let her mother and her sister enter.

Edith had said it would be a squeeze, and Ruth realised she was probably right, though the house was far bigger than any she, Ruth, had ever lived in. She, Helga and the twins were sleeping in the one big spare room and the two girls had folding beds in what was little more than a box room, down the landing from the other children, on the floor above. Anna had put the two suitcases into the spare room, and once the twins were reunited with their rabbits, and Inge with her silk scarf, they were happy to go back downstairs to the dining room. Laura had not taken her diary from the case, she simply checked that it was still there and then tucked it back among the clothes.

By the time they had got back downstairs, Paul had reappeared with his sister, Naomi. Naomi, aged nine, was as fair as her mother had been as a child. Her long, blond hair was neatly braided, with pale blue ribbons at the end of each plait. Wide-set blue eyes looked out on the world through the palest of lashes, and her skin was almost translucent. Although she was less than one year younger than Laura, looking at them the difference could have been two or three. She recognised her grandmother, but hung back shyly behind her brother at the sight of so many other people that she didn't know.

"Come along, Naomi," her mother said briskly. "Give Oma a kiss, then we can all sit down to lunch."

Helga held out a hand, and Naomi edged forward to take

it. Helga smiled at her. "Hallo, Naomi darling. It's so lovely to see you again." She made no move to hug or kiss the child; Naomi hadn't seen her for two years, and needed time to get to know her again.

"Now then, everybody," Edith called, "let's sit down at the table."

The lunch was served, and Ruth certainly couldn't fault her sister's cook. A meal had been produced that was both plentiful and filling. None of the Friedmans had seen so much food since they had left Kirnheim, and all of them ate hungrily, while their cousins ate with polite delicacy, and Edith picked at the food on her plate and pushed it away with most of it uneaten.

What a waste, thought Ruth as she remembered the times they had all gone hungry recently. She caught her mother's eye and knew that she was having the same thought.

When they had all finished Edith said, "Now then, Paul, Naomi, I want you to look after your cousins while I talk to Oma and Aunt Ruth. You can play in the playroom, or you can take them in the garden if you like, but make sure you all have your coats on, it's very cold today."

"Now," Edith said as she poured them each a strong black coffee, "let's take this into the drawing room, so Anna can clear, and you must tell me everything."

When they were settled in the drawing room, Ruth began her story. When she had finished, Edith was staring at her in horror, her coffee stone-cold in the cup beside her.

"I don't know what to say," she said. "You poor, poor things. Mother, how did you cope? It must have been terrifying with those Hitler youths throwing things at you." She took her mother's hand and squeezed it gently. "But at least you're safe now. David will be home from the hospital soon," she went on. "He'll know what to do for the best."

Even after all I've told her, she has absolutely no concept of what we've all been through, Ruth thought, looking across at the concern on her sister's face. Edith had aged well. At almost forty her face was largely unlined. Her blond hair was thick, cut into a fashionable bob, with no trace of the grey hairs now liberally threaded through Ruth's dark hair. Her clothes were well cut and clearly expensive. She had changed from being Ruth Heber's big sister, with whom Ruth had romped and played, into the perfect wife for David Bernstein, eminent orthopaedic surgeon.

When David came home from the hospital later that day, it was to find his wife's family installed in his house. He greeted his mother-in-law civilly enough, kissed his sister-in-law on the cheek and said he was delighted that they had been able to come on a visit. Then he went upstairs to change for dinner.

"David wants us out as soon as possible," Ruth whispered to her mother that night in the darkness. "I shall start looking for somewhere tomorrow. Will you be all right looking after the children? I'll have to find them a school as well. They need to get back to some sort of normality. And I'll need a job, too. I refuse to be beholden to David." She sighed. "Tomorrow's going to be a very busy day."

"You can't do everything in one day," said Helga. "David will have to put up with us until we are ready to move out. After all, we shan't be in his way…he's out all day."

Ruth lay in the warm comfort of the bed, but, despite her exhaustion, sleep still would not come. She listened to the regular breathing of the boys. When she had kissed them goodnight she had sat in the room with them until, each clutching his rabbit, they had dropped into exhausted slumber. Listening to them now, peacefully asleep in bed, she prayed that it would not be long before the last few nightmare weeks slid from their minds as she tried to provide them with a normal life. They were so young, surely the memories would recede and fade away as new, everyday experiences replaced them. Ruth was not so sure about the girls. Inge had become extremely clinging, needing her mother's attention, or that of her grandmother, all the time. She had always been a rather volatile child, but had now begun to throw temper tantrums, as if she were a two-year-old again; that or withdrawn silences when she sat, thumb in mouth, silk scarf against her cheek.

Then there was Laura. She had become Ruth's rock. Old way beyond her years, Laura knew what had been happening to them. She had learned to recognise the disdain in people's eyes; she had learned to keep a low profile, not to draw attention to herself. She was ten years old, but the look in her eyes was that of someone five times that age. She asked for nothing, expected nothing, except derision and contempt from the people she encountered. It would take a very long time for her to learn to trust again.

"Ruth, have you still got Kurt's passport?" Helga's whisper broke in on her thoughts.

"Yes, of course." Ruth was surprised at the question. "Why?"

"What are you going to do with it?"

"Do with it?"

"Yes. If you've got it, Kurt can't use it to get out of Germany, can he?"

"No, of course not. But I don't know where he is, do I?" Ruth sounded exasperated. "I can't send it to him, can I?"

"Well, I've been thinking about that," replied Helga,

ignoring her daughter's irritable tone. "If you were Kurt, and you came home to find the family gone, what would you do?"

"I'd go to Munich, to Herbert, but..."

"Hold on a minute, darling, let's really think this through. Suppose he does come home and then follows the trail, in the end he's going to draw a blank. You and the children will have vanished. He will work out that you must have come to Vienna to Edith's. Right?"

"Probably."

"Almost certainly. Where else would you go?"

"All right," conceded Ruth and waited for her mother to go on.

"If he knows you have the deed box, then he knows you have his passport. He'll hope you have left it for him somewhere...or sent it to him somewhere."

"But where?" Ruth's voice took on a tone of despair. "Where can I send it that he might think to look?"

"To those friends who took you in after the fire."

"The Meyers?"

"Yes, the Meyers. Think about it. If he goes home and finds the shop burnt out he will ask around to find out what happened. He will ask the Meyers. If you sent the passport there, addressed to him, they would give it to him when he asked."

"Leah Meyer asked me not to contact them again," Ruth said. "She's afraid the mail will be intercepted."

"I think you have to risk it."

"But suppose Kurt's been there already. It'll be too late!"

"I know," soothed Helga, "but surely it's worth a try. If the Meyers have the passport and he goes to them, they'll give it to him. If he doesn't, then we are no worse off than if you have it. If he contacts us here..."

"He won't," Ruth interrupted bleakly. "He won't remember Edith's address, and he certainly won't know the phone number..."

"He might. And if he did you'd be able to tell him where to go to collect his passport." Helga sat up in the darkness. "Come on, Ruth, this isn't like you! You've been so brave and done everything you could for the children. Now you must try and do this for Kurt. Let's face it, darling, his passport is no good to him in Austria if he's in Germany."

"All right, Mother," agreed Ruth wearily, "I'll send it tomorrow."

"Good!" said Helga with satisfaction. "Now then, stop brooding and try and get some sleep, or you'll be no good to anyone in the morning."

Ruth gave a shaky laugh. "Yes, Mutti!" she said.

Friday 10th December

We moved out of Uncle David and Aunt Edith's yesterday. Mutti has found us a home of our own. It is not very big, just three small rooms and a toilet in the passage. Oma, Inge and I sleep in one room, Mutti and the twins in another, and we live in the last. It has a stove, so it's quite warm, and there is a table and some chairs and a cupboard to keep things in, but we haven't got many things to keep. There is no room for anything else because the room is so small. I'm glad we have left Aunt Edith's house. Everyone was very strict and seemed to be cross with us all the time. I'm scared of Uncle David. I think my cousin Naomi is too, but she loves her Opa. Everyone else is frightened of him, but Naomi isn't. My other cousin, Paul, is nice, but he's much older than we are. He's at the gymnasium. He's very clever and says he is going to be a doctor like his papa when he leaves school.

Our apartment is near a big fairground. Mutti says we might be able to go there one day soon. I hope so, I want to go on the big wheel, but we haven't got much money for fairgrounds.

Mutti has found a school for me and Inge to go to. It is not very big, but my teacher is nice. She is called Fräulein Lowenstein. Inge is in the baby class, her teacher is called Fräulein Munt. We do arithmetic and write stories, and on Wednesdays we have art. I'm not very good at drawing, but Fräulein Lowenstein says it doesn't matter as different people are good at different things. I like Fräulein Lowenstein.

Oma looks after the twins as they are too little to go to school, and Mutti has got a job in a shop.

All the shops are decorated for Christmas. We don't have Christmas, but I do like the decorations.

Ruth had been determined they should move out of Edith's house as soon as possible, and she'd set about finding them somewhere to live the very next day. It took several more days, but eventually she had managed to find a three-roomed flat in a tall tenement, in the Leopoldstadt district. A twisting lane led off the street and halfway down there was an old brick archway leading into a courtyard, around three sides of which stood crumbling apartment blocks. From the court-yard, flights of outside steps led up to the flats above. Ruth and her family had moved into one on the first floor.

Edith was horrified that they should live in such an area. "It's all low Jews and working class," she cried, "not for families like ours."

"It is for a family like mine," Ruth retorted, "one that has no money and nowhere else to stay."

Edith looked slightly abashed, but she didn't suggest that they stay longer with her, and it was David who paid a month's rent in advance to secure them the apartment. Ruth was sure that this was more from the wish to get them out of his home than from true generosity, but she didn't care. They had a roof over their heads. Many of their neighbours were Jewish and as they settled in there was the faintest comforting echo of Gerbergasse in the community around them. They were living very much hand-to-mouth, but they were in a place of their own. Helga was there to look after the children, so Ruth set out in search of a job.

For several days she trod the streets looking for work, and because the shops were busy just before Christmas, she managed to get a job in a small haberdashery. The pay was poor and the hours were long, but Ruth, running her own shop for most of her married life, wasn't afraid of hard work, and it meant she could provide food for the table, and save enough for each week's rent. She enjoyed working in the little shop; it was interesting as always she enjoyed meeting the customers and helping them to find what they needed. Frau Merkle, the proprietor, soon realised that Ruth was an excellent sales assistant, and that the customers liked her. So, after the Christmas season was over, she decided to keep her on and offered her a full-time job. The rise in pay made all the difference, and before long the children each had a new set of warm clothes. Ruth treated herself to a new coat and skirt, even though it meant the repayment of a loan from Edith had to be delayed.

The girls had settled well into a small Jewish school not far from the flat, and Helga took on the care of the twins and the running of the household. Everything gradually returned to a sort of normality. All they needed now was for Kurt to join them and life would be tolerable.

Ten

Kurt got off the train in Munich. When Franz Beider had dropped him outside Dost, Kurt followed his advice and made straight for the railway station. He would get on the first train that came along, he decided, wherever it was going. It was going to Munich, so that was where he went.

When he arrived, Kurt left the station quickly, moving out onto the street amid the crowd of disembarking passengers, and headed back to the house where he had rented the room before. Walking quietly up to the front door, he knocked. No one came to the door, but there was a slight movement at the window beside him. He turned to see who was there, but the curtains were still and there was no sign of anybody. Yet Kurt was sure that he hadn't imagined it; there had definitely been someone peeping from the window to see who was outside.

And now they know, Kurt thought ruefully, they aren't going to open the door. He would have to find somewhere else to stay. He could, he supposed, go back to the station, but it was the kind of place the Gestapo made regular sweeps, picking up undesirables...like him.

He found a small café and bought himself a plate of stew. He had long since given up worrying about the dietary rules he had followed all his life. There was no question of kosher food in Dachau. You ate whatever you could get hold of, and were grateful.

Feeling better for the hot food, Kurt considered what he should do next. Get out of Munich, he decided. Time was running out, he had only another four days in which to produce the deeds to his home at the Jewish Emigration Office, and to get his family out of the country...or he would be back in Dachau. He broke out into a cold sweat at the thought of the camp. Whatever happened, he was not going back there.

If I can't find Ruth and the children in the next couple of days, then I have to disappear myself, he thought. I've nowhere to hide, so I'll have to keep moving. Try and keep one step ahead of the SS who will be looking for me.

He had no doubt that if he did not turn up with the documents as arranged, Oberführer Loritz would have his hounds out on the trail to bring him back. Defying an SS officer was an extremely dangerous thing to do, and although Kurt had no alternative unless he found Ruth and the title deeds, there would be no explaining that to Oberführer Loritz...and he would take delight in exacting his revenge.

There's only one thing to do, Kurt thought as he drained the last of his coffee, I must try and get out of the country myself. I'll never find them while I'm on the run in Germany.

The waitress was beginning to eye him suspiciously, and not wishing to draw further attention to himself, Kurt got to his feet, paid his bill with some of his fast dwindling cash and went out into the street. It was bitterly cold and he drew his thin overcoat around him, but the biting wind drilled through its fabric as if it wasn't there. He set off at a brisk pace, not because he was in any hurry, but simply to try and keep warm. Also important, he thought, to look purposeful, as if I've got somewhere to go, something pressing to do.

As he strode along the street he continued to consider his options. Ruth and Helga must have taken the children to Edith, he thought. That's the obvious place for them all to go. Franz said that Helga Heber was with them now. Surely they would head for the only safe place where they had family. Vienna.

He knew Ruth had her passport, with the girls on it. Had she managed to get the twins put on as well? She also had his passport, or he assumed she did, as it, too, had been hidden in the deed box. But much good did that do him. He tried once again to put himself in Ruth's shoes. He knew she had left nothing with the Meyers when she'd left Gerbergasse, but then she had thought she was going to safety with Herbert in Munich. If she'd had to leave the country she'd know he couldn't follow unless he had his passport.

If only I could get in touch with her somehow, he thought, and cursed himself that he did not know the address or telephone number of his sister-in-law, and had no way of discovering it. Even if David Bernstein's number was listed in the Vienna telephone book, where was Kurt going to find one? He knew David was a surgeon, but he had no idea in which hospital he worked. Kurt didn't know the names of any hospitals in Vienna. There was no way at the present time that Kurt could get in touch with Ruth or her sister.

She must have my passport, Kurt decided. What would she do with it? What would I do with it if it were me? I'd try and get it to her; try and think of somewhere where she might think to look for it. "There's only one place," he said aloud, "and that's the Meyers'. So I must go back to Kirnheim."

Once that decision was made Kurt felt better. He now

had a purpose, but before he could put it into action, he had another problem to solve...where to sleep the night. It was far too cold...and far too dangerous...to spend the night out on the streets. He had to find somewhere to stay and quickly. It was already beginning to get dark and he could feel the first spatter of rain on the wind.

Who would help a Jew? Other Jews...maybe. Almost certainly no one else. Kurt remembered the rabbi who had helped Ruth and the children, and had passed on the message to him when he traced them there. Rabbi Rahmer.

He let the family sleep in the meeting room behind the synagogue, Kurt thought, perhaps he'll let me do the same.

Grasping his small suitcase firmly, he set off in the direction of the synagogue. He had only a vague recollection of exactly where it was and the rain was turning to sleet before he finally presented himself at the door of the rabbi's house. Frau Rahmer opened the door, and confronted by a strange man in a soaking wet overcoat with water streaming off his hat, began to close the door again.

"Frau Rahmer?" Kurt placed an involuntary hand on the door to stop it closing. "Is the rabbi at home?"

Frau Rahmer did not open the door again, but neither did she continue to close it. She regarded the stranger through the gap and said, "Who wants him?"

"My name is Kurt Friedman, you were kind enough to give my wife and children shelter some weeks ago."

Frau Rahmer peered at Kurt more closely, opening the door a little more to do so. It was against her nature to turn away anyone who was in need of help, but in these increasingly difficult and dangerous times one had to be unusually careful. Still she didn't want him to be seen standing on her doorstep either;

reported in the wrong quarter, that too could be dangerous.

"You'd better come in," she said, pulling the door wider to let him enter, and closing it swiftly behind him. "Wait there. I'll call my husband."

Kurt waited, dripping on the hall mat, as she moved away and called down a passageway behind her, "Manny, there's someone to see you."

A door opened and the rabbi whom Kurt had met the previous week emerged. Rabbi Rahmer took one look at him and said, "You'd better come into my study." Turning to his wife he said, "I think our friend would welcome a hot drink, Ruth."

Frau Rahmer nodded and disappeared through another door. The rabbi led Kurt into his study.

"Ruth is my wife's name, too," Kurt said as he followed the rabbi into the room.

"I know," the rabbi replied. He waved Kurt to a chair. "Please take off your wet coat." And as Kurt did as he was bid he went on, "So you didn't find her."

"No," Kurt replied. "She...they had to move on. And now I am in trouble, it's a long story..."

The rabbi raised his hand and said abruptly, "Stop! I don't want to hear of your trouble. We all have enough of our own. So, no long story, just tell me why you have come here, now."

"Simply to ask if I may sleep in the meeting room at the back of your synagogue...just for one night."

"You ask a good deal from someone you don't know," the rabbi said sharply.

"I ask you as a pastor who looks after his congregation," replied Kurt. "I have nowhere else to turn. If I sleep out tonight, I shall die of cold. If I am picked up, I will be arrested. All

I ask of you is a safe haven for one night. Tomorrow I leave Munich, and you'll never see me again."

"You ask me something that may bring danger to my family and to my congregation," the rabbi pointed out, "if you are a wanted man."

"I'm not a wanted man," Kurt replied firmly. "Not for another four days," he added silently. "I am still searching for my wife and children. All I need is a place to stay for tonight before I move on after them."

There was a tap on the door and Frau Rahmer appeared carrying a tray. On it were two cups of coffee. She put it on the rabbi's desk and disappeared again without a word.

Rabbi Rahmer gestured to the cups. "Take one," he said, "it's all I can offer you." He reached for a cup himself, and Kurt took the other.

"Please, Rabbi, in the name of charity, let me sleep in the meeting room."

"The synagogue is already locked for the night. I'm afraid I have to lock up as soon as it gets dark these days," said the rabbi. "Now, if you'll excuse me, I have work to do. I think, when you've drunk your coffee, you should leave."

Kurt downed the coffee, almost scalding his mouth as he did so. It wasn't coffee at all, just hot brown liquid, but at least it was hot.

He got to his feet and pulled the damp coat round his shoulders. "Thank you, Rabbi," he said. " I quite understand your reluctance. You have to protect your own."

The rabbi stood as well, and calling to his wife said, "Herr Friedman is leaving now, Ruth. Please see him out." He didn't extend his hand, merely nodded to Kurt and sat back down behind his desk. Kurt was dismissed, and Rabbi Rahmer gave his attention to the papers in front of him.

Kurt turned and left the room, following Frau Rahmer to the front door. As she opened it she said softly, "The meeting room has a broken window. Smashed by the Hitler Youth. If my husband doesn't get it mended soon, anyone will be able to get in." She held out her hand. "Goodbye, Herr Friedman, I hope you find your family soon."

The door closed behind him and Kurt found himself back in the biting March wind. He walked away from the house and on up the street without so much as a glance at the synagogue opposite, not slowing his pace until he had rounded the corner and was out of sight of the rabbi's house. Then he drew into the shadow of an alleyway and considered what to do.

Had he understood Frau Rahmer's words aright? Was she telling him how to get into the back of the meeting room? Suggesting that he might rest there for the night after all? But would the rabbi think of that, too? Would he come out and check that his visitor hadn't tried to break in? Kurt decided that he had to take the risk. Better to be caught by an angry rabbi when camping in his meeting room than by a Gestapo patrol out in the street at night. He would wait for a quarter of an hour and then he would try and get into the meeting room through the window. He walked back a little way until, from the shadow of a tree, he could see the rabbi's front door. The minutes ticked by and it remained shut. There was no sign of the rabbi or his wife.

Kurt was chilled to the bone now, the wind knifing through his wet overcoat as he stood and waited. Frost was forming on the road and on the trunk of the tree that sheltered him. The sky was beginning to clear, and a half-moon sailed into the sky, lightening the street and deepening the shadows. At last Kurt thought it must be safe to try his luck. He looked at the outside of the synagogue and realised that the meeting room could not be seen from where he was. The alley he'd sheltered in earlier must run round the back of the building, so he would not be visible to any casual passer-by.

Stiff with cold, his teeth beginning to chatter, Kurt made his way back to the alley, and felt his way along it. It was almost pitch dark in here as there were no streetlamps and the moonlight did not penetrate between the high walls that enclosed it. The building on the opposite side had no windows, but halfway along there was a gate in the wall, which Kurt assumed led directly into someone's garden. As his eyes adjusted to the darkness, Kurt found that he could see more than he'd at first thought. Running his hands along the brickwork, he found a window, and sure enough the glass had been smashed, leaving jagged shards jutting from the frame. Pulling his hand up inside his coat sleeve, Kurt carefully pushed his arm through the frame and reached inside. The window was a casement, and it was not long before he had found the catch to release it. The catch was stiff, but, by shaking it up and down, he gradually loosened it until he was at last able to open the window. The rusty hinges screeched in protest as he pulled it open and he froze. Had anyone heard? The people who lived in the next house? Again Kurt waited, poised for flight if there should be a shout, a light, or the sound of investigating footsteps. But the night remained silent around him and he eased the window again. The hinges creaked again, but this time he was ready for the sound and it didn't seem quite so loud. It was enough, the gap was now wide enough for him to slide inside. One of the shards caught his coat and tore the sleeve, but apart from that he found himself inside, undamaged. Very gently he eased the window almost closed again. He didn't want anyone passing down the alley to notice that it had been opened.

He had no torch, and wouldn't have used it if he had, but a shaft of moonlight pierced the darkness through a window on the opposite side of the room, so he had enough light to make out his surroundings. The room was quite large, with chairs and tables stacked round the walls, ready for use. Several old armchairs stood in a group in front of a large iron stove at one end, and there were two large cupboards at the other end. The stove was quite cold, all the previous ashes swept away. No fuel was piled beside it, and Kurt could see nothing with which he could light a fire even if he dared. He had no idea who would be able to see lights in these windows. It was nearly as cold as the street outside, except there was no wind, and Kurt wondered, if he allowed himself to go to sleep, whether he would ever wake up again.

Still, he thought, at least I am off the streets. I should be safe here until the morning. He took off his wet coat and hung it over a chair in the vain hope that it might dry a little by the morning. Then he investigated the cupboards at the end of the room. They were locked, and unwilling to damage anything that might reveal he had been there, he didn't try and force them open. He was still shivering and so he began to do physical jerks. He thought back to his days at primary school when they had been made to do exercises before class every day. He swung his arms, raised his feet high, running on the spot, jumped, feet together, hopped round the room first on one leg and then on the other. As the blood began to flow more quickly through his veins, he began to feel a little warmer. He opened his suitcase and got out the few clothes that were inside it. He pulled them all on over what he was already wearing in an effort to retain the heat he had just generated.

I must try and get some sleep, he thought, and make an early start in the morning. He pulled two of the old armchairs together to make him a short bed. It was not long enough for him to lie straight, but if he curled himself into the foetal position, he could just about fit, and the sheltering arms of the chairs gave an illusion of warmth.

Kurt awoke several hours later, cold and stiff. His neck ached and one of his arms had gone to sleep. It was still dark outside, but it was, Kurt decided, a lightening darkness. It must be almost morning. He got out of the makeshift bed and stretched before going through the routine of physical jerks he had done the night before. Gradually warmth began to creep back into his body, but his stomach rumbled for lack of food. Kurt took out his money and counted it. He had enough for a cheap meal or a ticket back to Kirnheim... not both.

Time was not on his side, Kurt knew, so he would have to go hungry. He needed to get to Kirnheim, to the Meyers, before the last three days of his deadline ran out. As soon as the sky lightened to grey daylight, Kurt checked that there was no sign that he had used the room, put on his still-damp overcoat and picked up his now empty suitcase. He would still carry it, he thought, it gave him an air of respectability. He dropped the case out of the window and then climbed out into the alley. When he emerged at the far end he turned in the opposite direction from the rabbi's house. No point in risking being seen again now. He walked briskly back to the centre of the city, and when he reached the early bustle of the station bought himself a ticket to Kirnheim.

*

It was mid-morning before Kurt found himself at the end of Gerbergasse. The shops were all open and people were going about their business. Further down the street he could see the Meyers' bakery, and beyond it on the opposite side the ruined shell of his own grocery. At least that is what he thought he saw until, as he walked slowly down the street, he realised that things had changed. Work on restoring the building had begun. A new, sturdy door stood open, with workmen going in and out from a van parked in the street outside.

Kurt felt a shudder of fear. Who had instigated this work? He had passed the deeds to no one yet. Who would spend money rebuilding the place if it didn't belong to him? Kurt turned away and walked back up the street, out of sight, to consider this development and to decide what to do next. Oberführer Loritz must have decided not to wait for the deed before he seized the property.

If I had turned up at the Jewish Affairs Office in Munich with the deeds, Kurt thought with a stab of panic, he would probably have taken them and arrested me again anyway.

The more he thought about this, the more certain Kurt was that he was right. The Oberführer had had no intention of letting Kurt and his family leave Germany, he had simply used that as a way of appropriating a piece of property. Once he'd got his hands on the deeds, Kurt would have been back in Dachau. The icy chill of terror ran through him at the thought of his narrow escape. Thank God he hadn't had the deeds, thank God he hadn't taken them and handed them in. Now he had absolutely nothing in the world, no home, no money and nothing to bargain with.

But I'm still alive and I'm still free, Kurt thought with a surge of adrenaline. They haven't won yet! But as quickly as the rush went through him it drained away again, leaving him standing two hundred yards from his home, cold and frightened, trying to think what to do next.

Had Ruth thought of sending his passport to the Meyers? When he had left them last time, they were terrified. The arrival of the SS patrol and his own narrow escape from them had put the Meyers in danger. Even if Ruth had sent the passport, would they have held on to it? Wouldn't they simply have destroyed it, afraid to hold something belonging to another Jew, a Jew on the run? He could understand that they might. He might, too, in the same situation, if it put any of his family at risk. But without a passport, Kurt was going to find it almost impossible to escape. It must be worth the risk just to go and ask them. He wouldn't stay in the shop a moment longer than necessary. All he had to ask was, "Has a parcel arrived for me?"

Kurt knew that if he were going to do it, he had to do it now, before his own nerve broke. He retraced his steps to the top of Gerbergasse and walked briskly down to the bakery. The door was closed, but the bread and pastries were laid out in the window. Without looking across at the building opposite, Kurt pushed open the door and went in.

Leo Meyer was behind the counter, serving a customer. When he saw who had walked into the shop, the colour drained from his face, and the words he had been saying dried on his lips. At this reaction the woman being served turned round, and Kurt saw that it was Rudy Stein's wife. She stared at him for a moment, as if she'd seen a ghost, and then with a cry she pushed past him and fled from the shop.

"Kurt!" Leo's voice was a croak. "I thought you were long gone. What brings you back here?"

"I'm still looking for my family," Kurt replied. "And I wondered, Leo, if by any chance Ruth had sent anything to me, here, to your address."

Leo walked across the shop and flipped the open sign to closed, drawing the bolt across, turning the key in the lock and then pocketing it. "Something did come for you not long ago," he said. "I put it in my bureau upstairs for safekeeping. If you'll wait here, I'll go and fetch it for you." Without pausing for a reply, Leo went through the back of the shop and up the stairs to the apartment above. Kurt waited a moment and then followed him. He thought he heard a voice, and paused on the stairs; Leah must be up here. He knocked on the door and went in; Leo was standing by his bureau, but there was no one else in the room.

"I thought Leah was here," Kurt said, looking round. "I thought I heard a voice."

"No, she's away," Leo said. "I talk to myself...it's a sign of old age. Look, here's the packet that came for you. It was posted in Vienna. If it's from Ruth that must mean they're safe, mustn't it? You'll be able to go and find them there."

Leo thrust the package into Kurt's hand. "Go ahead and open it," he said. "I can guess how much you are longing for news of them."

Kurt was about to rip the brown paper from the parcel when he saw that it already had a tear across the top. He looked up sharply. "Did you open it, Leo?"

Leo gave a nervous laugh, "No, of course not. It arrived like that. I'm afraid the post is very badly handled these days." Leo's face was grey with fear and his eyes flicked from the desk, to the window, to the clock on the man-telpiece, back to the window. It was then that Kurt saw the telephone, remembered the voice he had heard as he'd mounted the stairs and in that moment he knew what Leo Meyer had done. With one despairing look at Leo, Kurt spun on his heel and pelted down the stairs. As he ran he heard Leo wailing, "What else could I do, Kurt? They've taken my Leah! They've taken my Leah!"

Kurt knew the front door was already locked, so he ripped open the side door and ran across the yard to the back gate. How long had he got? How long before the Gestapo arrived to grab him, to drag him back to Dachau? They would have people surrounding the place, covering the back alley as well as the front entrance. He drew back the bolts on the gate and flung it open. The alley was empty, each end out of sight as it curved away behind the houses. Both ends opened on to a main road, but unless he reached one before it was covered by the Gestapo, he would walk straight into a trap. How long had he got?

His answer came immediately. There was the crash of glass and splintering of wood as a jackboot broke down the shop door. No time to run. Kurt looked wildly round the yard for somewhere to hide. A small tool shed stood against the side wall. No good hiding inside...but the roof? It was his only chance. He jumped up and grasping its rough stone parapet, scrabbling with his feet, he managed to heave himself onto the top of the wall. With heart pounding, he scrambled onto the roof of the shed, but realised at once there was no hiding there. He slid back onto the wall, to lie, shaking, partially concealed by the jut of the shed roof. At that moment the back door of the bakery burst open and two men catapulted into the yard.

There was a roar from one, "He's gone through the back

gate! You go that way, I'll take the other! We've got him!"

"Yes, sir."

The sound of heavy boots pounding along the alley echoed back to him. Kurt raised his head a fraction. What to do now? It wouldn't be long before they realised that he had not tried to make his escape along the alley. They would be back to search the bakery and its neighbours properly. Two men. How many had come in answer to Leo's call? There were certainly more in Leo's apartment, he could hear shouting. No escape that way then. He would have to move on. He glanced down into the yard on the other side of the wall, and the back entrance of the tobacconist, next door to the bakery. Could he escape that way? There was nowhere else.

As softly as he could, Kurt slithered round and dropped into the yard. He edged his way to the back door, keeping close under the wall so that he should not be seen from one of Leo's windows. He tried the back door of the shop, but it was locked. If he wanted to get into the building, he would have to bang on the door. No point in that. He was about to try his luck at climbing the next wall and moving into the next yard, when he noticed the sash window beside the door. It had been left open an inch or so for ventilation. Kurt slipped his fingers under the frame and pushed upward as hard as he could. The window was well greased and slid up easily. It was a moment's work to slide in through the gap and roll the window down again, this time completely. For the moment Kurt was out of sight, but he knew that the whole area would soon be flooded with men looking for him; and if Leo saw him, that would be that. Leo would do anything to try and save his beloved Leah.

The room in which Kurt found himself was used as a laundry. There was a large sink with a tap, a copper for boiling water, a scrubbed wooden table covered with an ironing cloth, and on a wooden airer, slung from the ceiling, clothes had been hung up to dry. Kurt saw a dark blue boiler suit, and shedding his old overcoat he grabbed it down and pulled it on over his clothes, buttoning it high to the neck. There was a workman's cap on the back of the door, and Kurt crammed it onto his head, pulling it well down to shade his face. He checked that he had the precious packet in his pocket, and he was ready to move. As he was about to open the door, he saw a toolbox tucked under the table. It was Frau Hirsch who ran the tobacconist's, he remembered, and her husband was a plumber. Kurt's suitcase was somewhere in Leo's shop, but there was nothing in it anyway. Kurt picked up the toolbox. He was now a plumber.

He eased the door open and found himself in a narrow corridor. A flight of stairs ran up to his right, and further along another door to the right led into the tobacconist's shop. At the far end of the passage was a door onto the street, allowing entry to the apartment without having to pass through the shop.

For a moment Kurt tried to visualise the inside of the tobacconist's shop. The door from the back of the house came in behind the counter, he remembered. It was glazed, but if Frau Hirsch was serving a customer, she probably wouldn't see him slip past. It was a risk, but one he had to take. His only chance of escape was to get away from here as fast as possible.

Kurt drew a deep breath and walked swiftly and silently down the passage to the street door. It opened to his touch and he stepped out into the street. There was a large black car parked outside Meyer's bakery, and another across the road outside his own home. The street was almost deserted. At the sign of Gestapo interest in the neighbourhood, everyone headed for cover, hoping that they had come for someone else. Still clutching the toolbox, Kurt walked purposefully up the road, away from the parked cars. He passed several entrances to back alleys, but decided he was safer walking along the main roads as if he had nothing to hide. When he reached the corner, he turned left, away from the end of the alley that ran behind the Meyers'. There were a few more people around here, but even so Kurt was anxious to find somewhere busier where he could melt into the crowd.

It won't be very long before they know what I'm wearing, Kurt thought as he strode along, toolbox in hand. How long before they find my coat in Frau Hirsch's laundry? How long before she tells them I've stolen her husband's boiler suit and his toolbox? Not long, if they are thorough as they usually are. No one will try and protect me; no one will dare and who can blame them?

"This man is a thief!" the Gestapo will say to justify my arrest. "This man has stolen the tools of another man's trade, leaving him unable to earn his living and support his family!"

Kurt still had no idea as to where to go. They would surely be watching both the railway and the bus stations, and if he stayed on the streets it was only a matter of time before they picked him up. He was definitely a man on the run now, a man on the run with no money. The few coins that he had in his trouser pocket were the last he owned in the world. The only things he had of any value now were his watch and Herr Hirsch's toolbox. He would have to sell them...if he could find anyone willing to buy.

It was then he remembered Paul Schiller. He had been a good friend of Kurt's father, a jeweller who had a shop just a few streets away. Paul Schiller would probably give Kurt a fair price for the watch...if he were still in business.

Kurt set off to find the shop. As he waited to cross the road, a sleek black car swept round the corner, its wheels throwing up filthy spray from a puddle in the road. Kurt was not the only one to turn away as the car sped past, but even as he did so, he saw the pale despairing face of Leo Meyer, crushed between two Gestapo, in the back. Leo had betrayed Kurt to try and save his own wife, but it would seem that the Gestapo had not kept their side of the bargain. Perhaps, thought Kurt, because they didn't catch me, or perhaps simply because they are the Gestapo and they don't have to. Like Oberführer Loritz, who had taken possession of Kurt's property when there were still two days to run. Well, if they've taken Leo in for questioning, it won't be long before they know exactly where I'm going.

The sight of Leo in the back of the car made Kurt feel sick. The reputation of the Gestapo was well established, and no one who fell into their clutches was safe. Kurt quickened his pace and before long he reached the street where Paul Schiller had had his shop. Hardly daring to look, Kurt walked to the corner where the shop had been, and miracle of miracles, was still. He pushed open the door and went inside, if nothing else, pleased to get off the street for a while.

Paul Schiller was an elderly man, with snow-white hair standing in a halo around his head, half-moon glasses perched on his nose and piercing blue eyes. He was behind the counter when Kurt opened the door and he looked up as the bell jingled to announce the arrival of a customer. He had an eyeglass screwed into one eye and he squinted at Kurt, not recognising him.

"Good day to you," he said mildly. "How can I help you?"

"I have a watch I'd like valued," Kurt said. He put his hand into his pocket and pulled out the watch he had removed from his wrist before entering the shop. He held it out to the jeweller who took it and looked at it for a long moment. Then he looked up again.

"Where did you get this watch?" he asked.

"It was my father's. Now it's mine."

"Kurt Friedman? Is it you? Heinrich's boy?"

Kurt smiled and held out his hand. "Yes, Herr Schiller. It's me, Heinrich's boy."

The jeweller took Kurt's outstretched hand and shook it. "I heard your shop had burned down...and that you were arrested. Is that true?"

Kurt nodded. "It happened the night of the riot. Back in July."

"And you've been released? Where are you living now?"

"Nowhere," replied Kurt. "I am looking for my family. I'll be honest with you, Herr Schiller, I don't just want the watch valued, I want to sell it."

Paul Schiller looked at the watch in his hand and said, "Your mother bought that watch from me as an anniversary present for your father over thirty years ago. Swiss. A beautiful movement." He handed the watch back to Kurt. "It would be a pity to part with it."

"I don't want to part with it," Kurt admitted, "but I've nothing else of value to sell, indeed nothing else in the world, and I need money to eat and to find my wife and children. My father would think it was being put to good use."

"I see." The old man came round the end of the counter and pulled down the blinds on the windows. "Let's have a cup of coffee and talk about this," he said, locking the door.

"I often close in the afternoons these days, there's very little business. Come on through." He led the way to a room at the back of the shop. It was furnished as a small sitting room with armchairs and a sofa. A closed stove sent a steady heat into the room so that it was comfortably warm, and it was only as the warmth hit him that Kurt realised how cold he was.

Paul Schiller set the kettle to boil and then said, "Are you hungry?"

Kurt admitted he was. "It was food or a train ticket this morning," he said. "The train ticket won."

The jeweller went to a cupboard and drew out a large loaf of bread and some cheese. "I always keep some food here, to have for lunch," he said, and cutting a thick slice from the loaf, put it, with a large hunk of cheese, onto a plate and passed it across to Kurt. "You eat that while I brew the coffee."

Kurt fell on the food, and his father's old friend, watching him, realised what dire straits he was in.

When the coffee was made, he prepared another plate of bread and cheese, which he also handed to Kurt, and then he sat back nursing his coffee cup and said, "Now then, I think you'd better tell me everything from the start, don't you?"

Kurt looked across at him. "I'm not sure that is a good idea at all," he said. "It could well put you in danger."

"We're all in danger while the Nazis are in power," replied Paul. "I've only myself to think about. If I am prepared to take the risk, it is my decision, and you don't bear the burden of it." As Kurt still looked uncertain the old man said, "There are few enough able to stand up against this tyranny, even in small ways. They have families to protect, they have private scores to settle, they are just plain scared. For whatever reason they can't or won't say enough is enough. Now, tell me what's happened to you, what you are trying to do and what I can do to help you."

The grey afternoon faded to dusk, and still they sat in the warm room behind the shop, Kurt relating all that had happened to him and what he knew of what had happened to Ruth and the children. Paul listened almost without interruption, just occasionally asking a question to clarify something, and when at last Kurt finished he made no comment for several minutes. Silence lapsed round them, and neither man felt the need to break it. At last, Paul said, "Have you opened the packet from Ruth? Is it your passport?"

Kurt looked at him in surprise. "You know, I haven't had an opportunity." He reached into his pocket and produced the packet. He was about to slit it open when Paul stopped him.

"May I have a look at this first?" he asked.

"Of course." Kurt handed over the package.

Paul held it carefully between finger and thumb, looking at the flap, still sealed, and the tear across the top. "This has been opened and re-sealed," he said. "Look, you can see where there is extra glue at the edge of the flap...beside the tear."

"I thought it had simply got torn in the post," Kurt said.

"That is possible," Paul conceded, "but unlikely. I've had several packets and parcels arrive here in this condition. They intercept parcels like this addressed to Jewish firms and businesses. They are looking for the transfer of funds. In the current climate Jews are keen to get their money out, or at least spread it round so that they don't lose it all at once. The post is no longer inviolable. Anything suspicious, any regular post going to Jews, is opened, read and either disappears, or is re-sealed and sent on. The Gestapo know who is receiving what, and why. Take your package, for instance—" Paul held up the unopened packet. "It was addressed to someone who didn't live at that address. That was suspicious straightaway. It was addressed to someone already known to them...a definite reason for interest. Finally, it came from abroad. Post from other countries addressed to Jews can be worrying to the Nazis. They are still trying to protect an international reputation. They aren't quite ready for war yet."

"War?"

"Oh yes," Paul nodded his head as if in confirmation, "there will be one, mark my words. Eventually the world will realise what Hitler is up to, but, until they do, the Nazis try to keep the lid on what is actually happening in Germany."

"So you think the Gestapo opened this parcel before it reached the Meyers?"

"Almost certainly. And when they saw what it contained they decided to set a trap."

"They took Leah," Kurt said slowly, "and told Leo that he must tell them immediately if I turned up."

"It would seem that way."

"But what would have happened if I hadn't turned up?" wondered Kurt.

Paul shrugged. "They would probably have held on to her and used Leo as a spy in other ways."

"Leo said she was away when I asked," mused Kurt. "That must be the line he's had to use."

"He would be no use to the Gestapo if everyone knew that they were holding her hostage. Leo has to have credibility or people won't tell him anything he can pass on. I doubt if you are the only one he has betrayed."

"I'd probably do the same if they were holding Ruth," admitted Kurt.

"Would you? Well, one never knows until one is in that

position, so it's not fair to judge. However, I am in the happy, or unhappy position, of having no one they can hold hostage. If they come for me it's only I who will suffer."

Kurt tore the brown paper wrapping from the packet and saw that it did indeed contain his passport...and to his delight a letter written in Ruth's strong, upright hand.

"Leave it till I've gone," said Paul. "You'll want to read that when you're alone. Now, I suggest you stay here for the night. You should be safe and warm. I'll go home as usual, and come back in the morning with some more food and some different clothes for you. You're quite right, they will know about the boiler suit now." The old man got up and checked the curtains were covering the windows and no crack of light would shine through. "Keep the stove alight," he said, "there's plenty of wood. I'll be back to open the shop in the morning." He showed Kurt the lavatory, with basin and toilet, and then putting on his overcoat went to the door.

"I'll lock you in," he said. "Try and get some sleep."

As soon as he was alone, Kurt ripped off the last of the brown paper and took out the letter from Ruth. It was written on thick, stiff notepaper, her sister's address and telephone number printed in heavy dark type in the top right-hand corner:

My darling Kurt,

I don't know if you will ever get this letter. I have hesitated to send it to the Meyers as I know Leah was very worried that the post was no longer private and asked me not to write to her again. However, I've had to take the risk. You need the enclosed. We are all safely at Edith's now, Mother included.

I won't go into all that has happened to us, but should tell you that the price of our being allowed to leave Germany was the title deeds to the shop and apartment. Perhaps I shouldn't have handed them over, as they were not mine, but it seemed a small price to pay for our children's safety…their lives even. Things had been making life impossible both in Munich and Vohldorf, and so I did what I thought necessary.

Dearest Kurt, I have no idea where you are. Maybe you're still in prison somewhere, but if you do get this letter please come to us. The enclosed should make it easier for you to leave Germany and join us here.

Obviously we cannot stay with Edith and David indefinitely, so we shall find a home of our own in the next few days, for Mother, me and the children. They are all well, you'll be glad to hear, and constantly ask when you are coming back. I tell them soon. I just hope and pray that I am right.

Whatever happens, my dearest love, I shall be listening for your step, watching for your face at the window. Go with G-d.

Your Ruth

Kurt brought the letter up to his lips, closing his eyes and drawing a deep breath in an effort to conjure Ruth from the paper on which she had written. Tears of relief slipped down his cheeks. They were safe! They'd had to leave Germany, but they were safe in Vienna, a city where the Nazi writ did not run. He kissed her name at the bottom of the page and then read the letter through again. His wonderful Ruth had not only saved the children, but had found a way of getting his passport to him, so that he could try and reach them.

Then he thought of the Meyers. They had taken his family in when their home had burned down, they had done their best to help, as good neighbours should, and now, because Ruth had written to him at their address, they were in the hands of the Gestapo. Kurt's euphoria at having received Ruth's letter evaporated as he thought of the price that had been paid for him to be free. The letter had explained so much; why the shop and apartment were already being restored. She had given the deeds away already. Oberführer Loritz would never get his hands on the property now, which made Kurt's own position even more perilous. The Oberführer would find someone else in possession of the property he had thought would be his, and his fury at being tricked would know no bounds. He would hunt Kurt like a fox, and when he found him he would slam him back into the hell of Dachau and throw away the key. Kurt would be worked until he dropped dead like poor Rudy Stein. In the meantime, with no property and no money, he had nothing else to bargain with should the need arise, and Kurt thought, it probably will!

Leo and Leah Meyer had lost their freedom, but, as a result, he, Kurt, was still free. He must escape; he must ensure that their unwilling sacrifice had not been for nothing. He had a fleeting vision of Leo sitting in the back of the Gestapo car, pale and terrified. Where had they taken him? To Dachau? And Leah? Where had they taken her? Where did they take women prisoners? Kurt didn't want to imagine, but he knew the thought of the elderly couple who had lost everything, including each other, because they had been good neighbours, would haunt him forever.

He picked up the letter again and looked at the address so boldly inscribed at the top. At least he knew how to contact

Ruth now, he thought, as he memorised both the address and the telephone number. He could telephone Edith's house and ask for her, and he would hear her voice. Paul Schiller had a telephone in his shop, perhaps he could ring from there. Kurt pictured Ruth's face when she heard his voice on the phone at last, and it was all he could do to stop himself from creeping back into the shop to find the telephone tucked away under the counter and place the call...now, that very minute. He fought the temptation. In the morning, he would ask Paul if he might use it.

Kurt folded the letter carefully and put it into his pocket, then he stoked up the stove and made himself as comfortable as he could on the sofa and settled down for the night. Certainly warmer than last night, he thought. And despite the perils and fears of the day, he soon drifted into a deep and dreamless sleep, not stirring until the winter sun had risen to cast its light on the grey streets beyond the window.

Paul Schiller arrived early to open the shop. He carried a small case and a paper bag with him, and these he handed to Kurt. "Breakfast," he said, nodding at the paper bag, "and clothes in there," he indicated the case. "They should fit you all right...my son Günter's. He was about your size." He turned away abruptly, saying as he left the room, "Get changed, and then stay in the back here. I'll come back at midday. I must be in my shop all morning, or it will be noticed."

Kurt vaguely remembered Günter, a boy of about his own age, studious and solitary, and interested in different things. They had never been close at school. Where was he now, Kurt wondered? Paul had said "was". Was he dead then?

Kurt opened the suitcase and pulled out winter

underclothes, a shirt, jacket and trousers. There was a pair of woollen socks and a sturdy pair of boots. He quickly removed the boiler suit and the clothes he'd been wearing for the last week and went into the lavatory. The water was cold, but Kurt didn't care. Standing naked beside the little basin, he scrubbed himself from head to foot, the cold of the water making him gasp as he plunged his head to wash his hair. At last he felt clean and he towelled himself vigorously to restore his circulation. He dressed quickly in the clothes Paul had brought, enjoying the clean cloth against his skin, and then turned his attention to the paper bag. There was some bread and an apple. Kurt set the kettle to boil and made himself a cup of coffee to drink with his breakfast.

At midday Paul Schiller closed the shop and came through to the back room. He nodded approvingly at the sight of Kurt, sitting warmly dressed on the sofa.

"You look very respectable," he said with a faint smile. "Not at all like a man on the run. Now," he went on, waving away Kurt's thanks, "I have to go out. I'll go to the station and buy you a ticket for tonight's train to Hamburg…"

"Hamburg!" exclaimed Kurt, "I don't want to go to Hamburg…"

"No one said you had to," Paul said calmly, "but if there is someone keeping an eye out for you, they may not see you get on the Hamburg train. You do have to leave this town as soon as you can. Anyone might recognise you and report you to the Gestapo. And you can be sure they will be watching the trains to Vienna."

"Why…?" began Kurt.

"My dear boy! Don't forget, they've read your wife's letter. They know where she is. You have her address now, but so does the Gestapo. They will be watching for you to board the Vienna train."

Kurt hadn't thought about the Gestapo reading the letter, only about them finding the passport. He felt a chill run through him; now they knew where Ruth and the children were.

Kurt asked Paul if he might use the telephone in the shop to phone Ruth, but the little jeweller shook his head, horrified.

"Definitely not!" he said. "Who knows who is listening in at the exchange? The call could well be reported and immediately traced back here. You must wait until you can get to a public telephone, and then keep your call extremely short."

Kurt thought guiltily of how close he had come to using the telephone last night. Even though he knew Paul was right, Kurt longed to ring Edith's number, to hear Ruth's voice just once, to tell her that he was on his way.

Kurt dozed by the stove as the afternoon dragged by, but at last the early evening darkness fell, Paul Schiller closed the shop for the day and came through to the back room.

"There's a lot of activity out in the streets," he told Kurt as he made them more coffee. "Perhaps it would be better if you waited here for another few days."

"No!" Kurt was adamant. "Every moment I'm here in your shop puts you in greater danger. Enough people have suffered because of me and my family. I'll go tonight. I'll take the train to Hamburg as you suggest, and then somewhere along the way, I'll get off and head for the Austrian border."

"Are you sure that is the best thing for you to do?" Paul asked.

"What do you mean?"

"Going to find them in Austria. Is that really the best thing to do?"

Kurt stared at him. "What else should I do?" he demanded. "I've got to get to my family. They need me."

"Kurt, I understand that's what you *want* to do," Paul said, "but just think for a moment or two, is it what you *ought* to do?"

"Why ever not?"

"Well," Paul said slowly, "I've been thinking about this all day, and it seems to me that the most help you can be to your family is to get right out of the country..."

"But that's what I'm planning to do," Kurt broke in. "Get out of the country, into Austria."

Paul waved his hand in acknowledgement. "I know, I know, but you have to look at the overall situation. Have you considered that if Hitler has his way, Austria very soon won't be 'out of the country'?"

"What do you mean?"

"I mean," said Paul patiently, "that Hitler is set on annexing Austria. He has the power to do it and he will. Sometime in the next couple of months, maybe much sooner, Austria will become a province of Germany. The Nazis will rule and German laws will prevail. If you're in Austria with your family, you'll be just as badly off as you were before. You'll have jumped out of the frying pan into the fire...and it will be some fire, believe me."

"Then I should be with Ruth and the children," returned Kurt. "If what you say is going to happen does happen, then I should be there, with them."

"Where you will be arrested again, and of no use to them at all."

"But I can't just save myself and leave them there!" Kurt was almost shouting now. "I can't just walk away! I have to be there to help them, to be with them."

"I think," began Paul and held up his hand to cut off Kurt's interruption, "I think that you could do far more for them if you were safely in England, or Holland or France. In those countries you could arrange to get them out of Austria."

"How?" Kurt snapped. "How could I do that?"

"I've heard there are Jewish societies and groups in London and other places who are helping Jews to escape from the Nazis. Sending money, arranging sponsors, finding jobs. Remember, you were going to be allowed to leave once the Nazi colonel had his hands on your property. Jews are being allowed to leave, at a price. You have nothing to offer here anymore, so, now you should go to England and ask for help."

"Why would the English help me?"

"Why wouldn't they? There are English Jews who are doing their best to bring their fellow Jews out of Germany, and I think I am right when I say that soon it will be out of Austria too." Paul reached over and placed a hand on Kurt's arm. "If you go to Austria now, you will be trapped, too. You can do more for your family as a free man...in a free country."

Kurt stared blankly at the stove, his mind in turmoil. How could he possibly save himself and leave the rest of them to their fate?

"Kurt, it is your decision. Yours and yours alone." Paul spoke gently: "Whatever you decide, I will do all I can to help you. All I am asking you to do is to consider your options, and to remember that if the Gestapo are looking for you any-where, it will be trying to cross into Austria. They, too, know that's where you want to go." Paul sighed. "They call us Jews subhuman, but they recognise the very humanity in us that makes us love our families above all else and they use that

217

knowledge to their advantage and our destruction. Threaten a man's son, and you have the man."

Kurt looked across at him and said softly, "Paul, I don't know what to do, but I thank you from the bottom of my heart for all you have done for me. I will consider what you say, but whatever I finally decide, I must leave here now." He got to his feet, and taking off his watch again, tried to hand it to Paul, but the little jeweller waved it away.

"Keep it, Kurt. It was your father's, and it may yet provide for you if necessary."

"But I must have some money," protested Kurt. "And that's all I have to sell."

"Then keep it to sell another day," replied Paul, and, reaching into his pocket, he pulled out a brown envelope and passed it to Kurt.

Kurt looked at it uncertainly. "What's this?"

Paul shrugged. "You said you need money. It's money."

Kurt looked into the envelope and his eyes widened. "But I can't take all this!" he exclaimed dropping the envelope on the table.

"Of course you can," replied Paul. "Your father and I were friends, Kurt...and I have no one else who needs that money now. My Günter died in the 'flu epidemic last year. There's no one to have my money when I die...except the Nazis, and I'd rather they didn't." He gave a bleak smile. "I have something else for you," he said, and reaching again into his inside pocket, he produced a document, which he handed to Kurt. "Günter used to travel for me quite a lot. He often went to Amsterdam or London to buy stones for our business. This is his passport, I thought it might prove useful."

Kurt took the passport and opened it, staring at the

photograph inside. "It doesn't look much like me," he said doubtfully. "He had a beard for a start!"

Paul smiled. "So he did," he agreed. "But beards can be shaved off...or re-grown. You have the same dark hair, and are roughly the same age. I just thought there might come a time when it would be useful to have some papers in another name." As Kurt continued to stare at the picture, Paul went on, "It's still valid. No ordinary border guard will know that he's dead. It might get you through...wherever you decide to go. Take this, too. Learn the names and addresses and then destroy it." He handed Kurt a slip of paper. Kurt looked at it and saw two names and addresses written on it in Paul's neat script; one in Hamburg, the other in London.

"Two men I do business with," Paul said. "They both knew Günter, they may be able to help you." He sighed. "Who can tell in these dreadful times?"

"Come with me!" Kurt said suddenly. "Come with me, we could travel together."

The jeweller shook his head. "No," he said, "I'm too old to start running; too old to start another life somewhere else. I'll be all right here. They can see there's no harm in me... I'm too old for one of their labour camps." He picked up the envelope and thrust it at Kurt again. "Take it, Kurt, and use it to save yourself and your family. Go to America if you can, we shan't see the end of these Nazis in Europe for a long time to come. Take the money, Kurt, and the passport, so that I can meet my maker knowing that I did something that made a difference."

Kurt looked at the old man for a long moment and then reached forward and took the envelope, and tucking the addresses into it, put it, with Günter's passport, into his pocket.

"And now you must go," Paul Schiller said. "I've brought you an overcoat, scarf and a hat." He passed them over to Kurt who put them on. "And here's your ticket. It will take you all the way to Hamburg if you decide to go that far. Somewhere along the way you will find a telephone." He clasped Kurt's hands in his. "Leave by the back door," he said. "I'll go out through the front, locking the shop up as I always do. Good luck, my boy."

"I don't know how to..." began Kurt.

"Then don't. Just survive."

Eleven

Kurt slipped out through the back door of the shop and made his way to the station. Carrying the suitcase Paul had brought, he looked like any travelling salesman. That is, he thought ruefully, until they open it and find nothing but a few crumpled clothes and some toiletries. Not the boiler suit or the tools. They had been left for Paul Schiller to dispose of. The precious passport was tucked safely into the inside pocket of Kurt's jacket, worn beneath his new overcoat. Darkness had fallen and it was very cold, but for the first time in days Kurt felt warm as he strode along the streets to the station.

The train for Hamburg would pass through Kirnheim in less than ten minutes if it were on time, and that, thanks to Hitler, was something that could be relied on these days. Kurt had timed his arrival so that he would have the minimum time to spend standing on the platform waiting. As he showed his ticket at the barrier, he fought the urge to look round, giving the ticket collector a faint smile and then looking resolutely ahead of him, as if he had no reason in the world to wonder who was watching. The arrivals board told him that the train for Vienna was due about twenty minutes after his Hamburg train had left. Kurt could only pray that those who were hunting him would be concentrating their attention on that platform. Like many another, his scarf was wrapped high around his neck and his hat pulled low over his ears to keep out the cold, and there was very little of his face visible. If he were lucky he would be onto the train and away entirely unnoticed.

The Hamburg train arrived in a cloud of smoke and steam, rattling its way into the station and screeching to a halt beside the platform. Doors opened, people were disgorged onto the platform, and in the bustle of passengers coming and going, Kurt got into the train, found a seat, and opening the newspaper he'd bought outside the station, buried his head behind its pages. As the train drew out of the station, he allowed himself a glance through the window, and his heart froze. A dark-haired man, much of Kurt's own height and build, was being hustled, protesting, along a parallel platform by two men in dark overcoats.

"Oh God," Kurt prayed, "let him be able to prove he isn't me!"

The train gathered speed, and for the time being there was nothing Kurt could do but sit back and go where it took him. He had no intention of going all the way to Hamburg, but he knew he had to stay on the train long enough to escape those looking for him.

It was late when they reached Nuremberg. Kurt had spent the journey considering all his options, but mostly thinking about what Paul Schiller had suggested he do. Make for Holland or England, not for Austria. He went over and over what Paul had said. Hitler will annex Austria. Austria will become part of Germany. It will be run by the Nazis. Laws which now subjugate the Jews in Germany will become law in Austria. "It you go to Austria, you will be trapped there,"

Paul had said. Looking at everything unemotionally, there was a great deal of truth in what Paul had said, but Kurt could not look at everything unemotionally. He couldn't just turn away from his family and run for safety; everything within him shrieked against it. How could he escape to Holland or England and leave them behind to be swallowed up into the new German Empire? Paul's foreboding about Hitler's intentions with regard to Austria made it all the more important that Kurt get to Vienna, and sooner rather than later. He had very little faith in English Jewish societies rescuing Jews from Austria, and certainly not Jews of his background. Those societies, no doubt very well intentioned, would work to bring out eminent Jews, educated and highly skilled Jews, not humble shopkeepers like him. Part of Kurt's brain knew that Paul was right, it would help no one if he went to Vienna and was caught there. The other part urged him to get to Ruth as soon as he could. He didn't know if Hitler really would try and annex Austria, but it would not surprise him; then Ruth and the children would be trapped again. Would they be of less interest to the Nazis if he were not with them? Maybe. Who could tell?

As the train chugged north, Kurt's brain churned, his thoughts in turmoil as the plans he had made the night before now had to be completely reconsidered, and by the time he reached Nuremberg the only definite decision he had made was to get off the train and try and speak to Ruth.

He walked away from the station, and found a small hotel in a side street nearby. It had two bow windows that spilled yellow light out into the street, and the rooms beyond looked warm and inviting. Thanks to Paul Schiller he had plenty of money for now, and he thought that a public telephone in a hotel would be safe enough. To speak to his beloved Ruth, Kurt was prepared to take the risk.

He paused and looked around him. The narrow street was empty, though he could hear the traffic on the main road. No one was watching, no one was there to see him, so he took the plunge, walked up the steps to the front door and pushed it open. The lobby of the hotel was small, scarcely more than a passageway with a desk set into an alcove. A young woman sitting behind the desk looked up with a smile.

"Good evening, sir," she said. "May I help you?"

"Yes, thank you," Kurt responded with an answering smile. "I'd like a room for the night."

"Certainly, sir. Just the one night?"

"Yes, thank you, I have a train to catch in the morning."

"If you'd just fill in the registration card, please." The girl handed him a card. It asked for his details, and Kurt knew a moment's panic. Which name should he use? Best to use his own. He would also be asked for his identity card, and it had his true name and address on it…so he would have to risk putting those on the form; he had only a passport in Günter's name.

When he had registered, the receptionist said, "Room 4 on the first floor." Kurt thanked her, picked up his suitcase and asked, "Is there a public telephone I can use?"

"Certainly, sir. Just down the corridor." She pointed along the narrow passage that led into the depths of the hotel. "There's a booth there."

Kurt thanked her and went up to his room. It was nothing special, but compared with the places in which he had been sleeping the last few days it looked like heaven. There was a basin in one corner, a radiator under the window, but best of all was a wide, iron bedstead, covered with a folded feather-bed. Kurt took off his coat and sorted through his pocket to find money for the phone. Then he locked his door behind him and went back downstairs in search of the telephone. When he reached the hall the receptionist looked up and smiled at him.

"If you just give me the number, sir, I'll place the call and put it through to the phone booth."

"Surely," stammered Kurt, "I can place it myself?"

"Sorry, sir, but all calls have to be routed through our switchboard. It's no trouble."

"It's an international call," began Kurt. She had caught him completely off balance; unused to hotels, it had never occurred to him that the public phone would not be con-nected directly to the exchange.

"That's no problem, sir," replied the woman smoothly. "Just give me the number and wait in the booth." She picked up a pencil, poised to write down the number she required. Kurt had to make an instant decision; give her the number and risk her listening in to his conversation with Ruth, or not give her the number, and say he'd changed his mind, at the risk of arousing her suspicions. The longing to hear Ruth's voice was overwhelming. He gave the number and the woman wrote it down.

"Now if you wait in the booth, sir," she said, "I'll place the call, and when the phone rings in there, you'll be connected."

Kurt thanked her and went along the passage to find the phone. The phone booth was a small, glass-fronted cubby hole under the stairs, but it had a light, a stool to sit on and seemed to be completely private. As he waited for the call, Kurt was assailed by fears and doubts. He should have gone to the station or somewhere completely anonymous. He should have found a reason for changing his mind. Had there been a flicker of interest in the woman's eyes when he'd said he wanted to make an international call? He had to assume that she would be listening in, so he must make it clear to Ruth that they were being overheard without actually saying so. Would Ruth understand his warning? Be cautious in what she said? He could only pray that she would.

The phone jangled in his ear and he snatched up the receiver.

"You're through, caller," the operator told him. "You have three minutes."

Then another voice said, "Good evening. Herr Doktor Bernstein's residence."

"Please may I speak to Frau Ruth Friedman?" Kurt's breath caught in his throat, he could hardly get the words out.

"I'm sorry, but there is no Frau Friedman here."

"Frau Edith Bernstein, then. Please hurry, this is an international call."

"Whom shall I say is calling?" asked the voice, unhurried.

"Kurt Friedman, her brother-in-law. Please hurry."

"Please hold the line," said the voice, and then there was silence.

"Come on, come on," muttered Kurt as the seconds of his precious three minutes ticked away.

After what seemed like ages he heard another voice. "Hallo. Edith Bernstein speaking."

"Edith, it's Kurt."

"Kurt! How are you? Where are you?"

"Edith, never mind that, I'm running out of time. Is Ruth there?"

"No, I'm afraid not, she…"

"Where is she? How can I contact her? Has she got a phone?"

"No, she hasn't. Look, can I take a message for her?"

Kurt tried to keep his voice steady. "Please ask her to be at your house this time tomorrow. I will phone again."

"But Kurt…" Edith began

"Please, Edith, this time tomorrow," Kurt managed to say before the operator said, "Time's up, caller," and the line went dead.

Kurt slumped down onto the stool, his head in his hands. He could have wept with frustration and disappointment. Ruth wasn't there. He had so longed to hear her voice and she wasn't there. She had said in her letter that she was going to move the family out to a place of their own, and she must have done so.

"For goodness' sake," he admonished himself, "you've only got to wait one more day. Edith will surely have her there tomorrow."

With a sigh, Kurt got to his feet and went out into the hall. With the exception of one light at the foot of the stairs, all had been switched off, and the hallway was in semi-darkness. The reception desk was empty.

Kurt paused for a moment, looking at the empty desk. Where had the receptionist gone, he wondered, cold fear flooding through him – had she been listening in to his conversation? Was she even now reporting that he had phoned Austria to the authorities? Had she passed on his registration card? Was someone, somewhere checking his name against a list? His heart was pounding as fear tightened its grip. Should he leave the hotel, now, before they came for him? Where would he go? He glanced over the front of the desk and saw his registration card on the top of a pile of similar cards. It was still there, the young woman hadn't passed it on. The panic subsided a little. Why should she, he argued with himself as he crept back up the stairs – what suspicions could he have aroused? Surely his name and identity could not have been circulated this far yet. He reached his room, and closing the door firmly behind him turned the key in the lock.

There could be any number of reasons why she wasn't at the desk, he told himself. A call of nature, duty somewhere else in the hotel. Perhaps she'd gone home. It was unlikely such a small hotel would keep a receptionist on duty throughout the night. Surely he was as safe here as anywhere else, and a lot safer than in most places. He would leave first thing in the morning. But he was only half-convinced and the fear did not leave him; despite the wonderful warmth and softness of the bed, he slept little, dozing and waking until it was daylight.

In the morning he shaved carefully with the razor Paul had provided, packed his few belongings into the case and got ready to leave. He knew that he must keep moving. To stay in one place for too long was to invite discovery, and he felt that he had stayed too long here already. Picking up his suitcase he went downstairs. A different woman sat at the reception desk.

"I'd like to pay my bill," Kurt said, taking money from his coat pocket. "Room 4."

The woman wrote out his bill and as she handed it to him she pointed to an added figure just above the total and said, "That last amount is for the international phone call you made to a number in Vienna last night." Written beside the amount was Edith's phone number.

Kurt looked at it and said quickly, "Yes, yes, that's quite

right. Thank you." He proffered the money for the bill, but the woman did not take it straightaway.

"If you need breakfast," she said, "we can serve you in the dining room."

"Thank you, no." Kurt replied, "I have to catch the Hamburg train."

At this the woman finally took the notes he held out, tucking them into a cashbox with the carbon copy of the bill. Kurt bid her good morning and picking up his suitcase went out into the street.

During his wakeful night, Kurt had decided what he should do next. He still intended to go to Vienna, but he knew he was going to have to take a circuitous route. He found a small bookshop, bought himself a train timetable, and took it to a café he had seen, where he studied it over his breakfast. He would keep well away from Munich while still heading east. He was determined to get into Austria, and decided that he would try and cross the border at Passau. He would take the train to Regensburg and spend the night there. From there he could phone Ruth again, to tell her of his plans and then the next day he would use Günter Schiller's passport and try and cross into Austria. Once he was over the border, he could get another train to Vienna. It was Thursday 10th March; with luck he should be in Vienna with his family by Sunday the 12th at the latest. It would be exactly eight months since the night of the riot.

Kurt finished his breakfast and walked back to the station. It was busy and he hoped that one more man wearing a nondescript hat and coat would pass unnoticed among the crowds. He knew from his timetable that there was a train for Regensburg in half an hour, so he bought himself a ticket and a newspaper and sat on a bench reading until it was time to board the train. There were some uniformed men around the station, but most were the civil police, who seemed to be on normal duty. As the departure time approached, Kurt got to his feet and walked purposefully across to the platform where the Regensburg train stood, its engine blowing smoke and steam as it prepared to leave. He showed his ticket to the collector at the platform entrance and was passed through without a second glance. With his heart still pumping, Kurt walked along the train until he came to the third-class carriages. Choosing one that already had an elderly couple sitting in it, he opened the door and got in.

"Is this seat taken?" he asked politely, indicating one of the empty corner seats.

"Please," the old man said, and waved his hand towards it.

"Thank you." Kurt placed his case on the rack above his head, carefully laid his hat on top of it and sat down. The couple were watching him, so he smiled politely and opened his paper.

No one else came into the carriage and within minutes the whistle blew and the train drew slowly out of the station. It was not an express train, and it had no corridor. He and the elderly couple were on their own until they reached the first station. It stopped at several small stations as it headed south towards Regensburg, but that suited Kurt very well. He thought that the Gestapo or SS might take less interest in a slow, local train than an express. At each station he was alert to what was going on outside, trying to look at ease while being ready to leap from the train if there was any sign of police or storm troopers. He watched the country slide past the window, but all the time he was aware of the couple in the compartment with him. They didn't speak to each other, or to him, and something told him they were as nervous of him as he was of them.

When the train eventually reached Regensburg he got out. He had half a day to kill before he could make his second call to Ruth, but he felt safer here, in a different place. If the hotel had reported his call, if they were indeed looking for him, the receptionist would report he'd said he was going to Hamburg. If his fears were unfounded, then he was still as safe here as anywhere. He would phone Ruth from here at the appointed time and just pray that Edith had given her the message.

Eight months since his arrest! The thought of speaking to her after so long made his heart pound in his chest. He walked out of the station into the city and wandered the nearby streets in search of another small hotel. He found one, ten minutes' walk from the station, and arranged to take a room. As of the previous evening he had to fill in a registration card, giving his name and address.

The receptionist looked at the card. "What brings you to Regensburg, Herr Friedman?" she asked.

Kurt managed a smile. "Just some business...for my mother." It was all he could think of as he realised that his papers named him as a grocer, not a travelling salesman.

The girl handed him a key. "Room 3 at the top of the stairs."

Kurt took the key, thanked her and made his way upstairs. The girl watched him disappear round the turn in the stairs, then picked up the registration card and looked at it again. She glanced at the stairs again before lifting the receiver of the telephone on her desk and making a call.

Kurt left his case in the room, and went out to find something to eat. He'd had nothing since his early breakfast, and he was feeling hungry. He found a small café and ate a plate of cold meat for his lunch, and then decided to spend the afternoon in the anonymity of a cinema. When the film was over, there was still some time before he could ring Ruth, so he strolled through the town until he came to one of the canals that linked with the River Danube. As he walked along the towpath he watched a string of barges being towed out from the canal into the main waterway, heading east. He wondered where they were going and what they were carrying. He crossed a bridge and watched as the barges slipped away beneath him, like so many ducklings strung out behind their mother. He found a bench and sitting on it watched the barges disappear slowly into the dusk. He looked at his watch. Nearly time to make his call, to talk to Ruth. He must find a public phone, somewhere where he was sure he couldn't be overheard. He walked back past the station. There, in the ticket hall, were three telephone booths.

I'll ring from there, he thought, and turned into the entrance.

At exactly the time he had arranged with Edith, Kurt went into one of the telephone boxes and placed his call. He was lucky and the operator was able to put him straight through. His heart was thumping as he heard it ringing at the other end.

"Good evening. Herr Doktor Bernstein's residence." As before the maid answered the call.

"Please may I speak to Frau Ruth Friedman."

"One moment, please."

Then he heard her voice, breathless, shaky. "Kurt? Is that you?"

"Ruth, my darling Ruth!" He had planned exactly what he was going to say in the precious three minutes allotted to him, but when he heard her voice everything flew out of his head and he could only say her name.

"Kurt! Where are you?"

"Ruth? It's really you!"

"Kurt! Yes, yes, I'm here! Kurt, are you all right? Where are you?"

"I can't tell you that. I'm so glad you've got the children safely to Edith's. Are they well? Are they all right? Are *you* all right?" Now Kurt's questions came tumbling out.

"We're all fine," Ruth assured him. "Did you get," she paused before saying, "what I sent you?"

"Yes, but I'm not sure I can use it. They're looking for me."

"Oh God!" Ruth cried. "Can't you come?"

"Darling Ruth, I will if I possibly can, but it'll be dangerous."

"Then don't!" Ruth spoke sharply "Don't come. We're fine. We're all fine."

"I want to be there with you all."

"Please, Kurt, don't come if it is too dangerous. I'd rather you were free, and alive and somewhere else." Ruth's voice shook as she added, "You should go and visit Berta."

"Berta?" For a moment Kurt was bemused. Who on earth was Berta?

"You know Berta, Edith's daughter. Listen, Kurt, write to me," Ruth said, "our new address is…"

"No," Kurt interrupted, "don't say it! I'll write care of Edith."

"All right. Oh Kurt, I do miss you. I love you so much."

"I love you too, darling." There was a break in Kurt's voice as he went on, "Always and ever, whatever happens, remember I love you!"

233

"If you can't come, Kurt, don't! Stay safe. We're safe. Just try and keep in touch somehow!"

"I'll ring again... same time next week."

"Time's up, caller." The line went dead.

Kurt stood with the silent telephone receiver in his hand for a long minute. Had Ruth heard his last promise, to ring again next week? Who else had heard it? Who else had heard the whole conversation? Had the operator listened in? Was someone even now reporting a strange conversation to the authorities? One of the Nazis' triumphs was to make informers of everyone.

Time to get off the streets, he decided, and take shelter in his hotel, ready to move on again in the morning. He replaced the receiver in its cradle and walked quickly away from the station. Once out on the busy pavements, he slowed his pace and headed back towards the hotel, just one more nondescript man in a crowd returning home from work. As he approached the corner of his street, a car swept past him and turned down towards the hotel. Kurt had seen cars like that before, and a chill ran down his spine. When he reached the corner he paused, looking along the road towards the hotel. The car had passed it and pulled up a hundred yards further along, but he saw that the hotel door was closing behind someone. Someone had just gone into the hotel. Kurt waited in the shelter of a shop doorway and watched. After a few moments a man came back out of the hotel, looked both ways along the empty street and then hurried to the parked car. He spoke to someone in the car and a second man got out. Both hurried back into the hotel, and the car eased off down the road and disappeared round a bend. Men like these were all too familiar. Despite his warm clothes Kurt felt suddenly cold. If he hadn't stopped to make the call from the station, he would have been at the hotel when they arrived. Even if they had not been looking specifically for him, he would have been discovered. He stepped out of the doorway and walked briskly back the way he had come. Whether the men in dark coats were looking for him or not, he would not go back to the hotel. There was little there he needed, everything of importance was with him; his money was hidden about his person and both passports were in the inner pockets of his coat. He had his watch on his wrist and Ruth's letter in the inside pocket of his jacket. Shaving kit, vital to keeping himself looking respectable, he could replace.

He headed back to the station, but the crowds returning home were thinning out now, and he walked past. He glanced in through the main entrance, and what he saw made him want to break into a run. It took all his willpower to keep walking at a steady pace as if he had somewhere special to go. Standing at the ticket office was a man in the uniform of an SS trooper. Two more were standing at the entrance to the platforms, stopping everyone going through to the trains. They were looking for someone, and although Kurt had no idea if it was him, he was taking no risks.

Fighting the instinct to run, he continued to walk away from the station. How had they caught up with him so quickly? One of the receptionists must have suspected something and handed his registration card to the police. How had the police known that he was on the run? Someone very important must be determined to find him, someone who was powerful enough to have his details wired to main police stations, Gestapo offices...and, he thought, to all border crossings. Wherever he went they might have his passport details, be on the lookout for him. Was it because Loritz had been tricked out of his property, or simply because he refused to allow a Jew to get the better of him? Once he was away from Kirnheim, he had thought he would be safe enough, he had never truly thought that the net would be cast this wide. By pure chance he had escaped that net just now, but he knew he was not safely away yet. He had to get out of the town, disappear again, and not risk moving about openly.

He walked purposefully along Bahnhofstrasse and then cut up through the maze of smaller streets that led back towards the river. Here the streets were darker and there were few people around. Kurt tried to keep to the shadows; and more than once he reached a dead end and had to turn back, but at length he crossed the river. Somehow putting the river between himself and the railway station made him feel a little safer. He continued, more slowly now, with no particular direction in mind. He was looking for somewhere to spend the night, before he headed for Passau and the Austrian border in the morning. Tall buildings loomed on either side of the streets, warehouses, their windows dark, their gates locked, but Kurt continued to walk, searching for a doorway, or sheltered alleyway where he might take refuge for the night. He turned into another lane, twisting its way between blank-faced warehouses, but he found it ended in high metal gates, secured by a strong padlock and chain.

He was about to turn back when he noticed there was a smaller, Judas gate in the main gates and it was slightly ajar, allowing access into the yard beyond. Cautiously he looked around him. The lane behind him was in shadow, but the yard on the other side of the gate was lit by a lamp fixed high on the corner of a large building, some sort of warehouse, Kurt assumed. Another lamp, atop a tall stanchion, spilled light across the rest of the yard, glinting on the dark water of the canal beyond. All along one wall of the warehouse were large crates, stacked neatly as if ready to be loaded onto something, and beyond stood several machines of some sort, still and silent, waiting for morning.

All was quiet; no sign of guards or a watchman. Perhaps there was somewhere here he could spend the night. Kurt eased the small gate open. It moved surprisingly smoothly, with no hint of a squeak or rasp, as if the hinges had been recently oiled. Stepping through he moved quickly into the shadow of the warehouse. Still no sound. Taking care to stay in the patches of shadow, he edged his way along its wall, hands outstretched against the brickwork. He was looking for a door or window that might let him into the warehouse. As he moved he strained his ears for any sound that would warn him someone else was there, but there was nothing. He reached the front of the warehouse, and found that it had huge wide doors, which would slide open along a track in the ground. These were tightly closed and well lit by the overhead lights, and he shrank back into the sheltering darkness.

Then he heard them, soft voices behind him. He pressed himself flat against the warehouse wall, hoping that he would be invisible in the shadows if he stayed completely still. Looking back across the yard, he saw two men had come in through the small gate, one leading the other to where the canal boats were tied up to the wharf. There were three barges waiting there, and the man leading went straight to the last. He jumped down onto the broad flat deck, and then beckoned the second man to follow. This he did, though with far less agility than the first. Indeed he almost fell, and it was only the first man grabbing him by the arm that stopped him from falling headlong into the water. Again there was the murmur of talk, but Kurt couldn't hear what was being said. Then the first man leaned down and twisted something before heaving open a hatch. He lowered the cover quietly to the deck and then both men disappeared below. Clearly, Kurt thought, they don't want to be heard, which means they shouldn't be here. In a matter of minutes, the first man reappeared on deck, quietly closing the hatch behind him. For a moment he paused, looking across at the warehouse, and Kurt thought with a jolt of fear that he'd been seen, but after another moment the man climbed up onto the wharf again and left the yard as silently as he had come, pausing only to lock the small gate with a large padlock. Within a minute he had disappeared into the darkness of the lane, leaving Kurt locked inside the boatyard.

For a long moment Kurt stared at the locked gate, and then ran swiftly over to it, wondering if he could climb over; but the main gate, he saw now, was topped with barbed wire. The yard was bounded by the warehouse on one side and walls too high to scale on the others. The only other way out was the canal. Kurt moved back into the shadows again. He didn't want to be caught there if the first man came back. For a long while he leaned against the warehouse wall considering what he should do. It was very cold, and he shivered. A thin mist was rising from the water. There was no escape that way. He would have to wait until morning and try and slip out of the gates when they were opened by the men coming to work in the yard. In the meantime, perhaps he could find shelter on one of the moored barges…and that was when the idea struck him.

Barges from here travelled east, down the canals and the

Danube, he'd seen them earlier in the day. They would pass through Passau, through Austria and beyond...and through Vienna. His mind teemed with questions as he considered the idea. Was it possible that he could stow away on one of these and travel safely down the river until he reached Vienna? How long did barges take to go from Regensburg to Vienna? Certainly days, but how many? Maybe he could stow away just until they had crossed the Austrian border. Surely he could remain hidden until then, Passau wasn't that far away, was it? What about food? What about water? What about calls of nature?

He edged his way round the yard, keeping to the shadows, until he came to the wharf on the far side. Here the lamps were brighter, shedding light onto three heavy barges that waited to make their journey east. They were long and low, and lay silent in the still waters of the canal. Although there was living accommodation aboard there were no lights showing from below. He looked at the one the men had entered, the last in the string. There was no light from that one either, though he knew that one man, at least, was inside. Perhaps that man was an illicit passenger as well. Perhaps he was trying to get out of Germany...another Jew on the run? Kurt moved to the next barge and stepped silently down onto her deck. He found a similar hatch, and, grasping the wheel as he had seen the man do, tried to open it, but the wheel wouldn't budge, and the hatch remained locked. Kurt moved softly aft along the deck, and came to the wheelhouse door, but that too was locked, as was the aft hatch. There was no way of getting inside this barge. He moved to the third one, but had no better luck there. The only barge that might carry him along the river was the one that already had a man hidden aboard.

Kurt thought of the soldiers at the station, of the Gestapo at the hotel, and of his desperate need to get to Ruth and the children, and made his decision. If the man in the last barge was on the run, then he was hardly likely to question the arrival of another fugitive. If he was hidden somewhere below decks, Kurt was determined to hide there too. He didn't know if the bargee would be aware that he had passengers hiding on one of his barges, but, even if he did, it was unlikely he would check on the man before taking his string of barges out onto the river. If he did, Kurt would try offering the man money to allow him to stay on board. If he regularly smuggled men across the border, he would almost certainly take the bribe...but whether he would betray him when he got there was another matter.

Kurt stepped quietly onto the deck of the last barge and crept towards the hatch. He hoped that if the man below had heard him he would think it was his friend coming back. He twisted the wheel, which turned easily, and pulled the hatch open. Darkness and silence greeted him, but he didn't wait, simply slid over the edge and dropped down into the space below pulling the hatch closed over his head. At first the darkness was complete, but as his eyes grew accustomed to it, he realised that faint light was coming in through two grimy portholes. He stood quite still, straining his ears for sounds of the man already hidden, but there were none. He had no idea where the man was, all he knew was that he was somewhere down here. As he gradually began to make out more of his surroundings, Kurt edged away from the hatch and ran his hands along the curved sides of the barge. He was in a cabin. It was very small, fitted out as living accommodation for crewmen. His fingers felt a folding table with a bench seat on each side. These had padded tops and clearly doubled as bunks. Above each was some sort of locker or cupboard, but there was little else and no sign of the man he had seen climb down earlier.

Kurt sat down on one of the benches and considered his position. He was out of sight, and he was out of the cold. What would happen when the crewman came and found him there he didn't know, but for now he could do no more, so he wrapped his coat more firmly around him and lay down on the bench bunk to wait for morning. He was almost asleep when he felt the bunk shaking beneath him, for a moment or two he lay between sleep and wakefulness, wondering what had woken him. Then he felt it again, the bunk was shaking. Kurt got up quickly, and as he did so the bunk was heaved up and from underneath it a man's voice spoke in a hoarse whisper. "Heinz, is that you? Heinz?"

Kurt didn't answer. He moved silently away from the bunk, so that he was standing below the hatch. The voice came again. "Heinz? Who's there?"

"Me," replied Kurt. "Who are you?"

"Did Heinz bring you?" A man's head appeared from below the bunk, which had opened like a window seat. "Who are you? Heinz didn't say there'd be anyone else." The voice was quavering now, uncertain and afraid.

"Didn't he?" Kurt was thinking fast. Clearly Heinz must be the other man, the one who had brought this man to the barge, and Heinz must be smuggling men across the border. "Well, he didn't tell me about you either."

The man hauled himself up from the bunk and peered in Kurt's direction. "He told me to hide in the bunk if I heard anyone coming," he said.

"He told me that, too," Kurt replied.

"It's *my* hiding place," the man snapped.

"I expect there's space under the other bunk," Kurt said and pulled up the padded seat to look. It was dark inside and he could see nothing, but he leaned forward and groped round with his hands. The space was empty. "There you are," he said reasonably. " A place for each of us." He kept his voice even, afraid that if he antagonised this man he would betray him to Heinz…whoever he was. "Just as long as…" He broke off suddenly as the sound of voices came from outside.

"Someone coming," hissed the man, and slipped back inside the bunk, pulling the top down over his head.

Kurt slithered into the space below the other bunk and just had time to close it before the hatch above opened and someone dropped down into the little cabin. Kurt heard a soft tap on the other bunk and an answering tap from the man inside, then the scrambling of feet as whoever it was clambered back up on deck, and the thud of the hatch cover coming down.

There was more shouting from outside, and then Kurt felt the barge lurch forward as the towline tightened and they began to move along the canal. It was smooth enough at first as they moved slowly along the canal, but the motion changed abruptly as they joined the surge of the river, and the barge began swinging and rolling in the swirl of the Danube, before settling to a more even motion.

It was impossible to remain crammed into the tiny space below the bunk, and as soon as he realised that they were underway, Kurt heaved himself upward, lifting the bunk and hauling himself out. He sat on the edge, with the top still raised so that he could dive for cover again if they heard footsteps approaching on the deck. It was still dark outside, but occasional lights from the shore illuminated the cabin briefly, and he took stock of his surroundings. He took off his coat, and, rolling it carefully, stowed it deep in the hiding place under the bunk. It was bulky and might hinder him getting in and out swiftly if the need arose.

The other man also pulled himself out, and as a light caught his face, Kurt knew he had guessed correctly. His companion peered across at him and demanded, "Who are you?"

"I might ask the same of you," Kurt replied, but he already knew. "Are you just going across the border, or all the way to Vienna?"

"What's that to you?" snapped the man.

"Nothing, but once we're out of Germany, we may not have to hide."

"You're a Jew!" stated the man, defiantly.

"So are you," answered Kurt. "So we both need to get out. If one of us is caught, we both shall be."

The man did not reply. He stared across at Kurt, trying to see his face in the passing lights. "Heinz said to stay hidden till he came for me," he said, "but I hate it in there."

"We should hear them coming in time," Kurt said. "I'm not staying in there all the time either. Just keep away from the portholes and listen out for footsteps."

As daylight crept into the sky, they sat in silence, each deep in his own thoughts. When he could see properly, Kurt inspected the space under the bunk. It was about six feet long and two feet deep, and was clearly storage space for the crew who lived aboard the barge. Surely only two men could live on each barge, simply there to keep the boat in line with the others in the string as they were towed down the Danube, a river busy with steamers, boats and barges.

It was full daylight before they heard the footsteps approaching the hatch again. Both men were under the bunks in a trice, the tops lowered, holding their breath. Kurt could hear his heart pounding and wondered if the person who had slipped down into the cabin could hear it too. Then he heard what he'd been dreading. Whoever it was had opened the other bunk and was speaking to the man inside.

Within moments the top of the bunk was jerked open and Kurt was staring up into the furious face of the bargee.

"Ho yes!" growled the man. "And what have we 'ere then? Who the 'ell are you? And what are you doing 'ere?"

"He said you told him to come here, Heinz!" squeaked the other man.

"Shut up, Max," snapped Heinz.

Kurt started to get out of the hiding place but a knife appeared from nowhere in the man's hand. He was gripping it tightly, caressing the wicked blade with his thumb and pointing it straight at Kurt's throat.

"No, no," he said, "you stay put where you are, mate. I think you're a Gestapo spy."

Kurt gave a bitter laugh. "Gestapo! You couldn't be more wrong! Ask your friend Max."

"Max doesn't know who you are!"

"No, he doesn't know who I am, but he knows what I am!"

"Another dirty Jew," said Max flatly. "You've got two for the price of one."

Heinz leered at them. "No I bloody 'aven't," he said. "I've two for the price of two...maybe." He gave a chuckle. "Or none for the price of two. Depends if you've got any money, don't it?" He nodded meaningfully at Kurt.

"How much do you want?" asked Kurt, his brain racing.

"All you've got," answered Heinz cheerfully. "And if it's not enough, well, our tug captain don't like Jews much. If I tell 'im I found you two stowed away on my barge, well I reckon he'll 'and you over at Passau. We'll be there late this evening. There's Gestapo there."

Max gave a wail. "But I've paid you, Heinz, you can't betray me now!"

Heinz did not reply, simply gave a wolfish grin and turned his attention to Kurt. "So 'ow much can you pay for a safe passage into Austria?"

"Let me up and I'll give you the money," Kurt said. "I can pay."

"First of all, mate, tell me what made you get on this barge, eh? Who told you where to come?"

"No one told me," answered Kurt. "I saw you. I was in the boatyard, and I saw you bring him," he jerked a thumb at Max, "and leave him on board."

"And what was you doin' in the yard, then?" demanded Heinz suspiciously.

"Looking for somewhere to sleep the night. The gate was open, I thought maybe the warehouse was too."

Heinz looked at him, considering his answer, then he gave a curt nod, accepting it. "Let's see the colour of your money then."

The knife, which up till now hadn't wavered, was withdrawn but not sheathed, and Kurt was able to scramble out of the hiding place.

"Right, let's see what you've got," said Heinz. "Slow, now!" he added as Kurt reached into his jacket pocket and withdrew a small roll of marks. Heinz snatched the money and counted it quickly. Kurt watched him, praying Heinz would think it enough. He glanced across at Max, who sat white-knuckled, watching. Surely the man would decide that it was enough, and not turn them in. Now he'd been amply paid for both.

"So, across the border, then. No further," said Heinz, pocketing the roll of notes. "There's food and water in that locker," he pointed at the locker above Kurt's head. "You'll have to share. Heads in there." He opened a small door that Kurt had assumed was another locker to reveal a tiny space with a lavatory bowl. "Now," he went on, closing the door again. "Stay below and leave these drawn." He pulled some flimsy curtains across the portholes. "Stay away from the portholes, specially when we're going through a lock. You should be safe enough down here until we get to Passau, but if I bang on the hatch, get straight into them bunks and stay there until I say you can come out again. You'll have to get into them later anyway...for the border, but I'll warn you if there's any danger before that...and if you're caught I don't know nothing about you, right?"

The rest of the day they moved slowly along the waterway, the barge obediently following the tug. There was no bang on the hatch cover and they were able to sit at the cabin table. They shared a meal of very stale bread and some hard yellow cheese, but otherwise Max and Kurt spoke little. They had been thrown together by circumstance, but neither wanted to know more about the other. Knowledge could be dangerous, and each had withdrawn into his own thoughts. They simply sat in the stuffy cabin, the hatch closed, and waited.

It was early evening when Heinz opened the hatch and

dropped down into the cabin. "We'll be at Passau soon, and then it will be on over the border. Usually they don't bother much with us, but in case they decide to come aboard this time, you get in them lockers."

"What? Already?" Max sounded panicky.

"Now."

"But how long for?" asked Max, his voice shaking.

"Till I come and tell you you can come out again," snapped Heinz. "Now, get in there, the both of you."

Kurt slithered into the hiding place, and to his horror heard Heinz slide the catch closed. He was locked into the space under the bunk, and there was no escape. He heard a cry from Max as he realised what Heinz was doing.

"Shut up!" growled Heinz. "I'll be back to let you out when it's safe and not before." Kurt heard him clambering up through the hatch and then the thud of the cover dropping back into place. He could hear Max whimpering, and fought to keep his own panic at bay. The space was tiny, and although he soon realised that air holes had been drilled in the corners, he still felt as if he were suffocating. He drew deep, slow breaths, forcing himself to believe that air was coming in from the outside. As he gradually became calmer, it struck him that Heinz must regularly smuggle people out of Germany like this. The hiding place was prepared, with air holes drilled; the food, though dry and unappetising, was stashed in the locker, the lavatory provided. Others must have escaped this way before without being caught. Heinz must have a way of getting them off the barge once they were over the border. They'd had to trust him...because continuing to trust him was their only option.

"Be quiet, Max!" Kurt hissed, as Max continued to

whimper. "Someone will hear you. There's air, just breathe."

"It's all right for you," moaned Max, "but I'm claustrophobic."

Anyone would be, thought Kurt, crammed into this wooden box, it's like a coffin, and at that thought he had to begin his own deep breathing again to calm his taut nerves.

Gradually Max's whimpers subsided and the cabin was quiet. Kurt strained his ears to see if he could hear what was going on outside. He could hear the water slapping against the hull of the barge, and felt a change of motion as the river took hold of the barge on the end of its towline. Something was happening, but it was impossible to tell what. From outside came the sound of a horn, and loud voices shouting, and then the barge jolted sideways.

"What do you think is happening?" whispered Max. "Are we stopping?"

"I don't know," Kurt answered softly. "Maybe."

"I want to get out of here." Max's voice held a note of hysteria. "We're trapped, and we don't know what's going on!"

Kurt felt the same panic welling up in him. Turning awkwardly in the confined space, he managed to press upward on the roof of his prison. It did not move. He tensed his muscles and pushed harder, but to no avail. The top would not budge.

"What are you doing?" cried Max from the other bunk. "Can you get out?"

"No, at least not yet. Can you? Try and push up the lid."

While he continued to struggle against the top of his own prison, Kurt could hear Max doing the same with his.

"It's no good," Max cried. "He locked it. I can't shift it."

"Nor can I," said Kurt.

He heard Max begin to mutter, and, straining his ears,

Kurt realised that he was speaking in Hebrew; a continuous murmur in Hebrew. He was praying, repeating over and over again, "Hear, O Israel, the Lord our God, the Lord is one." Kurt, giving up on his efforts to force his way out of the bunk, lay still, listening to the words; but even as he did so, he found himself wondering if there was any point. He had prayed to his God every day of his life, even in Dachau and while he was on the run, but it seemed to him that God was no longer listening... if he was there at all. How could God ignore the prayers and pleas of his people and allow the persecution that was their lot now? How could God allow his children to be hounded from place to place, little children who had done nothing wrong? Kurt wanted to shout at God... to make him listen. But now, he continued to pray in a repetitive mantra: "Lord, keep my family safe."

The hatch opened with a crash and there was a thud as Heinz dropped down into the cabin. Suddenly the bunks were opened and the two men inside stared up in terror.

"We're being pulled over," growled Heinz. "The place is alive with soldiers. Out with you! You're on your own."

"What!" shrieked Max.

"Shut up!" roared Heinz. "Didn't you hear what I said? Place is crawling with soldiers. Now get out, or I'll say I found you stowaways and hand you over."

Kurt clambered out of the bunk, pulling his coat on.

"We'll be moored alongside another barge train in a minute," said Heinz. "Then, over the side with you and across to the quay. It's dark, you should make it."

He hustled the two men up onto the deck. Night had fallen, but the lights along the shore showed them another barge train already lying alongside the wharf. There was no sign of the bargees, but dim lights showed through some of the cabin portholes.

"When I tell you, you jump," ordered Heinz. "If you're quick you'll be across the next barge before they know you're there, then up onto the dock."

"But how?" began Kurt.

"There's ladders along the wall. Up one of those. Ready?"

They were closing in slowly on the moored barge train, and as they drifted alongside Kurt could see down onto the deck of the last one. It was slightly lower than the barge he was on, and the only way to reach it was to jump. The two barges bumped gently together.

"Now!" hissed Heinz.

Not allowing himself time to think, Kurt launched himself onto the deck of the other barge, hearing as he did so Max wailing, "I can't! I can't jump that far." Kurt landed awkwardly, and felt pain in his ankle, but he scrambled to his feet and moved softly across the deck, the barge rocking gently beneath him. He strained his eyes looking for one of the iron ladders clamped to the stone wall of the wharf, reaching to the quayside above. There was one several yards to his left, but as he crept along the deck, the moored barge rocked, bumping against the harbour wall, as it was once again nudged by the incoming barge. Behind him there was a sudden shrill scream and then a splash. Kurt spun round and saw the burly shape of Heinz peering over the barge's rail, before he turned and disappeared into the darkness. The barges bumped together yet again, and Kurt realised, with sudden horror, what Heinz had done. Max had not jumped when told to, so Heinz had pushed him. He had fallen between the two great barges and was either struggling in the water below their hulls, or had been crushed between them. Either way Heinz had left him to die. Kurt took a step back the way he'd come, but froze as a hatch opened and a man stuck his head out.

"Hey!" he called. "What's going on?"

There was no reply to his question, and he climbed up onto the deck as if to investigate further. The two barges continued to bump gently as they settled together in the water, and the man went across to look at the newly arrived barge beside his own. Kurt turned and crept away towards the ladder he had seen in the light from the quay. He reached it and grasped its lower rungs. He was just beginning to climb up when he heard a cry from the deck. "Hey! There's a man in the water here. Get a boat hook. Quick!"

Kurt didn't wait to hear more, but scrambled up the ladder onto the dock. There were people around, but no one paid any attention to a bargee climbing up from a moored barge, and Kurt was able to move away unchallenged. He walked quickly from the quayside towards the dock gates. They were open, but standing outside them in a pool of light cast from an overhead lamp was a uniformed guard. Kurt ducked back into the shadows while he considered what to do. Would he be challenged leaving the docks or was the guard only interested in people coming into the dockyard? Boldness was his best option, he decided, and he was about to stride purposefully forward when there was a shout from the moored barges below. The guard moved inside the gate, pausing to listen, and the shout came again.

"Hey, anybody up there? Hey, we need help!"

The guard hurried to the edge of the dock and peered down to see what was going on.

"There's a dead man down here!" called the voice. "We

"need help to get him up on the quay."

"Who is it?" called the guard, leaning over the wall to get a better look.

"How should I know?" called the man below. "We found him in the water. Are you going to help or not?"

Kurt didn't wait to hear the answer, but slipped silently out of the unguarded gate into the street beyond.

Once in the town, he found to his horror that Heinz had been right. Even at this hour, there were soldiers marching down the streets. There was the roar of motorised transports, lorries filled with troops, staff cars flying swastika pennants and the rumble of tanks. Townspeople were standing at the side of the road watching in awe as regiments of the German army passed by, heading for the Austrian border. There were some cheers from above him, and Kurt, who had joined the bystanders, looked up to see people in their windows waving to the troops.

"It's the Anschluss," said someone behind him. "Hitler has done it! He's really done it! We shall all be united with our German brothers across the border!"

"Will they fight?" asked a nervous voice.

"Why would they fight?" demanded the first voice scornfully. "Austria will welcome them. We shall all be part of the great German Empire! Heil Hitler!"

"Are you sure that's what's happening?" asked a third voice.

"Quite sure," asserted the first voice. "I heard it from my sister-in-law's husband. The troops are going to cross the border during the night."

"You mean they're invading Austria?"

"It's not an invasion," said the first man, "they are simply going in to help the Austrians deal, once and for all, with the Communists and the Jews that have been causing all the trouble."

"How does your sister-in-law's husband know all this?" asked someone else.

"Because, he was home on leave, but has been recalled to his regiment for duty."

"Doesn't mean they're going to invade Austria," pointed out a doubter.

"Well, it does," insisted the man. "They were told to be ready to cross the border during the night."

"Pretty poor security if people like you know all about it," remarked another man.

"We don't need security," replied the first man. "There won't be any resistance. Why would there be? The Austrians will welcome our troops...and the Führer when he goes to Vienna."

Kurt slipped away from the group before he was noticed, but his heart was pounding. Hitler was going to invade Austria, tonight, and even if the Austrians put up some resistance, they wouldn't have a hope against the might of the German army. Paul Schiller had been right, overnight Austria was going to become a vassal state to Germany, and Kurt's beloved family would be trapped in Vienna. Despair flooded through him. Even if he were able to slip across the border into Austria, which would be almost impossible in the circumstances, then he would be trapped as well. Paul had been right; right about the Anschluss and right in telling Kurt he would be far better able to help his family as a free agent in a free country.

He thought of the two names Paul had given him, Hans Dietrich in Hamburg and James Daniel in London. Perhaps he would have to call on them after all.

As the night lengthened, Kurt sat quietly in the porch of

a church, huddled in a corner, his mind warring with his heart, but as day broke and streaked the eastern sky with golden fire, he made his way into the town to look for the station...and to buy another ticket to Hamburg.

Twelve

"Sieg Heil! Sieg Heil! Sieg Heil!" The hundred thousand voices swelled to a roaring chorus, echoing round the vastness of the square, rebounding from the ancient buildings that surrounded it. "Sieg Heil! Sieg Heil! Sieg Heil!"

The crowds were packed into the Heldenplatz, crushed together, an amorphous mass of humanity, yet moving with a single purpose. Everyday people wearing everyday clothes, workmen in overalls, men in smart suits, women in overcoats pulled close about them against the chill in the spring air, people in hats of all descriptions pulled down over ears or perched jauntily on heads; gloved hands, ungloved hands, cracked, work-reddened hands, raised as one in their devotion to their new leader. "Sieg Heil! Sieg Heil! Sieg Heil!" Flags and banners on long poles waved above the crowd, each with its swastika, stark black within its white circle, emblazoned on a red ground. Uniforms everywhere, soldiers, drawn up in ranks before the Hofburg, police, their swastika armbands mirroring the floating banners.

Ruth looked down on the sea of faces from her perch on the plinth of the Prince Eugen statue. All were raised to salute the man in uniform on the balcony of the Hofburg, eyes aglow with the fervour of their welcome. Unwillingly she raised her own eyes to the small man who stood above billowing Nazi banners, addressing the crowd packed into the square below him. As he began to speak a hush fell over the huge square, heads craned forward to see him, hands shading eyes against the morning sunshine, but as his voice began to rise, so the excitement began to build within the crowd until, as he reached a crescendo, it burst forth. "Sieg Heil! Sieg Heil! Sieg Heil!" So great was his charisma that for a split second Ruth almost raised her own arm, her own voice, and almost fell from her place on the great statue.

"Careful, love," admonished a voice beside her, and a hand grasped her arm to stop her falling.

"Thank you!" she gasped, and looked up into the face of the young man balanced precariously on the plinth beside her. She regained her hold on one of the bronze carved wreaths beside her, clutching it firmly in both hands, afraid she might truly fall and be crushed in the crowd.

The young man smiled and said something else, but his words were drowned in the rising crescendo of Sieg Heils. She smiled back awkwardly at him and then appeared to turn her attention back to the Führer, whose voice now boomed out over the crowd, which fell silent once more, listening to him with rapt attention.

What am I doing here? Ruth thought. What is a Jew doing at a Hitler rally? What would that young man have thought if he'd realised I'm a Jew? Perhaps he's a Jew, too.

She stole another glance at him. His attention was on Hitler, his eyes filled with fervent delight. No, he was no Jew! No Jew would welcome Hitler to his city like that...unless he didn't want to be recognised. Like I don't want to be recognised. Arms were once more raised in salute, but Ruth continued to cling on to the wreath with both hands. No salute from her, but it was clear to anyone who might wonder why she could not. Who was to wonder? Everyone round her was carried away on a tide of euphoria, which had been building ever since the declaration of the Anschluss two days earlier. If Ruth had realised how the arrival of Hitler would take the city she would never have left home that morning, never ventured out into streets crammed with people ecstatic in their welcome for their new leader.

"I'm going to leave very early, this morning," Ruth had told her mother. "I think there'll be a lot of people out and about in the city today."

"I wish you wouldn't go at all," said Helga. "It could be dangerous."

"I'll be all right." Ruth tried to sound reassuring, though she, too, wished she didn't have to go. "You know I can't afford to lose this job, Mother." She gave her mother a quick hug. "Don't let the children out, though. No school for the girls today. You can give them some homework here, and then we'll see how things are later in the week."

She closed the front door of the flat and hurried down the flight of stairs that led to the courtyard below. Although it was still early, there were plenty of people about, and as Ruth made her way through the streets more and more flooded out of their homes to join the crowds. Ruth found herself being gathered into the stream of people, a surging floodtide, all heading the same way. At first Ruth allowed herself to be carried along, it was her direction too; but when she wanted to turn off and cut through the back streets to the shop where she worked, she found she couldn't. She was being swept along by an unrelenting tide of people, all excited, shouting, chanting, laughing. Overnight, banners had appeared, hanging from windows, draped down the fronts of buildings, jagged black swastikas proclaiming a welcome...a welcome for Adolf Hitler himself. Rumour had it that he was already in Vienna. He had travelled from Linz and was now staying, it was said, at the Imperial Hotel. Many of the people carried banners too, homemade flags to welcome the Germans to Vienna.

The excited tide of people continued to grow, and Ruth could not escape from it. She was pushed and shoved from every side, swept along inexorably. Once she stumbled, and someone grabbed her arm crying out, "Steady!" and then was gone again, swirled away in the crowd. Ruth allowed herself to be carried along too; there was no alternative, and after a while she found herself part of a seething mass of people, standing, swaying, pushing, surging to and fro, all packed into the Heldenplatz, all focussed on the Hofburg at the far end. More and more people poured into the square, crushing those already there, pushing them forwards, shoving them sideways, and all the time the excitement continued to grow, mounting to fever pitch when at last the Führer appeared on the balustraded balcony of the Hofburg. Immediately the crowd surged forward again, and Ruth found herself crushed against the plinth of the statue of heroic Prince Eugen.

"Here, lady, up here!"

Ruth looked up and saw that several people had already scrambled clear of the swarming crowd and were perched on the statue, some standing on the plinth, others, having climbed higher, actually clinging to the huge horse. A hand reached down to her and, grasping it, Ruth found herself hauled up from the crowd and onto a narrow ledge that ran round the base of the huge statue.

"Hold on tight!" ordered the young man who had pulled her up. "If you fall off here you'll be trampled to death." Ruth looked down fearfully and saw that he was right. She grabbed hold of a piece of the moulded edge above her, gripping it with both hands.

The young man grinned. "Good view from up here," he called. "Look at all those people!"

Ruth had looked and was astonished at the ocean of humanity that surrounded her. She looked at it again now, and wondered if she would ever get away from such a crowd. Men and women cheering, children hoisted on shoulders, old men waving walking sticks in the air, young men tossing their hats for joy…and all for Adolf Hitler, whose armies had marched, unopposed, into Austria, and who now stood, addressing a euphoric crowd, from the seat of the ancient Hapsburg Empire.

How has it all come to this? Ruth thought wildly. How can Hitler simply arrive and take over the country and proclaim it as the homecoming of Austria into the German Reich? How can all these people, Austrians not Germans, be here, cheering him? Saluting him? "Sieg Heil! Sieg Heil! Sieg Heil!"

Ruth had heard the announcement of the Anschluss three days earlier. She had been invited to join Edith, her family and parents-in-law for the family Shabbes dinner, and afterwards they had gathered round the Bernsteins' wireless to listen to Kurt Schuschnigg's final broadcast as Chancellor. They listened in complete silence, aghast, unable to believe what they were hearing.

"So I take leave of the Austrian people with a German

word of farewell uttered from the depth of my heart: God protect Austria!"

The sonorous voice boomed from the wireless that stood on a table in the corner of the room, but it was a voice edged with emotion. Kurt Schuschnigg, the Austrian chancellor, had done all he could to keep the Germans at bay, but, in spite of a brave rearguard action, he had only put off the time when Hitler would put his claim to Austria to the test. Now Schuschnigg had made his final speech, his farewell to an independent Austria, ending with the fervent prayer: "God protect Austria".

"Well, if God doesn't, no one else will!" David Bernstein said bitterly. He leaned over and switched the wireless off with a snap. "Schuschnigg has sold out to the Nazis."

For a moment there was silence as the family who had been listening tried to take in what they had heard, then Grandfather Friedrich shook his head, and sighed.

"That's it," he said. "We must thank God that at least Berta is safely out of the country."

"Hush, Friedrich," said his wife Marta, laying a finger to her lips and tilting her head towards the children who were sitting round the supper table. Don't frighten the children, her expression said, but her grandson, Paul, who had just turned fifteen, looked across at her and he saw the fear in her eyes as well.

"What's going to happen?" asked Naomi. "What was Herr Schuschnigg saying? Mutti, what was he saying?"

Edith, her mother, shushed her gently. She hardly ever spoke when in the presence of her parents-in-law unless directly addressed. She was in awe of her mother-in-law, so capable and strong, and she was just plain terrified of her father-in-law. "Nothing, darling," she murmured. "He was just talking to the grown-ups." But although she was only nine, Naomi sensed the atmosphere in the room, and, slipping down from her chair, went over to her mother and tried to climb up on her knee.

Her father got to his feet and paced the room. "He's given in," he said, bitterly. "He's given in to Hitler. Now there'll be no plebiscite on Monday. The Germans will be here by then, and Hitler will have won."

"Time you were in bed, young lady," Naomi's grandmother said, determined that there should be no more of such talk in front of the little girl. She reached for the hand bell on the table at her side and rang it loudly. Almost at once, Maria, the maid, came into the room. She responded so quickly that Paul wondered if she had been listening to the wireless broadcast through the door. He wouldn't have been surprised if she had. He'd noticed before that these days Maria always seemed to be close by, listening.

However, his grandmother didn't seem to notice. All she said as Maria came into the room was, "Ah, Maria, please take Miss Naomi up to bed," adding as she saw that Naomi was about to protest, "your mother will come up to tuck you in, in a little while. Say goodnight to Opa and Papa and then off you go with Maria, like a good girl."

Naomi did as she was told, saying goodnight to each of them in turn. When she reached her grandfather she reached up and hugged his neck, whispering in his ear as she did so, "Opa, what's a pleb...pleb thing?"

Friedrich Bernstein, who had been completely captivated by his granddaughter from the moment he had first held her, hugged her to him and smiled down. "Nothing for you to worry your head about, dumpling. I'll tell you all about it in the morning."

Naomi reluctantly allowed Maria to lead her away, and as the door closed behind her, Oma spoke quite sharply. "There was no need to frighten the child, David," she said.

"She'll know what's happening soon enough," replied her son. "We're all going to have to face up to what this Anschluss means. Austria has become a German province, that's what it means. We're now part of Germany, and we all know what is happening to the Jews in Germany."

"Poor Ruth!" cried Edith, her hand flying to her mouth in alarm. "What will you do now?"

"The same as before!" Ruth replied curtly. "Keep my head down and pray...the same as you'll have to."

"Us?" Edith sounded surprised.

"Perhaps our own people won't behave towards us as the Germans have been doing to their Jews," suggested her mother-in-law. "I mean, we don't know things are going to change here too."

"Yes, we do," David said quietly. "Hitler will come here and when he does, everyone will be falling over themselves to show him how dedicated they are to the Nazi line."

"But the Nazis were banned!" protested Edith. "Only in January. Why has the chancellor given in?"

"You really should try and keep up to date, Edith," said her husband sharply. "They were reinstated weeks ago."

"Well, I don't understand politics," wailed Edith. "Why did the chancellor do that?"

"I imagine he had no choice," replied David, wearily. "How does anyone stand up to a man like Hitler?"

"He's not a man, he's an animal," asserted Marta.

"Maybe," David agreed, "but now he's got his hands on Austria he'll be even more difficult to stop."

"But what about the plebiscite on Monday?" asked Edith.

"There won't be one!" answered David. He was pacing the room now, unable to still his nervous energy. "What is the point of asking people if they want to be part of the German Empire, when the Germans are already here?"

"But they aren't here...not yet."

"They will be...in a few hours."

"Hours?" Friedrich stared at him. "Surely it will take them longer than that."

"Father, this has been very carefully orchestrated. Hitler had to move before the plebiscite, in case Austria rejected him on Monday. I'll bet his troops are already across the border, and he'll be here himself in the next few hours.

"Is there going to be a war?"

His parents and grandparents looked at Paul in surprise. They had almost forgotten he was in the room.

"That depends on how the rest of the world reacts, and the English in particular," replied his father. "They don't want a war, not after the last one. Hitler knows that. He'll promise not to go any further, and they'll probably let him get away with it."

"And will he go any further?" asked Paul.

"Almost certainly. He's power crazy."

"Well, there's nothing we can do about it now," remarked Marta, rising from her chair. "We should go up and say good-night to Naomi, Edith."

Ruth also got to her feet. "I must go home, too," she said. "And tell Mother what has happened. She won't have heard yet."

Edith, ever obedient to her mother-in-law's wishes, stood up. "I'll see you out, Ruth, and then I think I'll read in bed, David. Goodnight, Opa." Edith had always addressed her parents-in-law as Herr and Frau Bernstein until the children had arrived, and then she, too, had begun to use "Oma" and "Opa". It had made them seem a little less frightening.

"You should go up, too, Paul," she added, and shepherded her son out of the room.

At the front door, when Ruth kissed her sister on the cheek, Edith said, "Will everything change very much, do you think?"

Ruth sighed at Edith's naivety. "I think it will," she replied. "I think you should be prepared."

But even Ruth hadn't been prepared for the thousands and thousands of people flocking to the Heldenplatz to welcome Adolf Hitler. She had had no illusions either. When she'd got home that evening, she told Helga about the chancellor's broadcast, repeating the solemn pronouncement, "God protect Austria." She looked across at her mother and said, "It's going to happen again, isn't it, Mother? Just when we thought we were safe."

Helga sat, pale-faced, in her chair. "The Anschluss may have been agreed," she said wearily, "but it's unlikely that anything will happen for a while. We'll just have to keep going as we have been and hope for the best."

When Vienna awoke the next morning, it was to the news that German troops had crossed the border and were already on their way to the city. A new chancellor, Dr Arthur Seyss-Inquart, an ally of the Nazis, had, on Schuschnigg's resignation, immediately assumed office, announcing, "Any opposition to the German army, should it enter Austria, is completely out of the question." He lost no time in being sworn in, and in naming his ministers…all of whom were Nazis.

As the day wore on, everyone listened to the wireless, to hear the latest news of what was happening. Ruth went to work as usual, and as she crossed the city, walking along the now-familiar streets, she could feel the difference in the atmosphere. Posters advertising the abandoned plebiscite for Monday, exhorting people to vote yes to an independent Austria, were still on walls and billboards, but many had been defaced. Austria's chance to say no to Hitler had been lost. The streets were busy. People had come out of their homes, full of the news. There was an air of suppressed excitement as they gathered on street corners, talking, passing on news. Ruth heard snippets of their excited chatter as she hurried by. One tall man, holding forth to his friends just outside the haberdashery, was saying:

"General Himmler, you know of the SS? Well, he landed here, in Vienna this morning. Now we'll get some action!"

Ruth froze. Could it be true? Could the monster, Himmler, architect of the terrifying SS, really be here already? She wanted to ask the man how he knew. If he was certain. But the smile of delight on his face as he passed on his piece of news made her move on, before he noticed her standing and listening to him. He was clearly a man who welcomed the Germans. He was not the only one. His words were greeted with a cheer. Ruth kept her head down and went into the shop.

Not the only one! Ruth thought now as she clung to the statue above the seething crowd. Was there an Austrian who was *not* here, crammed into the Heldenplatz, roaring his support? "Sieg Heil! Sieg Heil! Sieg Heil!"

Eventually the harangue from the balcony came to an

end and, when the band played "Deutschland, Deutschland, über Alles", the words were taken up by 200,000 voices. Tanks and armoured cars rolled past the square, squadrons of cavalry clattered by, pennants and standards flapping in the breeze; columns of soldiers goose-stepped their way past the teeming crowd who stood, some madly cheering, others with arms raised in the rigid Nazi salute. The Germans had arrived and were here to stay, and let no one doubt the might of their armies. High above in the clear blue of the March sky, Luftwaffe planes flew past in close formation; Germany was master of the Austrian skies. Germany would be the master of Europe.

Ruth watched from her perch on the statue, unable to get down, unable to escape and slip away to the safety of her home. Trapped in the middle of the mass rally, she had to remain where she was until the parades were over and the crowd began to disperse. The young man who had hauled her up now made a space beside him, so that although she still clung on to the statue she was able to lean against its base.

"I think we'll be here for some time," he said, "so we may as well try and get more comfortable."

Ruth smiled and thanked him. He held out his hand and said, "My name is Peter Walder."

"Peter," she repeated. "My son's name."

Peter grinned at her. "Good choice!" he said. "And you are?"

"Helga," Ruth said after a moment's hesitation, "Helga Heber." In that split second of hesitation, she decided not to use her own, Jewish-sounding name. Her mother's more Aryan name was safer. They shook hands, each of them hanging on to the statue with the other hand.

"Isn't he amazing?" Peter demanded, his eyes still glowing

with the excitement of the past hour. "Isn't he just amazing?"

"Unbelievable," Ruth agreed truthfully.

"What a leader! What a man to follow! And an Austrian! Can you believe it? An Austrian is the most powerful man in Europe?"

"Unbelievable," Ruth murmured again.

"With the Führer leading us, we Germans from all over Europe will be united!" Peter asserted. "Won't that be wonderful? All Germans equal citizens!"

"That would be a dream come true," Ruth said carefully.

"Your Peter will grow up in a brand-new world," Peter enthused. "He will be able to take his rightful place in the world! And we were here to see the start of it, you and I! Imagine! If I'd gone to my lecture at the university today as I should have done, I'd have missed all this!"

"What are you studying?" asked Ruth, anxious to turn the conversation away from the scene before her.

"Law," he replied. "I'm nearly qualified as a lawyer."

The parades continued around the square, the people continued to cheer, but gradually Ruth could make out a thinning in the ranks, and said, "I must try and get home. My . . . Peter will be wondering where I've got to."

"You should have brought him with you," Peter said. "This is an historic day! What did the Führer say? 'Before the face of history . . .' Today is the day in Austrian history that will never be forgotten."

Ruth managed a smile. "I'm sure you're right, Peter. Never forgotten."

He helped her to slip down from the statue, and she eased her way quickly into the crowds, anxious to get away from the Heldenplatz as fast as she possibly could. Once she glanced back. She could see Peter Walder still standing on the statue. He had climbed higher and now stood, one arm round the horse's leg, the other waving, shouting in furious joy as the mob saluted their beloved Führer yet again.

"Sieg Heil! Sieg Heil! Sieg Heil!"

God help us, Ruth thought as she threaded her way through the masses round her, God help us if all the young Austrians think as he does...and he's going to be a lawyer!

Once she was clear of the square and the surrounding streets, Ruth almost ran back to the apartment. What she had seen this day had made her realise just what she and all the other Jews in Vienna were up against, and it absolutely terrified her.

She thought of Kurt. It had been so wonderful to hear his voice on the phone. New hope had surged through her. She'd walked back to the flat after his call, her feet scarcely touching the ground. He was coming to her, to be with her and the children again, a proper family. She didn't tell the children, or even Helga, she simply hugged the secret of his return to herself. She could almost feel his body against hers. For that one night, Ruth had been overflowing with happiness, her eyes alight with the joy of her secret. The next evening all her hopes had been dashed. Germany had grabbed Austria, dragging it into the new and ever-expanding German Empire. The Nazis had arrived, joining with those already carefully placed in the Austrian government. The Nazis had swept into power, backed by the German army that had marched across the border. Ruth and her family were no safer now than they had been in Kirnheim or Munich.

Thirteen

The evening of the rally in the Heldenplatz, David went to see his father. His parents were surprised to see him, but when he had drunk a cup of coffee with his mother, he said that he needed a word with his father, if she would excuse them.

Marta Bernstein, who was quite used to the men retiring to Friedrich's study for a brandy, agreed readily enough and returned to her embroidery.

"Well, David? What's this all about?" Friedrich dropped into his favourite chair in front of the fire. His study was his refuge, the place where he was never allowed to be disturbed by the rest of the household, and the fire was always made up and the room warm.

David poured them each a generous brandy and carried one of the glasses over to his father. Taking the other to a chair across the fire from him, he raised his glass, looking at the flames through the amber spirit.

"I'll tell you what it's about," he said. "After what has happened today..."

"What has happened today?"

"This welcoming rally for Hitler in the Heldenplatz...I think we should seriously consider leaving."

"Leaving?" Friedrich looked up in surprise. "Leaving Vienna?"

"Not leaving Vienna," David said patiently. "I mean leaving Austria. You said yourself that it was a good thing Berta wasn't here, that she was safely in England. Perhaps we should be getting the other children out, too." He took a sip of his brandy, and then went on, "Ruth came to see me earlier this evening."

"Ruth? And what has she to say to anything?"

"She was in the Heldenplatz this morning and…"

"More fool her!"

"Father, will you listen, please! I know you don't think much of Edith's family, but over the last few weeks I've grown to have a great deal of respect for Ruth."

He thought again of the conversation he had had with his sister-in-law earlier in the evening. She had arrived at the house, and asked Anna if David was in. He had said he would call Edith, but Ruth had stopped him.

"No, David, don't call Edith yet. It's you I need to talk to."

"I see. Well, I suppose you'd better come into my study then." He had led her into the comfortable room off the hall where he, like his father, found refuge from his family. Despite the fact that spring was definitely in the air, there was a fire burning brightly in the grate, and Ruth went eagerly to warm her hands.

David closed the door behind them. She's going to ask me for another loan, he thought sourly. He gave her a tight smile and said, "Well now, Ruth, what can I do for you?"

"Do for me?" Ruth echoed. "Nothing, David. I've not come to ask you for a favour, I've come to tell you what I saw today and to warn you…"

"Warn me? Warn me about what?" David waved her to a chair. "You'd better sit down and tell me what this is all about."

Ruth sat, and still holding her hands out to the warmth of the fire, told him what had happened to her that morning.

"What I've come to tell you, David, is that you and Edith and the children should get out while you can. Your parents, too. You've got enough money to go anywhere in the world. You should leave Austria while you still can."

"I see. Well, thank you for that bit of advice, Ruth," David replied coolly. "I'll bear it in mind."

"Look, David," Ruth didn't trouble to hide her irritation at his tone, "I know you aren't particularly fond of any of Edith's family, but like it or not we are here. We've escaped from the Nazis once, we've lived through what they do to Jews. What I saw today terrified me. All Austria was welcoming Hitler, and what the Nazis have been doing in Germany is going to happen here. I tell you this, David, if *I* could afford to get my family away from Vienna, out of Austria, I would do it. I would do it tomorrow." She got to her feet then, and walked to the door. "Life is going to change out of all recognition from now. You're in a position to do something, if you act fast. That's all I came to say. Good afternoon."

She had left the room closing the door softly behind her, leaving David staring after her. He heard voices in the hall, Edith greeting Ruth with surprise, not knowing she was in the house, and then there was the sound of the front door closing. David moved to the window and saw Ruth striding off down the street, her coat held closely about her against the chill in the wind. He had to admit she had earned his respect the way she had brought her children out of Germany to the safety of Vienna, and how she had set herself to provide for her family since they had arrived. She had hardly called on his generosity at all, and the loans Edith had made her were all being paid back. Partly that irritated him, women in his circles did not take jobs in a haberdashery, but loath as he was to admit it, even to himself, it impressed him. He wished Edith showed as much spirit sometimes.

He sat down by the fire again and considered what she had told him. He realised things were not going to be easy from now, but as a well-established figure in Viennese society, he didn't think he or his family were in danger . . . not in any real sense. And yet . . . Ruth had been serious about her warning, and she spoke from bitter experience.

"She's a strong and determined woman," David said to his father now.

"More than can be said for your wife," Friedrich snorted.

"Father! For God's sake let's not go into all that again. Listen to what I am telling you now. Let's face it, Father, we've seen the way things have been going these last few weeks. We shouldn't have been surprised by Friday's announcement. Schuschnigg had been gradually giving in to Nazi demands for the past two months. He was never strong enough to take on Hitler . . . or our own Nazis, for that matter." David shook his head. "No, Father, it could well be time to get the children out, and fast."

"You'd all have to go," stated his father. "You could hardly send the children somewhere else on their own! Would you leave your home, your work, the rest of your family, just like that?"

"You and Mother could come as well. We'd all go."

"Just desert Austria, you mean? I never took you for a coward before, David!"

David sighed. "Father, I'm not a coward, I'm simply being realistic. Look at what happened to Ruth and her family. They were turned out of their home more than once, and they finally had to buy their way out of Germany. She's now living in three rooms in a tenement block, hoping Kurt can escape and find her."

"She was married to a shopkeeper," grumbled Friedrich, "a nobody. They aren't going to do the same to the likes of you, a well-known orthopaedic surgeon."

"We don't know that," David replied. "Yes, Kurt was arrested, so what happens if they arrest me…or you? How would Mother, or Edith manage?"

"Why would they arrest me?" demanded Friedrich.

"Because, Father, you're a Jew." David looked across at his father. Sitting upright in his chair, he stared back at David out of deep-set dark eyes, his nose prominent above a mouth hidden by his luxuriant white beard. His hair was combed back from his high forehead, and he wore his koppel on the back of his head. He looked as he had always looked to David, but now viewing him through the eyes of an Austrian, rather than a son, David could see that he was the archetypal Jew, the Jew of the caricatures and cartoons that had been filling the German newspapers for four years or more.

"It's just something we ought to think about," David said at last. "We have to try and protect our own. After all it's quite possible that I won't have my job at the hospital for very long."

"Why ever not? They'll still need doctors."

"I know, but Jewish doctors in Germany are only allowed

to treat Jewish patients now. The same thing could happen here."

"Well, we don't have to rush into anything. We've plenty of time to think about it," Friedrich announced, getting to his feet. "Now, I must have my quiet time."

David stood up, too. "I've got to get back," he said. "But do think about what I've said, and we'll discuss it again soon." He left his father, already turning to his books, and quietly let himself out of the apartment. He didn't go in to say goodnight to his mother, she would have quizzed him on the reason for his visit, and he wasn't ready to discuss the idea with her yet. Friedrich, he knew, would spend the rest of the evening studying his books.

David had long since given up study of the scriptures. He considered himself Austrian first and Jew second, only attending the synagogue near Liechtenstein Park with his family on special occasions, but he had seen what had been going on in Germany, and had heard firsthand from Ruth what was happening to the Jews there. What she had told him today simply reinforced what she had said before. He had no illusions, things were about to change, but how much and in what way he was far less certain, and taking the family out of Austria was a huge decision, not one to be taken lightly.

It was two weeks later that he received a telephone call at the hospital. Edith was on the line, sobbing so hard as she spoke that he couldn't make out what she was saying. All he could hear were the words "Come home! You must come home, now!"

He went at once, for there was a note of hysteria in her voice that he'd never heard before. When he reached the house he found his mother there, looking extremely pale, her eyes wide with fear. She held a cup and saucer in her hands, but they were shaking so much that the cup rattled against the saucer and the tea slurped over the rim of the cup onto the front of her skirt. She appeared not to notice, simply sat, shaking, as David greeted Edith and asked what on earth was going on.

"It's the Nazis, they've taken your father and…"

"Taken my father? Where? Where have they taken him?"

Edith wrung her hands. "We don't know! They simply took him away when he started to argue…"

"Argue about what? Edith, for goodness' sake pull yourself together and tell me exactly what has happened."

"The Nazis want Oma and Opa's apartment." David hadn't realised that Paul was in the room, but he turned to him now. His son was standing in a corner by the window, watching the street below. His face was pale, but he seemed calm enough.

"All right, Paul. *You* tell me."

"There are some top-brass Nazis who've arrived in Vienna and need places to live. They're simply taking them. They've found out where rich Jews live and they are just turning them out and moving in. When Opa said they couldn't have the apartment, they sent some soldiers. The soldiers pushed Oma out into the street and marched Opa away. Maria was still in the apartment, and she came out with Oma's coat and bag. The soldiers told Maria that she could pack one suitcase for Oma, and then she was to go back into the apartment and get it ready for its new owners." Paul fell silent as he came to the end of his story.

"What are we going to do?" cried Edith. "What are we going to do?"

"First you're going take Mother upstairs to her room and

make her comfortable. Then ask Cook to make her some nice hot soup." He looked at his panic-stricken wife. "Come on, Edith, you've got to be strong. Dissolving into tears isn't going to help anyone." He turned to his son. "You stay here with your mother," he said, then on a sudden thought asked, "Where's Naomi?"

"She's having tea at Hilda's."

"Right, well I want her home straightaway." David went to the door to call Anna, and found her on the point of coming in. "Ah, Anna. I want you to go round to Frau Schweiz's. Collect Miss Naomi and bring her home at once. If necessary you can say there is an illness in the family, but she must come home at once."

Anna glanced at the old lady sitting, still shaking in the chair, and gave a half-smile. "Yes, sir. Of course, sir," she said, and left the room.

"What about your father?" Edith had slumped into an armchair beside her mother-in-law. She looked up at David now, her eyes huge and staring in the whiteness of her face.

"I'll try and find out where they've taken him and see if I can get him released. I'm sure they'll let him go again now that they've made their point." David sounded far more assured than he felt. He had no idea how to find his father, or whether they, whoever *they* were, might release him. All he could do was go first to the police and work from there.

His car and driver, Jacob, were still waiting for him outside and he had himself driven straight to the local police station. Although it wasn't in the same area as his parents' apartment, he went there because he knew the local police chief.

"Wait here," he told Jacob, and went inside in search of Superintendent Müller.

When he asked for the superintendent, the desk officer looked him up and down and said, "Who shall I say wants him?"

"Dr David Bernstein."

"Wait here."

The officer disappeared and was gone some time. David waited in the front office. There was nowhere to sit down, so he stood, reading the posters up on the walls. One or two were quite old dealing with reported crime from several months ago; another explained how to register for the plebiscite that had been planned for Monday 13th March, but most of them were new, and mostly related to restrictions for Jews. Jews were not allowed to attend Austrian schools. Jews were to register as Jews on pain of deportation. Jews were not allowed to shop in Austrian shops. Jews were allowed to ride only in certain parts of public transport. David read them all and then read them again. He knew of many of the directives, but had not really understood the number of them, nor the heavy restrictions. Jews no longer had any rights as citizens, because they were no longer citizens.

The desk officer returned to his place, but did not speak to David, simply began writing notes in a ledger.

David approached the desk again. "Is Superintendent Müller there?" he asked.

The man looked up, as if surprised to be addressed while he was working. "He is in his office. He will see you when he has time."

David felt his temper rising at the young man's impudence. "I'd like to see him now, please," he said.

"He will see you when he has time," repeated the man, and returned to making his notes.

David waited another ten minutes, during which several people came into the police station, and were dealt with swiftly, efficiently and politely by the desk officer.

David looked at the door that led into the inner part of the police station. He knew the way to Superintendent Müller's office, he had been there several times when he had helped the police with some medical matters. Normally he would have been shown straight upstairs, given coffee, asked what he wanted. Today he faced the blank expression of a young desk officer and a closed door.

He was about to walk through the door and run up the stairs before the young man could stop him, when a bell rang and the desk officer looked up.

"The superintendent will see you now. Follow me."

"It's all right," David said mildly, "I know my way."

The young man stopped in the doorway, and turned to face him. "We do not allow Jews to wander round the police station," he said. "Follow me."

David followed him. They reached the superintendent's office and the young officer knocked on the door. When called to enter, he stepped inside and said, "The Jew is here to see you, sir."

"Thank you, Lombay."

Lombay moved out of the way and allowed David to go through the door, then he stood behind him as if to prevent his escape.

"Thank you, Lombay," repeated the superintendent. "Go back to your duties on the desk." Lombay looked disappointed, but he closed the door and David heard his feet on the wooden stairs.

Superintendent Helmut Müller was sitting behind his desk.

Once the door was closed he got to his feet, but he didn't extend his hand to David as he would once have done, and David was immediately aware of a difference in his attitude.

"Herr Doktor," Müller said, politely enough, "what can I do for you?" He did not offer David a seat, though he sat back down himself, leaving David to stand in front of him, making David feel like a schoolboy called up before the headmaster. He fought to quell a rising anger; he needed this man's help.

"I've come for your help," he replied. "My father has been arrested, and I don't know where they've taken him."

"And you think this has something to do with me?"

"No, I'm sure it hasn't," responded David quickly, "but I thought you might know where he would have been taken."

"So, who arrested him?" The superintendent sounded a little more relaxed.

"My mother says it was some soldiers. They came to move my parents out of their apartment so that some German officers could live there, and my father argued with them."

"That was very stupid of him," remarked the superintendent.

"Superintendent Müller, my father is an old man. He has lived in that apartment for the last twenty-five years. What would you have done?"

"If I were confronted by the SS and I were a Jew, I'd have left without a fuss, and thanked God that I had not been arrested," replied the superintendent. "Look, Herr Doktor, we have worked together occasionally over the years and I've nothing against you...or most Jews actually, but you are going to have to realise our political masters have changed. I cannot afford to be seen as a friend of Jews. I cannot afford to be seen taking a sympathetic line. I am in as much peril from my own men informing on me to the authorities as you are. The laws of Austria with regard to Jews are now the same as those of Germany."

"I understand," David replied quietly, "but I have to find my father and try to get him released."

Superintendent Müller sighed. "You know the Hotel Metropol in Morzinplatz?"

David nodded, the colour draining from his face. He did indeed know of the Hotel Metropol, who did not after these last few weeks?

"He will probably have been taken there. It's become the Gestapo headquarters...there are cellars..." His voice trailed off. "I'm sorry, I can't help you any further, Herr Doktor, except to say, if I were a Jew, I would go nowhere near the place. Heil Hitler!"

"Thank you, Herr Superintendent," replied David quietly. "Good day," and he left the room.

Jacob drove slowly along Franz-Josef-Kai until he was within two hundred yards of the Hotel Metropol, when David said abruptly, "Stop here and let me out. Keep driving round and pick me up again here." He opened the back door of the car as Jacob drew to a halt and was out before his driver could open his own door. David stepped onto the pavement and mingled with the throng going about their business there. He walked towards Morzinplatz where the Hotel Metropol stood in all its elegance and style. Four storeys high, its main entrance dignified with tall columns, its windows tall and wide, it was an imposing building. A beautiful building, once the preserve of the rich and famous, and now, draped with swastika banners, a house of terror. The Nazis had been in Vienna for only three weeks, but already the rumours were circulating about the horrors of what went on within. People disappeared inside, not through the graceful portico at the front, but through a small, back entrance that, it was said, led straight to the cellars where prisoners were kept and tortured.

David stood across the square from the hotel and looked at it in despair. How could he discover if his father was in there? There were SS guards outside the front door, and, even as he watched, a long, black sedan drew up at the front. The two sentries snapped to attention, while the driver of the car leaped out to open the door for his passenger. All three men saluted the man who strode inside, returning their salutes with a casual "Heil Hitler". David had seen pictures of that man in the papers, and seeing him in the flesh now he shuddered; Heinrich Himmler was an extremely powerful man, and every Jew with any sense of self-preservation was in mortal fear of him. David shrank back into a doorway, and watched as the black car glided away again, disappearing round the back of the hotel. He knew his nerve had failed; he knew he dare not approach the hotel. Keeping his head down, he crossed the street and walked beside the canal until he reached the Salztor Bridge. Standing on the end of the bridge, David looked along Salztorgasse towards the back of the hotel, but although he could see the building, he could not see the infamous door leading to the cellar. Could his father really be in the hands of the Gestapo? How could he find out? Müller's advice was good advice. No Jew should go within a mile of the Hotel Metropol. If his father was in there, there was nothing he, David, could do, certainly not immediately, certainly not without careful thought.

Shaken and frightened, and ashamed of his fear, David retraced his footsteps along the canal to the corner where

Jacob had dropped him, and as his car slid up beside him, he wrenched open the back door and scrambled in.

"Home," he said.

"There is nothing we can do if he has been taken to the Metropol," he said to Edith when he reached home again, and armed with a stiff drink told her what he had discovered.

Edith stifled a cry. "What will you tell your mother?" she asked. "What shall we tell the children?"

"We tell the children nothing more than they know already. That he has been arrested, but will be home again soon. As for Mother, we'll see how she is. Today she was in shock. Tomorrow she'll be stronger. In the meantime I will consider what, if anything, we can do."

"Can you really not go into the hotel and ask?" Edith looked at him with wide blue eyes. "He's your father. They must tell you if he's there. If it were one of my family..."

David turned away, his shame at his own fear making him harsh. "Your family! When your sister wrote to you and told you she'd been burned out of her home by the Nazis, you didn't even answer the letter," he snarled. "Don't talk to me about family duty."

It was Paul who found his grandfather. Coming home from school the next day, he saw a crowd gathered on a street corner. They were shouting and jeering, their laughter ringing out across the street. Paul walked over to see what all the fun was, only to stare in horror at what he saw. A group of people were on their knees and armed only with a scrubbing brush and bucket of water, were being made to clean the street. Two SS men stood over them, ready to deal with any trouble. Even as he watched, one of the guards kicked an old man in the ribs shouting at him to scrub harder, and as the old man's face jerked upward, Paul found himself staring down at his grandfather. The jeering crowd applauded the soldier's action, with shouts of, "That's right! Make the dirty Jew clean up properly! Come on, Granddad, get scrubbing. Time you did an honest day's work!" There were some small children in the crowd; one, high on his father's shoulders, chanted merrily, "Dirty Jew! Dirty Jew! Dirty Jew!"

Paul stood petrified, his face a mask of horror. His grandfather, looking up, saw him. Paul took a step forward and the old man hurled the scrubbing brush at him, screeching shrilly, "Seen enough, have you? Come for a good laugh? Here to see the Jews getting what's coming to them?" His shrieks were cut off by another boot in the ribs, and another roar of laughter from the assembled crowd as he crumpled forward on the ground. Paul turned away sickened, his legs like jelly as he walked away. Once round the corner and out of sight he began to run, and although the breath was screaming in his lungs, he didn't stop until he was home. David was already there, and came out of his study to see what was the matter as Paul crashed through the door and collapsed sobbing on the floor.

"Paul? Paul! What on earth...?"

"Opa! It's Opa!" was all he could say.

Gradually they calmed him down, and he managed to tell them what he'd seen. Opa, scrubbing the streets. Opa on his hands and knees with a scrubbing brush and bucket, the jeering crowd, the little boy chanting...and the soldiers with guns...kicking, kicking Opa in the ribs.

"Where, Paul? Where was this?" asked his father.

Paul still looked dazed but he knew where. He passed that street corner every day on the way to school.

"Antonstrasse," he said. "By the pharmacy."

283

David turned to Edith who, wide-eyed with fear for her son, was sitting beside Paul on the sofa, clutching his hand. "Edith, you must go and see what's happening," David said. "Go and find out where they are keeping him?"

"Me!" Edith shrieked. "How can I go? I have to stay here and look after Paul."

"Paul's fine," David said, trying to stay calm himself. "It has to be you, Edith. If I go anyone there will recognise me as a Jew. You look as Aryan as the best of them. No one will notice you in the crowd and maybe you can follow and find out where he's being held."

Edith stared at him in horror. "David, I couldn't," she stammered. "I really couldn't."

"Edith, my father earned himself a kicking so that your son, our Paul, wasn't recognised as a Jew by the crowd. You have to go."

"I'll go back, Papa," Paul said. He sat on the sofa beside his mother, white-faced, but determined. "I'll go back and see what's going on."

"No!" Edith was on her feet. "I'll go." Without another word she walked out of the room and they heard the front door slamming behind her.

Paul stared up at his father. "Will she be all right?" he asked. "You should have gone."

"No," replied David, "I would have made things worse, and might have been arrested as well, which would have helped no one. Your mother can pass as just a bystander, just another in the crowd. Now we'll just have to wait."

They didn't have to wait long. Less than ten minutes later Edith was back at the front door, calling David to fetch the car.

"They've moved on," she said, "and they've left your father in the gutter. Come on, David. Get the car, we can pick him up."

Within moments, they were in the car and on their way. They reached the street corner and saw what looked like a heap of old rags at the side of the road. As the car came to a halt, the three of them leaped out and ran to the old man. He was unconscious, his head bleeding, his arm twisted at an alarming angle, but he was breathing, his breath coming in painful rasps.

"Gently," David said as he ran exploratory hands over his father's body. "He's dislocated his shoulder, we must move him very carefully and get him onto the back seat of the car." Awkwardly the three of them lifted the old man and carried him to the car. He was a dead weight in their arms, and it was difficult to manoeuvre him through the car door, but at last they managed it.

"You'll have to walk home, Paul," said his father. "There's no room for you. Off you go, quickly. We'll see you at home." Paul set off at a trot, and, having made the old man as comfortable as they could, David and Edith got back into the car. As they pulled away and turned the car for home, there was a thud on Edith's door and she spun round to see a woman reaching for another stone to hurl at them, shouting as she did so, "Dirty Jews!" David accelerated away and the second stone fell short.

They got Friedrich upstairs and into bed, and, while he was still unconscious, David managed to ease his father's shoulder back into its socket. Then he bathed the cut on his head and gave him a thorough examination.

"He's very bruised," he told his mother as she waited

anxiously by her husband's bed. "His ribs are probably cracked and will be very painful when he wakes up, but as far as I can tell they aren't broken. The head wound looks worse than it is. They always bleed a lot." He gave her a reassuring smile. "He's lucky. It could have been a lot worse. He needs rest, but it won't be long before he's feeling much better."

"And when he is," David said to Edith much later when they were alone, "we'll have to decide what we're all going to do."

"What *can* we do?" Edith said bleakly. "Things are going to get worse."

"Yes," agreed David. "The time has come to leave. I spoke to my father about it before. Now we must give it serious consideration."

Fourteen

"So we are to leave Vienna," wailed Edith, "and go to Shanghai!"

"Shanghai!" echoed Ruth, staring at her sister.

"David says we have to go. After what happened to his father, he says it's too dangerous to stay here and we must get the children away to safety."

"But why Shanghai?" asked Ruth.

The two sisters were sitting in Edith's drawing room, coffee cups in their hands and a plate of pastries, such as Ruth never saw these days, on the table between them. Edith had sent Jacob with a message that she needed to see Ruth, and, tired as she was from a day's work in the shop, Ruth had trailed across the town to the house in Liechtensteinstrasse, when the haberdashery closed.

"He says Jews have been moving there for several years. There's a big Jewish community. We shan't be alone."

"But, China! Surely there are other, better places you could go, America, England, France?"

"Those countries won't take any more Jews," Edith moaned. "They have quotas or something. David says if we go to Shanghai we don't need visas to get in. We can just get on a boat and go."

"If the Germans let you," pointed out Ruth.

"Oh, they will. They want to get rid of us, we just have to leave everything behind," Edith's voice broke as she looked round her elegant drawing room. She said with a sob, "We're allowed to take thirty marks and a suitcase each."

"Thirty marks!" Ruth reached out and took her sister's hand. "How on earth will you live?" she asked gently.

"David says..." sobbed Edith, "David says there are several hospitals there, so he will be able to work." She pulled a handkerchief from her pocket and blew her nose, before saying a little more steadily, "He says, and I know he's right, that the important thing is to get the children to safety; and his parents, too."

"How is your father-in-law?" Ruth asked. "Has he recovered?"

Edith sighed. "He's recovered physically, though his ribs are still painful where he was kicked, but he's a changed man. He's morose and silent. He stays upstairs most of the time and we have to send his meals up on a tray. He's afraid to go out."

"I'm not surprised," said Ruth. "It was a terrible ordeal. What happened to him when he was arrested? Did he say?"

"We're not sure," sighed Edith. "He says he was taken to a prison and thrown into some sort of cell with lots of other people, but we don't know where it was. It was so crowded that they could only just sit on the floor, there was no room to lie down, and they were given nothing to eat. Then the next morning they were taken out onto the streets and told to clean them up. He had to scrub walls first, to get rid of the last of the posters about the plebiscite. Then he was set to scrubbing slogans off the street. That's when Paul saw him."

"Thank goodness he did. You might never have found him again otherwise."

"They left him for dead in the gutter," Edith said bleakly. "An old man. No one went to help him."

"No one dares," said Ruth, gently.

"No one wants to," snapped Edith. "They all hate us. Look at what's happening to all the Jewish families. David's parents have lost their home and it will probably only be a matter of time before we're turned out, too. Paul's not allowed to go to the gymnasium anymore, none of the Jewish boys are. It's not fair." Edith's voice was a childish wail: "It's not fair, he was doing so well."

Fair? Ruth stared at Edith in disbelief at her naivety. What did "fair" have to do with anything anymore?

"No," Edith was continuing, "no, Ruth, we have to go, David's right. The sooner we get the children out, the better, and of course we must take his parents with us too."

"Do his parents want to go?" enquired Ruth. "It will be an enormous wrench for them to leave Vienna. They've lived here all their lives."

"They don't have much choice," said Edith. "David's made up his mind. We're going, and his parents are going to come too."

"I see," Ruth said, adding, her voice deceptively calm, "and your parent?"

Edith stared at her. "My parent? You mean Mother?"

"Have you another?" asked Ruth tersely.

"Well, Mother's with you, isn't she?"

"Yes, she is," agreed Ruth, "but it doesn't mean she's safe. None of us is safe, Edith. We'd all like to go, but we can't."

"So you think that just because you can't go, we shouldn't?

289

Is that it?" Edith's eyes flashed with anger. "Is that what you think, Ruth?"

"No, not at all. Quite the contrary, in fact. If you ask David, you'll find that I told him you should all go sometime ago, well before anything happened to your father-in-law. But I just think you might have given Mother a thought."

"She wouldn't want to come," Edith said defensively. "She'd want to stay with you and the children until Kurt gets here."

"Kurt won't come here now," sighed Ruth. "It would be madness. Things are worse here than they were in Germany. I told him not to try, it's too dangerous."

"Oh, I nearly forgot," Edith interrupted suddenly, "what with Shanghai and everything, there's a letter for you. It came yesterday morning."

"A letter!" Ruth almost dropped her coffee cup. "Why didn't you tell me? Where is it? Give it to me!"

"I am telling you," Edith replied plaintively. "That's why I asked you to come, so I could give you the letter." She got to her feet and went to the bureau in the corner of the room. "I've got it in here. It's quite safe." She opened a drawer and drew out the letter. "Here you are. The postmark's Hamburg, so he must be there, mustn't he?"

Ruth snatched the envelope from her sister's hand, and after a quick glance at handwriting and postmark stuffed it into her bag.

Edith looked surprised. "Aren't you going to open it? I thought you'd want to read it right away."

"So that's why you kept it for a whole day?" fumed Ruth inside her head, but all she said was, "You could have sent it with Jacob when he came yesterday."

"But I wanted to give it to you myself," bleated Edith. "And I wanted to tell you about Shanghai."

"Are you going to come and tell Mother, yourself, that you're going to Shanghai?" Ruth asked, rising to her feet and preparing to go home, "or do you expect me to tell her?"

"Couldn't you bring her here?" wheedled Edith. "I'm sure she'll want to see the children before we go."

Ruth compressed her lips into a tight line, biting back the flood of anger that threatened to stream from her mouth. She was furious with Edith and her self-centredness, but she knew in her heart that Edith was right in this at least, her mother would want to see her grandchildren before they left.

"We'll try and come at the weekend," she said. "Do you want me to break it to her about Shanghai?"

"Would you?" The relief in Edith's voice was heartfelt. "Tell her I'll explain it all to her when I see her."

Ruth couldn't wait to get out of the house, and once she was safely back on the street she almost ran to catch the bus home. Several times on the way she slipped her hand inside her bag, to make sure the precious letter was still there. Hamburg! What was Kurt doing in Hamburg? She had heard nothing since their brief phone call nearly four weeks ago. He had not phoned again as he'd said he would and her fears for his safety had increased with every passing day.

At last she reached their courtyard, and climbing the stairs to the apartment was greeted with cries of delight from the younger children, and huge, relieved smiles from Laura and her mother. They knew how dangerous the streets were becoming for Jews, and her safe return every day was awaited with anxiety. Ruth no longer allowed the girls to walk to school through the streets on their own, where they were now prey to attack, both verbal and physical, from Austrian children, but insisted that Helga went with them, even though it meant that the twins had to trail all the way there and back again, too. Their small Jewish enclave lived under a canopy of fear. New laws and directives were published almost every day, and they all lived with the dread of being arrested for breaking one of these without even knowing it existed.

"So what did Edith want?" asked Helga once the welcome was over and she had sat down at the table.

"Oh, nothing much," Ruth said, her eyes flicking to the children. "I'll tell you all about it later." Even now she couldn't read the letter from Kurt. She needed privacy to do so. She had no idea what he was going to say, but clearly he wasn't coming to Vienna and she needed to be alone as she read the words that explained why. She washed her hands and face at the sink, and then, picking up her bag, went to the room she shared with the twins. When she had heard their prayers, she settled them into bed and read to them; waiting, watching over them as they fell asleep, top to tail in the single bed, each clutching a battered rabbit. Sitting on the mattress that was her own bed, she finally got out her letter. With trembling fingers she ripped open the envelope and withdrew the single sheet inside.

My darling Ruth, she read:

I wish I were with you now, but though I tried to reach you recently it was not possible with the recent change of affairs. At present I am in Hamburg where I am working in a shop. You can write to me here and let me know how you all are. I am working on the plan for a visit to Berta, as you suggested, and hope to leave in the next few weeks if I can get time off from work. Perhaps you and the children will be able to come and see Berta too before very long.

Write to me, my darling, and tell me how you and the children are doing. Is your mother still with you? Please remember me to her.

I have to go to work now, but I will write again soon with my news. Forgive the brevity of this letter but you know the circumstances.

Remember how much I love you, my darling girl, more than life itself.

Kiss the children from me and tell them I am longing to see them again.

All my love,
    Kurt

Ruth read the short letter through several times, wondering at the strange and stilted language. Kurt must have thought the letter might be intercepted, and was giving as little away as he could. She looked again at the envelope, but as she had torn it open she had destroyed any sign that it might have been opened before.

She read the letter again, trying to work out the subtext to what he had written. By recent change of affairs he must mean the Anschluss. The visit to Berta was the code she herself had used in their telephone call, so he was trying to get to England, and from there he was going to try and get them out as well. Was that possible? She wondered. Forgive the brevity of this letter, but you know the circumstances. Yes, that's what he meant, Ruth thought. He was afraid that the letter might fall into the wrong hands.

She looked at the address at the top of the page. It was a shop in Hamburg. He must think it safe for her to write there, or at least that the risk was small. She clutched the letter to her. Thank God it had arrived in time. If it had come to Edith's house in another week or so, when the Bernstein family had left for Shanghai, she would never have received it. Kurt did not know where she lived now, and they would have lost all contact. She shivered with fear at the dreadful thought. He wouldn't have known where she was in Vienna, and she wouldn't have known where he was at all. She found that tears were running down her cheeks, and for a few blessed moments she allowed herself the luxury of a good cry, before she scrubbed her cheeks with her handkerchief. No need for tears, she admonished herself. Kurt was alive. He was safe. He wasn't trapped in a daily-more-terrifying Austria, and he seemed to think he could get to England and send for them when he got there. She put the letter back in her bag and got to her feet. Gently she straightened the coverlet over the twins, kissed each one on his forehead twice, once for herself and once for Kurt, and then went back into the kitchen where the girls were sitting at the table, Inge drawing on a scrap of paper, and Laura writing in her diary:

When Oma took us to school today we saw some poor people scrubbing the road, trying to get some paint off the stones. They had only toothbrushes and bucket of water and two soldiers with guns were watching them. Two horrid boys came by and tipped a bucket of horse muck on them, and they had to clean that up as well. Oma told us not to look, just to walk by and take no notice, but one of the people was an old lady, and she was crying. Why aren't there proper sweeping men like before? When I asked Fräulein Lowenstein she told me not to talk about it. She was quite cross, but I think she is scared like all the grown-ups. Horrible things are happening to Jews like us, and everyone is afraid.

Helga looked across at Ruth as she came in, raising an interrogatory eyebrow. Ruth smiled. "They're sound asleep," she said, and turning her attention to the girls she said, "Now then, what would you two like to do before you go to bed? How about writing a letter to Papa?"

When at last they had the kitchen to themselves, Ruth told Helga about her visit to Edith. "Shanghai? In China? Why on earth is David taking them there?"

"Edith says there's already a large Jewish community there, but I think it's mainly because they don't need any sort of visa to go there. America has a quota system and other countries are taking fewer and fewer Jews. They could wait forever to be allowed to go there. Anyway, they're going and as soon as it can be arranged."

"What about David's parents? Surely they aren't leaving them behind? Specially not after what happened to poor Herr Bernstein." Helga broke off for a moment and then said bleakly, "We saw the same thing happening again today, as I took the girls to school. A group of Jews being made to clean the road on their hands and knees." She sighed. "David's right to get them out, of course, but Shanghai?"

"Edith says that his parents are going, too."

"To Shanghai? But they'll hate leaving Vienna."

"That's what I said," agreed Ruth. "But she says David's made up his mind and they don't have any choice."

"Poor things," sighed Helga, "but I suppose it's for the best."

"Edith also gave me a letter from Kurt," said Ruth.

"From Kurt?" Helga's eyes lit up with pleasure. "Oh darling, how wonderful. You must be over the moon. What did he say? Where is he? Is he coming here?"

Ruth took out the letter and handed it to her mother. "You can read it yourself," she said.

Helga looked doubtful as she took the letter. "Well," she said, "if you're sure," and adjusting her glasses on her nose, she read it through. When she looked up she looked a little bemused. "What a strange letter," she said. "What does he mean?"

Ruth explained what she thought Kurt had been telling her. "He doesn't know if the post is safe," she explained. "He's telling me things which no one else would understand. And at least now I know where he is, for the moment anyway."

"So you can write back to him and tell him what's been happening here."

"And I must do it quickly before he moves on," said Ruth. "If he writes to me care of Edith again, I shan't get the letter, and whichever Nazis are living in Edith's house will."

"Do you know when they are leaving?" asked Helga. "Did Edith say?"

"No, not exactly, but I think it will be as soon as possible. She asked us to come and visit them on Sunday."

"I can't believe they're going so far away," Helga said, a break in her voice. "My Edith in China. Shall I ever see her or the children again?"

Ruth was beside her at once, her arms round her comfortingly. "Of course you will, Mutti. It's only till this nightmare is over."

"It'll never be over," said her mother flatly. "The Nazis

will never be satisfied until they've got rid of every Jew in the country, and there's no one to stop them."

"You could go with them, Mutti," Ruth said gently.

Her mother's head jerked up. "And leave you here on your own! I would never do that. Edith has David to look after her and the children. She doesn't need me."

It was three more weeks before David, Edith and their family finally left Vienna. Getting all the exit permits from the Department of Emigration had taken longer than they had thought. David spent hours queuing up at the department, waiting with the required documents, only to be told that this form was incorrectly filled in, or that another one was now necessary. Their situation in society had changed radically. Anna and Cook had both left, neither prepared to work for a Jewish family anymore. Edith had to manage the house and do the cooking on her own, something she had not done since she had married David. Jacob, the driver, also left, because David no longer had a car. That had been confiscated. Two SS men had arrived at the house one afternoon, brusquely demanding the keys of the beautiful motor parked outside the house. David, remembering his father's fate when he had argued about the apartment, could do nothing but hand them over, his face pale with contained fury, as he watched the men drive away.

Once their application to emigrate had been lodged, they prepared for their journey. Edith had been right about the amount of luggage they could take, and they packed and re-packed the cases trying to cram in all the basic things they would need to set up their new home.

On the two Sundays before they left, Ruth and Helga took the children across the town to visit them. Summer was fast approaching and the children were allowed to play in the garden, under the eye of a disconsolate Paul. Watching young children play wasn't his idea of fun, but there was no Anna to look after them anymore, and he knew his parents were relying on him more and more these days. He was quite excited about moving to Shanghai. He'd never been out of Vienna, and thought that the whole trip would be a great adventure.

"You'll be able to go back to school there," his father had promised, "and then train as a doctor as you always planned."

"I don't want to go to China," Naomi confided to Laura as they sat together on the swing seat. "I want to stay here."

"I didn't like leaving my home either," Laura said sympathetically, "but it may not be as bad as you think."

"Yes it will be," asserted Naomi. "I shan't know anyone, and I shan't see Hilda again for ages."

"But you'll have both your mother and father," pointed out Laura, "and your Oma and Opa."

"Opa's gone all funny," Naomi said, "and Oma's fiercer than ever!"

At that moment the twins erupted from the house, chasing and yelling as they hared round the garden. They charged over to Paul, whom they both adored, and he swung them up in the air, one after the other, as they shrieked at him to do it again and again.

"Your Paul is a fine boy," Ruth remarked to Edith as they watched from the window. "Almost a young man now."

"We're getting him out just in time," said David who had overheard her comment. "On his sixteenth birthday he'd have had to register for a work permit, and he might have been sent anywhere."

"When are you leaving?" Helga asked her son-in-law.

"If I get the final documents tomorrow, as promised, we shall take the train to Odessa on Wednesday," he replied. "From there we travel by boat."

"They were promised last week," complained Edith, "but when David went to collect them, they sent him away and told him to come back next day. He's been going back every day since."

Ruth thought of her dealings with the Office of Jewish Affairs in Stuttgart and shuddered. She knew exactly how the Germans worked when dealing with Jews; the Austrians were clearly as bad.

"They'll have to give them to me this time," David said. "We have to leave on Wednesday, some high-ranking Nazi and his family are moving in here. They've given us until Wednesday to get out."

"But what about all your things?" asked Helga. "Your furniture, your pictures, all your glass and silver?"

"Our dear Anna made an inventory of it all," spat Edith. "She gave it to the Nazis, and we are to remove nothing from the house. They will have it all, and Anna will have her job back...working for them."

"Anna?" Helga was incredulous. "But she's been with you for years."

David shrugged. "So she has, but she has obviously decided to join the winning side."

The door to the drawing room opened and Friedrich and Marta Bernstein came in. Ruth was shaken by the difference in their appearance since she had last seen them, the night the Anschluss was announced. Both had aged ten years, particularly Friedrich, who no longer carried himself ramrod straight, as he always had, but walked with a stoop, leaning on an ebony cane. Marta still held herself erect, but there were new lines etched deep in her face, and her skin was pale and drawn taut over her cheekbones.

Helga and Ruth both got to their feet, Helga holding out her hands to them saying, "My dear Frau Bernstein, how do you do? Herr Bernstein, I hope you are recovering from your ordeal."

Friedrich shuffled over to the window, making no effort to take her hand or to reply, but Marta took the extended hand in hers for a brief moment, saying, "Yes, he is much better, thank you. The bruises have almost gone." She turned to look at her husband who stood staring out at the children playing below. Suddenly he swung round and addressing them all, said, "They will kill us all. The Nazis will kill us all."

"No, Father," David said firmly. "They won't. We leave on Wednesday, remember?"

"They have driven us out of our home, and now they're driving us out of our city. I would rather die here than live in Shanghai."

"Well, I would not," David said. "And we have the children to think of. I have to get them out of Vienna, and I can't leave you and Mother behind."

"David's only doing what he thinks is best for all of us, Friedrich," said his wife soothingly. "We need to take the children away from here to somewhere safe."

That evening, when they were back in their apartment and the children were tucked up in their beds, Helga finally allowed her self-control to snap and began to weep. When they had said goodbye that afternoon, she had remained dry-eyed, even when Edith dissolved into tears. She had hugged her grandchildren convulsively, but had talked brightly about the great adventure of going to China, making them promise to write and tell her about all the new and exciting things they had seen. Knowing how distressing they would find them, she had held her tears at bay until there was no one but Ruth to see them.

Ruth, too, had managed not to cry as she had said goodbye to Edith. Deep in her heart she knew it was unlikely she would ever see her, or her nephew and niece again, and, despite Edith's self-centredness, she was still Ruth's big sister and Ruth loved her. David had shaken her hand and then reached across to kiss her cheek. Startled, Ruth drew back, looking up into his face, and was surprised to see his expression was a mixture of affection and admiration.

"God bless you, Ruth," he said. "You're a brave and resourceful woman. I admire you for how you've coped since Kurt was arrested." He seemed about to say more, but simply gave a small shrug and turned to Helga.

"Look after my Edith," Helga had said, and David had nodded.

They had left then, no one wanting to prolong the painful goodbyes, and had brought the children home.

"Well," said Helga when, clasped in Ruth's arms, she had wept until she had no more tears, "we're on our own now."

Fifteen

Kurt sat on the bed in his tiny room in Hans Dietrich's house and pulled out the latest letter that had come from Ruth.

My darling Kurt, she had written:

They have gone now. They left for Shanghai on Wednesday. Goodness knows what awaits them there. Mother was very upset when we went to say goodbye on Sunday, though she's been very strong in front of the children, I know she's grieving inside, almost as if Edith was dead. Mother is certain she'll never see her again.

Life goes on here much as it did in Kirnheim, the children are well and though we haven't much money, provided I am able to keep my job they won't go hungry or cold. Hans and Peter are a real pair of monkeys and keep Mother on her toes during the daytime. Inge worries me these days, she is still very quiet, nothing like her old volatile self, though she seems to be settling at school at last. She has begun to make friends with some of the other girls in our little complex, but she is very clingy and always wants to know where I am and when I am coming home again. Laura is, as she has been ever since you left, my rock. She is so grown-up you would hardly recognise her. She never complains about what is happening to us and she is fiercely protective of the younger children. I enclose a picture of us all that David took a couple of weeks ago…just so you'll recognise us when we meet up again!

If you do manage to get to see Berta it would be lovely if you could arrange for us to come and see her too. The children haven't seen her for ages, and of course Mother would love to see her again as well.

Keep well and safe, my darling, we all miss you, but are happy to know you're with friends.

All my love,
    Ruth

The letter was dog-eared, and its enclosed photograph was decidedly ragged at the edges. Kurt stared down at the little group in the picture. In the ten months he'd been away the twins had changed from toddlers into little boys, grinning mischievously into the camera. Identical twins, and still so alike that if they walked in through the door now, after ten months' absence, Kurt was not at all sure he would know which was which. He looked again at the girls; Inge seemed to be clutching a piece of cloth against her cheek, and Laura, solemn-eyed, was staring into the camera. Standing behind them was Ruth, his beautiful Ruth, but now a shadow of the Ruth he remembered. Her face was thin, the flesh drawn tightly over her cheekbones, making her nose more prominent; her hair, even in the photograph, showed streaks of grey, and although she was smiling for the camera, there was a sadness in the eyes that struck at his heart.

Kurt could only imagine what life must be like for his family in newly Nazified Austria. He wished with all his heart that he'd managed to reach them in Vienna before the Anschluss, but even as his heart ached to be with them, he knew in his head that he had been right to come to Hamburg.

The train journey had been uneventful. There had been a couple of document checks, and, as the police came through the train, he braced himself to make a break for it, but his identity card was unquestioned and handed back to him. Perhaps his fear of Loritz was out of all proportion. Surely an SS camp commandant could not have such far-reaching tentacles, but even if it wasn't Loritz after him, he was still a Jew travelling between cities with no luggage and no apparent reason for the journey. Since his escape from the hotel in Regensburg, he'd had no chance to shave, and his clothes were looking decidedly slept-in, just the sort of scruffy individual to be picked up by the Gestapo as a vagrant. He slept for a good while, and when he arrived at last in Hamburg he was hungry, but wide awake. From a station kiosk he bought a street map and set out to find Festungstrasse and Hans Dietrich.

Festungstrasse turned out to be a side street in a smart part of the city, where exclusive shops offered expensive goods. Kurt felt completely out of place in an area where chic and fashionable women sauntered the streets, glancing into the discreet shop fronts of jewellers, furriers and couturiers, where a single item might be displayed, its price tag delicately turned inward. Hans Dietrich's shop was just such a one, the bow window holding one disembodied hand through the fingers of which trailed a three-row pearl necklace with a diamond clasp. Even as Kurt watched from the outside, a hand reached in and removed the pearls. The shop was closing for the day, the precious merchandise being placed in the safe overnight.

Kurt glanced along the street. There were few shoppers around now, and the couple who had been approaching flagged down a taxi, and drove away in the opposite direction. Kurt pushed the shop door, but it was locked. Anxiously he peered in through its frosted glass panel. A light shone through the window; there was definitely someone inside, moving round the shop. Then Kurt noticed a discreet bell beside the door with a sign: "Please ring for attention". Hans Dietrich was not going to allow just anyone inside his premises. Kurt drew a deep breath and pressed the bell. For a moment he thought there was going to be no response, but then a disembodied voice crackled in his ear, and he realised that there was a speaking tube from inside the shop.

"Yes? What do you want? We're closed."

"I'm looking for Herr Hans Dietrich," began Kurt.

"Who are you?" The voice was distorted by the speaking tube, and Kurt could not tell if he were being addressed by a man or a woman. Kurt had been about to give his own name but then realised that whoever was in the shop would have no notion who he was, so he replied, "Günter Schiller."

There was movement behind the glass. Kurt saw the silhouette of a man, and he stepped back from the door so that the streetlamp behind him would light his face. The door opened on a chain and a voice said, "You're not Günter Schiller. Günter Schiller is dead."

"His father, Paul Schiller, sent me," Kurt said. "I'm looking for Herr Hans Dietrich."

The door closed, the chain was released and then the door opened again. "I'm Hans Dietrich; you'd better come in."

Kurt edged through the partially opened door and the man immediately closed it behind him, pulling down a blind so that it was impossible to see through the glass panel from the outside.

"You'd better come through to the back and tell me what this is all about."

The man led the way through the shop, behind the counter and into a room beyond. It immediately reminded Kurt of Paul Schiller's backroom. An overhead lamp threw a pool of light into the centre of the room, and when he turned to face Kurt, Hans Dietrich was revealed. Aged about fifty, he was a small man with delicate features. His blue eyes were pale in the pallor of his face. His fair hair was too long, curling on his collar, and his mouth was small, lips pursed together as he surveyed his visitor. One long-fingered hand pushed a lock of hair from his forehead as he said, "Well, what's your name and why did Herr Schiller send you to me?"

Kurt looked at the strange man in front of him, and knew that he had no option but to trust him. Paul had said to go to him, and now he was here there was nothing to do but to tell him. "My name is Kurt Friedman...and I need to leave Germany," he said.

"You don't want much, do you?"

"He said I should come to you if I needed help," said Kurt.

"Did he now? What a cheek!"

"In which case," Kurt said, stepping towards the door, "I'll leave now."

Hans Dietrich made no move to stop him, but said, "You can't go out onto the streets round here looking like that. You look like a vagrant, and they aren't welcome in this part of the world, I can assure you."

"My luggage is lost," Kurt began. "I need a shave and…"

"Why did you say you were Günter?" Hans cut him off with a wave of the hand. "Why are you using his name?"

"Paul gave me Günter's passport and told me to use his name if I needed to." Kurt paused before adding, "And he said you might be able to help me."

"Did you know Günter?" asked Hans, dropping into a chair and waving Kurt towards another.

"We went to the same school," answered Kurt, ignoring the second chair, "but he was older than I am and we weren't close friends." He looked across at Hans Dietrich and said, "Were you just business acquaintances, or were you friends, too?"

"Oh, I think you can say we were friends." Hans Dietrich was inspecting his fingernails as he spoke, not looking at Kurt, but running the nail of his right forefinger under a nail on his left hand to remove a speck of dirt. "Günter used to stay here when he was in Hamburg." He looked up, suddenly irritable, and snapped, "For goodness' sake, man, don't tower over me like that, sit down."

This time Kurt took the chair Hans indicated, perching on the edge of it. He looked across at the jeweller, trying to decide why Paul had thought he might help. He was clearly not a Jew and yet Paul had been sure it would be safe to approach him in need; that was why Kurt had expected him to be Jewish. Why, Kurt wondered, would he put himself in danger to help someone he didn't know?

"Have you got the passport here?" asked Hans. "May I see it?"

Kurt reached into his inside pocket and passed it over to him. Hans opened it at the picture page, and stared down at it for a long moment, before looking up and saying bluntly, "Well, you don't look very like him do you?"

Kurt agreed that he didn't, but added that the beard made all the difference. "I have to decide whether to say I shaved it off, or to grow one myself."

"You'd look more like the picture if you grew one," Hans said, "but you'd also look more Jewish, which would be dangerous. Günter Schiller isn't a particularly Jewish name, if you stay clean-shaven, perhaps wear some spectacles, they might not look at you too closely. Whichever you do is a risk, but then we're all at risk, aren't we? Still," he went on, "the first thing, Kurt Friedman, is for you to have a bath. Not to put too fine a point on it, you smell. Come with me." Hans Dietrich got to his feet and opened what Kurt had supposed was a cupboard in the corner of the room, to reveal a narrow staircase leading to the floor above. He led the way up the stairs, which opened onto a tiny landing, off which were three doors. He opened one and said, "Bathroom in there." Opening a second door to show a small bedroom, he said, "You can sleep in here tonight. I'll put some clothes out for you to change into." He gave the surprised Kurt a little push. "Go on," he said, the irritability back in his voice, "have a bath. We'll talk when you're clean."

After luxuriating in the first hot bath he'd had for weeks, Kurt towelled himself dry and crossed the landing to the bedroom Hans had shown him. On the bed were some clean clothes.

They'll be far too small for me, Kurt thought as he picked up the shirt, but to his surprise they all, more or less, fitted him. Surely these couldn't be Hans Dietrich's clothes, they would hang off the little jeweller like those on a scarecrow.

When he was dressed, Kurt emerged onto the landing and was about to go downstairs again when he noticed the other bedroom door was ajar. Unable to stop himself, Kurt took a silent step and gently pushed it wider, ready to apologise should his host be in the room. But he was not, and Kurt, ashamed of himself even as he did it, took another step inside. It was a larger bedroom, furnished with a wide double bed, beside which stood a chest of drawers and a bedside table. On each of these was a framed photograph, the one on the chest showing two men laughing together, Günter and Hans; the other, on the bedside table, was of Günter, his head turned back over his shoulder, smiling into the camera. And Kurt understood; he now knew whose clothes he was wearing, why they were in the apartment and why Hans Dietrich, himself, was already at risk.

Very softly he pulled the door to, and went down the stairs to where Hans Dietrich was waiting in the little sitting room.

Hans looked up as he came in. "You've decided not to shave," he remarked.

"No, not decided," replied Kurt, "just kept my options open."

The next few weeks Kurt stayed with Hans Dietrich. He worked in the shop as an assistant during the day and with the help of a dictionary and with Hans himself as teacher, set about learning to speak English. During the evenings spent learning the new language, Kurt and Hans gradually got to know each other, and, each liking what he found, a real friendship was forged. Kurt told of his arrest and the troubles that had surrounded him ever since. He spoke of Ruth and the children and his desperate desire to get them out of Vienna. He found that talking about them, speaking of them aloud instead of simply thinking of them, brought them closer, made them more alive.

Hans spoke little of his past and never of family, but he revealed himself in his generosity to Kurt and in his hatred of the Nazis.

They had decided that the best way forward was for Kurt to travel to England through Holland, visiting another of Hans's business acquaintances in Amsterdam on the way. He would have letters of introduction to the Dutch jeweller and to James Daniel in London, and he would travel on Günter's passport, which named him as a jeweller. Other papers were needed before he was able to leave the country, and Hans, through unnamed contacts, set about getting these, all in the name of Günter Schiller. In the meantime, Kurt learned as much as he could about the trade, so that he could, at least, answer superficial questions without difficulty. He was seen in the shop, and though it was not the sort of establishment that encouraged idle chatter with its prestigious customers, they let it be known that Günter was a cousin of Hans, who had moved from Munich. After some discussion they had decided against the beard.

"It makes you look too Jewish," Hans said, "as it did with Günter, but it used not to matter as much." So, Kurt remained clean-shaven.

At last the day came for him to try and leave. All his papers were in order; he had the relevant permits, identity card, ration book and passport with its visas still in date, all in the name of Günter Schiller, jeweller. Each, including the passport, was adorned with a recent picture and stamped with the required stamps. How Hans had managed it, Kurt didn't know, and Hans had refused to tell him anything.

"What you don't know can't harm anyone but yourself," he said. "If you have a problem with the authorities, you can point them in the direction of no one but me…and with the current political thinking I am probably on one of their lists already. It is almost certainly only the high profile of several of my regular customers that has saved me from a knock on the door in the middle of the night." It was the nearest he ever came to explaining himself and the relationship he'd had with Günter.

The station was busy, reverberating with the noise of steam engines, announcements and whistles. Carrying a small suitcase, Kurt boarded the train that would take him on the first leg of his journey to Amsterdam. Once across the border into Holland he would be safe. In a wallet in his inside pocket were the required documents to leave Germany, including a return ticket from the Hook of Holland to Harwich.

"They won't let you into England, even on business, unless they think you will be leaving again," Hans had said. "Günter travelled over quite often, so if they decide to check their records they will find you there. Once you've contacted James Daniel you'll have to be guided by him as to what to do next."

The two men had said their goodbyes in the privacy of Hans's sitting room, with the firm grip of a handshake. Kurt was surprised to see tears in Hans's eyes, and reaching forward put his hands on the other man's shoulders.

Hans pulled him close for a brief hug and then broke free, saying as he did so, "You're more like Günter than you know. Now be off. Write to me from London, and I'll forward any letters that come for you here." He smiled a rueful smile. "Don't worry, I won't let her lose track of you."

Kurt settled himself in a corner seat and buried his face in a newspaper. As he scanned the inside pages, an item, tucked away at the bottom of a column, caught his eye. He read it and then reread it, hardly believing what he read, and he realised that he was getting out of Germany just in time to escape the next move against the Jews. All Jewish men were going to have to add the extra name of Israel to their names, and all the Jewish women, Sarah. There would be no protection afforded by a non-typical Jewish name. Every Jew would have to register, every Jew would be known. Every Jew would soon have to have a huge red J stamped on his passport. Kurt stared at the article and knew real fear. The Nazi grip was tightening, and his family were held within it. Now, even more, he must try and get them away to safety, and his best chance was to work from England.

The train pulled out of the station, and Kurt sat back in his seat, apparently at ease reading the news, but vitally aware of the people around him. The compartment was almost full and there was a steady flow of people up and down the corridor. Kurt watched them from behind his paper, but as the train gathered speed and steamed its way through the suburbs of the city, the flow decreased as people found seats and settled down for the journey. Kurt did not relax, could not relax, he felt as taut as a bowstring, but he closed his eyes, as if in sleep, to discourage any conversation with his fellow-passengers.

The train stopped in Bremen, and it was after this that the ticket collector made his rounds. Kurt passed over his ticket and it was clipped and returned without comment.

The hours passed and at last the moment that Kurt feared most arrived as the train reached the border. It pulled up with the squeal of brakes and a shriek of steam. Border guards in uniform swarmed onto the train, demanding passports, papers and permits. Everyone in the compartment pulled documents from their pockets and wallets, ready for inspection. Kurt did the same, rehearsing yet again his explanation for travelling, business in Amsterdam and London. Tucked in with the official papers was a letter on Hans Dietrich's headed paper stating "To whom it may concern", that Günter Schiller was "travelling on the firm's behalf to diamond merchants in Amsterdam and London".

Kurt could hear the border guards moving closer, and it was all he could do to maintain a calm expression, when his heart was pounding so alarmingly that he thought the whole carriage must hear it.

The compartment door slid open with a screech and a uniformed man blocked the way out.

"Passports!" he demanded. "Have your passports ready for inspection." Each person's papers were carefully scrutinised before being handed back.

"Which is your luggage?" he demanded of a woman sitting in the opposite corner to Kurt.

"It's up on the rack." The woman's voice was hoarse with fear.

"Get it down!"

The woman stood up and reached for her case. The man snatched it from her, and opening it on the seat upended it, searching through the clothes it contained. Then with a shrug and without a word of apology, he left the woman to repack her belongings and turned to Kurt.

Trying to keep his hand from shaking, Kurt passed across his papers. The official checked both the passport and the official permit to travel, squinting at first the picture and then at Kurt, before grunting and passing them back. He withdrew from the compartment and the door screeched protestingly shut behind him. His departure was greeted with palpable relief within the compartment, but no one dared relax until, with the sound of banging doors and much shouting, the German border guards left the train and it began to edge forward. Another hundred metres up the track it stopped again, and more uniformed men came on board, this time Dutch customs officials. Once again they all had to present their papers.

"And your reason for entering the Netherlands, Herr Schiller?" asked the official who inspected Kurt's documents.

"Business," Kurt replied. "I am going to see Herr Torben Stuyvesant in Amsterdam." He produced Hans's letter on the headed paper. The guard gave it a cursory glance before handing all the papers back and turning to the woman in the corner.

Ten minutes later the train moved forward once more, and picked up speed as if, Kurt thought, it was as anxious as he to leave Germany behind. He felt weak with relief and sank back into his corner seat, watching the flat Dutch countryside pass the window. The others in the compartment sat back too, and although no one spoke, the atmosphere was lighter as they sped onwards towards Amsterdam.

At last Kurt was safe, at last he no longer had to look over his shoulder, at last he was out of Germany. Now all I have to do, he thought, is to reach London and arrange, somehow, to get them all out. All I have to do! He knew a moment's despair at the enormity of the task, before giving himself a mental shake. "It's all I have to do."

Sixteen

Life was very difficult for Ruth and her family over the summer months. The first disaster was that Ruth lost her job at the haberdashery. She met Frau Merkle, the proprietor, at the door of the shop one morning sticking a notice to the window. *No Jews.*

Looking a little flustered, Frau Merkle said, "Ah, Frau Friedman. Please come inside for a moment."

For a moment? Ruth had come to work her normal nine-hour day. She followed Frau Merkle into the shop, and almost as if the act could stave off what the woman was going to say, began to remove her coat and hat. Frau Merkle went to the till behind the counter and took out some money. Turning, she thrust it towards Ruth.

"This is what you are owed, up to last night. I'm not able to employ you anymore. Trade is falling off, and it is clearly because there is a Jew behind the counter." The woman lifted her chin defiantly. "Understandably, no one wants to be served by a Jew."

Ruth stared at the proffered money for a moment, before reaching out to take it. The old Ruth longed to tear it in two and fling it back into her employer's face, but the new, wiser Ruth knew that those few notes were all that stood between her children and hunger. As she took the money, her fingers touched Frau Merkle's and the other woman, withdrawing her hand, wiped it on her skirt, as if to remove the touch of Jewish flesh.

Without a word Ruth turned on her heel and went to the door, with Frau Merkle's parting salvo ringing in her ears. "Ungrateful Jewish bitch! I didn't *have* to pay you!"

"What are we going to do now, Mother?" Ruth asked when she had told Helga what had happened. "We've enough money for a week's rent and a little food! The miserable cow didn't even pay me a full week's wages, let alone a week's notice!"

"We'll manage somehow," replied her mother, imbuing her voice with far more optimism than she actually felt. "We'll think of something."

They discussed the situation long into the night and decided that Ruth must approach all the Jewish businesses still operating in the area and try to find work with one of them.

"But there aren't many," Ruth said, "and they're all family businesses, so any jobs go to the family. They're all fighting for survival."

"I know," agreed her mother, "there was an SS soldier outside Liebermann's yesterday. He was stopping any non-Jews from going in to shop. There were a few of their old customers who tried, but the SS man turned them away and called them 'Christian pigs!' When I went in poor Frau Liebermann was in tears."

Ruth set out next morning and visited every Jewish shop in the area, but they all turned her away, and Ruth couldn't blame them.

It was Helga who had the idea. "Why don't you go to the

girls' school," she suggested. "I know it's school holidays now, but there might be something."

Ruth went to the school the very next day, to ask Herr Hoffman, the Jewish head, if there was any work available.

Herr Hoffman recognised her as a parent of two of his pupils, and saw the desperation in her eyes even as she said calmly, "I'd be happy to do anything round the school. I'm not afraid of hard work, Herr Hoffman."

He smiled at her. "I'm sure you're not, Frau Friedman," he replied. He thought for a moment and then said, "We could do with a temporary cleaner. The whole school has to be scrubbed from top to bottom and the classrooms repainted before the children come back in the autumn. But it wouldn't be permanent, I'm afraid."

"I'll do it," said Ruth. "The cleaning and the painting, too."

Herr Hoffman looked doubtful. "The painting is quite a big job," he said.

"I painted our shop last spring," Ruth told him. "I can do it. Please, Herr Hoffman, I'm a good worker, and I need the work."

Herr Hoffman saw the determination in her eyes and smiled. "I'm sure you'll do an excellent job," he said.

They agreed a wage, much less than she'd been earning at the haberdashery.

"But at least we've got some money coming in," she said to Helga, "and it's several weeks' work."

It was hard work, but Ruth found it very satisfying, seeing the dreary classrooms bright with new paint. At the end of each day she could see the progress of her work, but each day brought her nearer to its completion.

Once again she found herself tramping the streets, further afield this time, looking for Jewish-owned businesses, but so many had been "Aryanised", their Jewish proprietors simply pushed aside or made to sell out for a pittance, that there was no work to be had there.

She even went back to Frau Liebermann at the little grocery shop, pointing out that she used to run a grocery herself and was familiar with what was needed, but yet again she was disappointed.

"You're wasting your time," Frau Liebermann told her. "We shall have to close down soon. Twice our shelves have been raided by gangs of youths and though we called the police, they stood by and did nothing."

During the hot days of the summer, things in Vienna had calmed down a little, and Helga, along with so many other Jews, began to think that perhaps the worst was over. Ruth was nothing like as optimistic. So many things were closed to Jews now, cinemas, swimming pools, theatre and opera house, the parks and gardens, even the benches along the tree-lined boulevards were *for Aryan use only.*

As the weeks passed, more anti-Jewish directives were announced, all of them designed to oppress the Jews in every aspect of their lives. Oppression and exploitation were the weapons of choice for the everyday anti-Semitic Austrian; the true Nazis had something far more sinister in mind.

Many wealthy Jews, those with enough money to buy their way out as had David and Edith, were fleeing the country, leaving the poorer Jews to their fate. Ruth didn't blame them. Goodness knows, she thought, if I had the chance to get my family out there would be no stopping me.

She went to the Jewish Community Office, queuing

for hours before she was able to see anyone, and although the man she finally met was sympathetic, he pointed out that there were hundreds of others in the same situation or even worse.

"At least you have a roof over your head," he said. "Lots of families have been turned onto the street with nowhere to go."

However, he agreed to take her name and the names and ages of her family, wrote down their address and promised to contact her if there was anything else he could do for her.

"There is a fund," he said, "which we're building up to help families like yours to emigrate, but it isn't just a question of money, you know; there are all sorts of documents and certificates required if you are to leave. All this takes time, and we have to work with Herr Eichmann's Central Office of Jewish Emigration."

"I thought they *wanted* us to leave," Ruth said bitterly. "That's what Goering said back in March. Vienna, a Jew-free city!"

The young man shrugged. "They do," he said, "but only if we pay a fortune for going and leave everything else behind." He gave her a few Reichmarks, and told her that her family's wish to emigrate had been noted.

It was the very next day that the letter arrived, addressed in Kurt's handwriting...and it had English stamps. Ruth could hardly believe it. With shaking hands she slit open the envelope and drew out the letter, in which was wrapped a large, white, English five-pound note. Ruth stared at both the letter and the banknote through eyes flooded with tears. Kurt was safe...in England. She dashed the tears aside and began to read.

My darling Ruth,

I am here in London, staying a few days with my friend James Daniel. I had a smooth crossing and am now setting about my business. You can write to me at the above address and even if I have moved somewhere else, the letter will find me.

I think about you and the children every day and hope that things are not too awful. I loved the letters from the girls and the pictures the twins drew for me, and I carry them with me always.

I am hoping to start a new job here in the near future, but there are things that need to be sorted out before I can take up my post. James is being very helpful about it all, he has found me a job as a manservant with a family living in a place called Hampstead. It is in London, but there is a wide, open heath here, with trees and grass and lovely views, so there are times when it will feel like living in the country. Once I am settled I can work on your arrangements. Each of you will need a sponsor, so it may take some time to organise, but I will spend every waking hour trying to find people willing to act as such.

My darling, it is almost a year since I saw you all, but I carry the photo you sent me next to my heart. Give my respects to your mother, kiss the children for me and know that I love you, forever and always.

Kurt

Ruth read the letter over and over. He was safe. He was going to have a job. He was going to get them out.

The money from the Jewish Community Office and the

five-pound note would help tide them over for a little while, but Ruth knew she desperately needed to find work. Day after day she trudged the streets, but there were too many others, thrown out of their jobs; doctors and lawyers no longer allowed to practise, teachers banned from schools, professors from the university, all searching for work, no matter how menial.

Ruth was coming home despondently yet again, when a young man came hurrying round a corner and cannoned straight into her, almost knocking her over.

"Oh, I'm so sorry," he said, putting out a hand to steady her. Ruth looked up to respond to his apology and found herself looking into the cheerful face of Peter, the student she had met in the Heldenplatz on that fateful day in March. She recognised him at once, the cheerful young man who had helped her up onto the statue, the young man who had clapped and cheered and waved his hat at the sight of the Führer, who had said that the Anschluss was a great day for Austria...who was going to be a lawyer and approved of Hitler's laws.

"Wait a minute, don't I know you?" Peter demanded. "Yes, I do. Now don't tell me...Helga Heber. Am I right or am I right? I never forget a face. Remember me? Peter Walder?"

Ruth almost denied remembering him, but knew it would be stupid as he so clearly remembered her, so she managed to conjure up a smile and say, "Yes, I remember. A law student."

"Not a student anymore," Peter said proudly. "I've grad-uated. I'm working for my uncle in his law firm. I'm a real lawyer now!"

"Congratulations," Ruth said faintly, not knowing what

else to say in the face of the young man's enthusiasm.

"Your son is called Peter, too, isn't he?" Peter Walder went on, clearly delighted with having remembered this piece of information too. "How is he liking our brave new Austria?"

For a moment Ruth was at a loss for an answer to this, but then she said, "He's only just turned four, he doesn't realise what has happened."

Peter grinned. "Yes, well I suppose four is a bit young. But what does your husband think?"

"My husband is away...on business," replied Ruth, but this time Peter Walder picked up on her hesitation, and, still holding her arm, scrutinised her more carefully.

"Is he now? Where is he? What does he do?"

Becoming entangled now in her web of lies, Ruth said, "He works for a jeweller...he's gone abroad...to buy..."

Peter Walder's expression changed. He seemed to take in, for the first time, the worn state of her clothes, the gauntness of her face, the thinness of her body. He looked her up and down and said, "He's a Jew, isn't he?"

When Ruth didn't answer, he gave her a shake. "Isn't he?"

Ruth still did not reply and he said, "And so are you! Aren't I right, Helga Heber?" He peered into her face for confirmation and then said, "So, he's gone. But why didn't you go with him? You and little Peter? Austria's no place for any of you anymore."

"I have other children," replied Ruth at last. "We couldn't all go."

"So he skipped and left you!" Heavy sarcasm. "What a brave man!"

"It's not like that," Ruth asserted angrily. "He was able to go. We need sponsors from abroad. He went to find them."

"And in the meantime..."

Ruth's shoulders sagged suddenly. "In the meantime, I'm trying to find work to put food on the table, but as I'm sure you know, no one wants to employ a Jew anymore."

"Well, Helga..."

"Ruth, my name is Ruth."

Peter raised an eyebrow. "I see. Well, Ruth, what work can you do?"

"I can do anything that will feed my family," Ruth replied.

"What on earth were you doing in the Heldenplatz that day?" demanded Peter, suddenly changing the subject. "What the hell were you doing at a Hitler rally?"

"I was on my way to work and I was swept there by the crowd," answered Ruth. "It was go with the crowd or get trampled underfoot."

"Hmm, yes, it was a seething mass, wasn't it?" He gave a shout of laughter. "How ironic! How funny! A Jew at the Anschluss rally!" His face clouded for a moment. "Well, not funny for you, I suppose." He thought for a moment and then said, "And now you need a job. What can you do, I wonder?"

"I told you, I can do anything that will feed my family." Ruth tried to pull away from the hand that was restraining her, but his grip tightened.

"Come on," he said, and turning, he set off down the street, pulling Ruth along behind him.

"Where are we going?" she cried, trying to break free. "Let me go!"

"We're going to find you a job," he snapped, "so just be quiet. People are staring at you."

A job? Ruth followed the young man more meekly now, though he still had a firm hold of her wrist and she doubted if she could have broken away if she'd wanted to. He led her through the streets, and stopped eventually in front of an elegant apartment block. Four stories tall, with an arched portico, it was similar, Ruth thought, as he pushed her in through the door, to the one where David Bernstein's parents had lived. He opened a door on the first floor and led her into a spacious apartment. It was fully furnished with heavy furniture, long silk curtains, plush rugs on the polished floors, ornaments in glass-fronted cases, books on the bookshelves.

"My mother's coming to live here," Peter Walder said. "But it needs spring cleaning first. The previous owners—" he hesitated, "—have gone." He took her into the kitchen. "The whole place needs airing," he said. "Every inch of this needs to be scrubbed." The faintest aroma of food lingered in the air, a familiar breath of spices that Ruth recognised at once. Now she knew for certain. This had been a Jewish kitchen.

"And the bathroom, of course" – Peter led her further along the passage – "has to be totally refurbished." Ruth stared into what had been the bathroom, now completely gutted, no bath, lavatory or basin. "They're fitting the new bath and things tomorrow," he said, "and then the floor must be scrubbed, the walls washed and the tiles polished." He took her through the whole apartment, telling her what had to be done in each room. "And when you have cleaned it," he said, "I will pay you."

"How much?" whispered Ruth, staring round the huge apartment, recognising how much there was to do.

"Enough, but you'll have to trust me for that, won't you?" His face broke into its cheerful grin. "Don't worry, Ruth, I won't let little Peter starve. You've a week to get this place habitable, and, who knows, if you're any good, my mother might just keep you on."

"A new bathroom, Mother, simply because Jewish bottoms had sat on the lavatory!" exclaimed Ruth as she told her mother later that evening all about her encounter with Peter Walder. "Can you believe that?"

"Just be grateful for the work," Helga said, wearily.

"Oh, I am, believe me I am," replied Ruth. "It's just that he's such a strange mixture. One minute revelling in the new Austria, and the next finding work for a Jew...when he clearly doesn't like us."

"Don't question his motives," advised her mother, "just take the work on offer."

Ruth spent the next seven days at the Walders' apartment. She scrubbed floors, polished furniture, cleaned windows, washed curtains, beat rugs, swept and dusted. Many of the ornaments she cleaned were clearly valuable, and she wondered which wealthy Jewish family had lived there and had had to leave all their treasured belongings behind. Clothes still hung in the wardrobes, and when she asked Peter Walder what she was to do with them he said they were to be burned.

When he saw her reaction to this, he said, with a sort of casual generosity, "You can have them if you want them, just get them out of the place."

The next day Ruth took their two suitcases over to the apartment and filled them with as many of the clothes as she could. She carried them home to Helga, who marvelled at the quality.

"These are beautiful," she said, feeling the softness of a cashmere jumper, admiring the cut of a dark blue winter coat. "Imagine just leaving all these behind."

"They had to leave everything behind, Mutti," Ruth said sadly. "Not just their clothes. Everything."

They selected a new coat each, a skirt and blouse, some underclothes and a warm jumper.

"It's a pity there are no children's things," Helga sighed as she sorted through the rest of the clothes.

"But we can sell all these," Ruth pointed out, "and then get some winter clothes for the children with the money."

By the end of the week, the work on the apartment was finished. The new bathroom was fitted, and the whole place smelled of beeswax and lemon. Peter Walder came to inspect what she had done, and then, keeping his word, paid her. It was little enough, but Ruth pocketed the money gratefully. Another week's rent and a little over for food. With the money she had made from the sale of the remaining clothes, she knew that she and her family would eat for another couple of weeks.

Frau Walder moved into the apartment and sent for Ruth. She was a grossly fat woman, but her grey hair was expensively coiffed, and her jowls heavily made up. She had a small pug nose, and small eyes that peered out at the world through folds of flesh. They studied Ruth now, assessing her, faintly contemptuous.

"My son tells me that you are a good worker," she said. "I shall have my maid, of course, and a cook, but I'll need someone to do the rough work. Be here each day at six-thirty in the morning, and you'll be told what to do."

Ruth thanked her and promised to be there at half-past six the next day. With the new Jewish curfew ending at six in the morning, she knew she could just get there in time. There had been no mention of pay.

"But her son paid me," Ruth said to Helga, "so I have to trust her, too."

With the small amount of money Frau Walder paid and the occasional pound note in Kurt's letters, they survived; September slid into October, and the weather grew chilly. The girls had gone back to school, and found it crowded with new pupils; children expelled from the state schools, no longer allowed into mainstream education. The classrooms were crammed with children, the teachers struggling to teach so many and the parents continually worried about them. How long would it be, they wondered, before even the Jewish schools were closed?

Many Jews, forcibly ejected from their homes, had been forced to move into the increasingly overcrowded Jewish areas, Leopoldstadt and Brigittenau, working-class districts on the island between the Danube and the Danube Canal. There was nothing like enough accommodation and still they crowded in, many living several families in an apartment too small for even one. Rumour was rife; rumour fuelling fear, fear fuelling rumour. And always new directives to be complied with; everyone scrambled to comply...obey the rules and you might be safe, but there was no certainty. No certainty about anything. No prospects for a Jewish child.

There was no question of university for any Jew now, nor entry into the professions, and many of the older children left school immediately. The Jewish Community Office organised practical courses, training plumbers, mechanics, electricians, trying to equip young Jews with skills still needed in Vienna, skills that might make them "useful Jews", offering slight protection, and providing them with a trade should they ever have the chance to emigrate.

More directives were announced; all Jews must disclose their wealth and assets, Jewish firms must register with the authorities, all males over fifteen must apply for an identity card, the addition of Sarah or Israel as middle names for every Jew. All Jewish ration cards and passports must be stamped with the letter J.

Ruth had to take her passport and all their ration cards to be stamped with a large red J, and again she, like hundreds of others, had to queue for hours, simply to comply with this new directive.

As the autumn went on there were more arrests and skirmishes. Jews began to disappear again, and the fear that had eased a little during the quieter, summer months returned again, escalating to panic in many quarters. Although most of the borders had been closed and few countries were still prepared to take refugee Jews, the desperate wish, the desperate need, to leave the country drove hundreds to queue for hours outside the foreign embassies and consulates in the vain hope of getting visas or permits to enter their countries. Even though Ruth knew that Kurt was doing everything he could to bring the family to England, she queued outside the French and Belgian consulates, the American and Swiss. At each her name was taken, her family noted and absolutely no hope was given of a visa to travel. She knew the wait had been in vain, but she still felt that she had to do it.

"Supposing there was even the slightest chance, Mother," she said to Helga. "Supposing just one place said yes, they had a place for us."

"We're too many," Helga said. "You shouldn't even mention me."

"I'm not likely to leave you behind, Mutti," Ruth chided her gently.

"Well, you may have to," replied her mother. "It is you and the children who need to get away most. They have their lives before them, mine is almost over."

"Mutti, don't say such things," cried Ruth.

"Even if things were following their natural course I've only a few years left," said Helga. "The children are the future. I thought that maybe the worst was over, that things were settling down a bit, but they've been getting bad again these last weeks. I know Kurt is doing his best, but you're right to explore every avenue."

Helga was right, too, things were getting worse. Several times recently there had been fights on a Friday night, when the brave souls who ventured out to go to the synagogue were attacked by young Nazis lying in wait for them on the way home. Old men were beaten up by bands of thugs, who attacked them with impunity, while others cowered in their homes, their doors locked and their windows closed to the cries for help and the shouts of glee from the streets outside. Jews were being arrested, disappearing off the streets, simply not coming home one evening. Several of the men who shared their courtyard had just vanished, leaving their distraught wives trying to discover what had happened to them and where they had been taken; trying to provide for the families left behind.

Once again fear stalked the streets. If it were a Jew who was attacked, the police made no move to intervene, they simply stood aside and watched the violence taking place, walking away from the battered body left in the gutter. More and more Ruth kept the children at home, only allowing them out to go to school with Helga. Not that Helga, she knew, could do much to protect them if they were set upon by one of the bands of young Nazi thugs that had taken to roaming the streets.

Monday 31st October 1938

We had another letter from Papa, yesterday. He is working as a servant in London. He says the house is very large and the people who live there entertain a lot, so he's always busy. He has to clean the silver. He says it's the forks that are the most difficult because the silver cleaner gets between the prongs. I can't picture Papa cleaning silver. I can't picture Papa at all anymore. It's funny because I know what he looks like, only I can't see his face in my mind. I talked to the twins about him yesterday when the letter came, but they weren't interested to hear about him. I don't think they remember him at all.

Oma is very tired today. She keeps falling asleep when she's supposed to be looking after the boys. I know she can't help it because she's very old, nearly seventy I think, but the boys are so naughty, she needs to stay awake.

Mutti says Papa is trying to find people who will help us go to London to live with him. It would be an adventure to go, but only if we all went. How would we manage, we don't speak English?

I have a new friend at school. She is called Sonja Rosen. Her papa is a dentist. He is only allowed to look at Jews' teeth now, but he hasn't got anywhere for his surgery. They have had to move out of their nice house and now they live across the courtyard from us. We always walk to school together. Her mother takes me and Inge too, so Oma doesn't have to. Mutti doesn't like her taking the boys out.

Ruth got to know the Rosen family quite well, and it was a relief when Anna Rosen offered to see Laura and Inge to school each day. Daniel Rosen was no longer allowed to practise as a dentist except on Jewish patients, but, when forced to leave their home, he had also been forced to leave most of his equipment in the room he had used as his surgery. He still looked at people's teeth if they had toothache, but there was little he could do to help them, and most of the time he worked as a street cleaner. Anna couldn't find any work at all.

Ruth knew that she was one of the few lucky ones, with a regular job to go to. Frau Walder did not need her all day, just to do the rough work first thing in the morning, but Ruth had soon slipped into a routine, and although the work was heavy, she never complained; it put food on her table.

Every night she prayed that Kurt would write and say he had found sponsors for them, every morning she woke to face another day of uncertainty and fear.

Seventeen

As before it was the shouting that awoke Laura. She heard the chanting, the animal roar of a crowd in search of prey. She sat bolt upright in the darkness, petrified, as the terrifying sounds brought memories of the riot in Kirnheim flooding through her.

"Oma! Oma! Wake up!" She reached over and shook her sleeping grandmother. "Oma! Wake up!"

Helga stirred and then, as she heard the noise from the street outside, was instantly awake. "Wake your mother," she said. As Laura rushed from the room, Inge began to scream.

Ruth grabbed the twins and some clothes. "Get dressed," she instructed, "all of you." Moments later, dressed, all except Inge, with whom Helga could do nothing, they were in the kitchen. Ruth sat with the boys beside her, but although they had grizzled a little when awoken from their sleep, they now leaned drowsily against her, each holding his rabbit, apparently unaware of the fear in the room or the noise outside it.

Perhaps they don't remember, thought Ruth. Perhaps they're too young to remember.

Inge remembered. Helga held her in her arms, trying to soothe her, holding her close and rocking her like a baby. At last the little girl's screams dwindled to wails and then whimpers, as she buried her face in her grandmother's shoulder, rubbing her little piece of silk scarf against her cheek. Helga slid a comforting arm around Laura as the child stood close beside her. Laura's eyes were wide with terror, and fighting the urge to cry like Inge, she nestled against her grandmother, her whole body trembling.

The noise outside grew louder, there was the sound of smashing glass, and cheering, bangs and crashes and more broken glass, and all the time the growing snarl of a hunting animal. "Jews out! Jews out! Jews out!"

Beyond the tenement roofs etched black against it, the night sky was spiked with red and orange. The dancing glow of numerous fires filled the sky, and lit from below by the very flames that produced it, clouds of thick black smoke roiled above the rooftops.

Ruth, holding the twins close, looked across at her mother. "Should we try and escape?" she whispered. "Fire..."

"No." Her mother was adamant. "It's further over, on the main street. They may not even come down here."

"We must get out!" Ruth's voice rose in panic as the memory of fire at her back, the hiss of it, the smell of it, the heat of it, rose to engulf her. "We could be trapped again! We must get the children out!"

"Where to?" snapped her mother. "Into the street? Into the path of that mob? Listen to them, Ruth. They're already baying for blood. Don't give them ours!"

Ruth went to the window and looked down. The courtyard below was lit by the single lamp above the archway. Most of the apartments now had lights on; one or two, as if unoccupied, remained dark. Ruth reached over and switched off their own light, and as the room was plunged into darkness, Inge began to moan again.

"Ssh, ssh," Helga soothed her. "It'll be all right, darling, we're all here."

That's what Papa said, thought Laura, before they took him away. There was no papa with them this time. She pulled away from Helga and went to join her mother at the window.

"What's happening, Mutti?" she whispered. "Is it like before? Will they come here?"

"I don't know, darling," replied Ruth, who, though trembling, had mastered her panic. "But Oma's right. It would be very stupid to go out into the street now. They may not bother with our little courtyard, there's nothing worth anything here."

"Jews out! Jews out! Jews out!" The crowd was closing in now, and even as Ruth watched from the dark window, a crowd of men streamed under the archway into the courtyard, carrying staves and axes and sledgehammers. Others brandished flaring torches, held aloft to light the yard. Behind them, in less unruly fashion, followed armed SS soldiers. As windows of the ground-floor apartments were broken, and locked doors were smashed open with axes, the SS went into each apartment and reappeared, dragging out any men they found inside.

"They're taking people, Mother," Ruth's voice was a croak. "The SS. But it's just the men...I think."

As she watched, Daniel Rosen appeared at the door of the flat opposite, pushed out at gunpoint, his hands in the air. His wife Anna came running out, and although Ruth could not hear what she was crying, she was clearly pleading with the soldiers not to take him.

334

One of the mob shouted something, and the rest of them turned on her. A man with a pickaxe handle hit her on the head, crashing the heavy wood down hard against the side of her skull. She crumpled to the ground, and would have received a further beating or kicking had not Daniel dived forward, covering her with his own body. The men surged towards them, but the man with the rifle bellowed, "Leave him! We've got this one. See if there're any more hiding in these other flats."

The men paused for a moment, then dispersed round the courtyard, running up the staircases to the upper levels.

At that moment their own front door flew open with a crash. Ruth spun round in horror to find an armed man striding into the kitchen. He flicked on the light and surveyed the little family cowering away from him. He was dressed in civilian clothes, but he had the arrogant bearing of not just a soldier but an officer.

"Where's your husband?" he demanded.

"Not here," Ruth replied, her voice quavering. "He's away."

"Search the place, Neumann," the man ordered another behind him, and while he stood, his gun trained on the twins, who surveyed him solemn-eyed, a second smaller man went into each of the three rooms, flinging open cupboards, upending beds, and peering into corners that clearly could conceal no one. As he passed the kitchen dresser, he swept his hand along the neatly arrayed plates, dashing them to the floor in a heap of broken china. Inge began to scream again, and Helga clamped a hand over her granddaughter's mouth as the man with the gun swung it round to point at her.

"No one here," reported Neumann as he stamped his way

across the remains of the china and peered out of the window. "Got some more down there, though."

"Right, next floor," ordered the officer, and without another word the two men stalked out of the flat.

For a split second nobody moved, then Ruth ran to the front door and pushed it shut, wedging a kitchen chair against it as both latch and lock were broken.

Not that it'll keep them out if they come back again, she thought. But somehow it made her feel safer to have a closed door between them and the madhouse outside.

She returned to the window and watched as several men were marched away by the SS soldiers, Daniel Rosen among them. There was blood streaming down the side of his face, but Anna was no longer lying on the cobblestones of the courtyard. Ruth wondered what had happened to her.

The last few rioters streamed out of the courtyard in search of further prey, but not before one of them had smashed the light above the arch, and another had tossed a firebrand into a pile of smashed furniture pulled from one of the lower apartments. For a moment the fire flared, a blaze of hatred in the middle of the yard, and then it was being doused by women running in and out of their apartments with buckets of water, and all that was left was a column of drifting smoke carrying the message of hate into the night sky.

The howl of the crowd had faded somewhat as the rampage had moved on. The courtyard, now empty, was left in darkness except for faint illumination from lighted windows. Above the rooftops the sky was on fire and the dense black smoke hung in an impenetrable cloud.

It was still dark when Ruth ventured out the next morning. Although she was afraid of what she was going to see after the night of rioting, she did not dare be late at Frau Walder's apartment.

"I don't think you should go," Helga told her, in no uncertain terms. "It's madness."

"Mutti, I can't afford to lose the job."

"And we can't afford to lose you," replied her mother.

"Don't let the children out of the flat today," Ruth said. "We don't know how widespread the riot was last night, or what's going to happen next."

"Which is why I wish you wouldn't go to work either," insisted Helga.

"Mother, I have to. We still have rent to pay, food to buy and we need fuel for the stove. If I lose my job now I may never find another…and then we'll starve."

Ruth went down the steps into the courtyard and glanced across at the broken windows of the Rosens' apartment. Once she had resettled the children last night, she had crept down and across the yard to find out what had happened to Anna. The door was hanging slackly from its hinges, and she pushed it open to find Anna lying on the floor, her head on a pillow, and her daughter, Sonja, sponging her forehead. The child leaped to her feet, the colour draining from her face, as Ruth pushed open the door, but then relaxed as she saw who it was.

"Is your mother all right?" Ruth asked softly, and was profoundly relieved to see Anna's eyes open at the sound of her voice.

"Is that you, Ruth?" whispered Anna.

"Yes, it's me," Ruth replied. She knelt down beside the woman on the floor and took her hand. "Oh, Anna, thank God you're not dead."

"Just knocked out for a minute or two," answered Anna.

"That SS man let Daniel carry me inside before they took him away."

"He stopped the crowd from finishing you off, too," Ruth told her. "Perhaps he has a Jewish grandmother," said Anna bitterly.

Ruth had stayed for another half hour, helping Sonja get her mother into bed.

"Don't go out tomorrow," Ruth had told the girl as she went back to her own apartment. "You look after her here, and I'll come in again later in the day. But don't go out."

I seem to have been telling everyone else not to venture out today, thought Ruth as she skirted the remains of the fire in the courtyard and hurried up the winding lane leading to the main street. And here I am out before dawn myself.

When she turned out of the lane and began to walk along the street towards the bridge, what greeted her almost made her turn back. She had smelled the smoke still hanging heavy on the air as she came out of her own front door, but as she emerged from the lane, the acrid smell engulfed her, making her cough. The pavements were covered in glass, smashed from the shop windows. The few shops and businesses owned by Aryans were left untouched, while their Jewish neighbours had been wrecked, left open to the street and the looters, jagged shards still projecting from window frames, doors hanging askew. Brickwork daubed with paint demanded *Jüden Raus! Jews Out!* The light from the streetlamps glinted on the shattered glass and cast shadows on the damaged buildings, on the sticks of broken furniture, on small, personal possessions, photographs, ornaments and family heirlooms, dragged into the street and then tossed aside by avaricious looters; and hanging over it all was the thick, black, suffocating smoke.

Horrified, Ruth stared at the small synagogue on the corner of the street. It stood stark and jagged against the lightening sky, its roof gone, its windows smashed, its door lying flat in the doorway. From its blackened rafters smoke continued to rise in a straight, dark column. She picked her way along the pavement, pausing at the next street to look down the road towards the school building that she had scrubbed and repainted in the summer. It, too, had been attacked; its windows and doors broken open, the remains of a bonfire of books smouldering in the schoolyard. She need not have told Helga not to send the girls to school this morning, there was no school left to send them to.

A few other people were beginning to appear on the streets now, staring in silent horror at the devastation that met their eyes. Keeping her head down, her eyes fixed firmly on the pavement, Ruth hurried onward to Frau Walder's apartment. She dared not be late, but all the way through Leopoldstadt she was confronted with destruction, the havoc wrought by the incited mob. Rubble and glass and splintered timber littered the pavements, evidence of the violent use of sledgehammers; the contents of shop and office were strewn across streets, trampled in the dirt by a thousand rioting feet. Fire still smouldered among the ruins of businesses, pouring smoke into the early morning air. An inferno raged unchecked in one large synagogue, the flames leaping with crackling abandon through its upper windows, streaking the grey dawn sky blood-red and orange. Ruth was stunned to see firemen standing by, watching the building burn while making no effort to put out the fire. For a moment she stared at them in disbelief, but as one man turned towards her, a fire-axe in his hand, she turned and scurried away, dodging a heap of broken chairs as she hurried onward, out of his sight.

As she left the Jewish quarter, the streets returned, suddenly, to normality. There was no more broken glass, no further signs of destruction. The mob's violence had been confined to the predominantly Jewish quarters of the city. As if, Ruth thought when she turned the final corner and reached her destination, there had been lines, drawn on a map, a battle plan.

It was a long day. Ruth was greeted with the usual silent resentment she had come to expect from the other servants, and on the one occasion when, carrying a scuttle of coal to the drawing room, she saw her employer that morning, she was met with a lifted eyebrow, but no greeting at all. Ruth had no idea why Frau Walder continued to employ her, especially in the face of such opposition from the rest of the staff, but she was eternally grateful to her, and carried out everything she was asked to do without comment or complaint. Today she was kept late, far later than usual, and it was almost dark before she was able to leave. She walked briskly through the darkening streets, but as she drew nearer to home, the way seemed, somehow, sinister and unfamiliar. Smoke still hung in the air, and although some of the pavements had been cleared of the debris that had covered them that morning, others were still treacherous. Even now fires smouldered, gleaming red in the gathering dusk as the evening breeze stirred the ashes. There were people about, but all kept their heads down, never making eye contact, anxious not to draw attention to themselves. Ruth did the same, but as she neared the lane that led to their courtyard, she heard, once again, the dreaded chanting, the clatter of boots, and before she could duck into a doorway, a group of youths pelted round the corner, knocking her flying into the gutter before trampling over her and disappearing into the next street.

For a long moment she lay there winded, unable to regain her breath, her ribs aching from the casually aimed kicks delivered in passing; her hands were bruised where booted feet had stamped, her cheek slashed wide by a metal toecap. No one came to her aid. Neighbours scurried by, faces averted, terrified of being caught on the streets by another marauding gang.

Ruth struggled to her feet and dragged herself into the lane, and using the high walls that enclosed it to steady her, she edged her way into the courtyard and up the steps, home.

The days that followed were little better. Each day Ruth ran the gauntlet of the Leopoldstadt streets on her way to work, and each afternoon she returned, her ears strained for the sound of approaching feet.

It was as she was leaving Frau Walder's apartment one day two weeks later that she almost bumped into Peter Walder, coming up the staircase two at a time.

"I always seem to be crashing into you, Ruth," he cried cheerfully as he put out a hand to steady them both. Then, as she drew back from him, he looked at her more carefully. "What happened to your face?"

Ruth touched the partially healed gash on her cheek. "The streets aren't safe for Jews anymore," was all she said, and pressed herself against the wall to allow him to pass, but Peter Walder did not move on.

"You should get young Peter out," he said. "Things are going to get worse for you from now on."

"Thank you." As if she didn't know! Ruth struggled to keep the bitterness out of her voice. "But it's impossible."

"It may not be," Peter said. "I've been working with the Jewish Emigration Office recently. We've just heard that the English are prepared to accept a certain number of unaccompanied Jewish children. Lists are to be made at the Jewish Community Office. You should go and see them...get his name down."

"Unaccompanied?" repeated Ruth faintly. "They're too young."

Peter Walder shrugged. "It's a chance to save them," he said. "We don't want Jews in Austria anymore. I don't want Jews in Austria anymore, but the round-up of Jews last week..." He left the words hanging between them, then said, "Go to the Jewish Community Office and register his name, all their names. If the English want them, let them have them." Then as if he realised that he had said far more than he should have, his arm shot out in the Nazi salute. "Heil Hitler!" Opening the front door of his mother's apartment, he went inside.

"Unaccompanied!" echoed Helga, when Ruth told her about the children who might be allowed to leave the country. "How could you send children so young? Where would they go? Who would look after them?"

"I don't know," replied Ruth, "but I intend to find out. And remember, if they're being sent to England, Kurt is already there."

The word had spread like wildfire. When Ruth reached the Jewish Community Offices the next day, there was a queue of desperate parents out of the door and down the street, all determined to register their children for the children's trains to safety, the Kindertransports. When, hours later, Ruth finally reached the front of the queue she gave the names of all the children. "Only two from each family," stated the man. Ruth stared at him in horror. How could she choose whom to send, whom must stay behind? She had only just convinced herself it would be all right for the twins to go, even at the age of four, because they would have Laura to look after them, and now she had to choose.

"Which two, Frau Friedman?"

Ruth closed her eyes. "Laura and Inge," she replied. "Laura and Inge."

The man entered their names, ages and address on a form. "Your application will be considered, and you will be informed if it has been successful. Please be ready to supply photographs of each girl and her birth certificate."

"I didn't know what to say," Ruth told Helga later that evening when the children were all safely in bed. "Laura could go, and if the boys went she could look after them on the journey, but we can't split them up. Inge...what do I do about Inge? She's the one who worries me the most. She's not my Inge anymore. How can I let her go? How can I let any of them go?"

"How can you not?" asked her mother gently. "If it were you, I'd want you to go. Like I wanted Edith to go. It broke my heart, but I knew she had to go. There's nothing left for us here, and in the end we shall all have to go...somewhere."

"They may not be chosen," Ruth said. "There are a limited number of places. The English still insist on sponsors, but there are more and more groups coming forward with sponsors, the man said. There's a rabbi in London who is finding Jewish families to take them and give them homes." She looked at her mother in desperation. "Oh Mutti, I don't know what to do."

The next time she visited Anna Rosen, Anna told her that she had registered Sonja for the Kindertransport as well.

"At the Jewish Community Office," Ruth said.

"Yes, but at the Palestine Office, too," replied Anna. "Gives you a double chance."

"But I don't want the children to go to Palestine," cried Ruth.

"Better there than stay here," said Anna flatly. She had heard nothing from Daniel since he had been arrested on the night of the pogrom. Making light of the orchestrated rampage, the Nazis were calling it Crystal Night, the night of broken glass.

"More than broken glass," Ruth said bitterly. "Broken lives and broken hearts, more like."

Following Anna's advice, she went to the Palestine Office and registered the children with them as well.

Within a week she received a message. She was to come to the office, bringing the children with her, bringing birth certificates. She left the boys with Helga and took Inge and Laura across to the office. Once again the queue of desperate parents waiting with their children already stretched down the road, but eventually, after more than three hours of waiting, Ruth and the girls reached the front. They were shown into a large room furnished with several desks, and at each of these sat a man to take down details and to conduct the interviews. The interviewer who called them forward to his desk was a young man with fair hair and startlingly blue eyes. He smiled at the two girls and asked them their names. Laura answered up well, but when Inge was spoken to she simply turned her head away, looking round the room and smoothing the fragment of silk scarf against her cheek.

"Come along, darling," coaxed Ruth. "Don't be shy. Tell the man what your name is. He wants to know. And he wants to know when your birthday is. You know that too, don't you? We made a special cake for it the other day, didn't we?"

Inge looked at the young man with solemn eyes and he smiled encouragingly at her.

"I'm eight," she said at last, "and I'm called Inge."

Ruth could have wept with relief. She'd been sure if Inge didn't answer her name she wouldn't have been included. "You will put them both on your list, won't you?" she begged. "Their father is waiting for them in London. Please, please, put their names on the list to go."

The young man gave a sad smile. "It's not up to me," he explained. "All I'm here to do is fill in the forms and do the paperwork. Now, Frau Friedman, we have a photographer here to take their pictures and a doctor ready to check them over, to see if they're fit to travel." He gave Ruth a reassuring smile. "There will be several trains going in the next few weeks. Don't despair if they aren't on the first one. I promise you we're doing all we can to get the children out."

Several weeks passed, and Ruth had almost given up. She had been to the Community Office again and again, only to be told that lists were being collated, and if the girls were chosen she would be informed. She had gone back to the Palestine Office, but had received the same answer. If her daughters were chosen she would be told. She should have them ready to leave at short notice, just in case.

Ruth had written to Kurt, telling him what she was trying to do.

I know you are doing your best for us from your end, she

wrote, but this may be the only chance we have to bring the girls to safety. I wish I could come too, and bring mother and the twins, but the transports are only for unaccompanied children. They'll only take two from each family, and anyway the boys are too young to come on their own. As soon as we know when the girls are coming, I will write to you so that you can meet them in London.

"When" not "if". Ruth refused even to contemplate the thought that Laura and Inge might not be chosen.

I know they can't live with you, she wrote, but you'll be there to meet them at the station. You can introduce them to their foster parents and keep in touch with them. Oh, my darling, I am so glad you are in London waiting for them.

It was the middle of January when Ruth was summoned to the Palestine Office. She had not met the man who dealt with her this time, an older man with thin grey hair and sad eyes.

"Your daughters will leave on the next transport from the Westbahnhof," he told her, reading from a list. "In ten days' time. Here are their permits, issued by the British." He handed her an identity card for each girl, to which her photo had already been attached. "And their exit permits, allowing them to leave Austria." He passed across two more pieces of paper, each stamped with an official Nazi stamp.

Ten days! Ruth put the precious permits into her bag and went home to tell the girls.

"You're going to London, to see Papa," she said.

Eighteen

The Westbahnhof was a cavern of noise; the shriek of a train whistle and the hiss of the steam into the echoing canopy of the iron roof reverberated with the clamour of voices. Ruth and her family arrived to find the platform thronged with people. Parents and children crowded together in an anxious and bewildered swarm, under the steely eyes of the SS soldiers ranged round the station, waiting for the slightest excuse to lash out at troublemakers.

Although it was almost midnight, the whole family had come to say goodbye to Laura and Inge...on their way to meet Papa in London. Helga held each twin by a hand, hanging on to them for dear life as she followed Ruth, pushing her way through the press of people.

"Hold tight to my skirt," Ruth instructed Inge. "Laura, hold Inge's hand." In her own hands were the two small suit-cases permitted by the authorities. Nothing but clothes, a few personal possessions and a packet of food. Anything else, they had been told, anything valuable, would be confiscated, and the owner put off the train. The girls had few enough clothes as it was. Ruth had dressed them in several layers to keep them warm on the long winter journey, and had scraped together enough money to buy a warm hat and coat for each. In the suitcases were an extra skirt and blouse, thick woollen stockings and another set of underclothes. The last pound note that Kurt had managed to send had been hidden inside a piece of sausage, and tucked into the package of food in Laura's suitcase.

"Remember not to eat that sausage, darling," Ruth had warned her. "I can't have you arriving in a foreign country with no money at all."

Laura had looked at the money doubtfully. "It's not like real money," she said.

"It's real money in England," Ruth assured her. And worth a lot more than I'd have been able to exchange it for here, she thought ruefully.

The young man from the Palestine Office was on the platform. He looked harassed as he checked off the girls' names on a typed list, checked that they had the required documents with them and then handed Ruth two labels.

"Please attach these to the children's clothes," he said, "then there will be no question of them getting lost." He consulted his list again. "Mr and Mrs Gladstone will be at the station in London to meet them and take them to their new home. Girls travel in the front three carriages, please." And with that he turned away to deal with the next family demanding his attention, leaving the Friedmans to fight their way across the crowded platform to the train.

"Come on, darlings," Ruth said, brightly. "Let's get you onto the train and find you some seats." She looked down at her two young daughters, white-faced in the unforgiving lights of the station, and had to fight every instinct that told her to gather them into her arms and take them home. "Look at all the children travelling with you!" she cried. "What an adventure it will be!"

Ruth led them to an open carriage door, and was about to climb on board to find them seats and to put their luggage up onto the rack when her way was barred by a burly SS man.

"No adults on the train!" he barked. "Children only."

"I only want to find them a seat..." began Ruth, but he shoved her roughly aside. "No adults on the train," he repeated.

Ruth pulled the girls back from the doorway, so that they could say a proper goodbye to their grandmother and brothers before they got on the train, but when she turned to find Helga and the twins, they were nowhere to be seen. They had got separated from her and the girls by the heaving crowd on the platform. Ruth looked round frantically, but there was no sign of them. She glanced up at the station clock; it was ten minutes to twelve. She dare not go in search of them now; she would never find them in time in the confusion of the station. As the hands of the clock moved round to the hour, children were being pushed up into the train. Pale, tear-streaked faces appeared at the carriage windows, peering out helplessly for a final look at mother or father left on the platform.

Ruth was determined not to break down in front of her children. She fought the lump that rose so painfully in her throat, struggled to keep the brimming tears from flooding down her cheeks as she looked down at her two little daughters, one just eight, the other eleven, about to embark on a journey into the unknown. How could she let them go? How could she send these two young children off on their own across Europe? Surely they'd be safer with her here in

Vienna, where she could look after them properly. Surely she should take them back home with her, and look after them as a mother should.

Then an SS officer started shouting into a megaphone. "The train leaves in five minutes, any child not on board in the next two minutes will be refused leave to travel. There will be no waving to the train, no calling out to the children. Anyone who does so will be arrested."

And Ruth knew why she was sending her daughters away; so that they should be safe from monsters like him, men who refused a parent the right to wave goodbye to her children, who would arrest a parent for waving or calling out an encouraging word to a small and terrified child.

Sonja Rosen had also been chosen for this particular transport, but at the last minute Anna had changed her mind.

"I can't let her go!" she cried to Ruth. "With Daniel gone, she's all I have left."

Despite the soul-destroying ache in her heart, Ruth thought Anna had made the wrong decision. The only way to protect her children was to send them away, but it was breaking her heart.

"Where's Oma?" cried Inge suddenly, staring with terrified eyes at the crowds around her. "I want Oma!"

"She'll be here in a minute," Ruth promised, knowing it was a lie. "She and the boys got caught up in the crowd."

She knew it was time, time to kiss her daughters goodbye, and with a conscious effort forced a reassuring smile. "Darlings, you must get on the train. Laura, look after Inge; Inge, do what Laura tells you. Give Papa great big hugs from me and the twins. We'll be there to join you in no time."

She pushed her way forward, and pausing only to give each

girl a convulsive hug helped them up onto the train. She just had time to pass their cases up after them, before she was shoved aside by another terrified parent, trying to hoist her small son into the carriage.

The SS soldier was there again. "Only girls in this carriage," he snarled, hauling the little boy back out of the train and pushing him towards his terrified mother. "Boys in the back carriages."

As the last few frightened children were pushed onto the train, Ruth stood back a little and craned her neck to see Laura and Inge appearing, white-faced, at a window, Laura lifting Inge up so that she could see out. Other parents swirled round her as Ruth stood, blank-eyed, staring at her girls for what could well be the last time in her life. She had no illusions. Her girls would be safe, but almost certainly they would grow up without her.

"Be good for your foster parents," she had told them. "Mr and Mrs Gladstone are very kind to take you in, and to offer to have both of you, so that you can stay together."

"I thought we were going to Papa," Inge had wailed. "I don't want to go, Mutti. I don't like Mr Gladstone."

"Papa will meet you at the station," Ruth promised, "but you can't live with him. He has to live where he works and there isn't room for you as well. He'll come and visit you whenever he can, and as soon as he's arranged it, the twins and I will be coming to London too."

"And Oma?" demanded Inge.

"And Oma," Ruth said, almost certain that she was lying. Her mother had made it fairly clear that she would not leave Vienna. But Inge and her grandmother had become very close over the last few chaotic months, and Ruth wanted to make their parting easier, offering illusory hope.

Vain promises, she thought now as she stood, rigid, watching her daughters' faces pressed against the compartment window.

The SS officer with the megaphone repeated his announcement, amending it to one minute to embark or be left behind.

"No waving!" he bellowed. "No shouting. No wailing! Or you will be arrested."

As the train doors were slammed shut, Ruth felt a tug at her sleeve and looked down to see Hans at her side, still in the firm grasp of Helga who had Peter wedged onto her hip.

"Where are they?" Helga asked, her voice breaking. "I didn't say goodbye!"

"In that window, look," Ruth said, nodding towards the train. She was unwilling to point out exactly which window, in case the watching SS man decided she was waving.

All the doors were shut now, the children locked into the train, but although the whistle shrilled several times, and the engine blew energetic steam into the roof, the train didn't move.

"Where's Laura?" demanded Peter, suddenly. "Is she…?"

"…on the train?" finished Hans.

"Yes," replied Ruth as she hoisted Hans into her arms, holding him tightly against her. "She's going to see Papa, remember? She and Inge are off to see Papa. Aren't they lucky?"

It was another ten minutes before the train finally began to move, chugging its way slowly out of the station. Some of the parents tried to run along the platform, tried to keep up so that they could have one last glimpse of their children. With the boys in their arms, neither Helga nor Ruth attempted to run beside the train; they simply stood and watched it growing smaller and smaller until it disappeared round a corner. They had gone. For better or worse, Ruth had sent two of her children, unaccompanied, to England.

The officer with the megaphone was ordering everyone to leave the station and go home, with more threats of instant arrest for any who still stood there, staring down the empty track, long after the train had gone.

As the bereft parents streamed out of the station into the cold night outside, many were openly crying, their keening rising up into the night sky, like the smoke from the train that carried their children away.

Again the megaphone roared. "Jews who are making that dreadful caterwauling will be arrested, instantly."

The SS soldiers began moving through the crowd, grabbing the arms of anyone outwardly showing emotion and dragging them away.

"You're all breaking curfew," bellowed the officer, "we'll arrest anyone still here in five minutes."

Panic ran through the crowd, and they began to scatter, slipping away into the darkness of the surrounding streets.

Each carrying a twin, Ruth and Helga ducked into the first side road they saw, and threaded their way through back streets and pathways, until they crossed the canal and reached the comparative safety of their home.

Exhausted, the two women put the boys to bed and then sat by the dying embers, finally allowing the tears to stream down their cheeks, as they thought of the two frightened little girls on the train.

"Did you see the age of some of those children tonight?" Ruth said at last.

She had been amazed at how young some of the children

on the train were. "Some were scarcely more than babies; some had older children to look after them, but others were simply pushed into a carriage before the doors were closed."

"Yes, I saw," agreed Helga bleakly.

"Toddlers!" cried Ruth. "How could they do that?"

"Fear and desperation," answered her mother.

"I have to get the twins out now," Ruth said with sudden determination. "If other parents can send their babies away to safety, so can I. I shall go to the Palestine Office and the Jewish Community Office and register them tomorrow."

Then she broke down once again, weeping, and her mother gathered her into her arms and rocked her as she had rocked her when a baby, trying to calm her, to soothe her as any mother should, until the dawn came up on their misery, and it was the beginning of another day.

Nineteen

The train started with a jolt. All the children who were pressed against the windows, staring out for a last glimpse of their parents, were flung sideways, grabbing at each other to maintain their balance. Those who had been unable to reach the windows and stood on the seats behind in a second rank clung to the luggage racks as the train began to move. All craned their necks for one last sight of their parents who stood frozen on the platform or ran beside the train. Laura clutched at Inge, holding her closely, as the train picked up speed. Some children were crying, others stared mutely out of the window at the darkness rushing past them, lit only by flying sparks from the engine so far ahead. Yet others, mostly the older ones, turned away from the darkness and regained their seats, checked their suitcases were on the rack above, comforted the younger ones, tried to be grown up. Laura led Inge, silent and expressionless, away from the window to two seats in the middle of the compartment.

"Come on, Inge," she said, hugging her. "We're going to see Papa."

Inge didn't reply, didn't return the hug. She simply curled into her seat and buried her face in her piece of silk. Laura watched her for a while, but she didn't move.

"Inge? Inge? Are you asleep?" Laura whispered. She knew that she wasn't; Inge's eyes were open, staring blankly and unseeing. She didn't move, didn't reply, hardly seeming to breathe, she simply stared. Pale-faced and pinched, she had withdrawn into a world of her own. Laura reached over and took her hands. Inge seemed warm enough, but she didn't respond to Laura's touch. Reluctantly Laura let go of her hands and left her alone, curling up in her own seat and trying to lose herself in slumber. But sleep eluded her. As soon as she shut her eyes, all she could see was Mutti, standing on the platform, her eyes fixed on the train, her face pale in the harsh light of the station. Mutti, suddenly smaller than she had seemed at home, waiting for the train to pull away, to carry them away from her; Mutti, small and tired and afraid...and left behind.

"When you get to London," Mutti had said, "Papa will be at the station, and so will Mr and Mrs Gladstone. They have no children, but have always wanted little girls, so they'll be so pleased to see you."

Laura fought the tears that threatened to overcome her now. Mr and Mrs Gladstone will be kind people, she thought, they'll look after us until we can go home again. But her deepest fear continued to assail her. Suppose we never go back?

"Never go back. Never go back. Never go back," clacked the wheels of the train, their rhythm taking root in her brain. "Never go back. Never go back. Never go back."

At last, exhausted, Laura slipped into a restless sleep, from which she awoke some hours later, stiff and cold, her neck aching. For one moment she had no idea where she was, and then she remembered, with awful clarity; remembered the sight of Mutti, Oma and the twins on the platform, getting smaller and smaller, until they disappeared into the darkness.

Laura was fully awake now. All around her were children she didn't know, children of all ages. Some asleep, snuffling as they slept; others awake, staring white-faced out of the window at the pearl-grey dawn. Some were eating the food they had brought, others shuffled to one of the two toilets at the end of the carriage, queuing to relieve themselves. Laura knew she should join the queue, but she looked across at Inge, who seemed exactly as she'd been the night before, curled into her seat, eyes closed now, the silk against her cheek.

As the morning drew on, the train stopped several times, but the children were not allowed to get off. The carriage doors remained locked, and as they looked out of the windows, they saw people on the station platform staring at the train, turning away if a child waved.

Laura had woken Inge at last, scared by her sister's long sleep, but although Inge's eyes were open again, she still stared into space, and when Laura offered her some of their packed food, she did not even seem to see the proffered sandwich, let alone take it and eat it. Laura took Inge to the toilet, going in with her to make sure that she used it, and although Inge allowed herself to be led along the train and into the cubicle, she never once spoke, simply did what Laura told her and then went back to her seat.

They travelled all day and all night. Some of the older children tried to make them sing, some children joined in, others just listened. Laura got her diary from her case and tried to write, but the words wouldn't come; how could she write about leaving Mutti, Hans, Peter and Oma behind? Later, she thought, I'll do it later, and she tucked the diary back among

357

her clothes. Inge sat, unmoving, eating and drinking nothing, her eyes blank, her face a deathly white, and Laura sat beside her, holding her hand.

Once again the train slowed down, and, peering out of the window, Laura was horrified to see a group of SS soldiers climbing aboard.

"SS!" cried someone in panic. "They're coming on the train!"

Cold fear gripped them all; most of the children had enough experience of the dreaded death's head soldiers to know true terror. Some of the younger ones, while not knowing the cause, caught the atmosphere of fear and began to cry.

The carriage door slammed open, and a young SS soldier strode in. He was tall with cropped fair hair, cold blue eyes and a long scar down one cheek. Instinctively the children shrank back into their seats as he towered over them.

"Papers!" he barked, and waited, tapping the whip he carried impatiently against the polished leather of his boot. The children hurried to find their passports and permits. As he scrutinised each, he peered at the label round the child's neck, his face thrust into theirs, his pale eyes alight with pleasure at his own power to instil fear.

Inge did not move, she seemed entirely unaware of his presence. Laura, having charge of both sets of papers, passed them over to the soldier. He looked at them and then pointed at Inge. "What's the matter with her?" he demanded.

"Please, sir," Laura whispered, "she's scared."

"Half-witted, more like," snapped the soldier. "Retards like her should be put to sleep!" He looked at the cases on the rack. "Those yours?"

"Yes, sir," replied Laura.

"Get them down!"

He stood and watched as Laura struggled to get their cases down from the rack.

"Open them!"

Laura opened the first case, Inge's. The man lifted the few clothes from the case, running his hands round the bottom as if he expected to find contraband in there. He tossed Inge's uneaten food onto the floor, casually crushing it with his boot. Obviously disappointed he turned his attention to Laura's case, growling, "And the other one."

Once again he rifled through it, pulling out her clothes and the last of her food. He picked up the sausage that contained the pound note, and looked at it. He saw Laura watching him with frightened eyes.

"Not hungry, little Jew?" he taunted, and with a wolfish grin, he sank his teeth into the sausage. For a moment he chewed on the rich-flavoured meat, and then he spat it out into his hand.

"Oh yes? What's this then?"

He pulled away the last of the meat to reveal the pound note. He turned avaricious eyes on Laura, and, carefully unrolling the note held it up and looked at it. "No valuables allowed," he said, and pushed it into his pocket.

"Wonder what else we've got hidden in here then," he remarked, as he upended the suitcase onto the seat. He made a more careful examination of its contents, throwing her precious diary onto the floor, tipping her underclothes after it, clearly checking for anything else that he might purloin. The only other thing that interested him was the double picture frame that Oma had given her, her grandparents smiling out from one side, her mother and aunt out from the other. He pulled the pictures out, ripping them across and throwing them on top of the clothes. Then, with a smirk, he pocketed the frame.

"I will report you, little Jew," he said, his eyes gleaming malevolently, "for carrying valuables…and you will be put off the train."

He moved on to the next carriage, leaving Laura white-faced and terrified. She picked up the torn photographs, staring at them for a moment through eyes blurred with tears, before tucking them inside her diary and returning them to the suitcase. With shaking hands she began stuffing the rest of their things back into their cases. What would happen to Inge if she, Laura, was put off the train? What would happen to her? The welling tears overflowed and began to pour down her cheeks.

"He can't report you unless he admits taking the money," said a voice behind her. Laura turned to find one of the older girls watching her. "If he tells them you had English money, he'll have to admit he took it and then he won't have it either."

"He might not care about the money…" began Laura. "He might not want it himself, and…"

"Oh, he wanted it himself," the other girl said. "I saw his face. Still," she went on, "it might be best though if you went into the toilet until we move on again." She saw Laura glance, panic-stricken, across at Inge, and added, "I'll watch your sister for you, go on."

Laura pushed her way through the carriage, where several other children were repacking cases that had been searched, and went into the toilet. The SS soldiers had already searched there, so unless they came back looking especially for her, she should be safe enough. She shut the door and locked it, then sitting down on the closed lavatory seat she began to weep. She wept for her mother, great heaving sobs that she had stifled at the station and ever since. She wept for Oma and the twins, whom she was sure she'd never see again, and when it seemed that she had no more tears left, she wept for herself. How was she going to cope in a country where she didn't speak the language? How was she going to look after Inge who had simply shut out the world, disappeared inside herself and didn't speak at all? She and Inge were cast adrift from everything that they knew, and although Papa would be there to meet them at the station, they would still have to live with people they didn't know, in a house they didn't know, in a country they didn't know, and all of a sudden it was too much.

It seemed an age before there was a clanging of doors, more shouting and a whistle blowing and the train started clanking its way slowly onward again. Drained from her bout of weeping, with red eyes and blotchy face, Laura crept out of the toilet and went back through the crowded carriage to find Inge. Good as her word, the older girl was sitting beside her, holding her hand, but throughout the whole episode Inge had remained silent. She had shown no fear of the soldiers, no interest in the other girl, indeed no reaction at all, and when Laura returned to her seat, she showed no reaction to her either, still not answering when Laura spoke to her.

"I was right," the girl said, ignoring Laura's tear-streaked cheeks and speaking cheerfully. "He didn't come back for you." She smiled at Laura. "You were very brave," she said. "What's your name?"

"Laura. Laura Friedman. And this," she indicated Inge, "is my sister, Inge."

"I'm Gerda Berger," the older girl said, and held out her

hand. Solemnly they shook hands. "Your sister is very quiet," Gerda said, as she moved aside to let Laura sit down beside Inge. "Is she always like this?"

"She won't eat or drink," answered Laura. "She hasn't had anything since we left Vienna. I don't know what to do."

At that moment the train, which had been rattling forward, began to slow again. Laura stared at Gerda in horror. All round them the chatter of children died away as they waited, resigned to the next search of the train.

"Do you think they're coming back for me?" whispered Laura, her face ashen.

"I don't know." Gerda, despite her earlier courage, looked pale too. She peered out of the window. "We're stopping at another platform."

Once again the carriage door burst open and another man in uniform came in. Instinctively the children shrank back, but he greeted them with a huge smile on his face. "Welcome to Holland," he cried in heavily accented German. "Welcome to Holland!"

Someone gave a cheer, but most of the children were too tired and frightened to take in what the man had said. He moved on to the next carriage, but almost immediately two women climbed in, both carrying baskets.

"Welcome to Holland," they said. "You're safe now, all of you. Anybody hungry?"

It was as if they had broken an evil spell that had bound the children for as long as they could remember. Suddenly everyone was talking at once, some laughing, some crying, some simply holding out their hands for the bread and cheese and milk and, wonder of wonders, chocolate. The women's smiles were the first any of the children had seen on the faces of strangers for months. These welcoming women, many of them Dutch Jews, went through the carriages, into every compartment, feeding the hungry children, hugging them, holding the little ones close as if they were the most precious things they'd ever seen.

One lady stopped beside Laura and Inge. Seeing Laura's still blotchy face she said in stilted German, "Are you all right, little girl?"

"I am," replied Laura bravely, "but my sister…" Her voice trailed off before she added, "Mutti gave us some food, but Inge won't eat any."

The woman smiled, and kneeling down beside Inge gently took her hand. Inge did not respond, simply continued to stare, blank-eyed, into space. The woman produced a small piece of chocolate, and breaking off a sliver slipped it between Inge's slack lips. At first Inge still did not react, her eyes still blank and unseeing, but as the tiny piece of chocolate began to melt in her mouth, her tongue slid across her lips as if seeking more. Laura watched as the Dutch woman slid another crumb of chocolate into Inge's mouth. When that, too, was swallowed down the woman poured milk from a bottle in her basket into a cup and held it to Inge's mouth.

"Come on, little girl…"

"Her name's Inge," said Laura.

"Come on, Inge, just a little sip. It's milk. You like milk don't you? Just a little sip, there's a good girl."

Gradually, coaxed by the lady's soft voice, Inge drank the milk. A piece of bread and butter followed, but then, as several blasts on a whistle came from outside, the lady got to her feet.

"I've got to get off now," she said. She handed the bottle of milk to Laura. "Take this," she said, "and give her some more later. You're a brave girl looking after your little sister, your mother would be proud of you."

There was another blast on the whistle and the woman scurried to the door and jumped down onto the platform. As the train began to move slowly out of the station, all the women stood along the platform, smiling and waving. The children on the train smiled and waved back. Flags fluttered in the breeze above the station roof, Dutch flags, blowing freely in the wind; no sign of a swastika anywhere.

Gerda stared out of the window at the flat countryside as it slid by. "Look, Laura," she said, "Holland. We're free. The Nazis can't touch us here."

"No," whispered Laura, "but I wish Mutti, Oma and the twins were here too. We're free, but they're not."

"No, but at least your papa will be waiting for you," Gerda said. "Mine's disappeared." Then making a valiant effort she said, "But my brother Bruno is with the rest of the boys, somewhere on the train. So I'm not quite alone."

When the train reached the Hook of Holland it was late evening. All the children were unloaded and made to stand in line, as their names were checked on a register. Laura held tightly to Inge's hand as they went up the gangplank onto a waiting ship. Inge still hadn't spoken, but she had lost the blank stare and, seeming more aware of the strangeness of her surroundings, kept a firm hold on Laura's hand. They were given some food and assigned a place to sleep, and sleep they did for a while, curled up together like puppies on a bunk, each drawing comfort from the closeness of the other.

The crossing was not rough, but there was a steady swell, and the rise and fall of the boat made both girls feel queasy, so it was with great relief that some hours later they found themselves being led off the ship onto the quay. It was a cold, grey morning, but after the stuffiness of the cabins on the ship, the air was fresh and clean, and Laura gulped down lungfuls, grateful to be on dry land once more.

"We're here, Inge," Laura said, still holding her sister's hand. "We're in England. When we get off the next train, Papa will be there."

Yet again the children were mustered, checked and loaded onto a train. Gerda had found her brother. Laura saw her hugging a tall dark boy, as they emerged onto the quay, but she didn't get a chance to talk to her again as they were put into different compartments.

The train sped through the cold morning air, and as the grey sky lightened, and shafts of early sunshine struck the trees and meadows, Laura stared out of the window at the unfamiliar countryside; small villages with houses clustering round the church, a stand of trees on the skyline, a solitary farmhouse with grey stone outbuildings, cows coming in from the fields to be milked, a man on a bicycle riding to work. Countryside at peace with itself, waking up to a new day. For the first time since she had left Vienna, she felt her spirits lift a little. They were going to live here, somewhere in this new country, where there were no Nazis, no SS, no Hitler. Soon, very soon, they would be with Papa.

"Look, Inge," she said, turning to her sister, "look at the villages. This is England. This is where we're going to live." But Inge had, once again, retreated into herself, and showed no interest in their new country.

The train did not stop at any of the stations through which it passed, and the towns, with strange names like Ipswich and

Colchester, passed by and gave way to the outward sprawl of a great city. Houses in rows, pocket-handkerchief gardens, brick warehouses and tall factory chimneys all warned of the approaching city. London.

The train slowed right down and edged its way across a multitude of tracks, clattering over the points and finally drawing under the echoing roof of Liverpool Street Station. All the children had had their noses pressed to the window, anxious to see the sort of place they had come to. As the train finally came to a halt, its great engine blowing off steam as it reached the buffers, there was nervous chatter and noise in all the carriages. Now they were going to meet their foster parents, their new families, where everyone would speak English, no one German.

Laura collected their two cases, and held one out to Inge. "Here's yours, Inge," she said. "You can carry it."

Inge made no move to take the case, and one of the escorts called out to them, "Come along there. Get down from the train." He reached up and took the cases from Laura, so that she could help her sister down onto the platform, then he handed them both back to Laura. "Take your sister over into the line," he said and turned away to help another child.

Carrying both cases, Laura led Inge to the group of children waiting patiently, lined up in pairs.

"You'll all wait on the platform until everyone is off the train," they'd been told. "Then keeping together, everyone with a partner, we'll go to the hall where your relatives and foster parents will be waiting for you."

Gerda was standing with her brother. She waved when she saw Laura again. "This is my brother Bruno," she said.

Bruno was tall, almost grown up. He smiled at the two

girls. "Hallo," he said. "We've made it, then."

At last the train was empty. Once again the young man from the Palestine Office checked their names against his list.

"He has to go back to Vienna," Bruno told them. "The Nazis only let him come as an escort. If he doesn't go back, they won't let any more children come."

"He's very brave," remarked Gerda, "going back."

I'd go back, thought Laura bleakly, watching the young man checking each child against his list. If I could, I'd go back to Mutti, Oma and the twins.

Once they were all assembled, the crocodile of children was marched off towards the hall where they would finally meet their new families. As they walked along the platform, still wearing their labels and each carrying a small suitcase, people stopped to watch them.

"Refugees," remarked one man, "poor little buggers."

"Never mind, darlin'," called another, smiling at Gerda as she walked beside her brother. "You're safe now. 'Itler ain't comin' 'ere!"

What were the men saying, wondered Laura? The only word she recognised was "Hitler", and it made her shiver.

They were led to a lofty, echoing hall. It was gloomy inside, its dirty windows, high in the wall, only allowing dull, grey light to filter through. As they came through the door, each child was handed a packet of sandwiches and then told to sit down on the benches that ran along one wall. The children filed in obediently, and took a seat. One or two opened the sandwiches straightaway and began to eat them; experience had taught them that you never knew where the next meal might come from, so it was best to eat food immediately, before it vanished again.

Laura, still struggling with both cases, pushed the sandwiches into her coat pocket and said, "Inge, stay close."

There was a great shuffling of feet and edging sideways as the children moved along the hall, trying to get a glimpse of the people who waited for them on the other side.

"Sit down, children," called out one of the escorts. "Sit down and wait for your name to be called."

The children sat on the hard wooden benches and waited in nervous expectation to hear their names. On the opposite side of the room were the group of sponsors and foster parents, who also waited, peering across at the assembled children, wondering. Who? Which?

Suddenly Inge let out a shriek, and leaping up from her place on the bench, she shot out across the floor, speaking for the first time in forty-eight hours; speaking...calling...crying out, "Papa!"

One of the escorts made a move to pull her back to the bench, but she pushed him aside and flung herself across the room into the waiting arms of Kurt Friedman. Laura dropped the suitcases and followed her, erupting from the bench, tears streaming down her face as she, too, found herself safe at last within the circle of her father's arms.

The noise around them faded, the business of matching child to foster parent blurred behind them as the three held and hugged and laughed and cried. Kurt on his knees, his daughters crushed against him. A middle-aged couple stood behind them, watching the ecstatic reunion. They looked at each other. "Can we really be parents to these little girls?" their eyes seemed to say. "They already have a parent here." They waited patiently for another few minutes and then the man stepped forward and coughed.

Kurt looked up and forced a smile to his lips. The Gladstones. He had met them already, had thanked them for offering to take his daughters into their home, but even as they stood there waiting to be introduced to their foster children, he could hardly bear it. His girls were here safe, and within minutes he was going to have to give them up again. He got to his feet, and still holding the girls against him, turned them towards the Gladstones.

"Laura, Inge, here are the kind lady and gentleman who are going to give you a home. Mr and Mrs Gladstone. Say how do you do."

Neither girl moved at first, but at a gentle push from her father, Laura stepped forward and dropped a small curtsey. "How do you do?" she said in German.

"You must be Laura," said the woman and coming forward took Laura's hand.

Laura, recognising her own name, although it wasn't said quite right, smiled and said, "Laura." Then she pointed to Inge, who had buried her face in her father's stomach, and said, "Inge."

The woman pointed to herself, "Aunt Jane," she said, "and this," she pointed to her husband, "is Uncle Frank."

Gradually the echoing hall was emptying as the children were claimed by their new families. Kurt picked up the girls' suitcases and led the little group over to the man with the clipboard, explaining who he was and where the children were going.

"That's right," said the man marking them off. "To Mr and Mrs Gladstone." He shook the Gladstones by the hand and said in careful English, "Thank you for taking these children, your generosity has brought them to safety."

Kurt travelled with them to their new home, having agreed with the couple beforehand that he would see the children into the house and then leave. So, after drinking a cup of tea in the Gladstones' parlour, he stood up to take his leave.

Immediately Inge burst into tears. "I don't want you to go, Papa," she wept. "I don't like it here. I want to come with you."

"I can't stay, my darling," Kurt said gently. "And you can't come with me, because there is no room for you where I live, but I promise I will come and see you on Sunday, all right?"

It wasn't all right, and Inge continued to cry, clinging to him, burying her face against him. Kurt looked over her head at Laura, who was fighting tears of her own.

"Be brave, my darlings," he begged. "Be brave and I will tell you some wonderful news. I have found a sponsor for Mutti. It won't be long before she and the twins will be here as well. So be good, my darlings. It won't be forever. In a few weeks we shall all be together again. Mutti's coming to England."

Wednesday, 30th August 1939

Inge and I are so excited. The twins arrive in London today. They've had to come by themselves, like we did. They're such little boys, I hope they weren't too scared. Aunt Jane and Uncle Frank are taking us to the station to meet them. I can't wait to see them! Will they remember us, I wonder? It's more than six months since we saw them. I wish Mutti was coming with them, but Papa says she'll be coming next weekend and then we'll all be together. She would have come sooner, but Oma was ill and she had to stay and look after her. Poor

Oma has died now, but she was very old. Poor Oma.

Aunt Jane and Uncle Frank have been very kind and we shall still have to live in their house, but we shall all be safe. The boys at school say, "We ain't afraid of Ole 'Itler." I am, and I think they should be too.

The Kindertransports

As the orchestrated persecution of the Jews intensified in the late 1930s, more than ten thousand unaccompanied Jewish children were brought to England from Germany, Austria, Poland and Czechoslovakia, between December 1938 and August 1939. Sent by parents, desperate to save them from the Nazis' "Final Solution", children aged from three months to seventeen years old travelled on trains that carried them across Europe and then over the sea to England. When they arrived they were fostered in families all over the country. Jewish, Methodist, Quaker, Catholic and Protestant families opened their homes to the children so brutally taken from their own families. For some no foster parents could be found and these were housed in hostels or went to boarding schools; but all had escaped the Nazi terror.

Some were lucky, and their parents managed to escape as well, so they were reunited; others found remnants of family who had survived the death camps after the war, but most of them never saw, again, the parents, grandparents, brothers and sisters they had left behind.

The strength of the love and courage of the parents who sent their children away is hard to imagine...their hearts were broken, but their children were saved.

A letter from the publisher

We hope you enjoyed this book. We are an independent
publisher dedicated to discovering brilliant books,
new authors and great storytelling. Please join us at
www.headofzeus.com and become part of our
community of book-lovers.

We will keep you up to date with our latest books, author
blogs, special previews, tempting offers, chances to win
signed editions and much more.

If you have any questions, feedback or just want to say hi,
please drop us a line on hello@headofzeus.com

@HoZ_Books

HeadofZeusBooks

www.headofzeus.com

 HEAD *of* ZEUS

The story starts here